THE USBORNE

Pocket Scientist

The blue book

CONTENTS

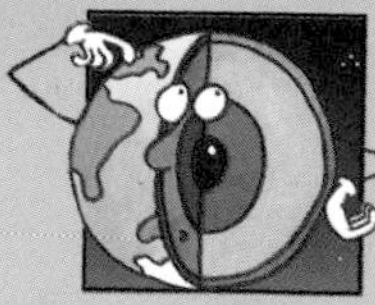

HOW DO ANIMALS TALK?

Susan Mayes

Designed by Claire Littlejohn, Brian Robertson and Mary Forster
Illustrated by Angela Hargreaves, Philip Hood and Colin King

Consultant: Joyce Pope

CONTENTS

Ways of talking

People talk to each other for all kinds of reasons. They talk using words, but they also say things in other ways. Different movements, sounds and faces all help you say what you mean.

This face shows sadness.

A "shhh" sound helps you say "be quiet".

You may greet your best friends by stretching your arms out to them.

Life in the wild

In the wild, animals have to "talk" to each other so that they can survive and bring up their families. For example, this is important for the cat's wild relative, the lion.

A lioness's special scent tells males when she is ready to mate.

Watching your pets

Animals say things to each other all the time. They don't use words, but they do "talk" in other ways, just as we do. Try watching your pets to see what they do.

You may see your dog bow to another dog like this. He is saying "play with me". He may do this to you too.

If your dog pokes another dog in the side with his nose, he is saying "stand still".

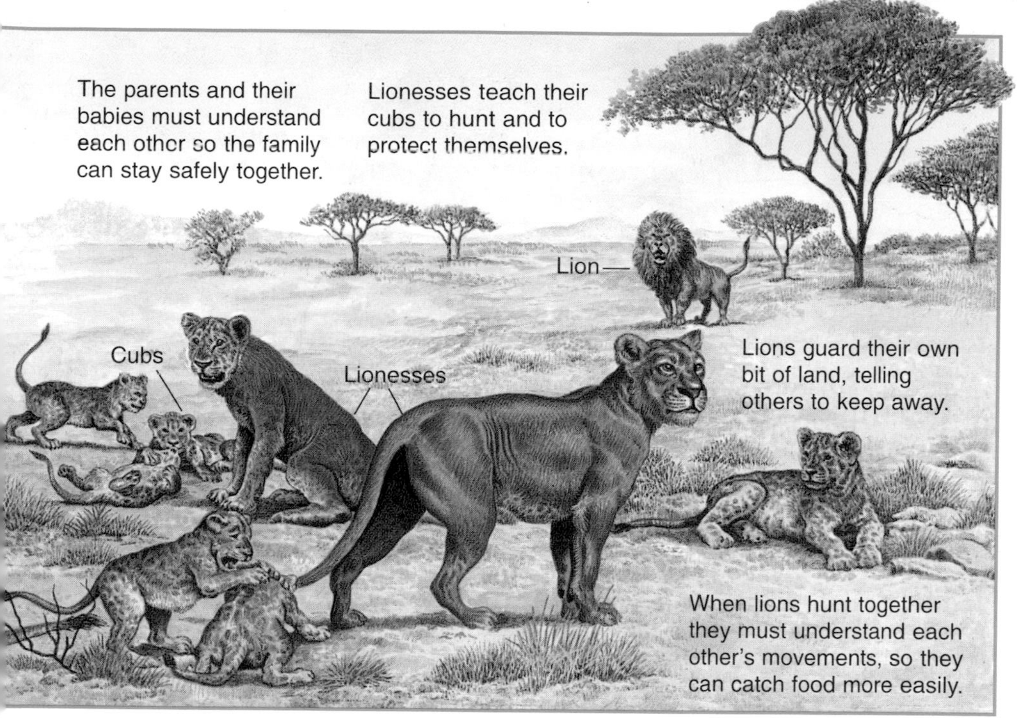

The parents and their babies must understand each other so the family can stay safely together.

Lionesses teach their cubs to hunt and to protect themselves.

Lions guard their own bit of land, telling others to keep away.

When lions hunt together they must understand each other's movements, so they can catch food more easily.

If you have pet cats you will often see them rubbing noses like this in a friendly greeting.

Animals "talk" to each other with many movements, sounds and smells. Some have special colours and patterns.

These all make clear messages which are full of important information for family, friends and even enemies.

Pictures with the symbol can be downloaded from ***www.usborne-quicklinks.com***

Saying "keep out"

The place where an animal finds food, water and a mate is very important. The animal guards part of it, to keep away others of its own kind.

The area the animal guards is called its territory. Territory owners must make clear warnings which tell others "keep out, I live here".

Making a noise

Many animals make sounds to warn others "this is my territory". Noises are a good warning because they travel a long way.

Birds such as gulls make a simple call which says "this is mine". Other birds, such as thrushes, sing more complicated songs.

Each kind of bird has a different song. Usually, the male sings it. He learns it by listening to the adult males when he is young.

When the bird is ready to guard terrritory of his own, he adds new bits to his song. This makes a stronger "keep out" signal.

A bird's song is usually meant for birds of his own kind. This thrush is singing to warn other thrushes nearby.

This thrush recognizes his neighbour's song and will keep out of his territory.

Rat-a-tat-tat

A male woodpecker marks his territory with a loud rat-a-tat-tat. He makes the sound by drumming his beak on a hollow branch or tree.

The woodpecker in this picture makes about 25 drums a second. When he is feeding he only makes a short tap-tap.

The lion's roar

Lions live in groups called prides. A pride's territory can be up to twenty kilometres across.

An adult male warns other males away with an almighty roar. It can be heard eight kilometres away.

Noises underwater

The male haddock guards his underwater territory by making noises. He moves special muscles so they drum against a part called his swim bladder.

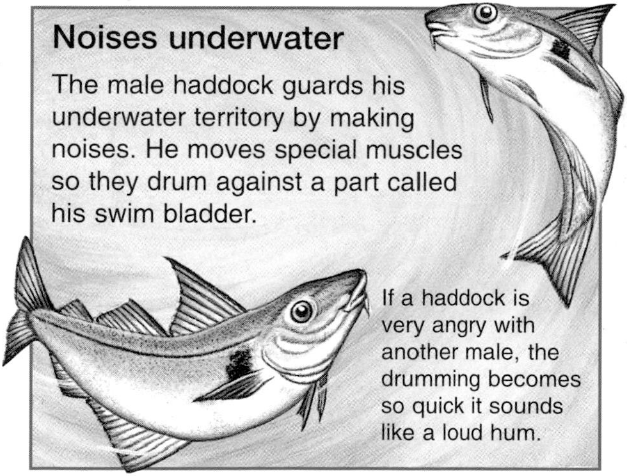

If a haddock is very angry with another male, the drumming becomes so quick it sounds like a loud hum.

Internet link *Go to* ***www.usborne-quicklinks.com*** *for a link to a Web site where you can find out more about how animals protect their territory and themselves.*

More warnings

Different animals have different ways of saying “keep out of my territory”. Bright colours, claw marks and strong smells are all warnings to strangers.

Some animals make themselves look bigger than they really are.

You may have seen a cat’s hair stand on end if a strange cat comes into the garden. This is called a display.

The Australian frilled lizard raises its bright neck flap and opens its mouth wide if an enemy comes too close.

Warning colour

When a male stickleback fish is ready to build his nest and look for a mate, his tummy turns bright red.

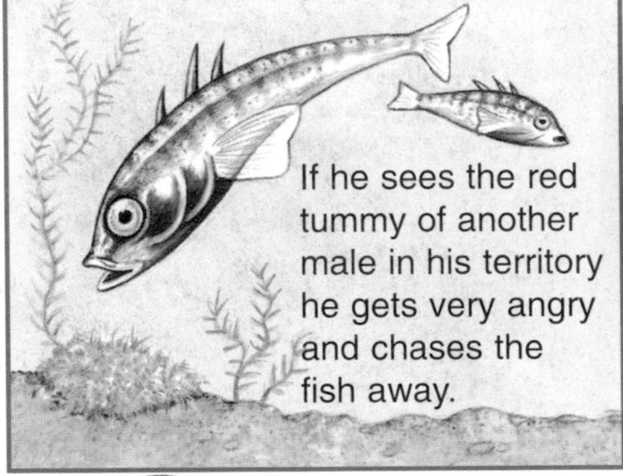

If he sees the red tummy of another male in his territory he gets very angry and chases the fish away.

A male elephant seal opens his mouth in an enormous gape to frighten other males away from his territory.

***Internet link** Go to **www.usborne-quicklinks.com** for a link to a Web site packed with interesting facts about how animals defend themselves.*

Smelly messages

Many animals have a very good sense of smell and they mark their territories with smelly messages.

An otter marks its exit from the water by leaving droppings on a stone.

The scent of a dropping can last for many weeks.

Dogs mark places where they live and walk by urinating (weeing). First, they sniff to smell who else has been there.

Stink fights

Male ring-tailed lemurs have stink fights to win territory. Their smelly scent is made under the skin of their arms.

Each lemur pulls his tail between his arms, then he waves it about. The one with the strongest scent usually wins.

"I was here"

Bears mark their territory by scratching at trees. The claw marks warn other bears "I was here".

Finding a mate

Most kinds of animals look for a mate each year, so they can have babies.

Usually, a male makes signals to a female, inviting her to be his partner.

The meeting place

Each year Uganda kobs meet at a place called a lek. The males gather there to fight for small bits of territory. A female visits a male's territory when she is ready to find a mate.

These male kobs are fighting for territory. The weaker animal will give in.

This male is displaying to a female who has come into his territory. He is showing off by dancing near her, to see if she will be his partner.

Beautiful birds

Male birds are usually more colourful than female birds. They use their brightly coloured feathers to make beautiful displays to the female birds.

A male blue bird of paradise hangs upside down and fans out his blue and green feathers.

Calling out

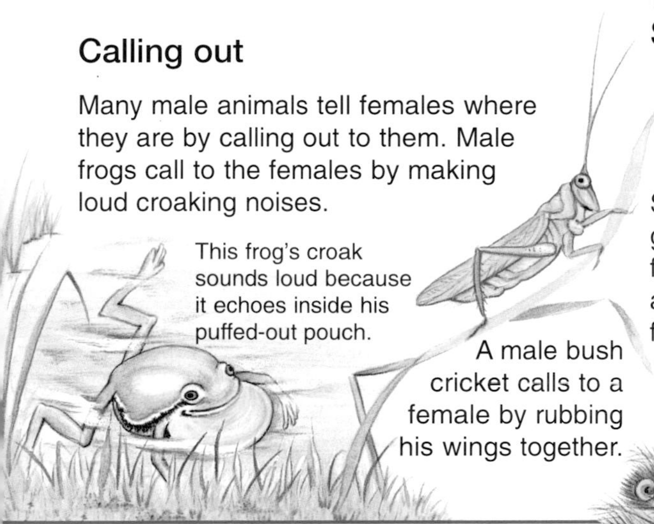

Many male animals tell females where they are by calling out to them. Male frogs call to the females by making loud croaking noises.

This frog's croak sounds loud because it echoes inside his puffed-out pouch.

A male bush cricket calls to a female by rubbing his wings together.

Smelling the air

Some animals, like this male gypsy moth, can smell a mate from far away. The moth's big antennae help him smell a female moth's special scent.

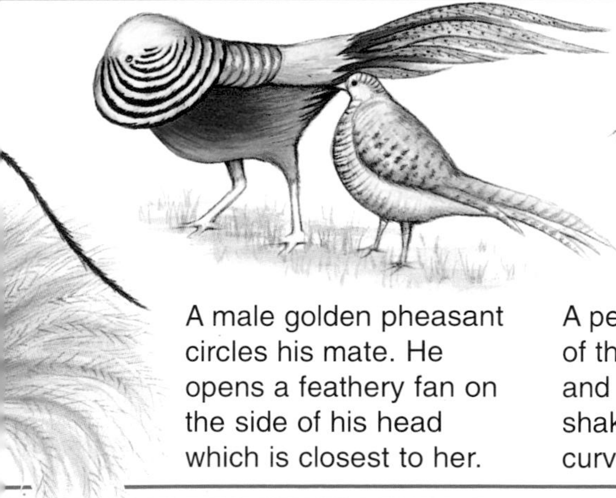

A male golden pheasant circles his mate. He opens a feathery fan on the side of his head which is closest to her.

A peacock stands in front of the female, the peahen, and displays to her by shaking his enormous curved feathers.

***Internet link** Go to **www.usborne-quicklinks.com** for a link to a Web site where you will find some beautiful photographs of birds of paradise displaying and find out more about them.*

Family talk

Animal parents and their babies must talk to each other for many reasons. They need to know how to recognize each other, so the family can stay safely together. They must also understand each other when they feed.

A voice from the egg

Some baby animals talk with their mother even before they are born.

A female Nile crocodile buries her eggs in the sand. When the babies are ready to hatch they make a peeping call. The mother hears the noise and uncovers the eggs, so the babies can get out.

Chicks make cheeping noises while they are still in the shell and the hen answers.

"Are you my mother?"

Many baby animals learn to recognize their parents almost as soon as they are born. This is called imprinting.

When birds hatch, their parents are usually the first things they see. These ducklings are following their mother.

***Internet link** Go to **www.usborne-quicklinks.com** for a link to a Web site where you can listen to the different noises made by crocodiles and find out what they mean.*

Hungry chicks

Many kinds of chicks have brightly coloured throats. This colour is a signal to the parents. When they see it they feed their hungry babies.

In some birds, the parents have colourful signalling marks.

An adult gull has a bright spot on the bottom part of its beak. When a chick sees the colour it taps the spot. This makes the parent bring up food which it has been storing inside its body.

Sometimes, the first thing a baby animal sees is not its real parent, but another animal.

These baby geese have never seen their real mother. They have imprinted on a dog and they follow it everywhere.

Important smells

Some animals recognize each other by smell. A female sheep learns the smell and taste of her lambs. She will not look after another mother's lamb.

This sheep can recognize the voice of her lamb among the bleating of all the other lambs.

Living together

Many animals spend their lives together, in a group. Here are some of the ways they say things to each other with their bodies and faces.

Chimpanzee language

Chimpanzees often talk using different movements, just as we do.

Chimps sometimes show they are friendly by kissing when they meet.

A chimp greets a more important member of the group by holding out its hand. The other one shows it is friendly by touching the hand.

Chimps calm each other by hugging and touching.

Making faces

Chimps make many different faces to say how they feel. They also add to their messages with different calls.

This chimp's smile shows that it is happy. Your smile says the same thing.

This chimp seems to be laughing, but it is not happy at all. It is frightened.

This hard stare means that the chimp is angry and may attack.

An angry gorilla

An adult male gorilla makes a frightening and noisy warning display if he feels threatened.

As part of the display the gorilla beats his chest. The loud booming sound can be heard far away.

Showing who is boss

In many groups each animal has a place in order of importance. This is called the pecking order. Wolves in a pack signal with their faces and tails to show their position.

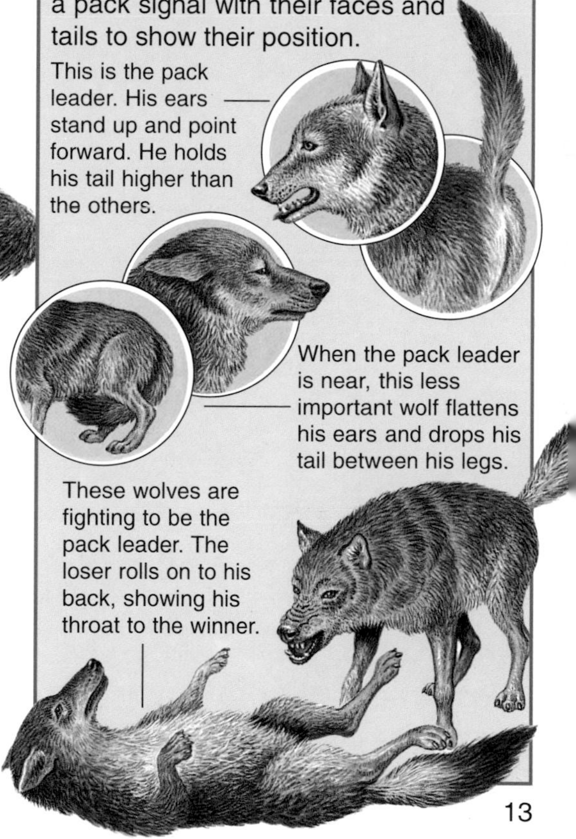

This is the pack leader. His ears stand up and point forward. He holds his tail higher than the others.

When the pack leader is near, this less important wolf flattens his ears and drops his tail between his legs.

These wolves are fighting to be the pack leader. The loser rolls on to his back, showing his throat to the winner.

Looking for food

Some kinds of animals hunt and feed in groups. It is easier to find food when there are lots of pairs of eyes keeping a look-out. It is also easier to spy danger. Here are some of the ways different animals say things to each other when they are looking for food.

African hunting dogs

Before a hunt, African hunting dogs get ready by licking and nudging each other. They soon get excited and set off together.

On the hunt, the dogs' strong scent helps them keep in contact. Their white-tipped tails help them to see each other.

Afterwards, the hunters will go back to their den to feed the puppies and dogs who stayed behind.

The hungry dogs ask for food by licking the hunters' lips. Then the hunters bring up bits of meat which they ate at the kill.

 Internet link *Go to* ***www.usborne-quicklinks.com*** *for a link to a Web site where you can see photographs of some of the things ants eat, including caterpillars.*

Smelly trails

A family of ants is called a colony. The worker ants search for food. They leave scent trails as they go. When a worker ant finds plenty of food it takes some back to the nest.

Some more workers leave the nest and find the food by following the trail. They smell the scent with their antennae.

Worker ants are females. This one is tapping the ground with her antennae so she can smell where to go.

"Come and help"

Sometimes an ant finds a bit of food which is too big for it to carry, so it tells the others to "come and help". It does this by hitting them with its antennae and front legs.

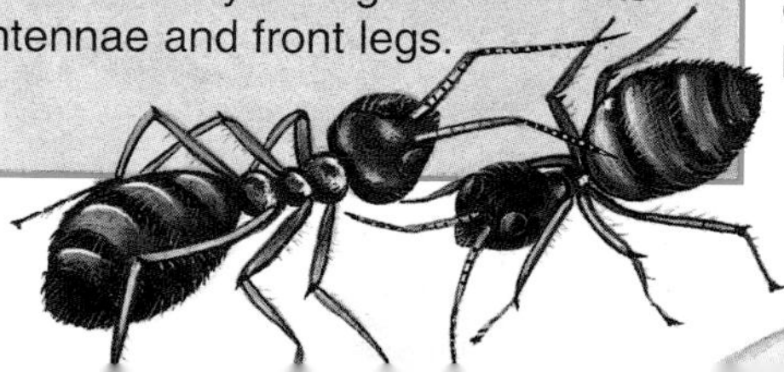

Feeding the flock

Different kinds of small songbirds sometimes gather in a flock to hunt for berries and seeds. They call to each other to say where there is food or to warn enemies.

The birds make about 25 different sounds, each with a special meaning.

Different kinds of ants eat different food. Some eat plants and some eat other creatures. These black ants eat both.

Busy bees

There can be as many as fifty thousand bees in a honeybee colony. Colonies are made up of three kinds of bees.

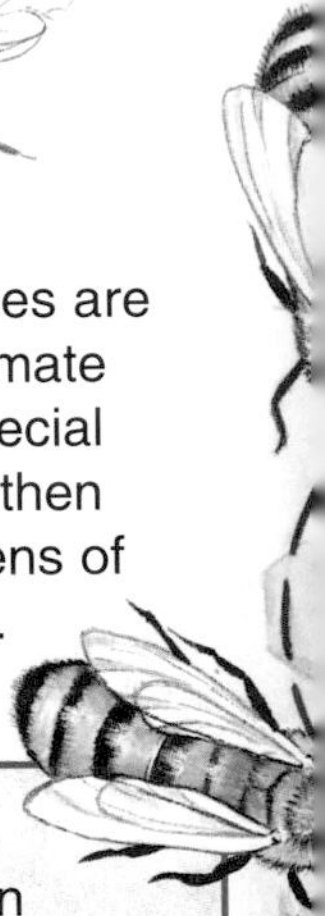

The queen is the biggest and most important bee. Each hive has one queen. She lays eggs and is the mother of all the bees.

The worker bees are females. They collect food, do the cleaning and feed the queen. They do not lay eggs.

The drone bees are males. They mate with a few special females who then become queens of new colonies.

The queen's scent

Bees crowd around the queen. They try to touch her and lick her.

The queen bee has a strong scent which has a powerful effect on the rest of the colony. As long as the queen is there the bees work calmly.

Strangers beware

Every bee colony has its own scent. Sometimes, a stranger from another colony tries to get into the hive, but the bees recognize its different scent and push it out.

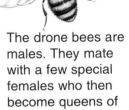

The intruder curls up. This tells the other bees "I give in".

 Internet link *Go to* ***www.usborne-quicklinks.com*** *for a link to a Web site where you can watch video clips of bees waggle dancing.*

"Food is this way"

Honeybees visit flowers to collect pollen and sweet food called nectar. When a worker bee finds plenty of food, she tells the others where to find it by doing a special dance.

The round dance

If the food is nearby the dancer moves in a circle, going one way then the other way.

The bees touch her and copy her. They can smell the pollen on her fur, so they know which kind of flower to look for.

The waggle dance

If a bee finds food far away from the hive she dances in the shape of a squashed figure 8. In the straight part she waggles her body very quickly.

This waggling part of the dance is called the waggle run.

The speed of the dance and the direction of the waggle run tell the bees how far away the food is. They also tell the bees which way to fly.

When the bees find the flowers they collect food. They then return to the hive and do the dance themselves.

Staying safe

Animals mostly say things just to their own kind, but if they are in danger, they say things to other creatures too. They even say things to their enemies.

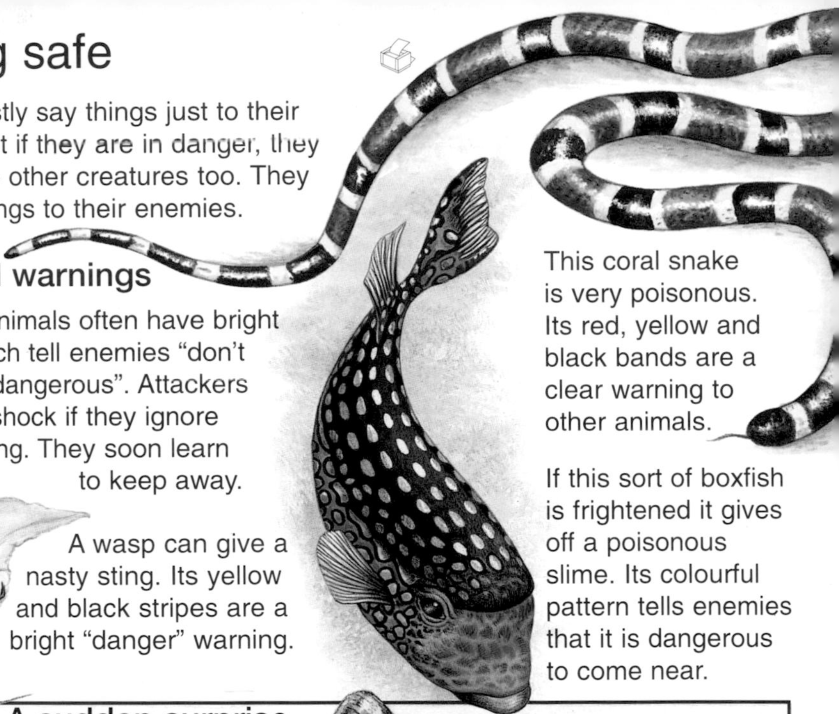

Patterned warnings

Poisonous animals often have bright patterns which tell enemies "don't eat me, I'm dangerous". Attackers get a nasty shock if they ignore the warning. They soon learn to keep away.

A wasp can give a nasty sting. Its yellow and black stripes are a bright "danger" warning.

This coral snake is very poisonous. Its red, yellow and black bands are a clear warning to other animals.

If this sort of boxfish is frightened it gives off a poisonous slime. Its colourful pattern tells enemies that it is dangerous to come near.

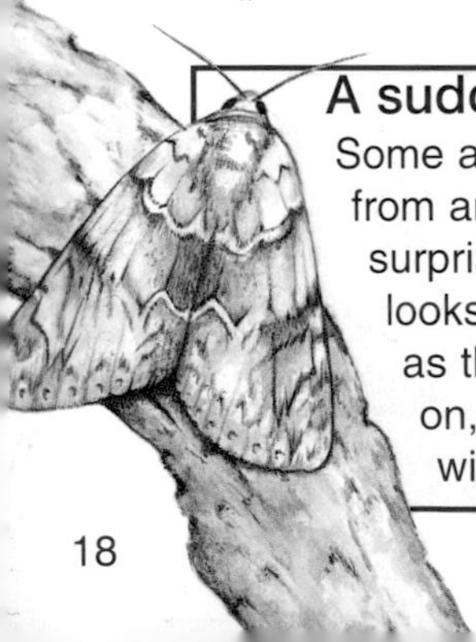

A sudden surprise

Some animals escape from an attacker by surprising it. This moth looks the same colour as the tree it is resting on, but its bright hind wings are hidden.

If the moth is disturbed, it flies and startles the attacker with a flash of colour. Then it settles again. The attacker thinks the moth has gone.

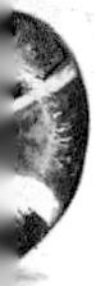

"I'm watching you"

Some animals are born with a clever disguise. They have markings which look like big eyes, which can frighten or confuse an enemy.

If the eyed hawk-moth is disturbed it moves its front wings to show two big spots underneath. They look like the eyes of a big animal.

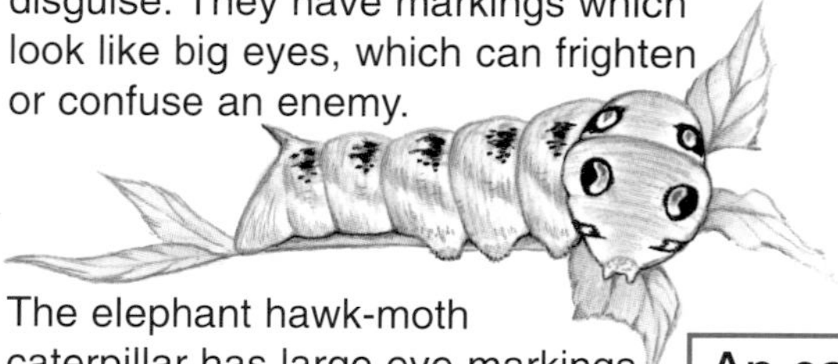

The elephant hawk-moth caterpillar has large eye markings. These make the front of its body look like a snake's head.

Many kinds of butterfly fish have a dark spot near the tail. This confuses enemies as they think they are looking at the head.

An early warning

When some birds sense danger they make a loud, frightened call. Other kinds of birds understand there is something wrong and join in.

If you hear lots of excited bird-calls in a garden, it may mean there is a cat about.

***Internet link** Go to **www.usborne-quicklinks.com** for a link to a Web site where you can read about how different animals manage to stay safe.*

Talking underwater

Whales, dolphins and many kinds of fish use sounds, movements and even smells to say things in their underwater world. Sound is a strong signal as it travels well in water.

Dolphin language

Dolphins live in groups called schools. They say things with lots of noises, including squawks, whistles, groans, burps and clicks.

Hawaiian spinner dolphins are most noisy in the evenings, when they are about to go hunting.

When they are ready to leave, they all join in a special chorus of noises. They also leap and slap the water with their bodies. This helps to show where everyone is before they go.

Whales

Whales call to each other with loud sounds which other whales can hear from far away. They make high trumpeting noises and low grunting sounds.

Scientists think the noises may help the whales keep in touch with each other when they are far apart.

Mystery songs

Humpback whales make sounds which they repeat in long, complicated patterns. Scientists call these "songs", but nobody knows what the songs mean.

A humpback whale usually sings when it is looking for a mate. A song can last for over 30 minutes.

 Internet link *Go to* ***www.usborne-quicklinks.com*** *for a link to a Web site where you can listen to the noises that whales make.*

Noisy fish

Many fish make sounds by rubbing their teeth, bones or fin spines together. Some even make sounds by moving muscles in their bodies.

This is called a grunt fish. It makes a grunting noise by grinding teeth which grow in its throat.

Scientists think these sounds help the fish say things to the rest of its group.

Alarm signal

If a minnow is hurt by an attacker, its body sends out a special liquid from the wound.

This signal says “danger” and the other minnows keep away.

Dancing fish

This colourful male guppy fish is showing the female that he wants to be her mate.

He does this by dancing up to her and fanning out his beautiful fins.

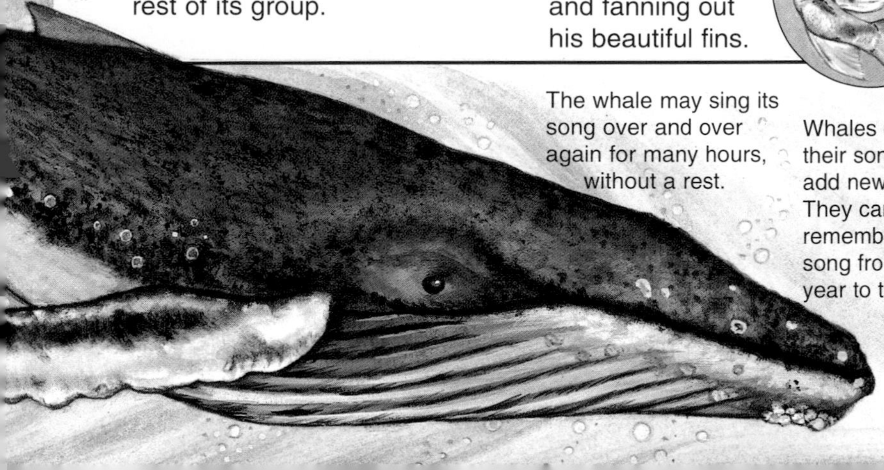

The whale may sing its song over and over again for many hours, without a rest.

Whales change their songs and add new bits. They can even remember a song from one year to the next.

Dogs and people

For hundreds of years people have trained dogs, using a language of signals and commands. Dogs are very sensitive. They can tell a lot from small changes in their owner's voice. This helps to make them easy to train.

Trained to help

Wolves and wild dogs follow their pack leader and do what it tells them. Animals who live or work with people obey a human leader instead.

Dogs can be trained to herd sheep. The farmer whistles signals which tell the dogs what to do.

Sheepdogs are good at their job because their wild relatives herded their prey when they hunted.

Some dogs are trained to guide blind people. They obey their owners, but if there is danger, the dog gives the orders. If there is something in the way, the dog stops its owner from moving.

Police dog handlers are taught to train their own dogs. The handler and the dog must learn to trust and understand each other.

This dog is being trained to track down criminals.

Internet links

Go to **www.usborne-quicklinks.com** and type in the keywords "pocket scientist 2" for links to these Web sites about animals.

Web site 1 On this Web site there is lots of information about animals, and pictures which you can print out, colour in and label. Click on a letter, then on a picture of the animal you would like to find out about.

Web site 2 At night you can hear animals but you can't see them. Listen to twenty different animal noises, and guess which animal makes them.

Web site 3 Sight is an important part of communication between animals, and an important part of catching food, for many of them. On this Web site you can find out more about how different animals see.

Web site 4 Discover more about how different animals communicate and look at photographs of they way they do it.

Web site 5 Although animals make the same sounds around the world, each language describes those sounds differently. Find out what the different descriptions are and listen to some animal noises.

Web site 6 Find out more about animals by playing some amazing interactive games. On this site you can click through a tree in search of insects, help five baby sea turtles reach the sea, and journey across the globe in search of strange creatures.

For links to all these sites go to www.usborne-quicklinks.com and type in the keywords "pocket scientist 2".

More internet links

Here are some more Web sites to visit to find out about animals. For links to all these sites go to **www.usborne-quicklinks.com** and type in the keywords "pocket scientist 2".

Web site 1 Read animal myths and legends from all around the world. You can test your knowledge of the stories with crosswords and try out some animal craft activities.

Web site 2 This Web site is packed with fun games. You have to gather clues about birds, mammals, insects, reptiles and fish to guess the mystery creatures. As you collect information, you'll also see parts of a picture of the hidden animal. There are lots of interesting facts on this site.

Web site 3 On this site you can find out about gorilla sign language by playing a game matching a gorilla's actions to words.

Web site 4 Find out all about Australian animals, including kangaroos, koalas and wombats. You can also print out pages to color in and do a word search.

Web site 5 Listen to a variety of animals sounds, from whales to tigers and elephants, and then click on the links to read some fascinating facts about them.

Web site 6 How can I stop my rabbit from biting people? Why does my cat sometimes pace up and down for hours on end? These are some of the questions answered on this Web site, which is all about pets, and how to communicate with them.

For links to all these sites go to www.usborne-quicklinks.com and type in the keywords "pocket scientist 2".

HOW DO BEES MAKE HONEY?

Anna Claybourne

Designed by Lindy Dark
Illustrated by Sophie Allington and Annabel Spenceley
Additional illustrations by Janos Marffy
Edited by Kamini Khanduri
American editor: Carrie Seay
Consultant: James Hamill

CONTENTS

Bees and other insects

Bees are amazing insects. There are lots of different kinds, but honeybees are the most common – and they are the ones that make honey. In this section, you can find out about honeybees, and about lots of other insects.

Honeybee

Tawny mining bee

Buff-tailed bumblebee

Busy bees

Some people are frightened of honeybees, because they can sting. In fact, bees are usually busy looking for flowers, and don't sting very often.

Bees only sting if they are frightened. If you leave them alone, they probably won't hurt you.

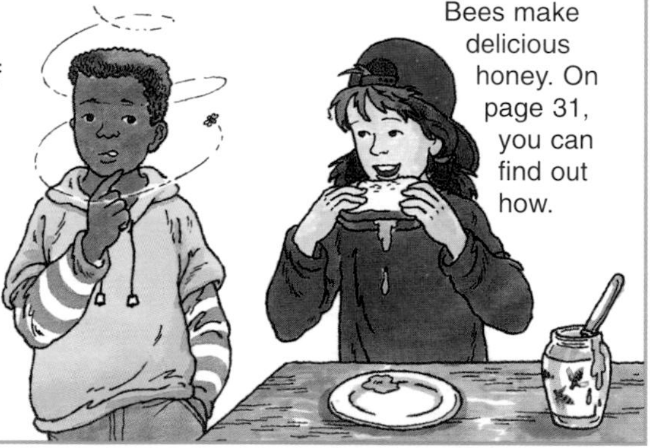

Bees make delicious honey. On page 31, you can find out how.

Insects all around

There are over a million kinds of insects. They live in all sorts of places – in the ground, on plants, under stones, and even in houses.

You can often see houseflies inside houses.

Honeybees fly from flower to flower, collecting food.

Butterflies fly around plants.

There are many different kinds of beetles. Some live on trees.

Dragonflies live near watery places.

These ants dig tunnels in the ground to live in.

Internet link *Go to* ***www.usborne-quicklinks.com*** *for a link to a Web site where you can find out lots about honeybees and their more dangerous relatives, the killer bees.*

A closer look

This picture shows a honeybee ten times bigger than it is in real life. You can see the different parts of its body.

A bee has a large wing and a small wing on each side of its body. When bees fly, their wings make a buzzing sound.

This is a close-up picture of a bee's eye.

A bee has a sharp point on its tail. It can use this to sting enemies.

Bees have big eyes made up of lots of tiny eyes joined together.

Like all insects, a bee has six legs – three on each side of its body.

Bees use their two antennae to feel, taste and smell things.

A bee has a long tongue called a proboscis. It uses it to suck up food.

A bee's body has three sections: a head, a thorax and an abdomen.

Internet link *Go to* ***www.usborne-quicklinks.com*** *for a link to a Web site where you can click on a picture of a bee to discover more about the different parts of its body.*

A bee or not a bee?

Lots of insects have black and yellow stripes. People sometimes mix them up with bees. Only one of these is a honeybee. Can you tell which one?

Look on page 48 for the answer.

Bees at home

Honeybees live together in big groups called colonies. Today, most colonies live in beehives built by people.

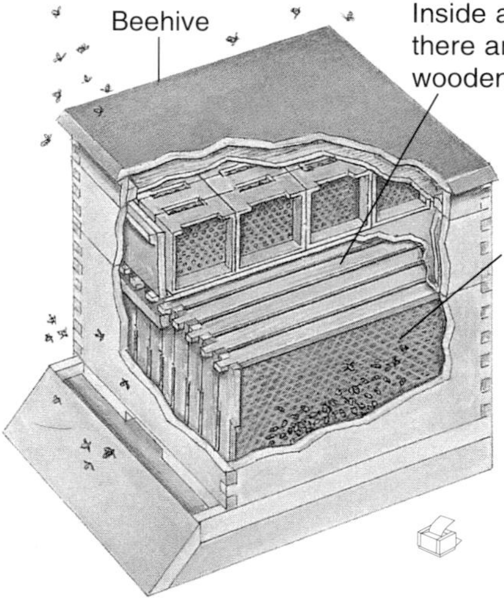

Inside a beehive, there are lots of wooden frames.

The bees build a wax honeycomb in each frame. They store their honey there.

There can be over 50,000 bees living in one hive.

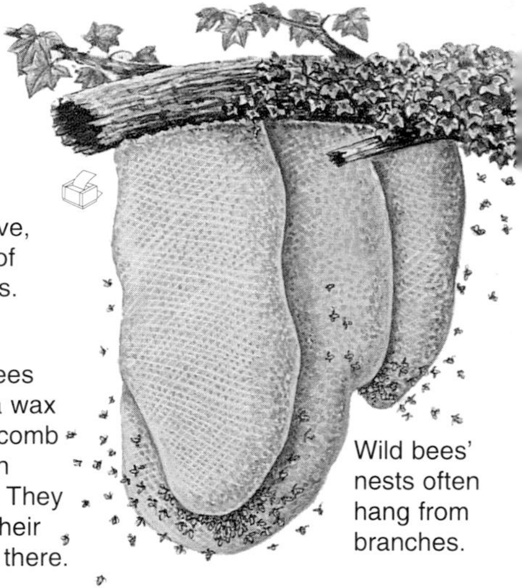

Wild bees' nests often hang from branches.

Some honeybees live in the wild. They build honeycomb nests out of wax.

Honey

The honey you buy all comes from honeybees. They make honey as food for themselves and their babies. People take some of the honey, but they leave enough for the bees.

Honey milk shake

To make this milk shake, measure out a cupful of milk. Add a scoop of ice-cream and two teaspoons of honey.

Whisk or blend the mixture. Pour it into a glass.

Top with banana slices.

Collecting honey

People who keep bees and collect their honey are called beekeepers. They wear gloves and veils when they are working, so they do not get stung. Their clothes are white, because this makes the bees feel calm.

The beekeeper lifts each frame out of the hive, takes out the honey and puts the frame back.

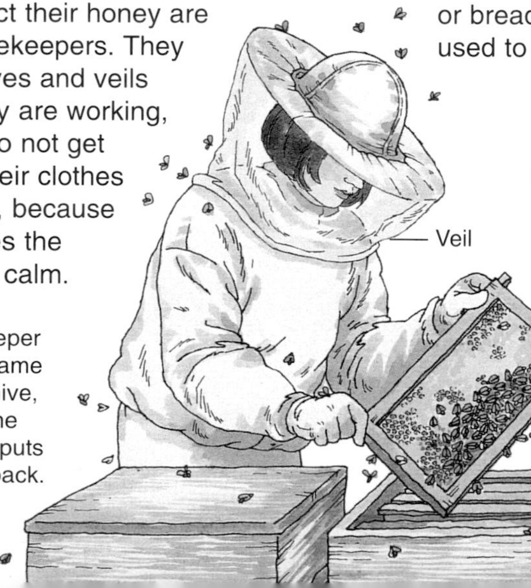

You can eat honey on toast or bread. Some honey is used to make other things.

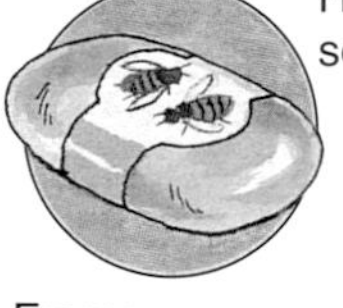

Honey soap

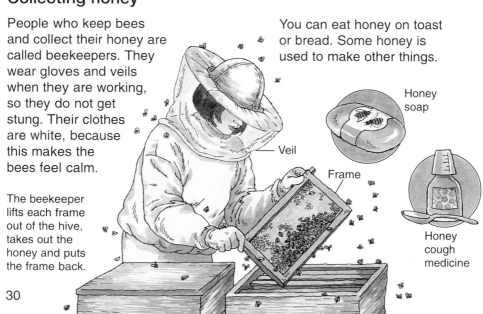

Honey cough medicine

How bees make honey

Honeybees make honey from a sweet liquid called nectar, which they suck out of flowers. Older bees collect the nectar and pass it on to younger bees.

This picture shows how bees make honey inside their bodies.

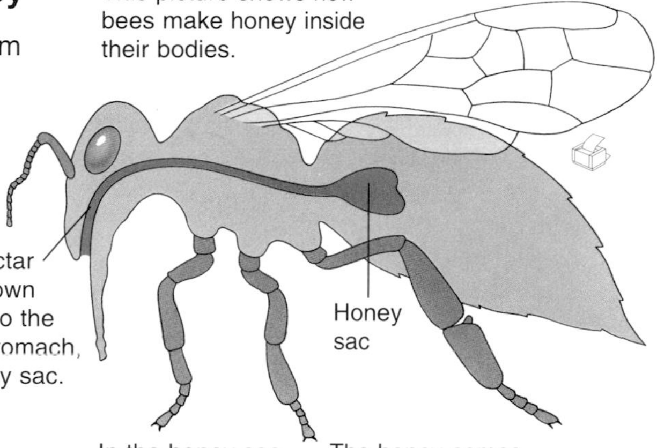

The nectar goes down a tube to the bee's stomach, or honey sac.

In the honey sac, the nectar gets thicker and turns into honey.

The honey comes out through the bee's mouth. It is kept safe in the hive.

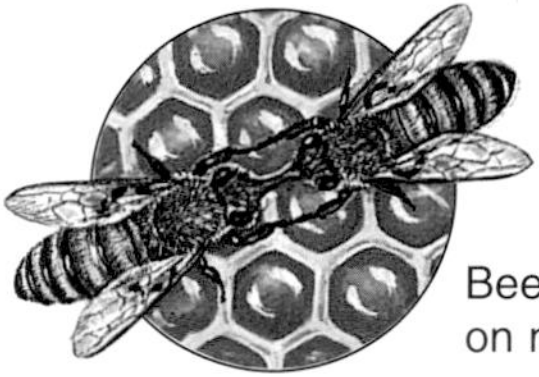

Bees passing on nectar.

Different kinds of honey

Apple blossom honey is thick and yellow.

Borage flower honey is pale and runny.

Next time you go shopping, try looking for different kinds of honey. How many can you find?

Bees and flowers

On warm days, female honeybees visit flowers to collect nectar and a kind of yellow powder called pollen. They use pollen as food for their babies.

Did you know?

A honeybee can visit up to 10,000 flowers in a day, but all the nectar she collects in her whole life is only enough to make one teaspoon of honey.

The bee lands on the flower and sticks her proboscis, or tongue, into the middle to reach the nectar.

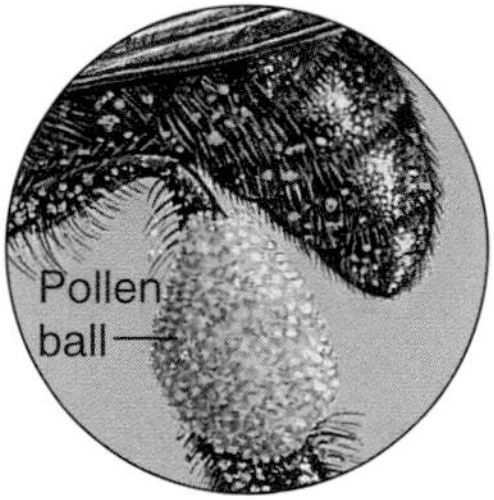

Some pollen sticks to the bee's legs and body. She rolls it into balls which she carries on her back legs.

Tiny drops of nectar are hidden in little hollows at the bottom of the flower's petals.

Pollen is found on little stalks, called stamens, in the middle of the flower.

Busy helpers

Flowers need to swap pollen with each other to grow seeds. Bees and other insects carry pollen from one flower to the next. This is called pollination.

This bumblebee is visiting a dog rose. Her fur gets covered in specks of pollen.

When the bumblebee flies to another dog rose, she carries some pollen with her.

The pollen helps the second dog rose make seeds. These can grow into new dog roses.

Making a beeline

Many flowers have bright markings and strong smells. These attract insects to pollinate the flowers. Some flowers also have dark lines called honeyguides.

Scientists think that honeyguides may help insects find their way into flowers.

Flower feeders

It's not just bees that like flowers. Many other insects, such as butterflies, visit flowers to feed on nectar.

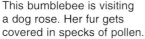

Monarch butterfly feeding on nectar.

Inside a beehive

This picture shows part of a honeycomb inside a beehive. It is made up of lots of little compartments called cells. There are three types of honeybees in a hive.

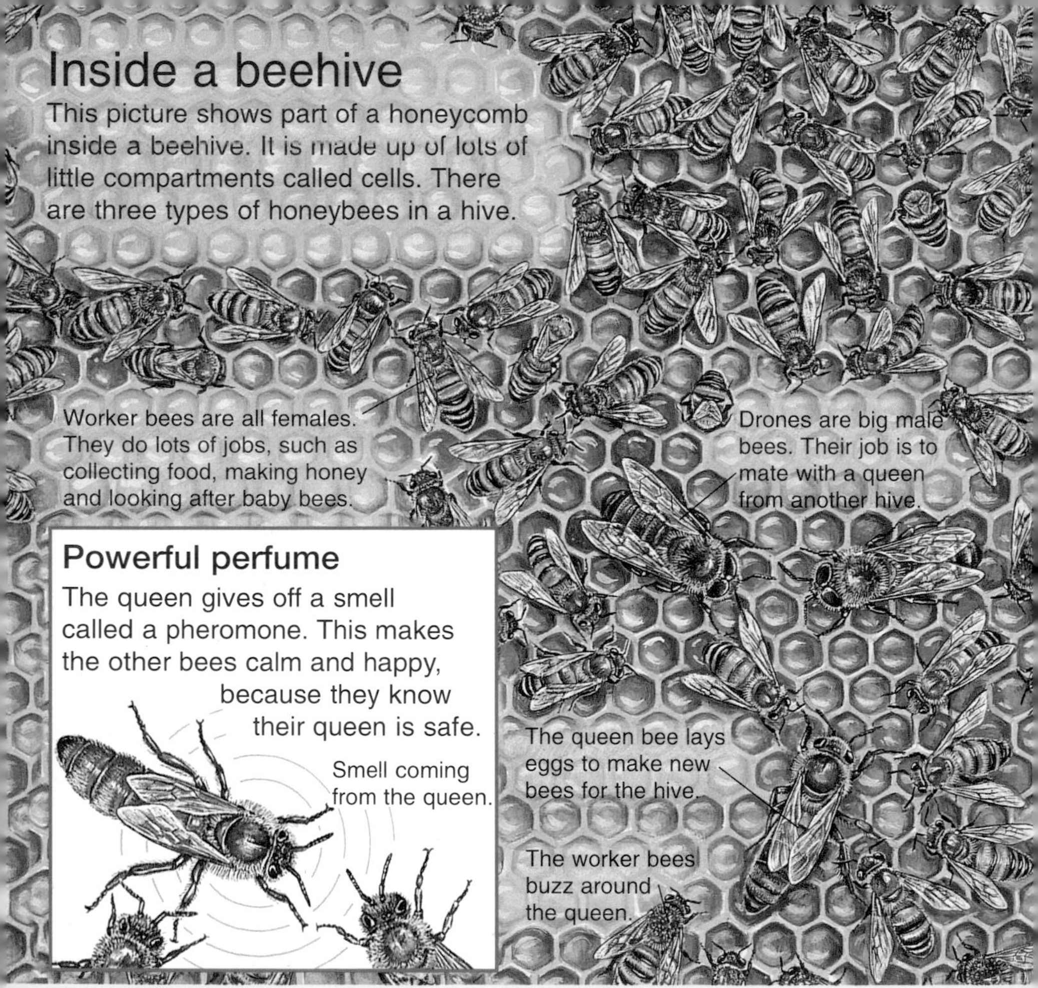

Worker bees are all females. They do lots of jobs, such as collecting food, making honey and looking after baby bees.

Drones are big male bees. Their job is to mate with a queen from another hive.

The queen bee lays eggs to make new bees for the hive.

The worker bees buzz around the queen.

Powerful perfume

The queen gives off a smell called a pheromone. This makes the other bees calm and happy, because they know their queen is safe.

Smell coming from the queen.

***Internet link** Go to **www.usborne-quicklinks.com** for a link to a Web site where you can enter a beehive and find out about the daily life of the honeybee.*

Making cells

Worker bees build cells from wax, which they make in their stomachs. The wax comes out in flakes under their bodies.

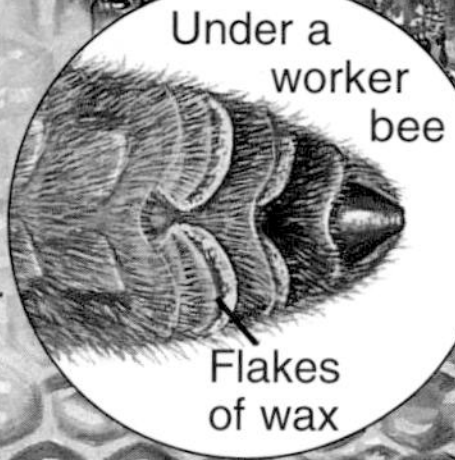

Under a worker bee
Flakes of wax

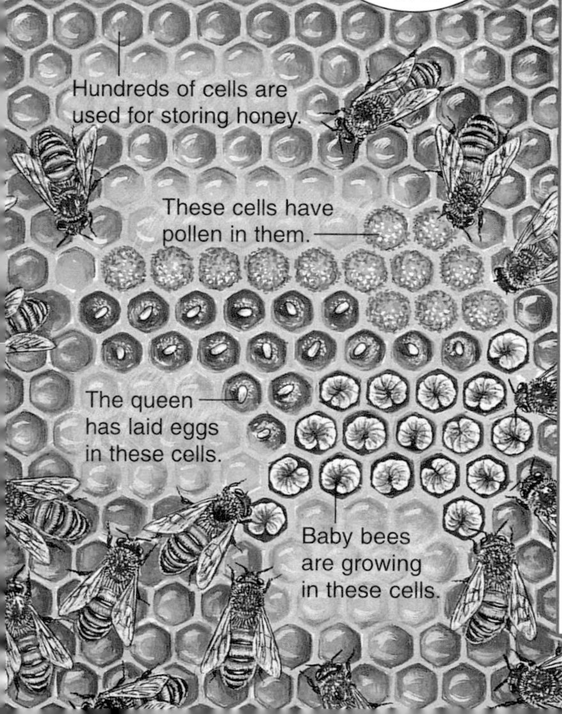

Hundreds of cells are used for storing honey.
These cells have pollen in them.
The queen has laid eggs in these cells.
Baby bees are growing in these cells.

Useful shapes

The cells in a hive are almost round, but not quite. Honeybees give the cells six straight sides. Can you guess why this shape is better than a round shape?

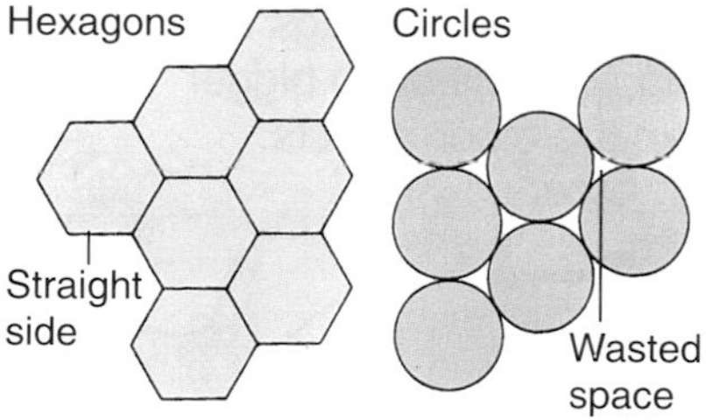

These cell shapes are called hexagons. Hexagons fit together well. This means the bees can build lots of cells next to each other, with no wasted space.

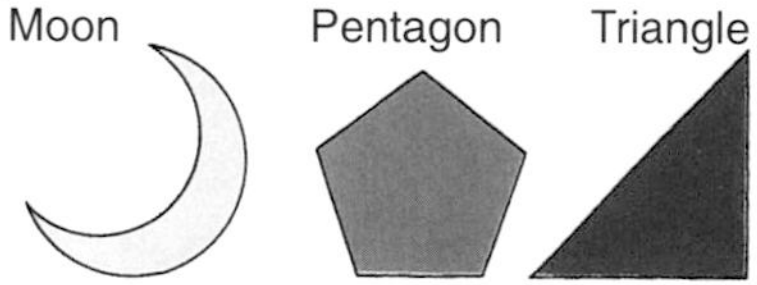

Can you see which of these shapes fit together without leaving spaces? Find out on page 48.

Living in groups

Honeybees are not the only insects that live in groups – many other kinds do too. Insects that live together are called social insects.

Queens and kings

Social insects usually have a queen. She lays eggs for the colony and is often bigger than the other insects.

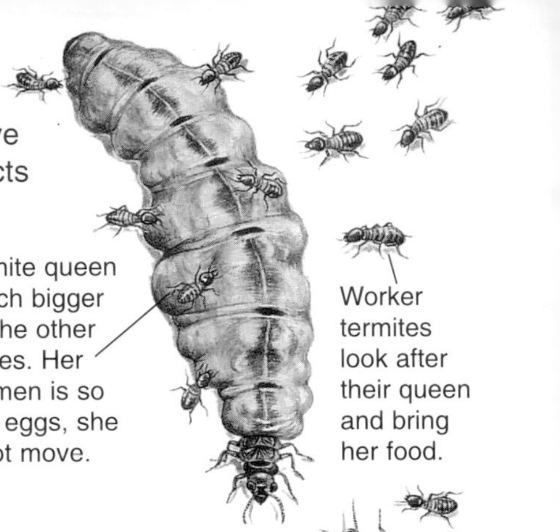

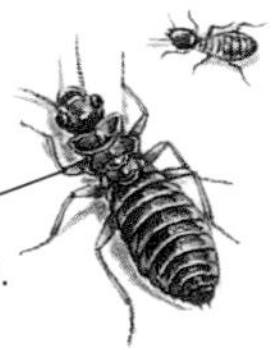

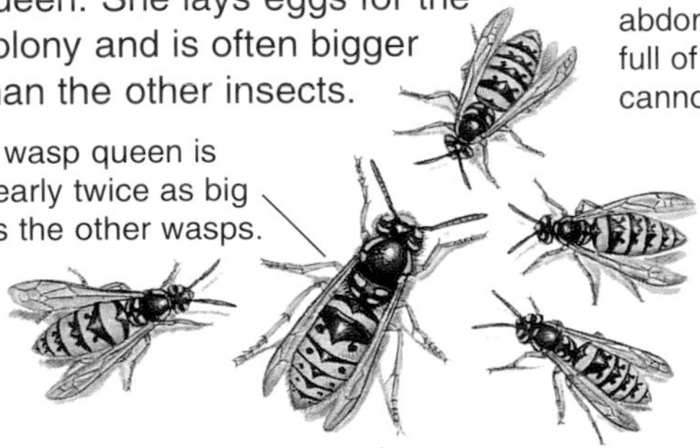

A wasp queen is nearly twice as big as the other wasps.

A termite queen is much bigger than the other termites. Her abdomen is so full of eggs, she cannot move.

Worker termites look after their queen and bring her food.

Termites have a king too, but he is much smaller than the queen.

Sharing food

Most social insects share food. These leafcutter ants are carrying bits of leaf back to their nest to make a store.

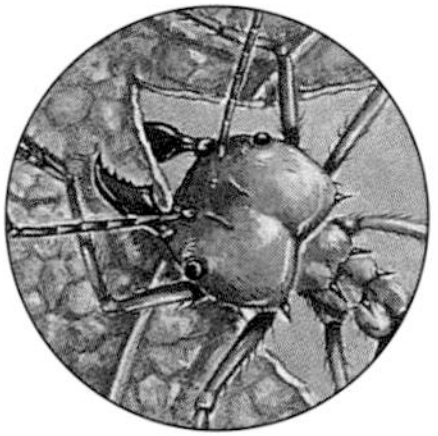

Leafcutter ants cut pieces out of leaves with their jaws.

An ant can carry a piece of leaf bigger than its own body.

Termite towers

Social insects often build themselves a home to share. Termites build tall towers out of soil, saliva (spit) and droppings. The termites live in the bottom part of the tower.

A termite tower can be up to 9m (30 ft) high – much taller than a giraffe.

This picture shows the tunnels and tiny rooms inside the tower.

Unusual jobs

Some members of insect colonies have special jobs to do.

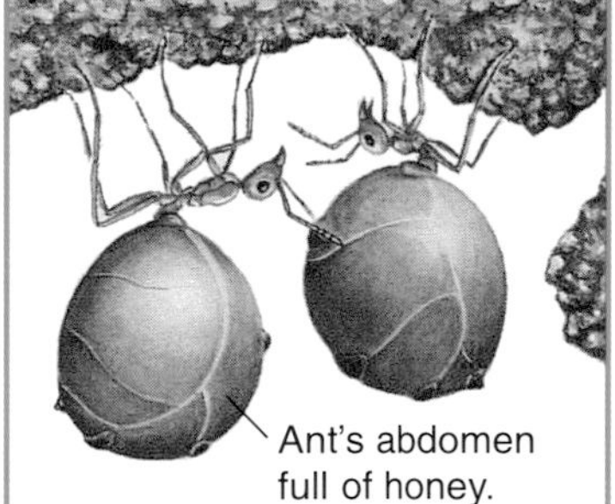

Ant's abdomen full of honey.

These honey ants store honey in their abdomens.

In an army ant colony, soldier ants use their huge jaws to fight enemies.

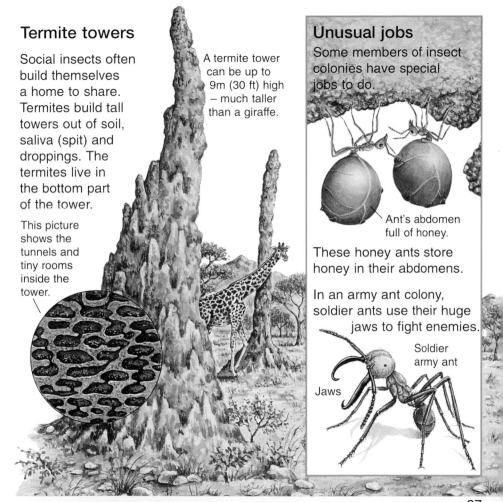

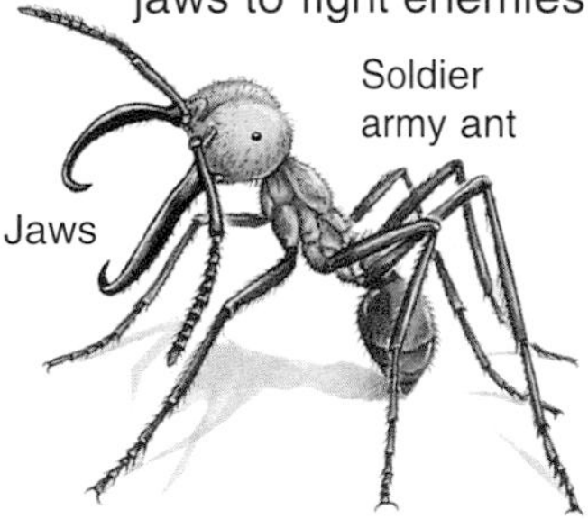

Soldier army ant

Internet link *Go to* ***www.usborne-quicklinks.com*** *for a link to a Web site where you can watch leafcutter ants on a Web cam and find out fascinating facts about them.*

Baby insects

All baby insects hatch out of eggs. Many of them look completely different from the adults.

Becoming a butterfly

Baby butterflies are called caterpillars. They have to change a lot before they become adults.

Most butterflies lay their eggs in spring on a plant.

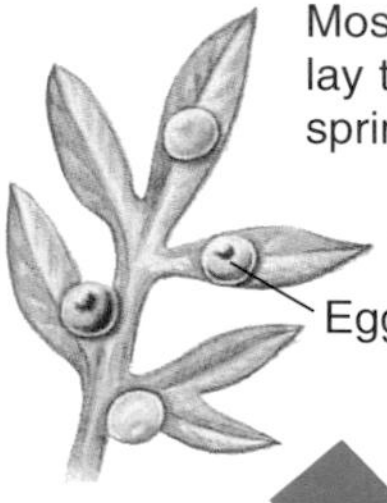

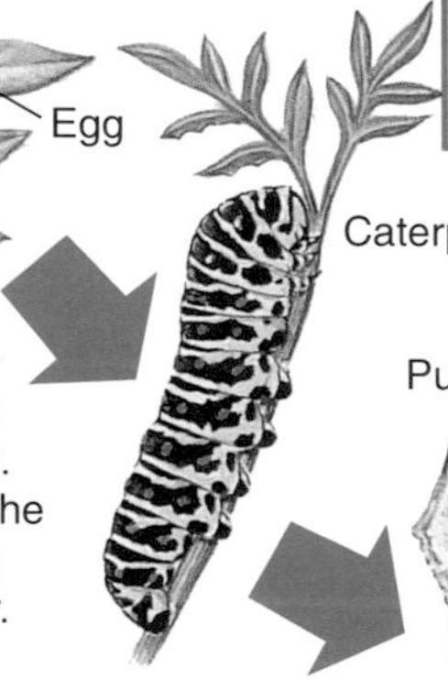

Caterpillar

A caterpillar hatches out of each egg. It feeds on the plant during the summer.

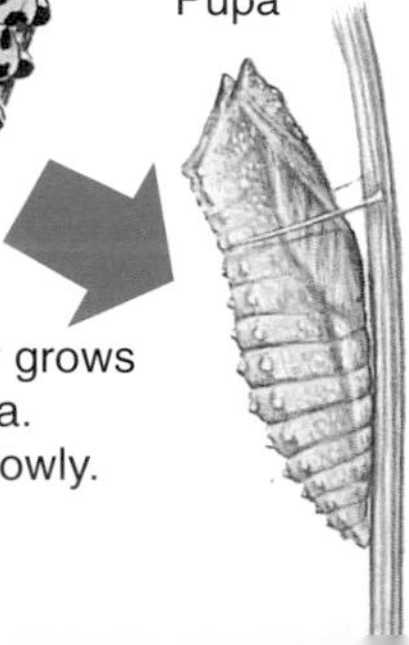

Pupa

In autumn, the caterpillar grows a hard shell called a pupa. Inside, it changes very slowly.

When it breaks out of the pupa a few months later, the caterpillar has changed into a butterfly.

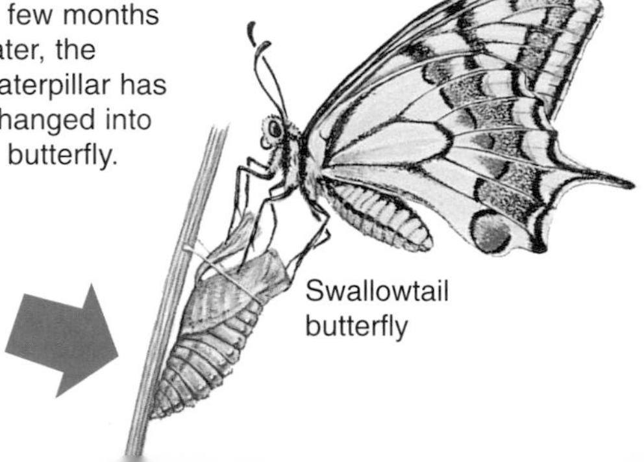

Swallowtail butterfly

Water babies

Dragonflies lay their eggs in water. When the babies hatch out, they live underwater for up to five years. Baby dragonflies, or nymphs, are small but very fierce.

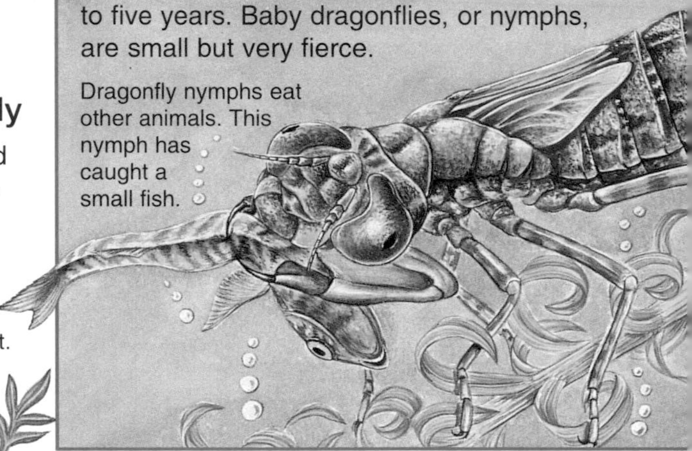

Dragonfly nymphs eat other animals. This nymph has caught a small fish.

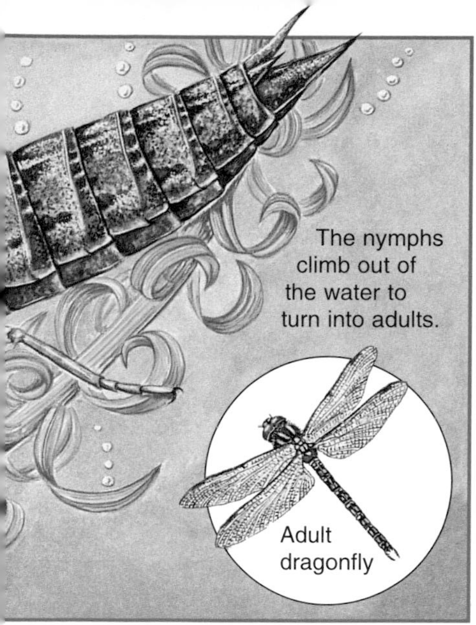

The nymphs climb out of the water to turn into adults.
Adult dragonfly

Which is which?

Can you tell which caterpillar turns into which butterfly? Follow the lines to find out.

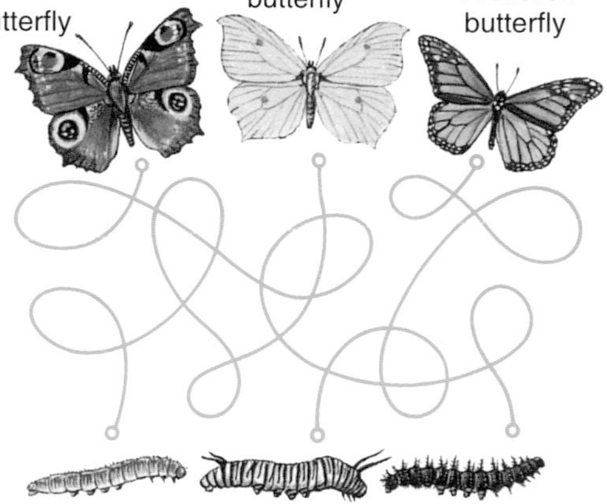

Feeding time

Some kinds of baby insects need to be fed by adults, but many can look after themselves.

This worker honeybee is bringing food to a baby in its cell. Baby bees, called larvae (say 'lar-vee'), can't fly or even crawl.

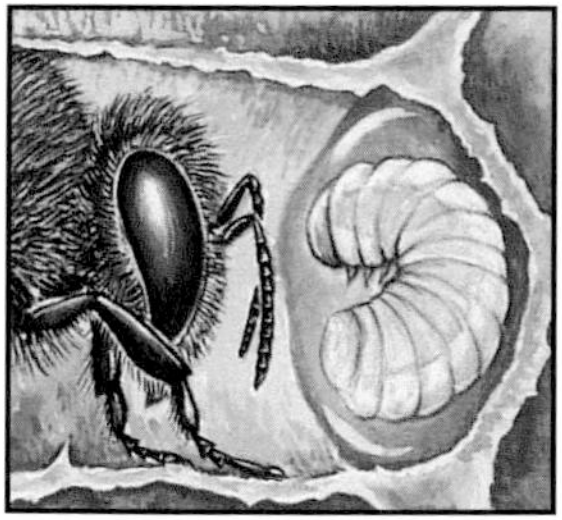

The caterpillars of large white butterflies find their own food. They can eat whole fields of crops.

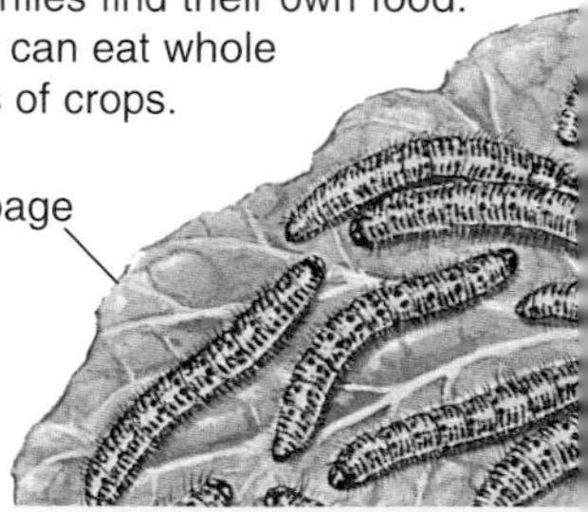

Internet link *Go to* ***www.usborne-quicklinks.com*** *for a link to a Web site that has lots of interesting information about butterflies, pictures of butterflies and caterpillars and a quiz to test your knowledge.*

Hunters

Some insects hunt other animals and eat them. Many hunting animals use clever tricks or secret traps to catch their food. The animals they catch are called prey.

Surprise attack

Mantises hunt by sneaking up on their prey and taking it by surprise.

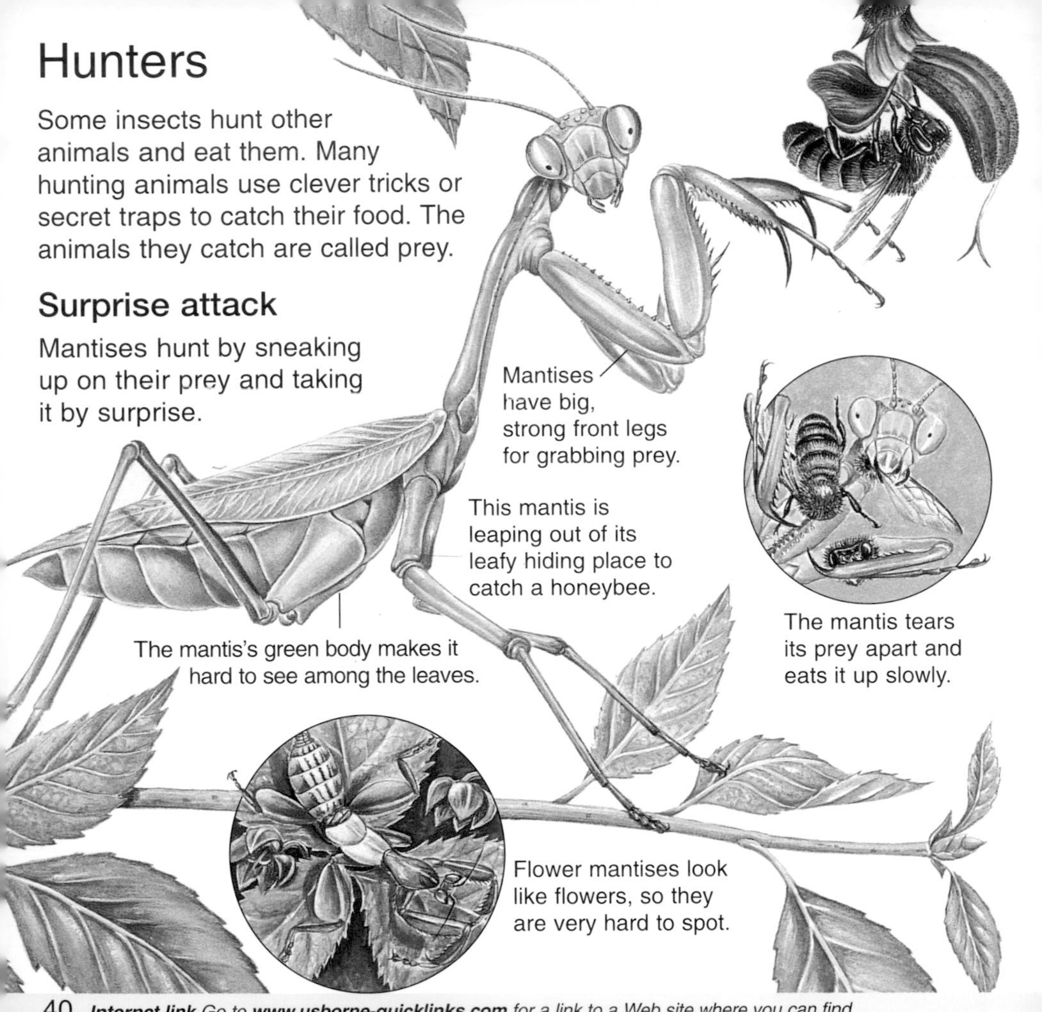

Mantises have big, strong front legs for grabbing prey.

This mantis is leaping out of its leafy hiding place to catch a honeybee.

The mantis's green body makes it hard to see among the leaves.

The mantis tears its prey apart and eats it up slowly.

Flower mantises look like flowers, so they are very hard to spot.

 Internet link *Go to* ***www.usborne-quicklinks.com*** *for a link to a Web site where you can find out where praying mantises live, and what they eat.*

Digging a trap

Antlions catch their prey by trapping it. They dig a hole and hide at the bottom.

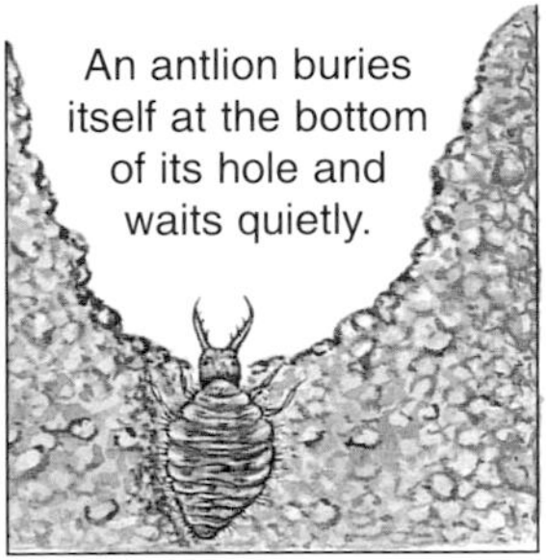

An antlion buries itself at the bottom of its hole and waits quietly.

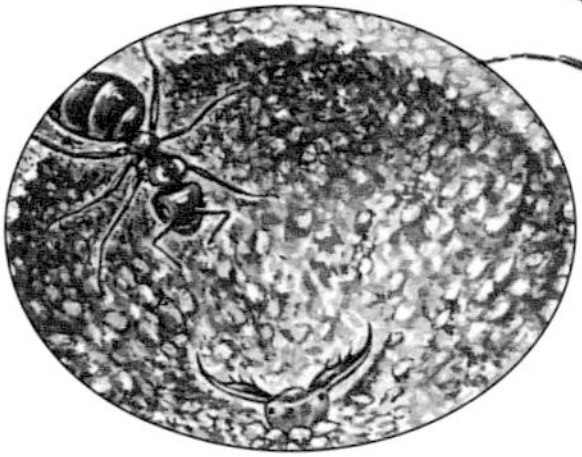

If another insect wanders near the edge of the hole, it may fall in and get trapped.

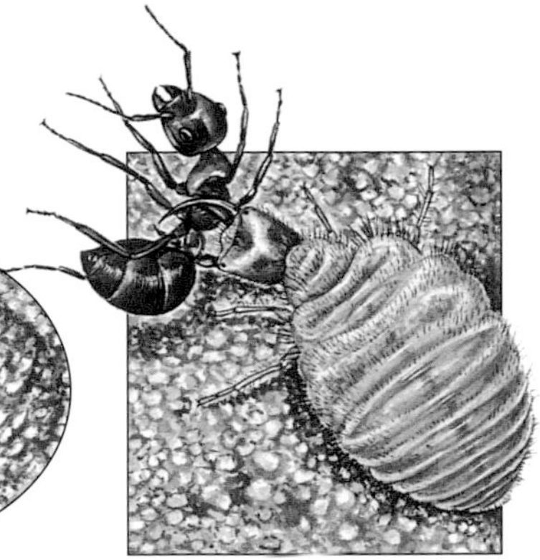

The antlion suddenly jumps out of the sand, grabs the insect and eats it up.

Liquid lunch

An assassin bug squirts a special juice into its prey, using its hard, pointed tongue. The juice turns the prey's insides into liquid, which the assassin bug sucks out.

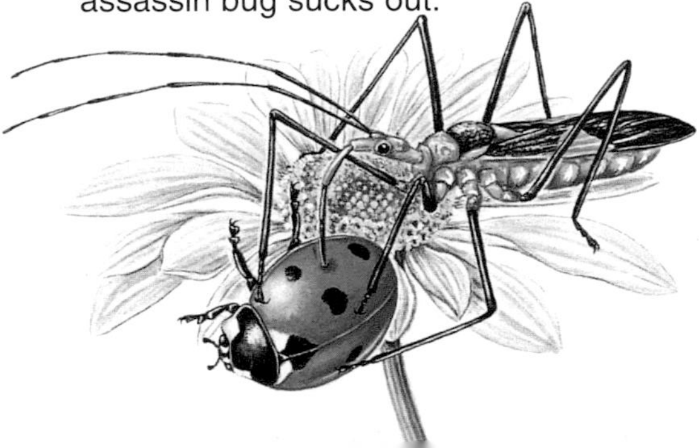

Blood suckers

Mosquitoes feed on the blood of people and other animals. They stick their long, sharp tongues into their prey's skin and suck out some blood.

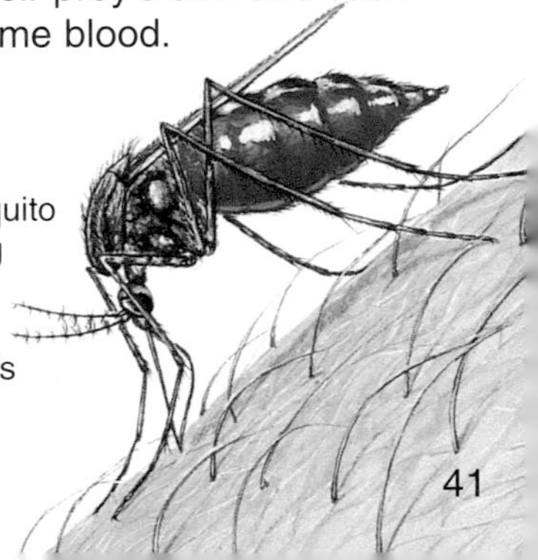

A mosquito sucking blood from a person's arm.

Staying safe

Because they are so small, insects are always in danger of being eaten or attacked by other animals. They have different ways of staying safe.

Stinging attack

Honeybees often scare away enemies by stinging them. Bees die after stinging, so they don't do it unless they are very scared.

Warning signals

Sometimes, bright markings can tell enemies that an insect tastes bad or is poisonous.

Jester bugs taste horrible. Their red and black stripes warn other animals to keep away.

Bees usually sting to protect the other bees and larvae in their colony.

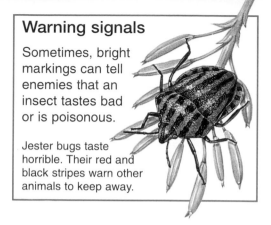

This bear has tried to steal honey from a beehive. Some of the bees are chasing after the bear and stinging it.

This bee is stinging a person. It injects its poison into the skin.

Bombardiers

If a bombardier beetle is attacked, it sprays its enemy with hot gas from the end of its abdomen. The gas hurts the enemy's eyes and skin. This bombardier beetle is spraying gas at a frog.

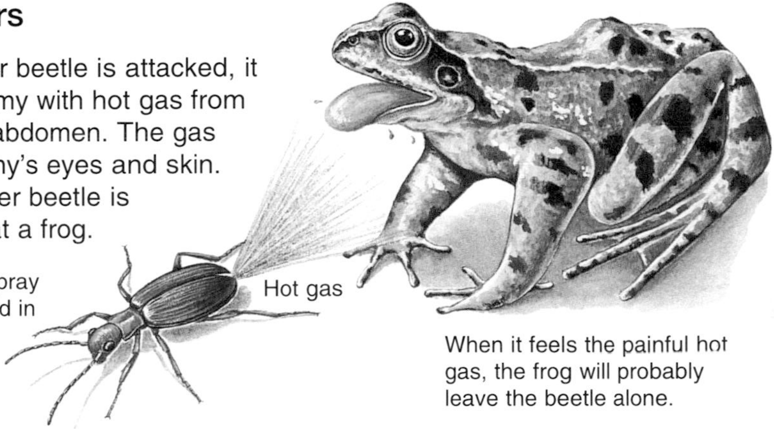

The beetle can spray very suddenly and in any direction.

When it feels the painful hot gas, the frog will probably leave the beetle alone.

Find the insects

Some insects match their surroundings, so they can hide easily. This is called camouflage.

Can you find five merveille du jour moths hiding on the lichen on this tree bark?

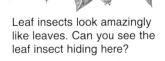

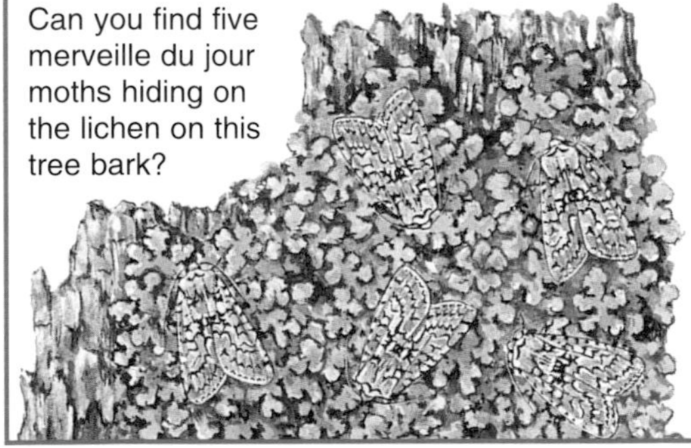

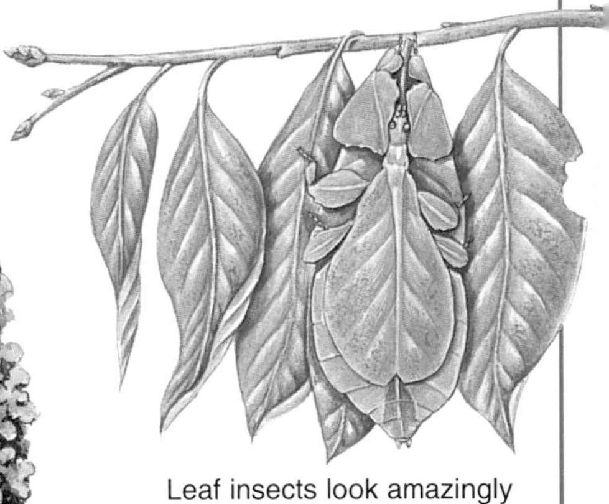

Leaf insects look amazingly like leaves. Can you see the leaf insect hiding here?

Internet link *Go to* ***www.usborne-quicklinks.com*** *for a link to a Web site where you can see amazing photographs that show how well insects can camouflage themselves.*

Sending messages

Insects can't talk to each other in words, like people do, but they can send messages and signals in lots of different ways.

Floral dances

When a honeybee has found a patch of flowers, she goes back to the hive and does a dance to tell the other bees about it.

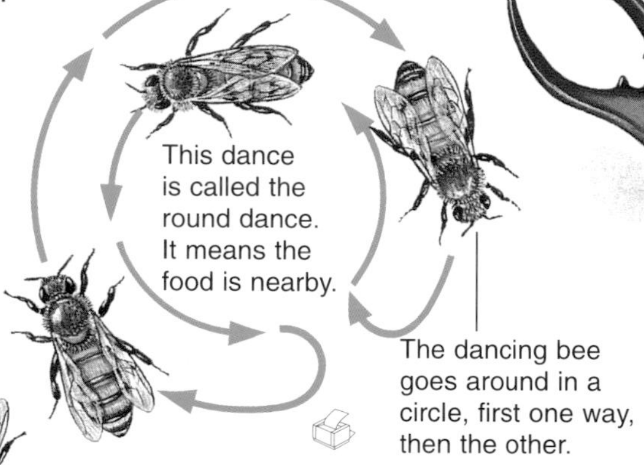
This dance is called the round dance. It means the food is nearby.
The dancing bee goes around in a circle, first one way, then the other.

This dance is called the waggle dance. It means the food is quite far away.
The faster the bee waggles her tail, the closer the food is.
Path of bee

Metal messenger

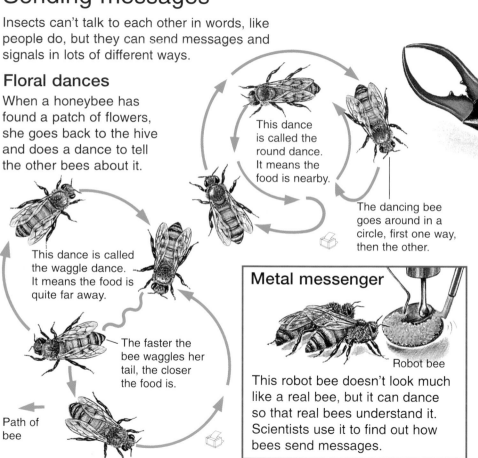

Robot bee

This robot bee doesn't look much like a real bee, but it can dance so that real bees understand it. Scientists use it to find out how bees send messages.

 Internet link *Go to* ***www.usborne-quicklinks.com*** *for a link to a Web site where you can see photographs of bees waggle-dancing and find out more about how they communicate.*

Keeping in touch

Insects use their antennae to pick up messages and signals.

This close-up picture shows a luna moth's feathery antennae. It uses them to smell other luna moths.

When male and female earwigs meet, they recognize each other by brushing their antennae together.

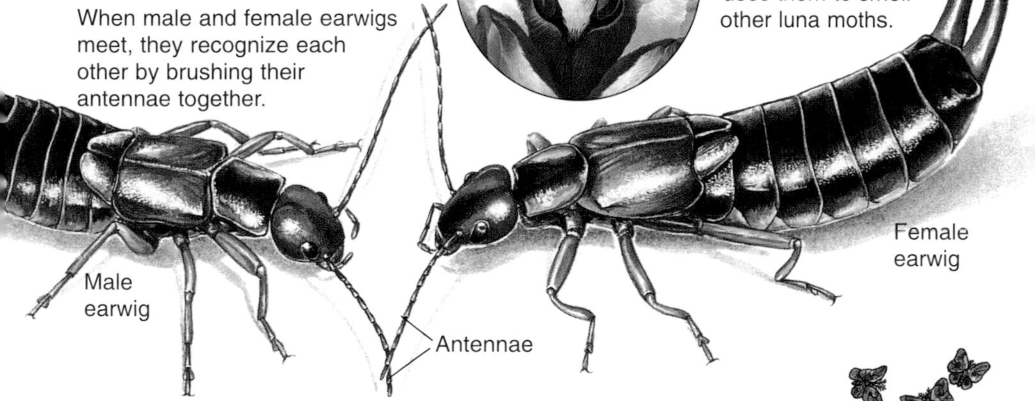

Long-distance love

Some moths give out a special smell when they want a mate. A scientist named Fabré discovered this over a hundred years ago.

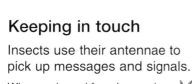

One day, Fabré caught a female emperor moth and put her in a cage in his study.

That evening, Fabré was amazed to find the room full of large male emperor moths.

The male moths had smelled the female and come to find her.

Insects and people

Although many people think that insects are a nuisance, some insects are very useful. They can provide food, and even cloth, for people.

Honey in history

People have been eating honey for a very long time. The wall painting in this picture is over 7,000 years old. It shows a woman collecting honey from a honeybees' nest.

Cloth from a moth

Silk comes from the caterpillars of the silk moth. The caterpillars, called silkworms, spin thread around themselves.

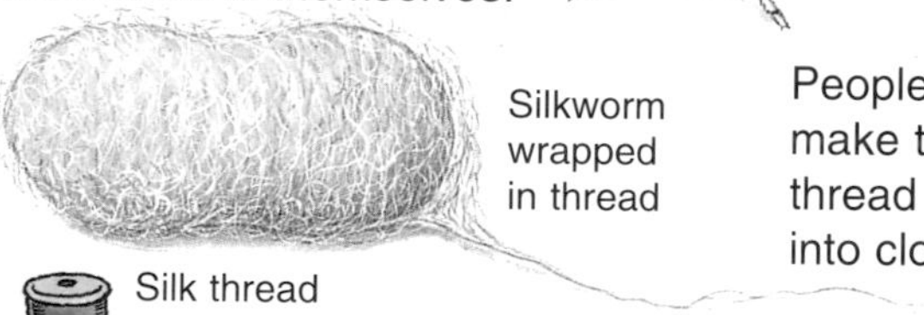

People make the thread into cloth.

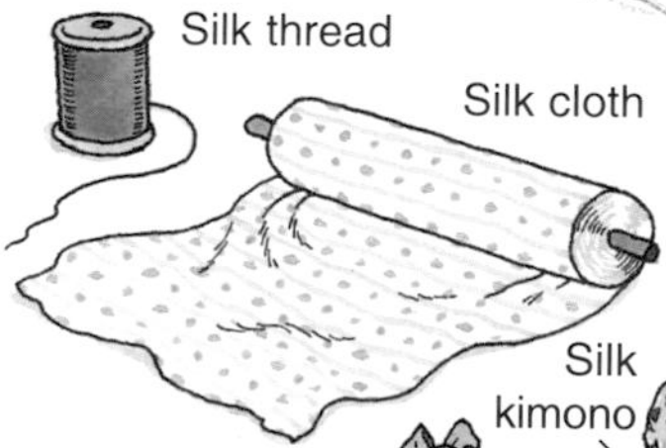

Clothes can be made from silk cloth.

Internet link *Go to* ***www.usborne-quicklinks.com*** *for a link to a Web site where you can find out more about how silkworms make silk.*

Internet links

Go to **www.usborne-quicklinks.com** and type in the keywords "pocket scientist 2" for links to these Web sites about bees.

Web site 1 How much do you know about honey? See how many of the answers you get right when you try out the quiz on this Web site. You can also look at a honey glossary, where lots of words about honey and bees are clearly explained.

Web site 2 Have you ever wondered how a bee sees the world? On this Web site you can find out. There are lots of pictures and patterns, and you can discover how a bee would see each one.

Web site 3 On this site you can look at some amazing photographs of bees, find out more about beekeeping and try out an interactive crossword puzzle. There is also a honeybee trivia quiz and interesting information about how bees have been used as weapons of war.

Web site 4 This Web site has lots of information about many different kinds of animals, including bees. You can also see pictures of each animal and click to find out the answers to some interesting questions.

Web site 5 Find out about bee stings and what you should do if you get stung. There is also some useful information on how to avoid getting stung in the first place.

For links to all these sites go to www.usborne-quicklinks.com and type in the keywords "pocket scientist 2".

More internet links

Here are some more Web sites to visit to find out about bees. For links to all these sites go to **www.usborne-quicklinks.com** and type in the keywords "pocket scientist 2".

Web site 1 This Web site is packed with insect arts and crafts activities, with photographs of what the end result should look like and templates to download. You can discover how to make a butterfly kite, a bumblebee fingerprint picture and much more. You can also find some great recipes, such as chocolate bar bugs, spider cookies and butterfly cake.

Web site 2 Look at amazing close-up photographs of many different kinds of insects, including lice, butterflies, caterpillars and beetles.

Web site 3 On this site you can read all about insects. Find out about good and bad bugs, the way in which spiders help farmers and how plants can fight back against insect attacks.

Web site 4 Find out about all the ways you can cook with honey and why honey is good for you. You can also read about different types of honey, what each type tastes like, play honey games and discover more about honeybees.

Quiz answers

Page 29 – Number 4 is the honeybee. Number 1 is a fly, number 2 is a beetle, number 3 is a wasp and number 5 is a moth.

Page 35 – Only triangles would fit together with no wasted space.

For links to all these sites go to www.usborne-quicklinks.com and type in the keywords "pocket scientist 2".

WHY ARE PEOPLE DIFFERENT?

Susan Meredith

Designed by Lindy Dark
Illustrated by Annabel Spenceley and Kuo Kang Chen

Consultants: Dr Michael Hitchcock, Indu Patel and Dr John Kesby

CONTENTS

What is a person?

Have you ever wondered why you are what you are? Why are you the same as other people in so many ways, yet different as well?

People everywhere are like they are for two main reasons. One is that they take after their parents. The other is that they are affected by the sort of life they lead.

There are millions of different kinds of living things in the world.

What made you a person, not some other living thing like a cat or a daisy, are thousands of tiny things inside you called genes. People's genes are different from animal or plant genes.

Where you live

Your genes are only part of the story. You are also the way you are because of where you live: your surroundings. Another word for surroundings is environment. Your environment affects the way you live.

This picture shows life in a part of West Africa.

These women are pounding vegetables called yams. They are made into a kind of porridge.

Young children stay close to their mothers.

This woman is carrying pots.

 Pictures with the symbol *can be downloaded from* ***www.usborne-quicklinks.com***

You got, or inherited, your genes from your parents.

Your parents inherited their genes from their parents.

Genes are the instructions which make your body work in the way it does. Everyone gets their genes from their parents, at the moment when they start to grow inside their mother.

Overhanging thatch keeps rain off the walls.
Houses are made of mud bricks which have been dried in the sun. They are cool inside.
The weather is hot. Long, loose cotton clothes help people keep cool.
Oven

Some things about you, like the way you look, depend a lot on your genes.

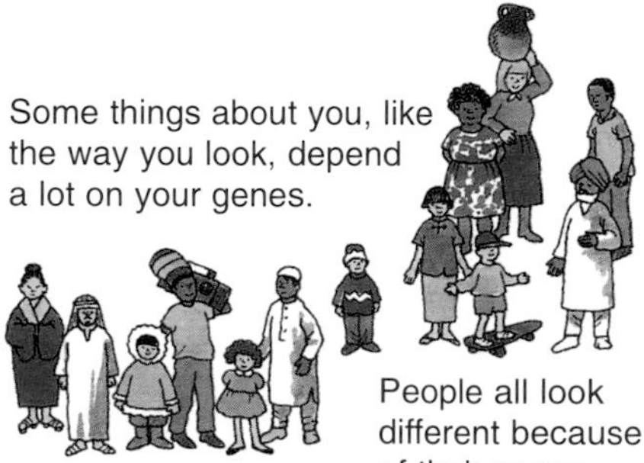

People all look different because of their genes.

Although everybody has genes, they are arranged in a different pattern in different people. That is one of the reasons why one person is not quite like another.

One big family

Everyone everywhere is really part of the same huge family which scientists call humans or human beings.

Everyone's bodies and brains are made in the same way.

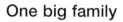

Where did people come from?

Jellyfish have been around for hundreds of millions of years; people for only about two million.

Creatures which were a bit like small apes lived about 10 million years ago.

There have not always been people in the world. There were plants and animals long before any humans. So where did people come from?

Most scientists think that living things gradually change, or evolve, over a very long time. They think people evolved from ape-like creatures.*

Out of Africa

Experts think that the first people evolved in Africa. They think they gradually spread all over the world from there, in the directions of the arrows on this map.

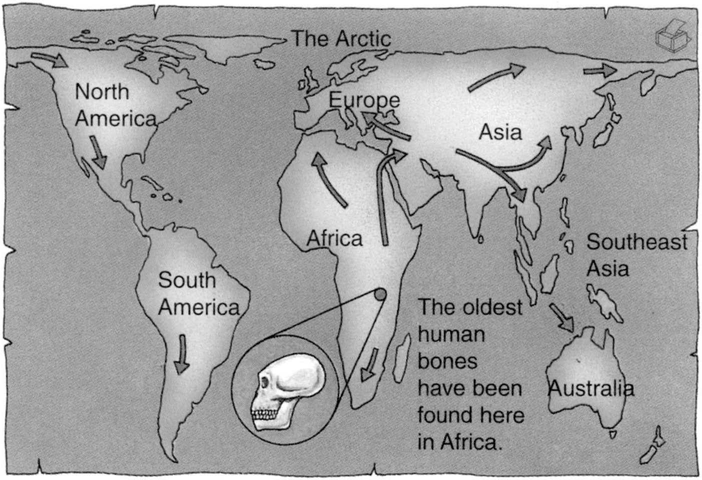

*Some people do not believe things evolve. They believe God created people as they are today.

The first people

The humans who lived two million years ago walked on two legs and had hands which could use tools. They hunted animals and gathered wild plant foods.

Young humans are very much like young chimps.

Chimps

The animals people are most like today are chimps. Nine out of every ten human genes are almost the same as chimp genes. The main difference is that people are brainier.

Our oldest relations

The first people whose bodies and brains were like ours evolved about a hundred thousand years ago. They made many weapons and tools, and could probably talk. This picture shows life in a cool place.

These people hunted with spears.
They lived in caves and in shelters made from animal skins.
They made fires: for warmth, for cooking and to frighten off wild animals.
They sewed animal skins to wear.

Internet link *Go to* ***www.usborne-quicklinks.com*** *for a link to a Web site with an interactive activity about how people evolved.*

Taking after your parents

The genes you get from your parents control the way your body lives, works and grows. The picture below shows just a few of the things about you that depend on your genes.

Your hair: whether it is dark or fair, curly or straight.

Your voice

Your eye colour

Your face

Your skin colour

The way you live cannot change your genes. It can affect how your body copes with some genes though.

Some people seem to inherit genes which make them more at risk of tooth decay than others.

If they do not eat much sweet food and clean their teeth very thoroughly, their teeth may stay healthy.

How genes work

Most things about you are decided by several genes.
A few, such as hair and eye colour, depend mainly on one gene from each parent. The example on the right will give you an idea of how genes work.

Your hair colour depends on the mixture of your two hair colour genes. A dark hair gene is dominant (strong). It blocks out genes for other colours. A fair hair gene blocks out a red hair gene.

Jessica's mother has a dark and a red hair gene. Her dark gene blocks out her red gene.

Jessica's father has a fair and a red hair gene. His fair gene blocks out the red one.

Jessica happened to inherit both her mother's and father's red hair genes.

What are your genes?

Your body is made of millions of tiny living parts called cells. Your genes are stored in your cells, on special threads called chromosomes.

There are 46 chromosomes in each of your cells: 23 from your mother, 23 from your father.

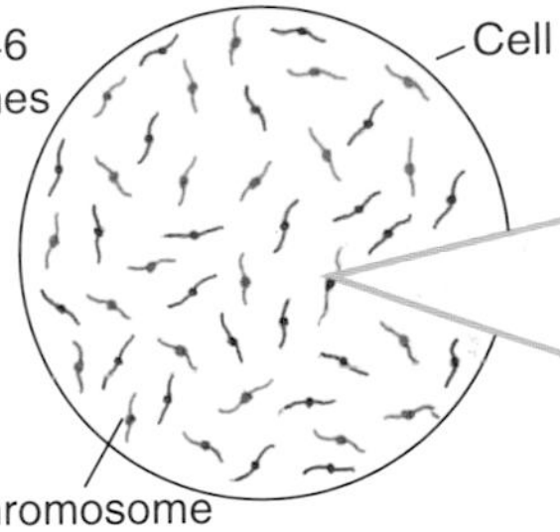

Chromosomes are made of a chemical (DNA) which looks like a twisted ladder. There are hundreds of genes on each chromosome.

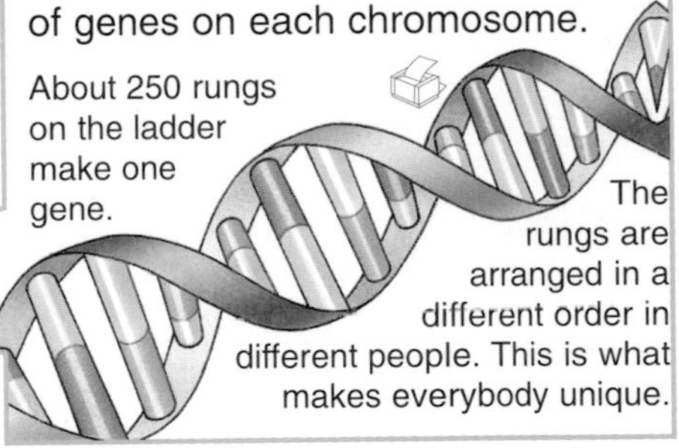

About 250 rungs on the ladder make one gene.

The rungs are arranged in a different order in different people. This is what makes everybody unique.

Exactly which of your parents' genes you get seems to be a matter of chance. That is why brothers and sisters do not always seem alike.

Only identical twins have exactly the same genes.

Genes or environment?

Simon walks with his feet turned out. Is this because of his genes or because he has copied his Dad? Nobody knows.

There is a lot that is still not known about genes. Nobody really knows whether some things about you depend mainly on your genes, your environment or both.

Internet link *Go to* ***www.usborne-quicklinks.com*** *for a link to a Web site where you can see a movie about genes and DNA.*

People and the weather

Living things evolve (change) to fit in with their environment. This is called adapting to the environment. Things that do not adapt, die.

Things that do adapt, survive and pass on their genes to their children. Gradually there come to be more and more of the well adapted things.

Woolly mammoths were well suited to life in the ice age. When the weather warmed up, they did not adapt and died out.

Humans evolved skilful hands and good brains. This makes them well adapted to their environment.

Body build

Over a very long time, people's genes have helped them adapt to the weather in different parts of the world.

In families that have lived in cold places for a long time, people have adapted. The people who had more fat were more likely to survive the cold. They passed on their genes to their children.

All people have a layer of fat under their skin, which helps protect them from the cold.

In cold places, people often have a thicker layer of fat, which helps keep them warm.

These people live in the Arctic, where it is very cold.

 Internet link *Go to* ***www.usborne-quicklinks.com*** *for a link to a Web site where you can find out about people who live in the Arctic.*

Dark or fair skin?

In very sunny places people evolved dark skin. This blocks out some of the Sun's harmful rays.

Dark skin helps to protect people from too much sun.

In cloudier places people did not need so much protection from the Sun. They evolved fairer skin.

People need some sunshine because it gives them vitamin D.

Ways of life

It is not only people's genes which have adapted to the weather. People have also adapted their way of life. Clothes, houses, even food and jobs can all depend on the weather.

A headdress and veil give protection from the sun and wind of the Sahara Desert.

Houses are built on stilts in Southeast Asia, where there are often floods.

Living apart

Groups of people came to look different not only because of the weather but also because they lived far apart.

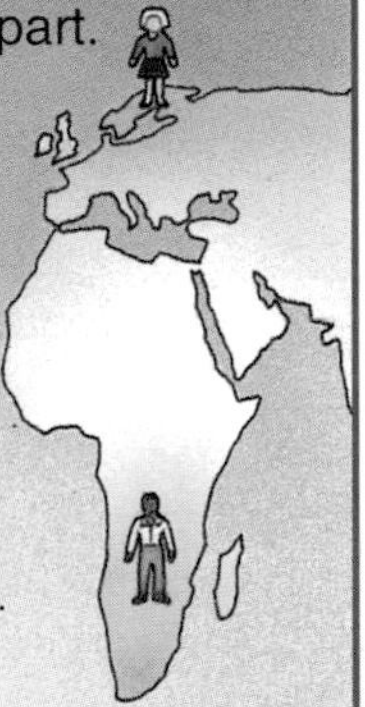

In the past, people did not tend to travel far, so they did not meet people from other parts of the world.

Today people from opposite sides of the world marry each other. Their genes get mixed together in their children.

Learning to fit in

Right from the time you are a baby, you have to start learning to fit in with the people around you. Different people have to learn to fit into very different kinds of worlds, depending on where they are growing up.

Showing the soles of your feet when you are sitting down is very impolite in Arab countries.

Eating in public places is impolite in Japan.

How you are expected to behave depends on your own family's way of thinking and on the general ways and rules of the place where you live.

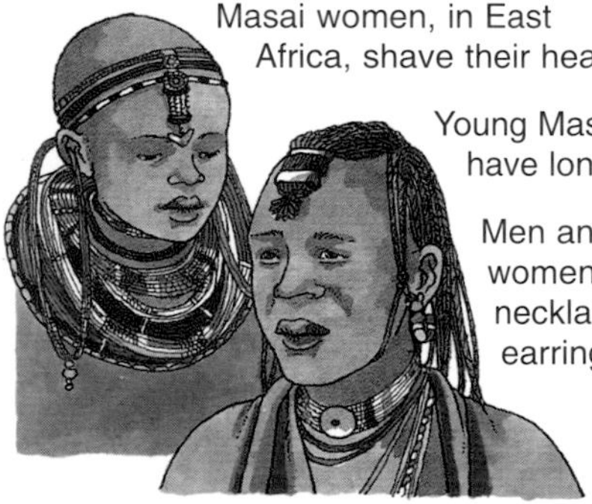

Masai women, in East Africa, shave their heads.

Young Masai men have long hair.

Men and women wear necklaces and earrings.

How you dress depends on what people in the place where you live think is suitable and attractive.

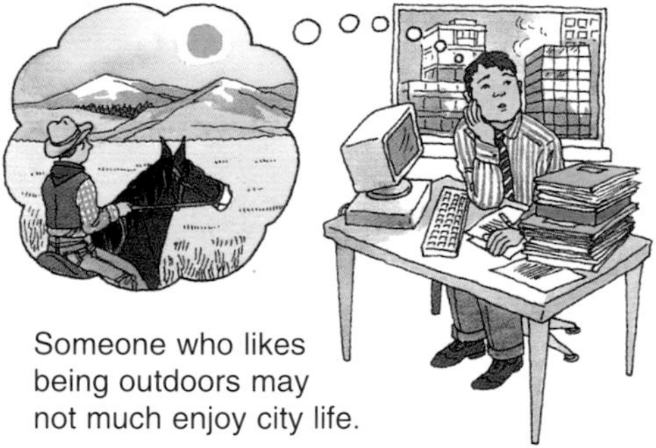

Someone who likes being outdoors may not much enjoy city life.

How happily people fit in depends on the kind of person they are and the type of environment they live in.

 Internet link *Go to* ***www.usborne-quicklinks.com*** *for a link to a Web site where there's more interesting information about how people are expected to behave in different countries.*

How do people learn?

Children learn to behave by following the example of people they admire such as parents, teachers and friends.

Behaving well is sometimes rewarded by smiles, praise or even presents. This encourages someone to be good another time.

Babies

Young babies do not fit in all that well with other people. When they need something, they just cry for it. This is the only way they have to tell people something is wrong.

Babies cannot wait for things, or imagine how other people feel.

Children

As babies grow up, they learn to fit in, for example, eating at mealtimes, not just when they are hungry.

At school, you learn skills which will help you to cope with life in the wider world outside your family.

You also learn by playing with other children, for example, how to share and take turns in games.

Making a living

People everywhere need things like food and shelter. Most people have to earn money to meet their needs. The work people do depends largely on where they live and what kind of jobs there are in the area.

Farming

Around half of the people in the world live in villages rather than towns.

In places where most people are farmers (Africa, Asia, South America) a lot of work is still done by hand.

In some parts of the world machines are used.

Harvesting in America.

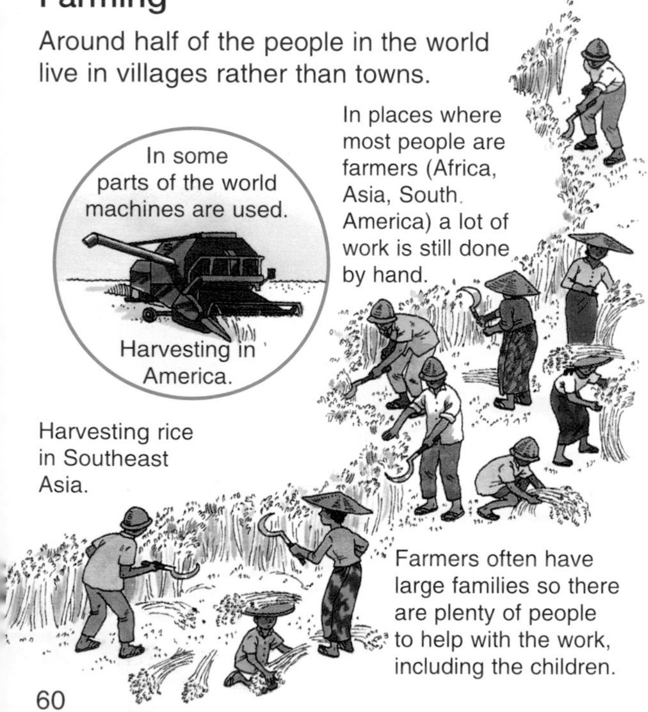

Harvesting rice in Southeast Asia.

Farmers often have large families so there are plenty of people to help with the work, including the children.

Factory work

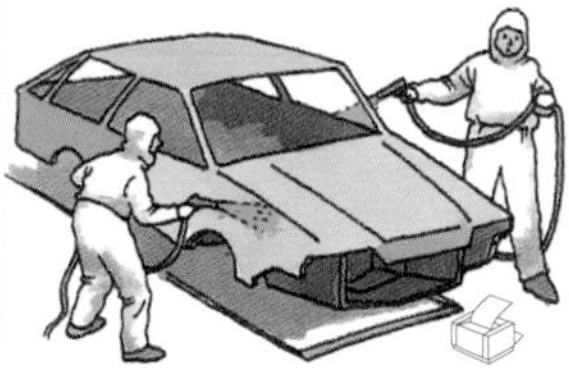

In places like Europe, North America, Japan and Australia there is a lot of industry. Many people work in factories, making things to be sold, or in offices. They get paid a wage.

People in industrial places often live in small families. They may move to find work.

In some places farmers do not get paid but keep some of what they grow.

Herding animals

In a few places, where it is too dry to do much else, some people herd animals for a living. They have to keep moving from place to place to find water and grazing land for the animals. These people are called nomads. They get most of what they need from their animals.

These people in Central Asia live in felt tents. (Felt is made from animals' wool.)

The tents are warm, and can be taken down and moved fairly easily.

The people keep sheep, goats, yaks, horses and camels. They sell animals to buy things they need such as wheat.

From the animals they get meat, milk and cheese; and wool and skins to make into clothes, tents and blankets.

They use the animals for getting around.

Fishing

Some people by the sea depend on fishing for their living, especially in places where there is no farming or industry nearby.

In the Arctic it is too cold for crops to grow. This man is fishing through a hole in the ice.

Other jobs

Some jobs are done all over the world, for example, teaching, nursing, or office work. Others are only done in certain places.

Picking tea

Tea will only grow on hills in warm wet places. It is grown in India and China.

Talking to each other

There are thousands of different languages spoken in the world today. The languages with the most speakers are English and Chinese.

How did language begin?

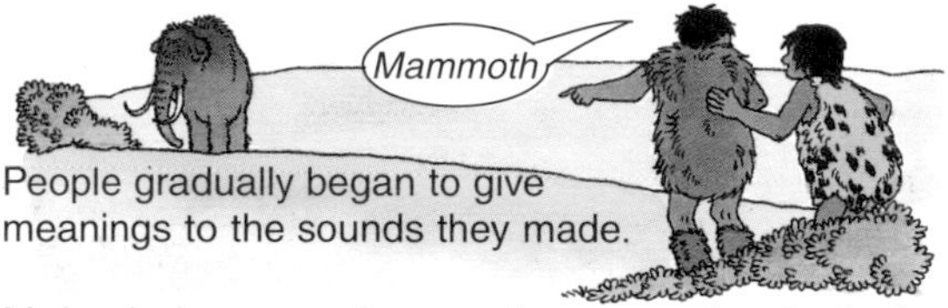

People gradually began to give meanings to the sounds they made.

Nobody is sure when or how people started to talk. They may have begun with noises such as grunts, and signs such as pointing.

Borrowing words

As people move around the world, their language goes with them. Words from one language often creep into another. Below are just a few words which have come into English from other languages.

potato (Native American), *anorak* (Inuit), *tea* (Chinese), *jungle* (Hindi), *garage* (French), *pyjamas* (Urdu), *orange* (Arabic), *robot* (Czech), *coach* (Hungarian).

Body language

In Indonesia it is rude to point with your finger. People use their thumb.

You do not only talk in words. You also use your face and body. Some things, like laughing and crying, mean the same everywhere. Some do not.

Language families

Many languages are related. French, Spanish and Italian all evolved from Latin, the language of the Ancient Romans. English is similar to German and Dutch.

 Internet link *Go to* ***www.usborne-quicklinks.com*** *for a link to a Web site where you can find out how to say hello in over 100 different languages.*

Learning to talk

By the time they are one, most babies can speak a few words and understand many more.

Babies' babblings include all the sounds it is possible for the human voice to make.

Young children gradually learn to speak the same language as their parents just by hearing and copying the sounds they make.

Same but different

The same language is often spoken differently in different places.

Even the same person can speak differently in different situations. Do you talk the same way to your friends as you do to your teachers?

Writing

There are over 50 different alphabets. Most West European languages have used the Roman alphabet since the time the Romans were rulers. On the right are some letters from different alphabets.

Chinese does not have an alphabet like that of most other languages.

This one symbol means horse in Chinese.

Moving around

Right from the time the first people moved out of Africa, groups of people have left one area and gone to settle in another. Journeys made long ago help to explain why people live where they do now.

Where from?

As people move around, they take their ideas and the things they use with them. Here are a few examples of where things started out.

Guinea pigs Potatoes	South America
Fireworks Ice Cream	China
Arithmetic Oranges	The Middle East

Hunger

Sometimes people move because their crops die through drought (lack of rain), floods or disease.

In 1845, the potato crop in Ireland failed and people were starving. Thousands left for America or England.

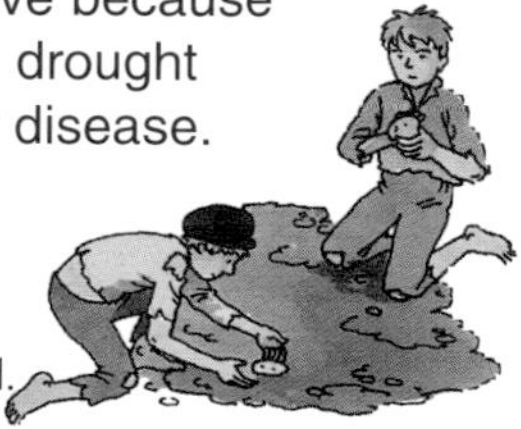

Slavery

In the 1600s and 1700s, millions of Africans were forced to go to America and work as slaves in the fields where sugar, tobacco and cotton were grown.

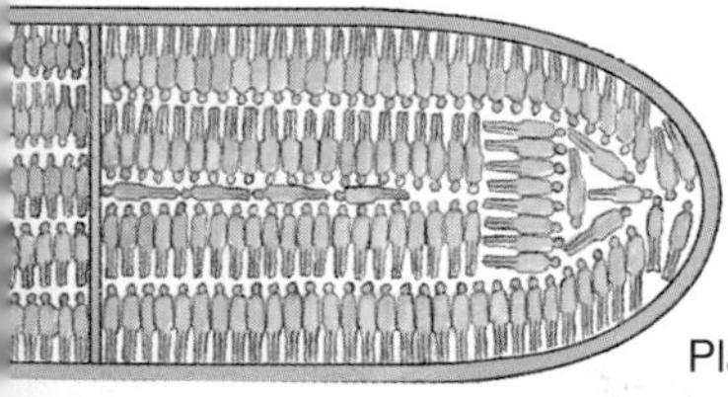

Huge numbers of slaves were packed into ships for the journey to America. Many of them died.

Plan of a slave ship.

Jobs

People often move from the countryside into towns to find work. Sometimes they move to a completely foreign country, often one which has close links with their own.

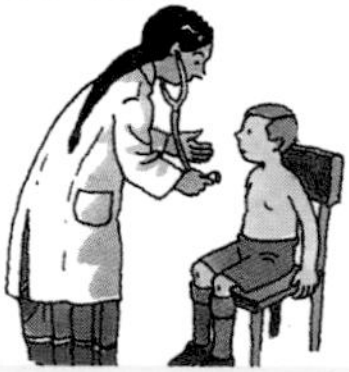

In the 1950s, many doctors moved from India to Britain, where more doctors were needed.

***Internet link** Go to **www.usborne-quicklinks.com** for a link to a Web site where you can see a slide show about the history of African Americans.*

Power

There have been many times when one group of people has moved in on another and tried to rule them.

In the 1500s, Spain conquered many parts of South and Central America and ruled them for years.

Spanish is still spoken in those countries (shown yellow on this map), making it the third most spoken language in the world.

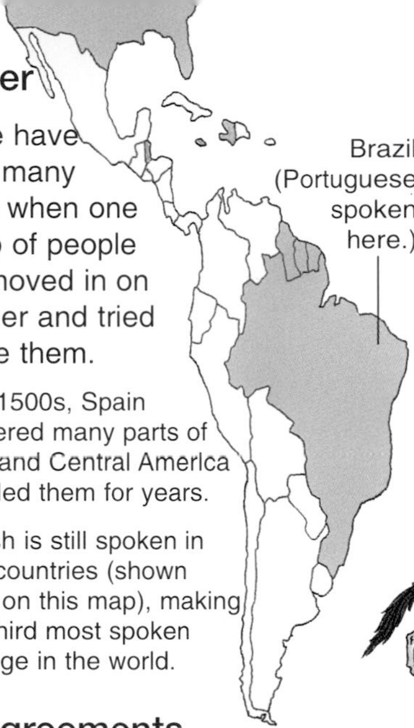

Land

Sometimes people have moved to find new land to live on and farm. This has often led to trouble.

In the 1800s, many Europeans went to North America. There were fierce battles as they tried to take land there.

The Native Americans were pushed into living only in certain areas called reservations.

Disagreements

Sometimes people are badly treated just because of what they believe or even who they are. This often happens in wartime.

Many Jews fled from Central and Eastern Europe at the time of World War II to escape being killed.

Prisoners

In 1788, the British government began sending prisoners far from home to Australia as a punishment.

Many stayed and made their living in Australia when their time in prison was over.

What people believe

People's beliefs depend a lot on what their families believe and on the religion and ideas that are taught in the place where they grow up. There are many different religions. Some have a lot in common.

The Japanese Shinto religion teaches that gods are in nature.

People pray at places like this.

Festivals

Many religions involve believing in some kind of god or gods. Believers may pray to their god, often asking for help or giving praise and thanks.

Religions try to explain how the world and people were made. It is only fairly recently that scientists have worked out the idea that living things evolved.*

The Christian and Jewish religions teach that God made the world and the first man and woman: Adam and Eve.

This Muslim is going from door to door, collecting rice for the poor.

Religions give rules for how to behave. For example, Muslims are expected to give to the poor and old.

*See page 52.

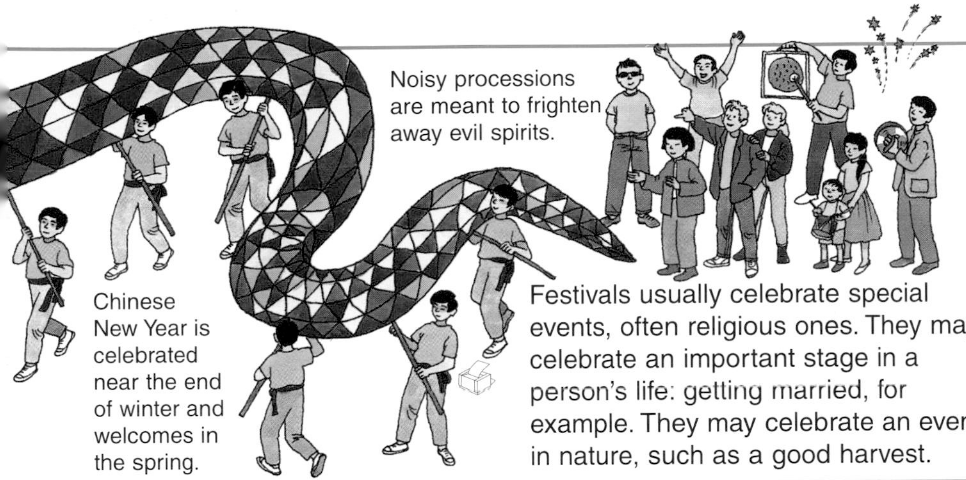

Noisy processions are meant to frighten away evil spirits.

Chinese New Year is celebrated near the end of winter and welcomes in the spring.

Festivals usually celebrate special events, often religious ones. They may celebrate an important stage in a person's life: getting married, for example. They may celebrate an event in nature, such as a good harvest.

Many religions involve believing in some kind of life after death. Hinduism, for example, teaches that people are reborn into the world. If you are good in this life, your next life will be a better one.

Hindu holy men give up their possessions and try to live a good and simple life.

Politics

People with different political ideas disagree about the best way to organize and rule a country.

Environmentalists believe it is all-important to improve the environment before it is totally ruined.

In some places people have no say in who rules them. In most countries elections are held. Then people can vote for those they think will run the country best.

Voting in India

Internet link *Go to* ***www.usborne-quicklinks.com*** *for a link to a Web site where you can find out lots more about what happens at the Chinese New Year and see photographs.*

People in groups

People everywhere are much more alike than they are different. However, it is sometimes interesting to think about people as different groups.

Male and female

Without the bodily differences between men and women, human beings would soon die out because no babies would be made.

What makes the difference between a boy and a girl is just one chromosome out of the 46 you have in each cell in your body.

The way men and women behave differently and do different tasks has a lot to do with where they live and how they were brought up.

Ethnic groups

People of the same ethnic group have relations who lived in the same part of the world long ago. They often share the same language, customs and beliefs.

In Australia, a lot of people whose relations originally came from Britain eat British Christmas dinner.

In Bali, Southeast Asia, women do the heavy work on building sites.

 Internet link *Go to* ***www.usborne-quicklinks.com*** *for a link to a Web site where you can watch a movie about what happens as people get older.*

Friends

Friends may be quite different in some ways.

People may become friends because they have similar hobbies, interests or ideas; or just because they like each other. Friends often help each other.

Young people

Young people* are learning to manage without their parents. They often go around in groups; this gives them a feeling of belonging while being free of their families.

Old people

Old people may not be as fit as they once were but the things they have learned during their long lives can be very interesting and useful to younger people.

Countries

People living in the same country live under the same government and have to obey its laws. Laws vary from one country to another.

Alcoholic drink is banned in some countries.

Disabled people

Disabled people cannot easily do some of the things most people take for granted. There are different types of disability. Some can be overcome.

A wheelchair marathon

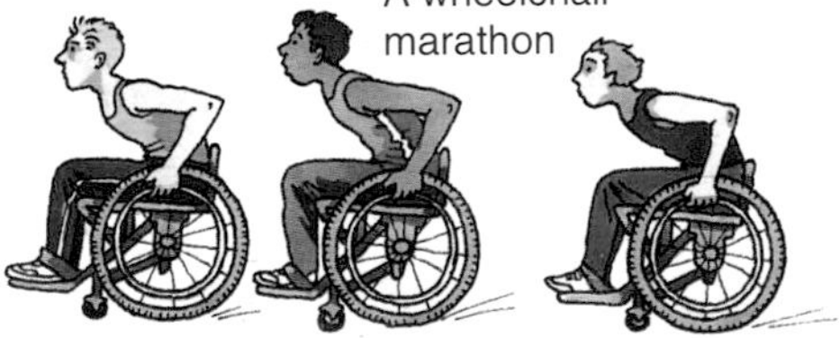

*To find out about children, see page 59.

One world

Humans have always had to adapt to survive and still need to adapt today. They need to change how they live before they damage the environment so much that they can no longer live in it. Here are some things they can do to improve their environment:

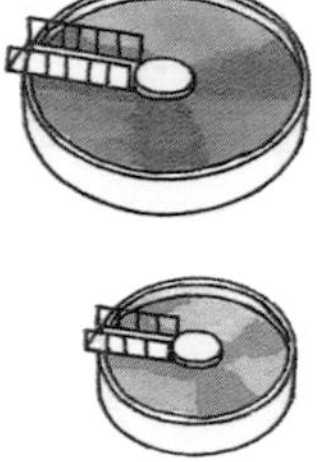

Sewage works

Clean sewage (waste from toilets and drains) properly so that it does not pollute rivers and seas.

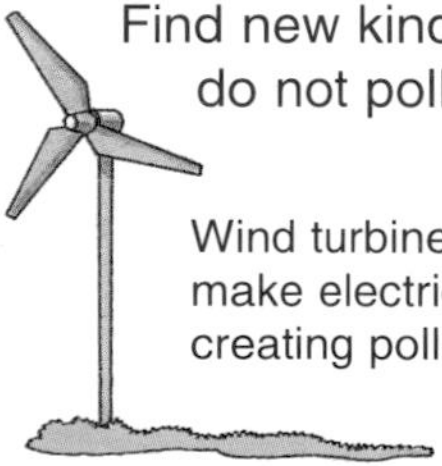

Find new kinds of energy which do not pollute the air.

Wind turbines like this make electricity, without creating pollution.

Stop dumping harmful chemical waste into rivers and seas.

Bottle bank

Make things from materials which do not harm the environment. Better still, make them from materials which can be re-used.

Stop letting wild animals and plants die out. As well as being important in themselves, they may be useful to humans in the future.

Use farming methods which do not damage the soil.

Stop cutting down forests. This destroys the homes of animals and plants, damages the soil and even causes changes in the weather.

Internet links

Go to **www.usborne-quicklinks.com** and type in the keywords "pocket scientist 2" for links to these Web sites about people.

Web site 1 On this Web site you can find out fascinating facts about different countries around the world. You can read about the histories of each counry, their different religions and what they are like to live in today.

Web site 2 Find out how you can help stop people damaging the environment by reading the action sheets on this Web site. There are also fact sheets so you can discover more information about the environment.

Web site 3 Lots of different festivals are celebrated in countries around the world. On this Web site children from all over the world describe how they celebrate the festivals in their country.

Web site 4 The world's population is growing all the time. On this site you can see how fast it is growing, find out what the world's population was in the past and what it may be in the future.

Web site 5 Read lots of fun facts about people, including how to address royalty and what the most popular children's names are.

Web site 6 Find out about different places around the world, and the people that live in them. There's descriptions of the different games people play and recipes to try out.

For links to all these sites go to www.usborne-quicklinks.com and type in the keywords "pocket scientist 2".

More internet links

Here are some more Web sites to visit to find out about people. For links to all these sites go to **www.usborne-quicklinks.com** and type in the keywords "pocket scientist 2".

Web site 1 Watch a short movie to discover how people around the world celebrate the coming of the new year. You can find out the different things people eat, how long celebrations can last and what people in different countries wear.

Web site 2 Learn about the environment and people of the Amazon, Greenland, Iguazu, Madagascar, Namib, Okavango and Tibet. There are lovely photographs to look at, videos to watch, experiments and games.

Web site 3 On this site you can find out the latest news about what is happening to people and animals in different parts of the world. There are interactive quizzes to try out and slide shows with photographs from around the world.

Web site 4 Explore a clickable map that will take you around the world to learn about different languages, customs, cultures and religions. There are also photographs, maps, recipes and fun things to make that show the everyday life of people around the world.

Web site 5 Read about different disabilities and find out what life is like for children with special needs, from daily injections for children with diabetes to those confined to a wheelchair. You can also learn how to help classmates or others with special needs.

For links to all these sites go to www.usborne-quicklinks.com and type in the keywords "pocket scientist 2".

WHAT MAKES YOU ILL?

Mike Unwin & Kate Woodward

Designed by Non Figg
Illustrated by Annabel Spenceley and Kuo Kang Chen

Consultant: Dr Kevan Thorley

CONTENTS

All about being ill

Most of the time you probably feel well. Your body can do lots of things without you even thinking about them.

Your brain lets you think clearly.

Most of the time you are happy and feel comfortable inside.

Your skin looks smooth and healthy.

You feel energetic and want to run around and play.

Your arms and legs feel strong.

You get hungry if you have not eaten for a while.

Ill or well?

You can usually tell if you are ill because things feel wrong with your body. These things are called symptoms. You can often tell what is wrong by the kind of symptoms you have.

You may feel hot one minute, then cold the next.

Your tummy may feel upset and you may need to be sick.

You might feel tired and achy and want to lie down.

You may feel miserable and not want to join in with your friends' games.

You might have a pain somewhere.

You may lose your appetite.

What is pain?

Having a pain is one way your body tells you something is wrong.

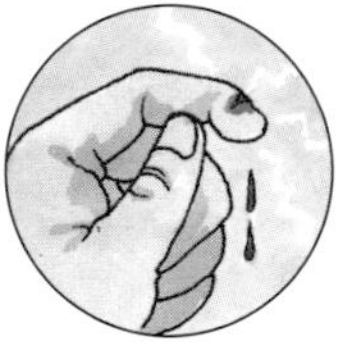

Sometimes you can easily see what is wrong because of where it hurts.

Sometimes you have a pain in one place when really the problem is somewhere else. Tonsillitis causes a tummy ache, even though your tonsils are in your throat.

Keeping well

Looking after yourself helps you stay well. Eating the right food and exercising keep you fit. Being fit helps you to fight illness and get better more quickly if you are ill.

Getting better

Your body is good at getting better by itself. You can help it mend by resting. There are lots of things you can do while you rest.

Plenty of love and attention from your family or friends can make you feel better too.

If resting doesn't help, and you don't get better on your own, you may have to visit your doctor.

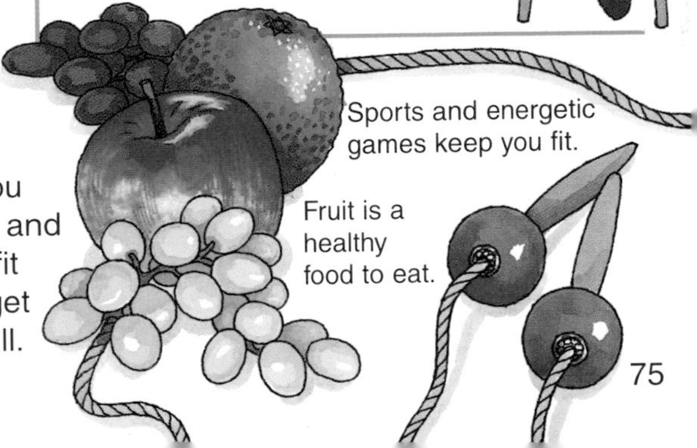

Sports and energetic games keep you fit.

Fruit is a healthy food to eat.

Why do you get ill?

People become ill for many different reasons. Most everyday illnesses are caused by germs. Your body usually fights off germs but sometimes they make you ill. This is called having an infection.

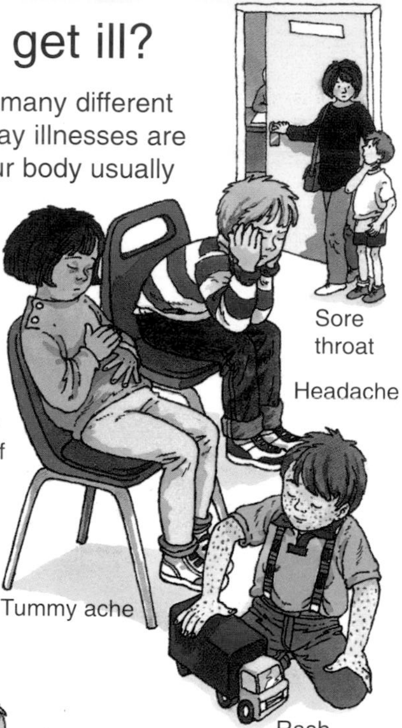

There are many different kinds of germ. They cause different symptoms of infection.

Sneezing sprays millions of germs into the air.

Most germs are spread through the air. When you have a cold you breathe out germs all the time. If people around you breathe them in, they may catch your cold.

Where you live

Where you live can affect your health. For example, traffic fumes and factory smoke can pollute the air you breathe. This can make people ill.

 Internet link *Go to* ***www.usborne-quicklinks.com*** *for a link to a Web site where you can find out more about colds.*

Accidents

Sometimes accidents can hurt you or make you ill. Many accidents happen at home.

Falling can give you cuts or bruises or even break your bones.

Hot things can burn you. Always be careful with hot food.

Feelings

Your feelings can make you ill too. Worrying may upset your tummy and make you feel sick.

Feeling nervous about your first day at a new school can make you feel ill.

Family illnesses

Some illnesses tend to run in families. Scientists now know someone is more likely to get asthma if one of their parents has it. Asthma makes it difficult to breathe properly.

People with asthma can take medicine to help them run around and play sports.

Allergies

Ordinary things like cat hair, pollen from plants, and certain foods make some people feel poorly. This is called having an allergy.

An allergy to strawberries can give you a rash.

What is a germ?

Germs are tiny, living things. They are everywhere: in the air you breathe, on your skin, in your food and on the things you touch.

The three main kinds of germs are called bacteria, viruses and fungi.

Germs are so tiny you need a microscope to see them.

There are germs inside your body all the time. Most of them don't do you any harm. Some can even be helpful, but others make you ill.

Some useful bacteria live in your tummy. They help you to digest your food.

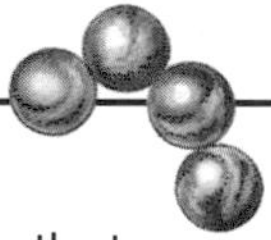

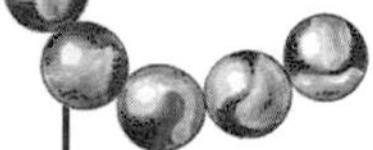

Bacteria

Bacteria are so tiny that over a thousand could fit on a pinhead. Some can cause illnesses such as ear and skin infections.

These bacteria cause earache. They are magnified many times so you can see them.

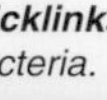

Viruses

Viruses are over a million times smaller than bacteria. They cause many common infections such as colds, tummy upsets and sore throats.

If you look at viruses through a powerful microscope, you can see their strange shapes.

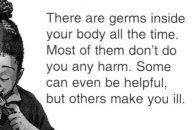

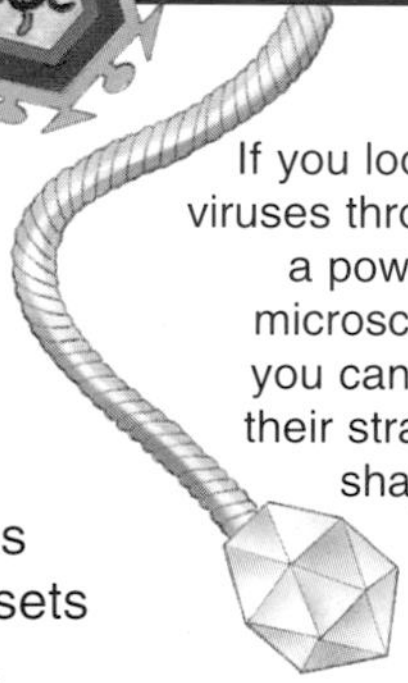

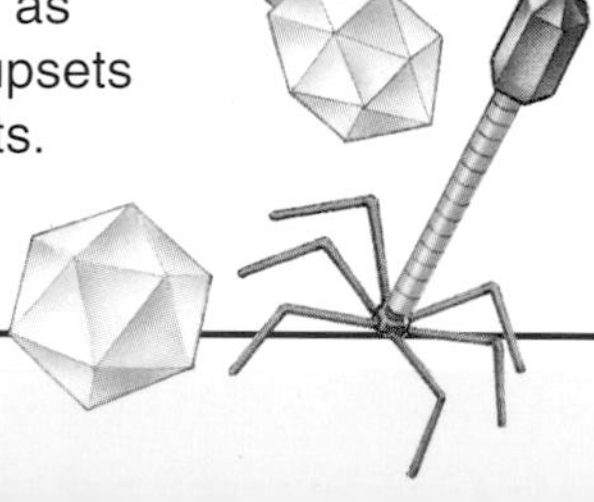

This kind of virus causes sore throats.

Internet link *Go to* ***www.usborne-quicklinks.com*** *for a link to a Web site where you can do a quiz about bacteria.*

Keeping germs out

Your body is built to keep harmful germs out as much as possible. This picture shows how your body protects you.

Your skin keeps germs out as long as you have no cuts or scratches.

Eyelashes stop dirt and germs from getting into your eyes.

Germs come out of your nose in slimy stuff called mucus, when you sneeze or blow your nose.

Your have tears in your eyes all the time. They help wash out germs.

Your mouth and throat are always wet and slippery so that germs don't get stuck there.

Tiny hairs in your nose catch any germs you breathe in.

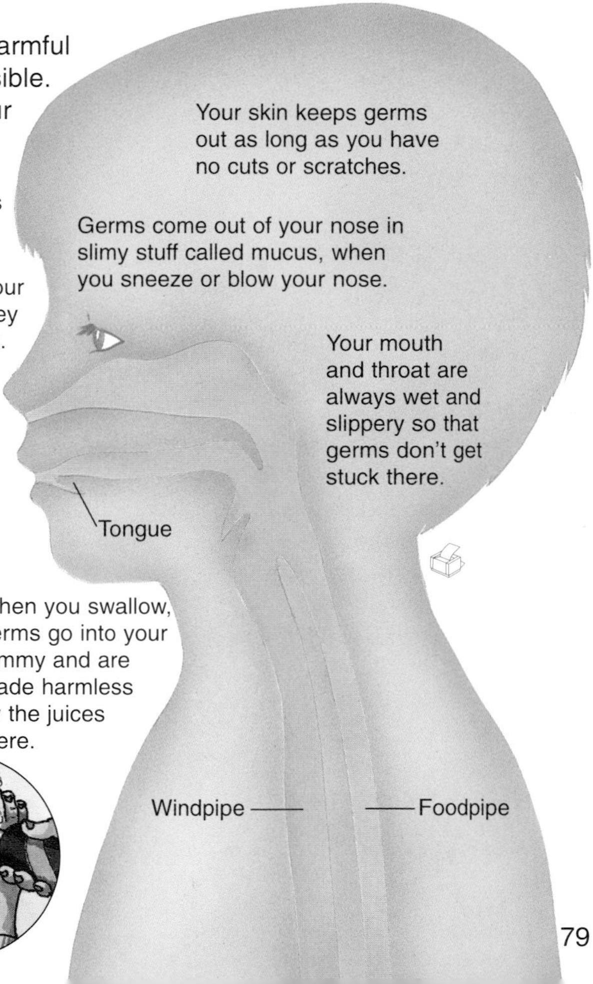

When you swallow, germs go into your tummy and are made harmless by the juices there.

Fungi

These are germs which grow on your body and cause infections. Athlete's foot is a fungus which can grow between your toes. It makes your skin sore and flaky.

You can get rid of athlete's foot with special powder.

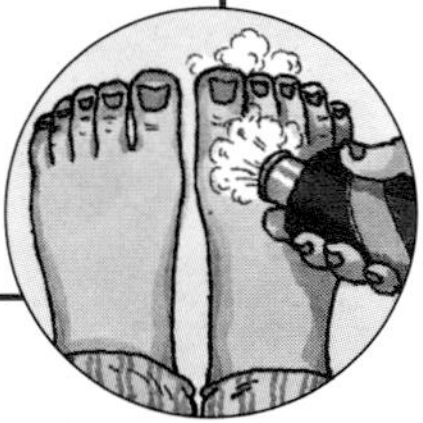

Germ attack

Your whole body is made up of millions of tiny living parts called cells. When germs such as bacteria or viruses get into your body they start to multiply and feed off your cells. This makes you feel ill.

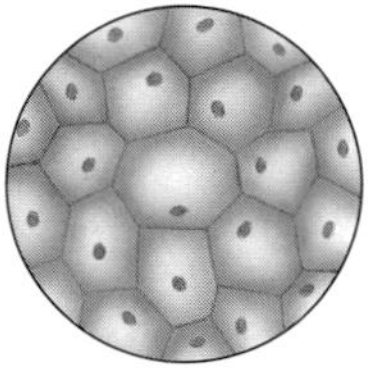

This is what cells from your skin look like through a powerful microscope.

Bacteria invasion

Your body is a warm, damp place with plenty of food, so bacteria grow and spread quickly inside you. Within hours there can be millions in one small part of your body.

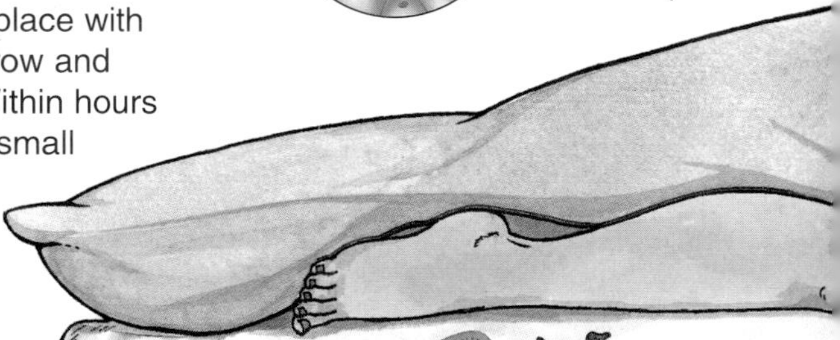

Some bacteria attack your cells by giving off poisons. These can also spread infection around your body in your blood.

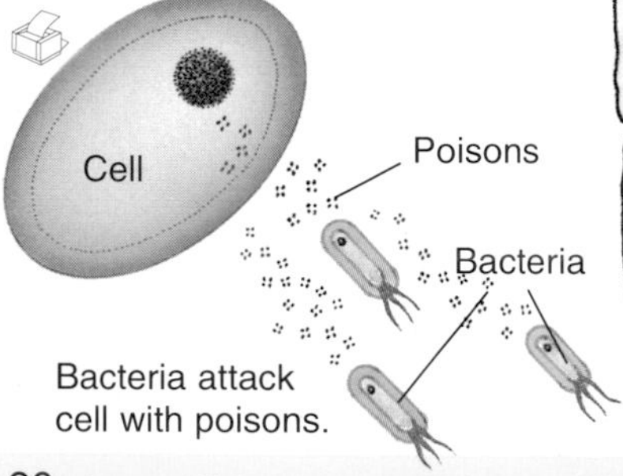

Virus invasion

Viruses attack by getting inside a cell. The cell becomes a kind of factory for making new viruses.

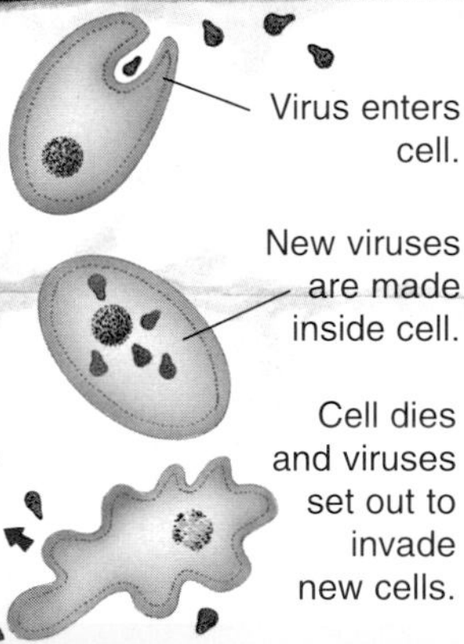

Virus enters cell.
New viruses are made inside cell.
Cell dies and viruses set out to invade new cells.

 Internet link *Go to* ***www.usborne-quicklinks.com*** *for a link to a Web site where you'll find lots of facts about germs and the diseases they cause.*

Germs and symptoms

Symptoms are caused both by germs damaging your cells, and by the way your body fights back. Different germs cause symptoms in different parts of your body.

An area infected by bacteria, such as an aching tooth, often feels sore and swollen.

Your temperature rises as your body starts to fight the germs. This is an early sign of infection.

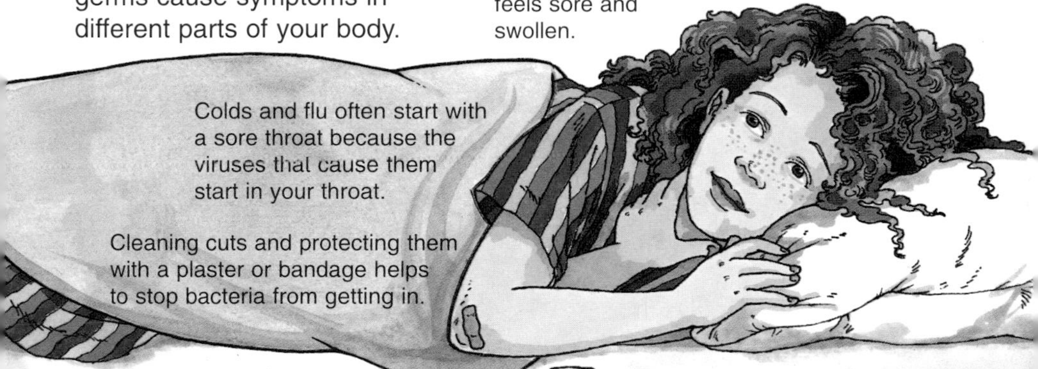

Colds and flu often start with a sore throat because the viruses that cause them start in your throat.

Cleaning cuts and protecting them with a plaster or bandage helps to stop bacteria from getting in.

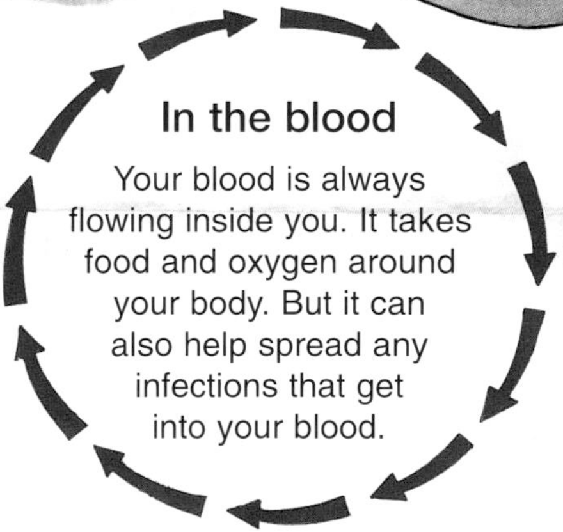

In the blood

Your blood is always flowing inside you. It takes food and oxygen around your body. But it can also help spread any infections that get into your blood.

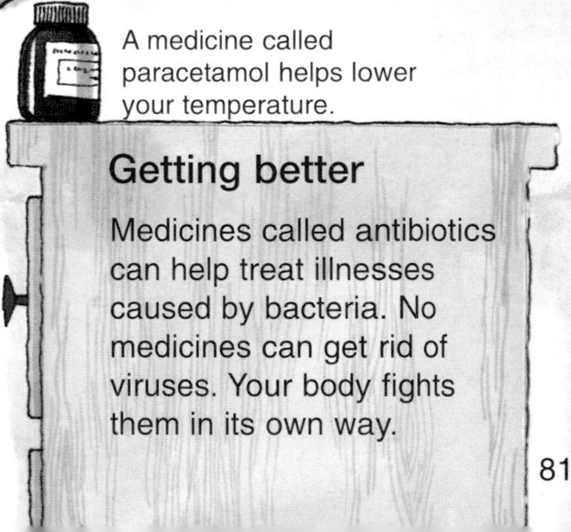

A medicine called paracetamol helps lower your temperature.

Getting better

Medicines called antibiotics can help treat illnesses caused by bacteria. No medicines can get rid of viruses. Your body fights them in its own way.

Fighting back

When you get an infection your body fights off the invading germs. In your blood there are special cells which try to stop them from spreading further.

In your blood

This page shows a close-up picture of blood vessels. These are the tubes that carry blood around your body. Blood contains millions of cells in a liquid called plasma. Red blood cells carry food and oxygen. White blood cells have the job of killing germs.

The germ eaters

When germs damage your cells, more blood flows to the infected place. White blood cells then devour the germs.

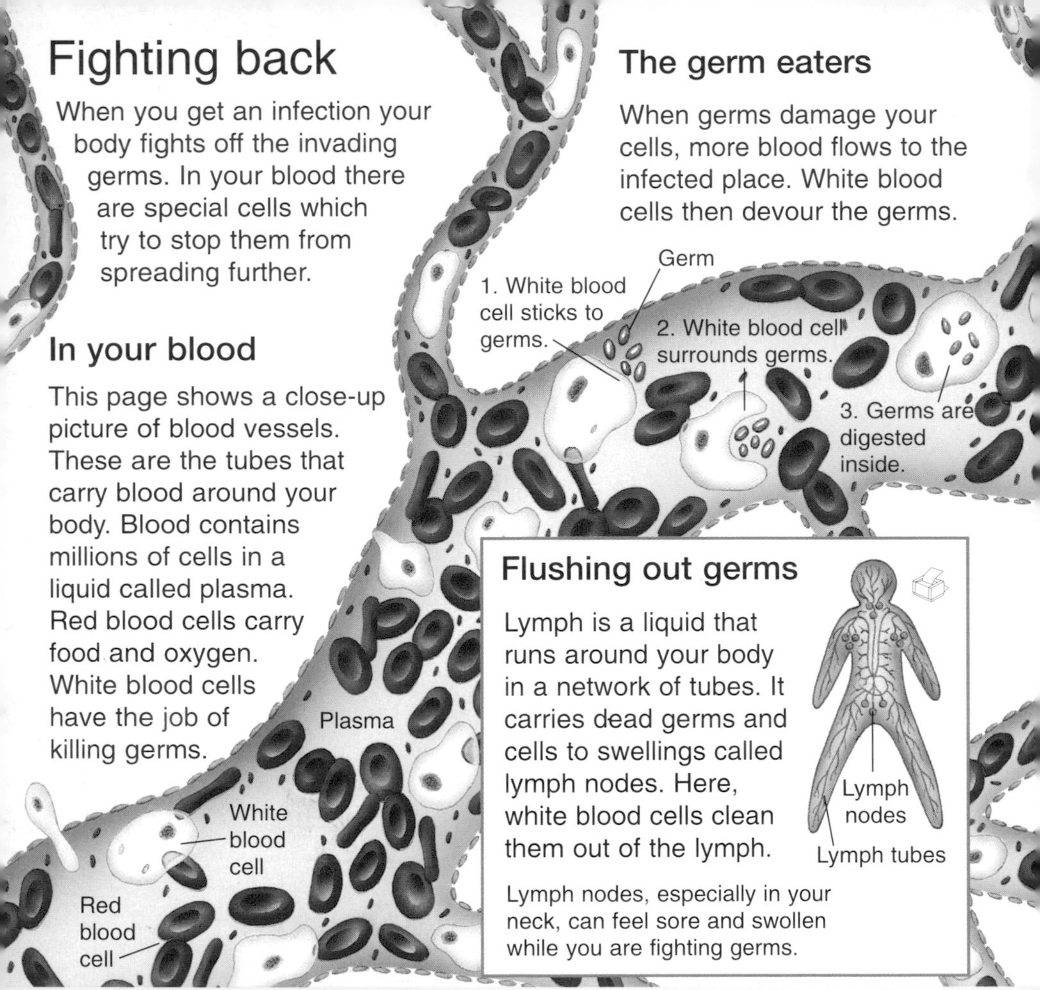

Flushing out germs

Lymph is a liquid that runs around your body in a network of tubes. It carries dead germs and cells to swellings called lymph nodes. Here, white blood cells clean them out of the lymph.

Lymph nodes, especially in your neck, can feel sore and swollen while you are fighting germs.

 Internet link *Go to* ***www.usborne-quicklinks.com*** *for a link to a Web site where you can watch a movie about blood.*

Permanent protection

During an infection, special white blood cells called lymphocytes kill germs using chemicals knows as antibodies.

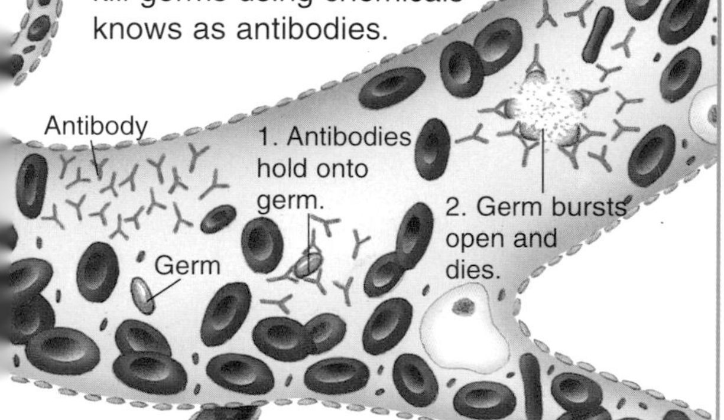
Antibody
1. Antibodies hold onto germ.
2. Germ bursts open and dies.
Germ

Antibodies can recognize germs that have attacked you before. They stay in your body to stop the same germs from attacking you again. This means you only catch most infections once. Being protected like this is called being immune.

Immunization

Immunization is a way of making you immune to an infectious illness without you having to catch it.

When you are immunized, you are given a tiny dose of a germ. The dose is too weak to make you ill, but it helps your body to produce the antibodies that will protect you against that illness in the future.

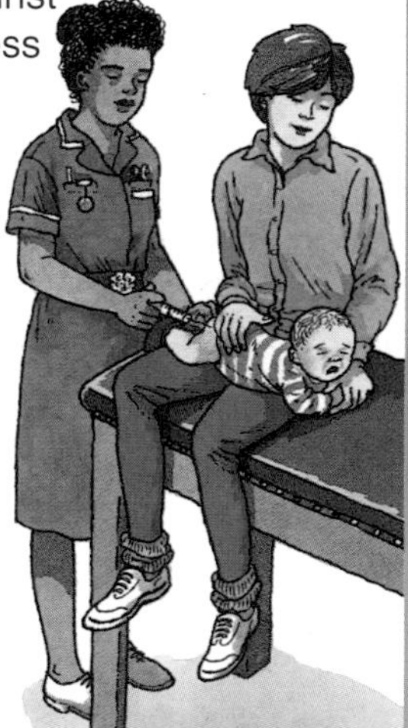

Babies are usually given injections that immunize them against some serious diseases.

Allergies

An allergy is when your body fights ordinary things as if they were germs. This can cause symptoms such as a rash, wheezing or tummy ache. Anything that causes an allergy in somebody is called an allergen.

Breathing

Some people are allergic to things they breathe in, such as dust, pollen, feathers or pet hairs.

Hay fever can be caused by an allergy to pollen. It makes you sneeze and your eyes become watery and itchy.

What happens

When an allergen invades the body of an allergic person, white blood cells send out antibodies to fight it. A chemical called histamine is produced, which causes the allergic symptoms.

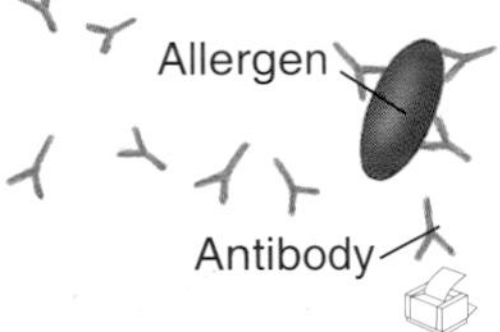

Antibodies stick to allergen.

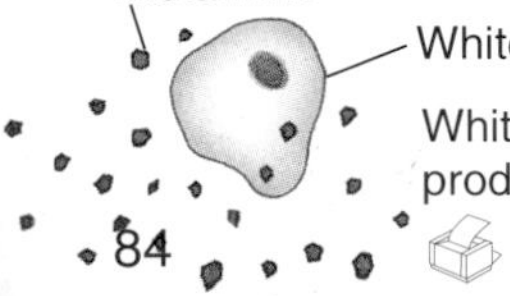

White blood cell produces histamine.

What is asthma?

Asthma can be caused by an allergy. It makes it difficult to breathe air into your lungs, so you wheeze or cough. Here you can see what happens.

You breathe air into your lungs along tubes called bronchioles.

Asthma makes the bronchioles narrower so less air can get through.

Breathing in medicine from an inhaler like the one below helps open up your bronchioles again.

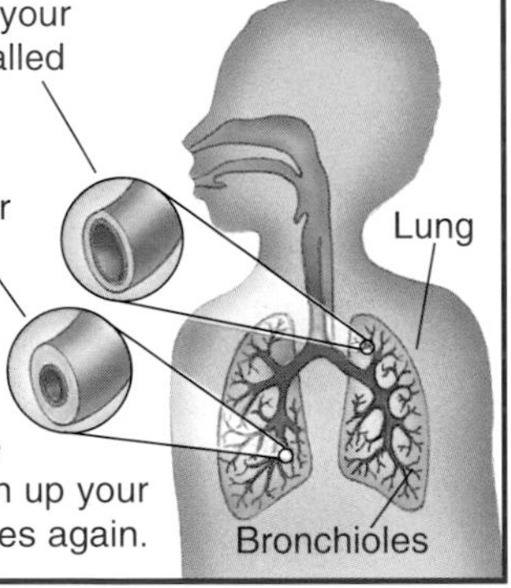

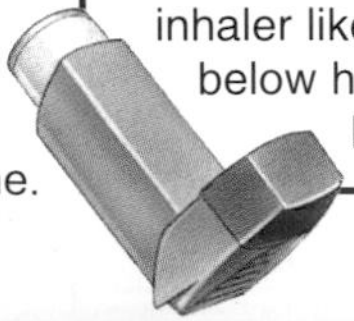

Touching

Some people have to be careful what they wear against their skin. Metal, for instance in earrings, and materials such as wool, can cause a rash.

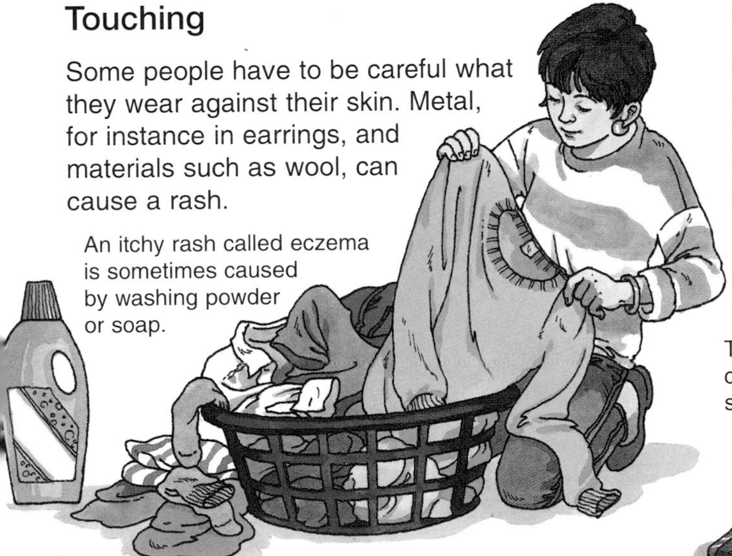

An itchy rash called eczema is sometimes caused by washing powder or soap.

Eating

Some people are allergic to certain foods. Eating them can cause allergic symptoms including a tummy ache or rash. Food allergy can play a part in asthma.

These foods can cause allergies in some people.

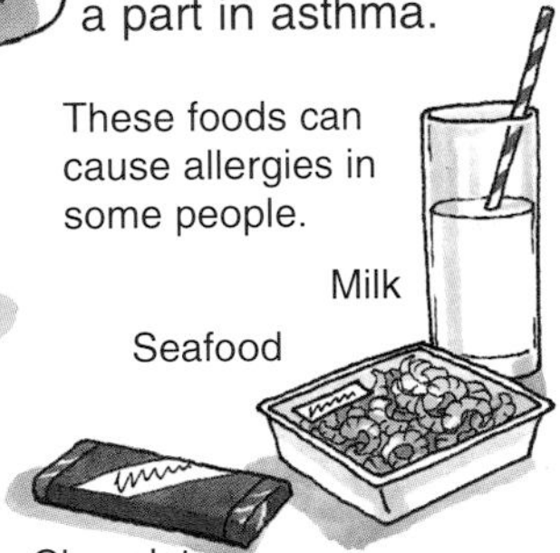

Treating allergies

You cannot catch allergies from other people. The best protection against them is for people to try to avoid things they know they are allergic to.

It is hard to avoid allergens such as dust which get everywhere. People who are allergic to dust need their bedrooms cleaned or dusted regularly.

Medicines called antihistamines can ease some of the symptoms caused by allergies.

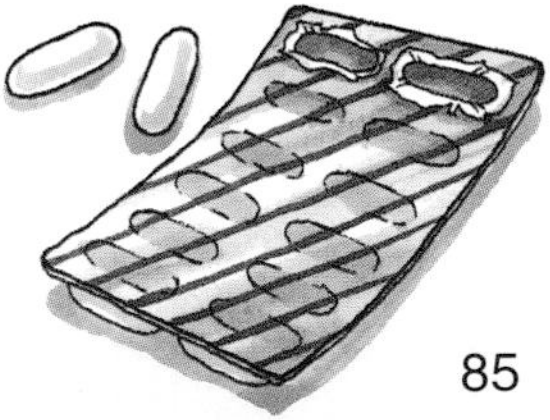

***Internet link** Go to **www.usborne-quicklinks.com** for a link to a Web site where you can discover more about what causes allergies.*

How illnesses spread

The most common way that illnesses are spread is through the air. When you cough, sneeze or breathe out, you spray tiny droplets into the air. This can spread illnesses such as colds, flu and chickenpox to other people.

Covering your mouth and nose when you cough or sneeze helps stop germs from spreading. One sneeze can shoot germs over three metres (10 feet).

Touching

Some skin infections, such as cold sores or warts, can be spread from one person to another by touching the infected place.

Try not to share other people's things, such as towels or unwashed dishes and cutlery, if they have an infection.

Food

If you do not take enough care with food, germs can make it bad and cause illness. Bacteria grow on foods such as meat and milk if they are kept for too long.

Fresh food should always be washed before cooking or eating.

Food lasts longer if it is kept somewhere cold.

A cover protects food from flies, which can carry bacteria.

Washing hands

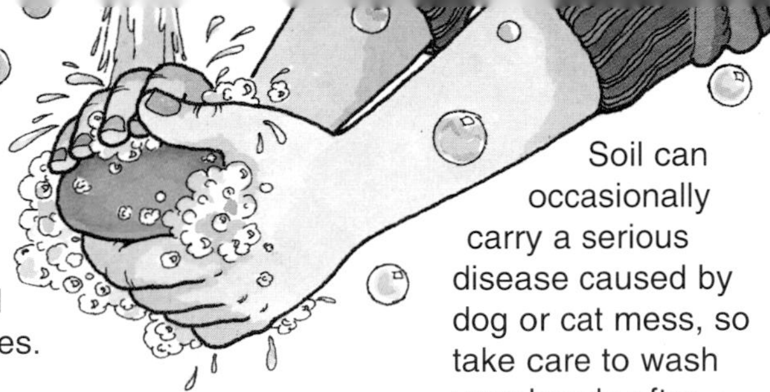

Always wash your hands after going to the toilet, and before eating or handling food. Dirty hands can spread germs onto food and cause bad upset tummies.

Soil can occasionally carry a serious disease caused by dog or cat mess, so take care to wash your hands after playing outside in parks or gardens.

Occasionally some pets can pass on diseases. It is always best to wash your hands after handling animals, and not to kiss them, or let them lick your face.

Headlice

Headlice are tiny creatures that live in your hair and make your head feel itchy. Lice and their eggs (called nits) can get from one person's head to another's.

Tie long hair back for school, and don't share brushes or combs.

Bad water

Water can also carry diseases. This sometimes happens in poorer places where people have to share the same dirty water for washing, drinking and cooking.

Infected water can spread diseases to many people.

Internet link *Go to* ***www.usborne-quicklinks.com*** *for a link to a Web site where you can do a quiz and find out how much you know about food safety.*

Accidents

If you get hurt or injured, whether it is a tiny cut or a broken leg, your body has its own ways of mending itself.

Cuts and grazes

If your skin is broken by a cut or graze and your blood vessels are damaged, blood flows out of your body. Tiny blood cells called platelets soon stop the bleeding by making a sticky plug called a clot.

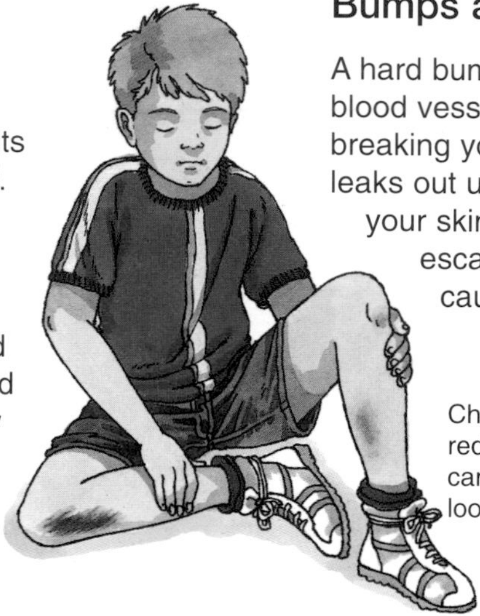

Bumps and bruises

A hard bump can damage blood vessels without breaking your skin. Blood leaks out underneath your skin, but it cannot escape. This causes a bruise.

Chemicals from red blood cells can make bruises look purple.

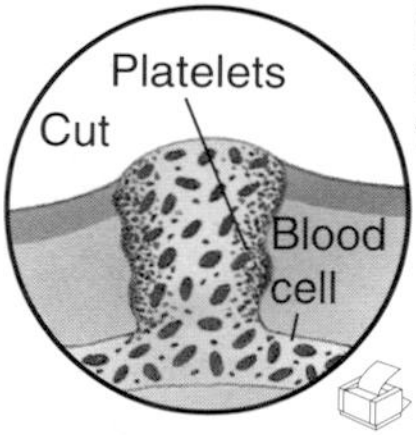

Platelets clump together in the blood around the cut.

The platelets catch other blood cells and make a clot.

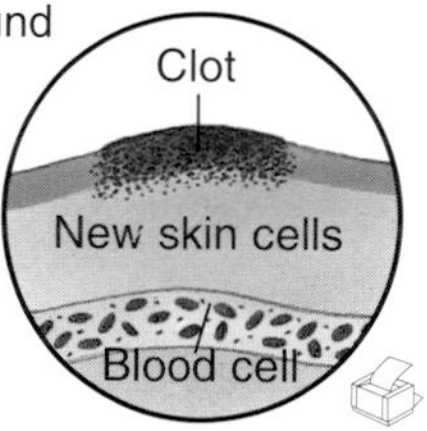

A bump on a bony part of your body, such as your shin or head, can cause a lump. Your skin swells because there is less room underneath for the blood to drain away.

A blood clot becomes a scab which protects the cut while it heals. Underneath, new skin cells are made to replace the damaged ones. Soon the scab dries up and falls off.

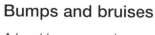

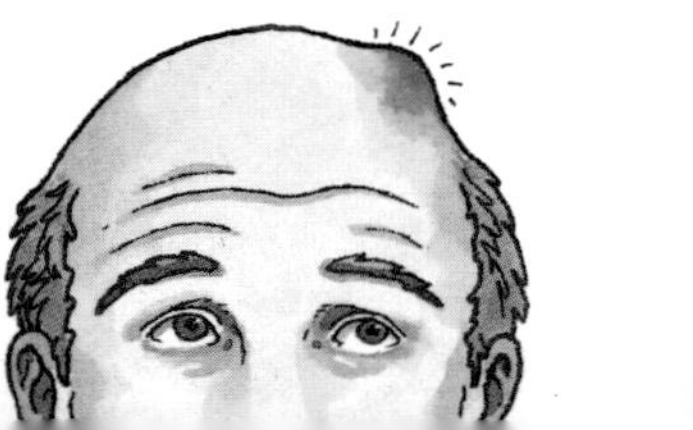

Broken bones

If a bone gets broken, your body has to make new cells to grow over the break and join the bone together again. The bone must be set (put) in the right position and kept still while it mends.

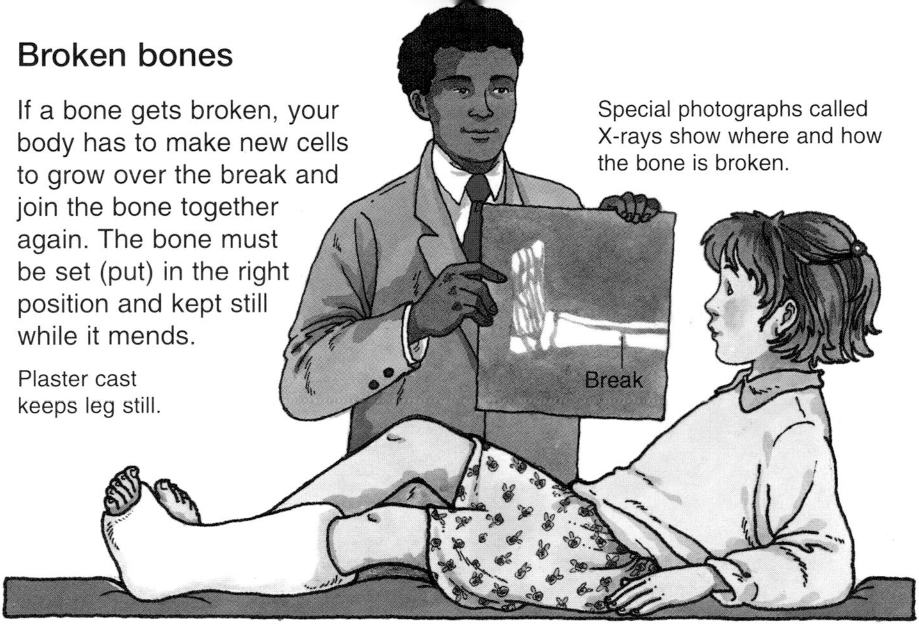

Special photographs called X-rays show where and how the bone is broken.

Plaster cast keeps leg still.

Burns

When a burn damages your skin, watery fluid wells up from underneath and forms a blister.

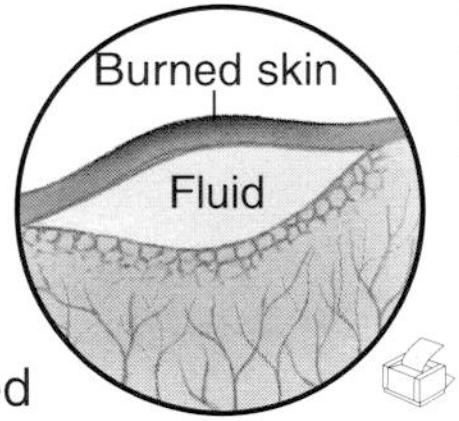

Blisters help protect damaged cells. When new cells grow underneath, the fluid disappears and the old, damaged skin peels away.

Cold water can ease the pain of a burn and help stop the damage from spreading.

Internet link *Go to* ***www.usborne-quicklinks.com*** *for a link to a Web site where you can see a fascinating movie about how bones mend.*

Going to the doctor

Sometimes you may need help from a doctor to get better. A doctor's job is to recognize an illness and try to put things right.

Finding out what's wrong

The doctor asks you questions about how you are feeling. If you can describe your symptoms clearly, it helps her to tell what is wrong. She also looks and feels for any signs of illness such as a rash or swelling.

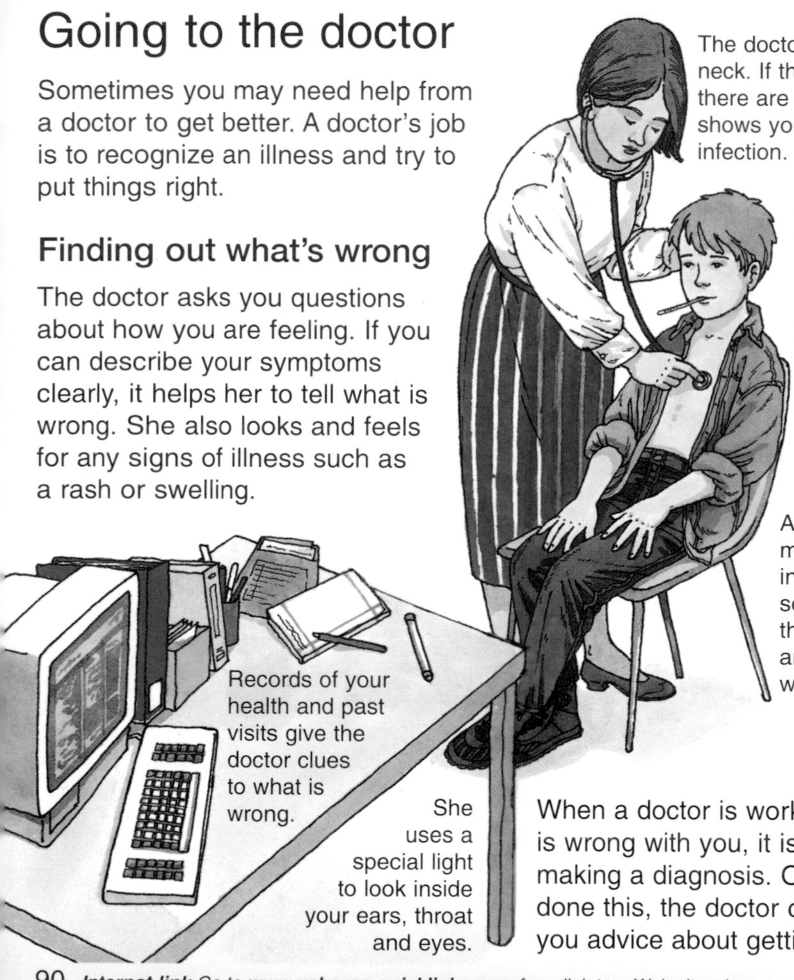

The doctor may feel your neck. If the lymph nodes there are swollen, it shows you have an infection.

She may put a thermometer under your tongue to take your temperature. It should be about 37°C (98.4°F).

A stethoscope makes sounds inside you louder so she can check that your heart and lungs are working properly.

Records of your health and past visits give the doctor clues to what is wrong.

She uses a special light to look inside your ears, throat and eyes.

When a doctor is working out what is wrong with you, it is called making a diagnosis. Once she has done this, the doctor can then give you advice about getting better.

 Internet link *Go to* ***www.usborne-quicklinks.com*** *for a link to a Web site where you can find out what happens when you go to hospital.*

Hospital

Occasionally your doctor may decide to send you to a hospital. Here you can see another doctor who knows all about your particular illness. In different parts of a hospital, doctors treat different illnesses.

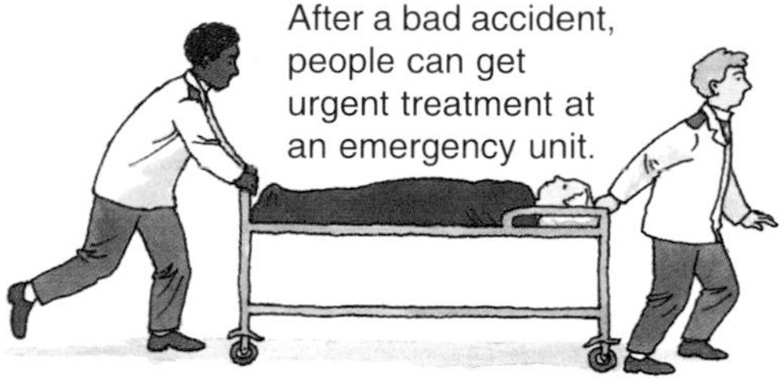

After a bad accident, people can get urgent treatment at an emergency unit.

If you have to stay in a hospital for a while, nurses will look after you. A close member of your family may be able to stay with you and friends can visit to cheer you up.

Medicine

Sometimes doctors have to prescribe medicine to help you get better. Medicines must be used just as the doctor says, otherwise they may not work, or could be dangerous.

Doctors on the move

In parts of the world far from towns, people cannot easily get to a doctor, so doctors travel to see them. They stay a short while in each place to give people treatment, and advice about staying healthy.

Where you live

People's health is affected by where they live, what they do and how much money they have. Different illnesses are found in different parts of the world.

Weather

The weather can affect people's health. For instance, in hot, wet parts of the world, mosquitoes can spread a serious disease called malaria.

Mosquitoes can infect people with malaria when they bite them.

Food

In some poorer parts of the world, there is not always enough food to go around. Without all the goodness they need from food, people can get very ill. This is called malnutrition.

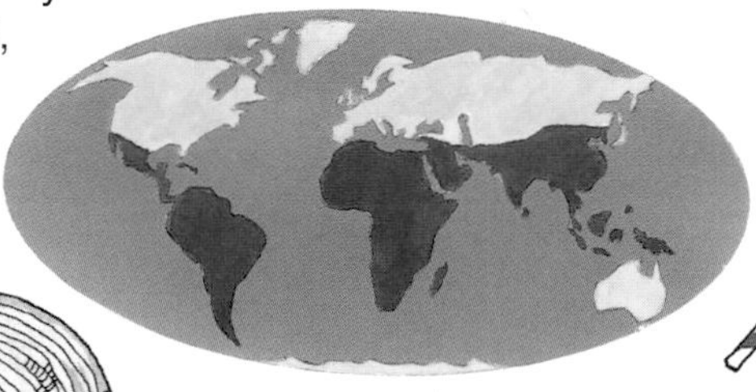

Red areas on this map show poorer parts of the world.

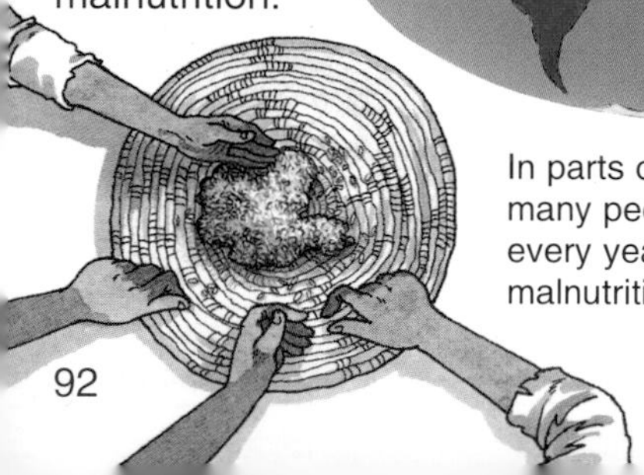

In parts of Africa, many people die every year from malnutrition.

Not all food is good for you. In richer parts of the world many people suffer from diseases which doctors think may be caused by eating too much of the wrong kind of food.

This meal has lots of sugar and fat, which can be bad for you.

Pollution

Pollution can harm all living things, including people. For instance, polluted lakes and rivers can make people ill if the water gets into their drinking supplies.

Epidemics

Illness can spread quickly in places where people live crowded together without good health care. A disease that infects many people at one time is called an epidemic.

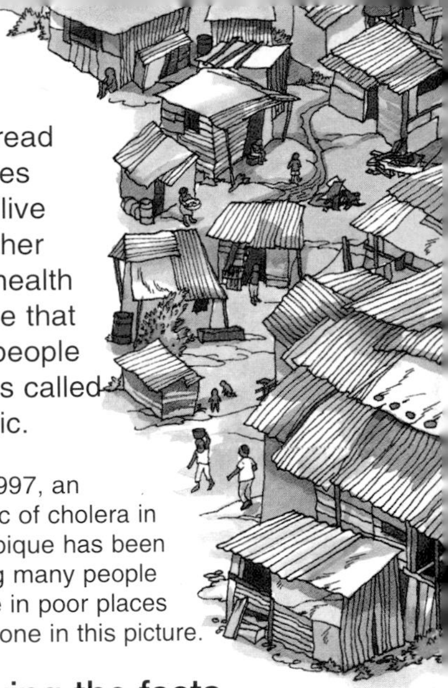

Since 1997, an epidemic of cholera in Mozambique has been affecting many people who live in poor places like the one in this picture.

Jobs

The places where people work, and the jobs they do, can affect their health.

People who work down mines can suffer breathing problems from the dust.

Knowing the facts

Learning about how your body works and how illnesses can happen helps you live a healthier life.

Years ago nobody knew that smoking caused serious heart and lung diseases. Now people know that it is healthier not to smoke.

Staying healthy

There are lots of things you can do to help you stay healthy. These are some of them.

Eating well

You need to eat many different types of food to stay really healthy. How much you eat is important too. Eating too much or too little can be unhealthy.

Keeping yourself clean

Keeping your body clean can help stop germs from causing infections.

Exercise

Exercising is a good way of looking after your body. It keeps it in good working order and helps prevent illness. Swimming is good for people with asthma because it helps improve their breathing.

Different foods help your body in different ways.

Internet links

Go to **www.usborne-quicklinks.com** and type in the keywords "pocket scientist 2" for links to these Web sites about what makes you ill.

Web site 1 On this site you can find out about everyday illnesses and injuries and how to stay healthy. There are lots of health questions and answers and a great glossary of medical terms.

Web site 2 You can look at lots of amazing photographs of what bacteria looks like under a microscope on this site. Click on each photo to see a larger image.

Web site 3 Find out what happens when you go to see a dentist or doctor, or to hospital, and read about the people, places and things that help keep you healthy.

Web site 4 This Web site has a health section, where you can watch movies all about your body and how it works.

Web site 5 At this Web site, you can find out about different parts of the body, how to stay healthy and about the different kinds of food the body needs.

Web site 6 Find out about the illnesses you can get at your age and how to avoid them. There is information about healthy eating, how to look after your teeth and an A-Z explaining different illnesses. You can also e-mail in any questions you might have.

For links to all these sites go to www.usborne-quicklinks.com and type in the keywords "pocket scientist 2".

More internet links

Here are some more Web sites to visit to find out about what makes you ill. For links to all these sites go to **www.usborne-quicklinks.com** and type in the keywords "pocket scientist 2".

Web site 1 Watch an animation that explains how your heart and circulatory system work, then try some fun activities including a heart diagram that you can print out and label.

Web site 2 Watch a video clip of medicine attacking bacteria and see amazing photographs of blood clots, white and red blood cells and bacteria. This site is packed with information and diagrams.

Web site 3 See pictures taken with a high powered microscope and read quick facts. At this site you'll also learn about bacteria in food, infections, flu, and the scientists who study microbes. There are lots of games, pictures, interactive activities, a mystery to solve and much more.

Web site 4 Learn about food allergies, read tips on how to keep yourself safe if you have an allergy and play games and quizzes to find out more.

Web site 5 Follow some children as they take you on a virtual tour of a hospital. There are photographs to look at and lots of information about what it is like to be in hospital.

Web site 6 On this site you can find out about different types of pollution and discover what you can do about it.

For links to all these sites go to www.usborne-quicklinks.com and type in the keywords "pocket scientist 2".

WHY IS NIGHT DARK?

Sophy Tahta

Designed by Christopher Gillingwater, Kim Blundell and Lindy Dark
Illustrated by Guy Smith, Joseph McEwan and Brin Edwards

Consultant: Sue Becklake

CONTENTS

Dark nights

In this section you can find out why night is dark. But there is a lot more to know about night and what happens then. Here are some things you may have noticed. They are all explained later on.

Have you ever noticed that the Moon can be different shapes?

On a clear night you can see lots of stars. Do you know what happens to them during the day?

Sometimes the Moon and stars are hidden by clouds or fog. They are still there, even though you cannot see them.

Town lights

Electric lights in towns or cities can also make it seem less dark at night.

If you live in a town or city, you may have noticed how the sky glows at night.

All the lights you see here run on electricity. Have you ever wondered how electric light bulbs work?

Did you know?

When it is day where you are, it is night on the other side of the world.

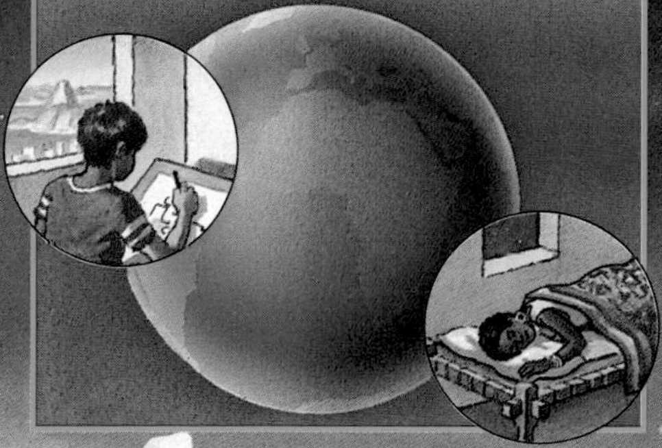

As you go to bed some animals are waking up. They sleep in the day and look for food at night.

Do you know how these animals find their way in the dark?

The Sun never sets here in summer. It is called the midnight Sun.

Some places do not get dark at night in summer, or get light during the day in winter.

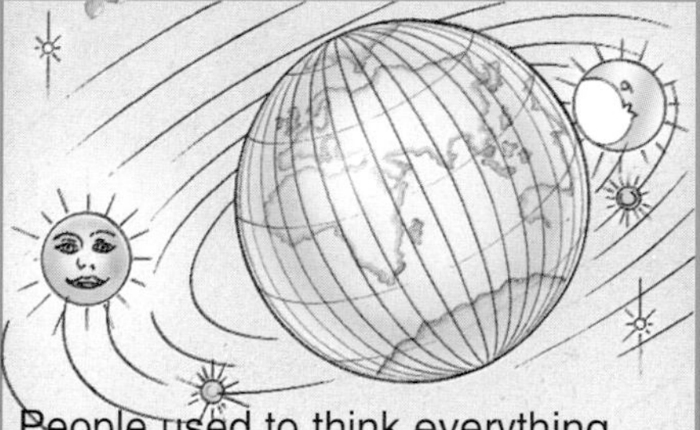

People used to think everything in space moved around the Earth. They invented reasons to explain night and dark. In this section you can find out what really happens.

Light and dark

It would always be dark on Earth if the Sun did not rise every morning. The Sun gives us light each day.

The Sun is a giant ball of incredibly hot, glowing gases. It gives out a huge amount of light and heat. Without it nothing could live or grow on Earth.

The Sun always shines, even when clouds stop you from seeing it.

A chariot of fire

The Sun is so important to life on Earth that hundreds of years ago people worshipped it as a god.

The Ancient Greeks believed that their Sun god Helios drove his chariot across the sky in the day. He rested his horses at night.

The Sun in the sky

On sunny days you can see the Sun rise, move across the sky and set.* People used to think this was because the Sun moved around the Earth.

In the morning the Sun rises in one part of the sky.

At midday you can see the Sun high above you.

In the evening the Sun sets in another part of the sky.

*NEVER STARE AT THE SUN. IT CAN DAMAGE YOUR EYES.

The spinning Earth

Now people know that the Sun does not move around the Earth. It is really the Earth that spins around and around in space.

The Sun only shines on one half of the spinning Earth.

The half facing the Sun is in the light. It is daytime there.

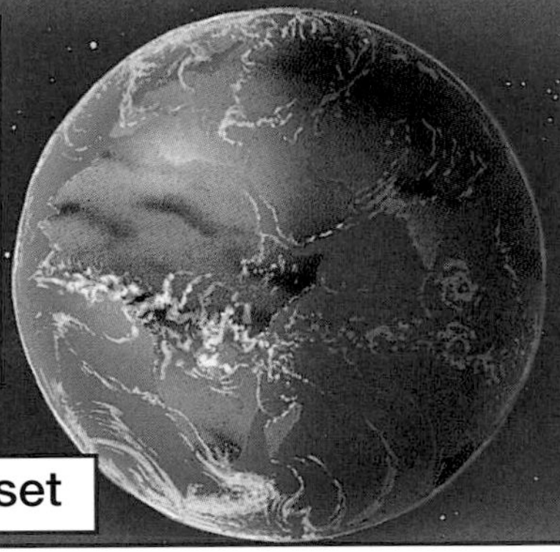

The sunlight cannot reach the other half of the Earth.

The half facing away from the Sun is in the dark. It is night there.

Sunrise and sunset

As your part of the Earth turns towards the Sun it begins to get light. This is when the Sun seems to rise.

As your part of the Earth turns away from the Sun, it begins to get dark. This is when the Sun seems to set.

See for yourself

You need a torch and a ball. Mark a spot on the ball for your home with tape or a pen. Make your room dark.

Ask someone to turn the ball while you shine the torch on it. See how the spot goes in and out of the light.

Hold the ball at the top and bottom and turn it this way.

Internet link *Go to* ***www.usborne-quicklinks.com*** *for a link to a Web site where you'll find some fascinating facts about the Sun.*

Day turns to night

The Earth makes one full spin every 24 hours. During this time most places have a day and a night.

But not all places have day and night at the same time. As one place spins into the light, another spins out of it.

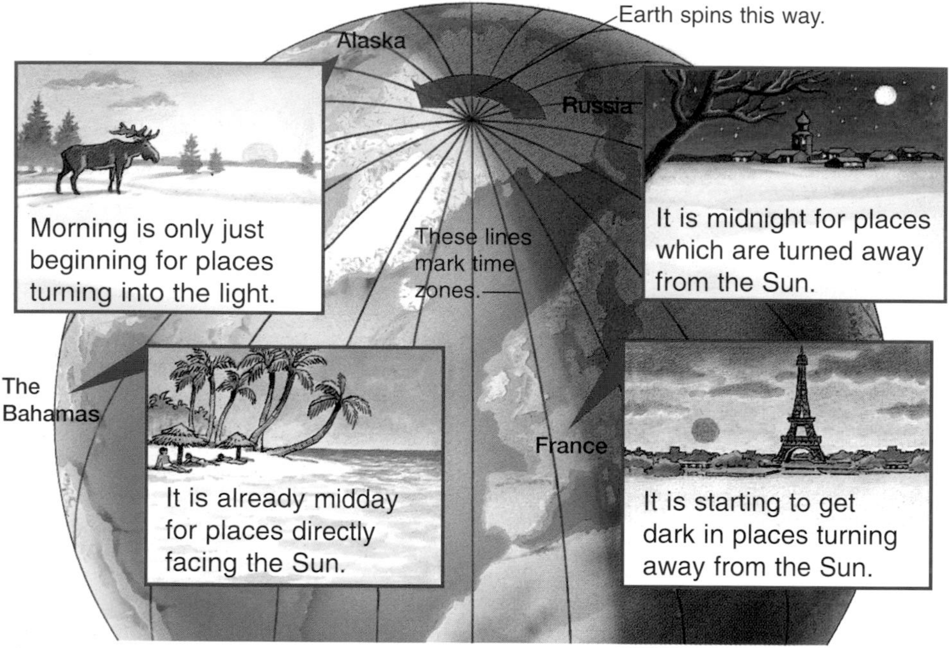

Earth spins this way.
Alaska
Russia
Morning is only just beginning for places turning into the light.
These lines mark time zones.
It is midnight for places which are turned away from the Sun.
The Bahamas
It is already midday for places directly facing the Sun.
France
It is starting to get dark in places turning away from the Sun.

Sometimes we need to know what time it is in another country. To help us, people have divided the world into 24 "slices" called time zones.

You can see them in this picture. Each place in one zone has the same time. But it is one hour earlier or later in the zones on either side.

How time zones work

Some very big countries, such as the United States of America, go across many time zones. America is made up of smaller parts called states. The time lines on this map bend to keep some whole states in one zone.

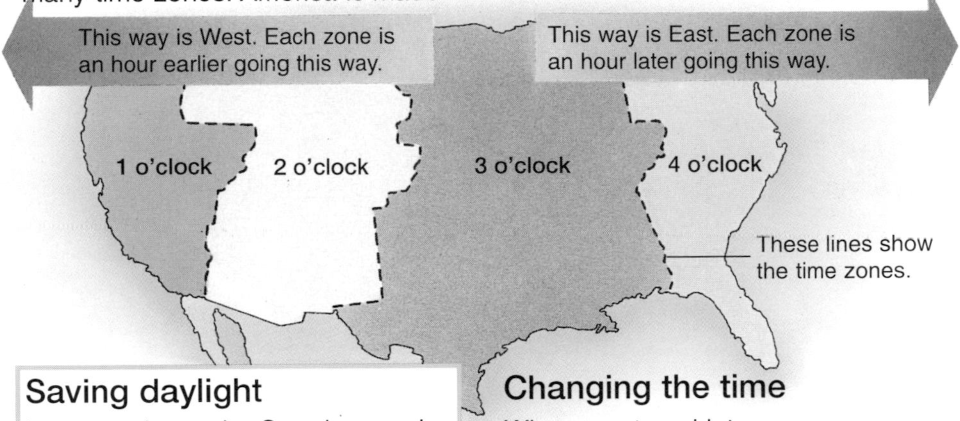

This way is West. Each zone is an hour earlier going this way.
This way is East. Each zone is an hour later going this way.
1 o'clock
2 o'clock
3 o'clock
4 o'clock
These lines show the time zones.

Saving daylight

In many places the Sun rises early in summer when most people are asleep. This seems a waste of daylight. So lots of places put their clocks forward one hour in summer.

Now the clocks say it is time to get up one hour earlier than in winter.

The clocks go back again one hour in winter.

Changing the time

When you travel into a new zone you change the time on your watch. You put it forward one hour for each zone you cross going East, and back one hour for each zone going West.

There is one special line called the International Date Line. When you cross it, you change the day of the week, as well as the time.

Internet link *Go to* ***www.usborne-quicklinks.com*** *for a link to a Web site where you can find out more about the International Date Line.*

The seasons

As well as spinning around once each day, the Earth also moves around the Sun. It takes a year to go around once.

The Earth is not quite upright as it spins in space. It leans to one side.

North
North Pole
The top half is the Northern Hemisphere.
This imaginary line around the middle is the Equator.
The bottom half is the Southern Hemisphere.
South
South Pole

The way the Earth leans makes the seasons change in both hemispheres during the year.

The Sun's rays

The Sun's rays shine more directly on the half leaning towards it. Direct rays feel hot. It is summer here.

Direct ray

The Sun always shines almost directly on the Equator. It is always hot here.

Direct ray

The Sun's rays slant across the half leaning away from it. Slanting rays feel cooler than direct rays because their heat spreads over more ground. It is winter here.

Slanting ray

A journey around the Sun

This picture shows the Earth moving around the Sun. The Earth always leans the same way so the Sun shines more directly on the Northern half and then on the Southern half. This gives each half summer and winter. When it is summer in one half, it is winter in the other.

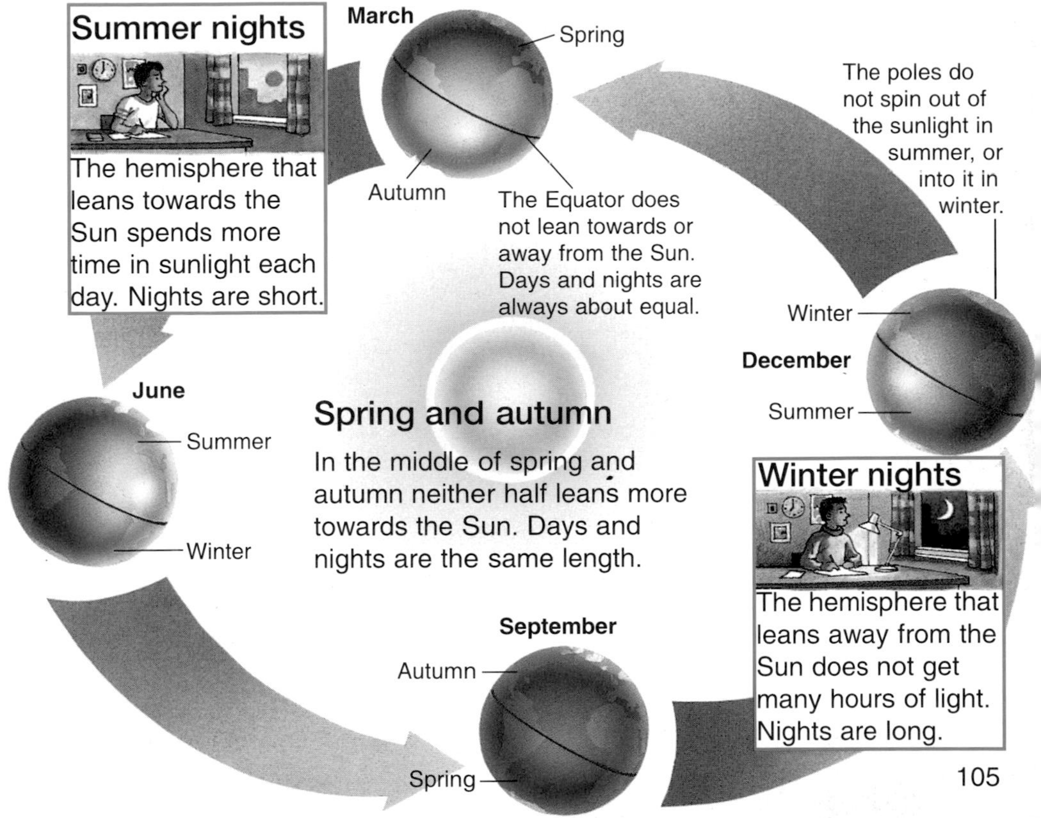

March
Spring
Autumn
The Equator does not lean towards or away from the Sun. Days and nights are always about equal.
The poles do not spin out of the sunlight in summer, or into it in winter.
December
Winter
Summer
June
Summer
Winter
September
Autumn
Spring

Summer nights

The hemisphere that leans towards the Sun spends more time in sunlight each day. Nights are short.

Spring and autumn

In the middle of spring and autumn neither half leans more towards the Sun. Days and nights are the same length.

Winter nights

The hemisphere that leans away from the Sun does not get many hours of light. Nights are long.

The Moon

Some nights are less dark than others. On a clear night you can usually see the Moon shining brightly.

The Moon looks big and bright in the night sky. But unlike the Sun it does not make its own light.

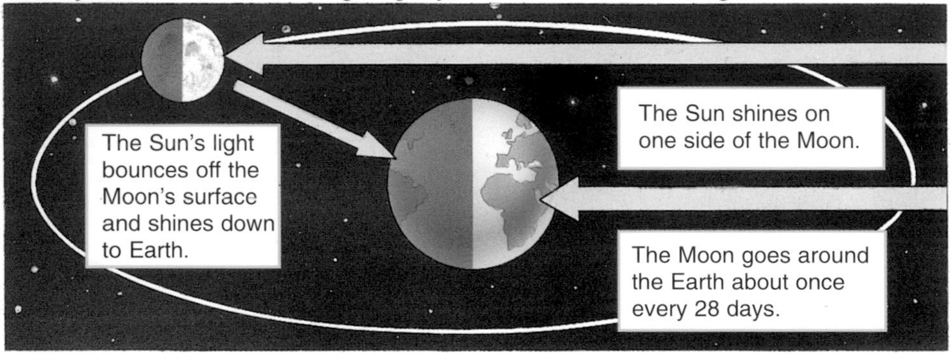

The Sun's light bounces off the Moon's surface and shines down to Earth.
The Sun shines on one side of the Moon.
The Moon goes around the Earth about once every 28 days.

The changing Moon

As the Moon moves you see different amounts of its light side. You could record the shapes on paper.

Draw the shape you see inside a circle. Do it each evening you see the Moon for 28 days. See how it changes.

You cannot really see a New Moon. The Sun lights up the other side.

This is a Crescent Moon. You can see a little of the Moon's light side.

This is a Full Moon. You see all of its light side. After this you see less.

 Internet link *Go to* ***www.usborne-quicklinks.com*** *for a link to a Web site which will tell you what shape the Moon will be tonight.*

Exploring the Moon

The Moon is nearer to Earth than the Sun or stars. It is the first place that people have visited in space.

12 astronauts have been on the Moon so far, between 1969 and 1972. Some took a Moon buggy to drive.

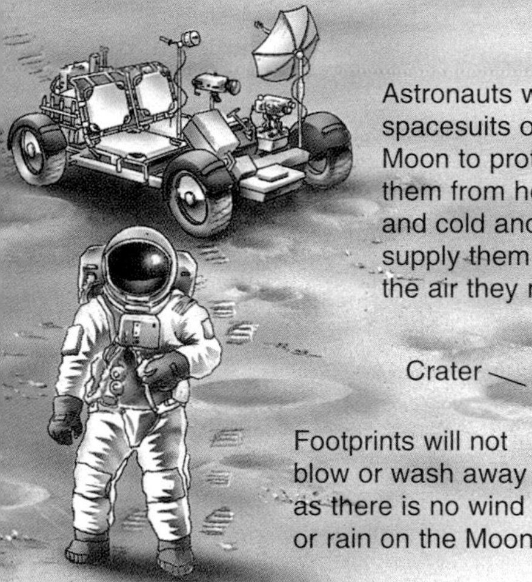

Astronauts wear spacesuits on the Moon to protect them from heat and cold and supply them with the air they need.

Footprints will not blow or wash away as there is no wind or rain on the Moon.

There is no air, water or life on the Moon. It is a still and silent place, covered with craters made when space rocks crashed there.

The Man in the Moon

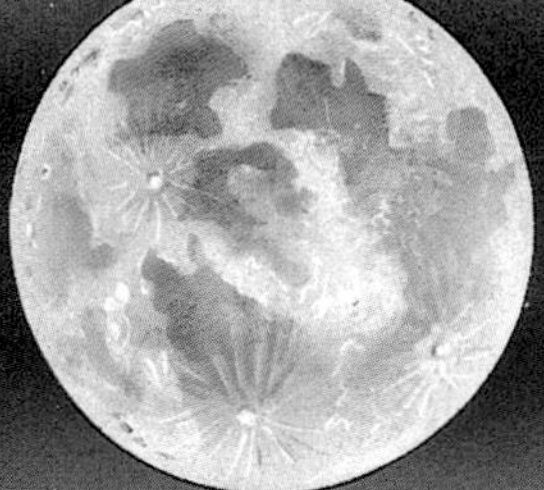

The dark patches you can see on the Moon are flat plains. Some people think they look like a face and call it the Man in the Moon. See if you can see it next time there is a Full Moon.

The Moon's pull

The Earth and Moon both pull things and people down towards them. This pull is called gravity. It makes things feel heavy when you lift them.

The Moon's pull is weaker than the Earth's. This makes things and people feel lighter there. Astronauts' spacesuits and backpacks are not so heavy on the Moon. Astronauts walk with great bouncy steps.

Internet link *Go to* ***www.usborne-quicklinks.com*** *for a link to a Web site where you can find out about the different parts of an astronaut's spacesuit.*

About the stars

On clear nights you can see hundreds of stars. Each one is a giant ball of hot, glowing gases like the Sun.

The stars look tiny because they are very far away.

The Sun is really a star too. It looks so big because it is our nearest star. Others are bigger but further away.

You cannot see the other stars during the day because the Sun is so bright.

A star is born

Stars are born in a gas and dust cloud. The cloud squeezes into a ball. It gets very hot and glows as a new star.

After millions of years a star swells up and cools. It is now called a red giant. Later, its outer layers drift into space.

Some of the biggest stars explode at the end of their lives. They leave behind new clouds of gas and dust.

A gas and dust cloud is called a nebula.

Red giants leave behind white dwarfs.

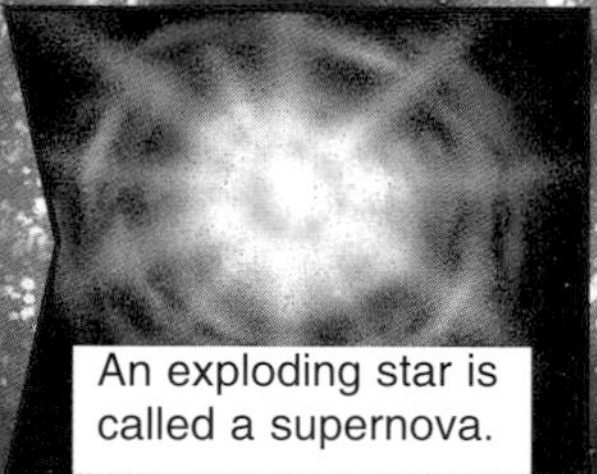

An exploding star is called a supernova.

Internet link *Go to **www.usborne-quicklinks.com** for a link to a Web site where you can do a quiz and watch a great movie about the life cycle of stars.*

The Milky Way

Stars belong to huge groups called galaxies. The stars you see belong to a galaxy called the Milky Way.

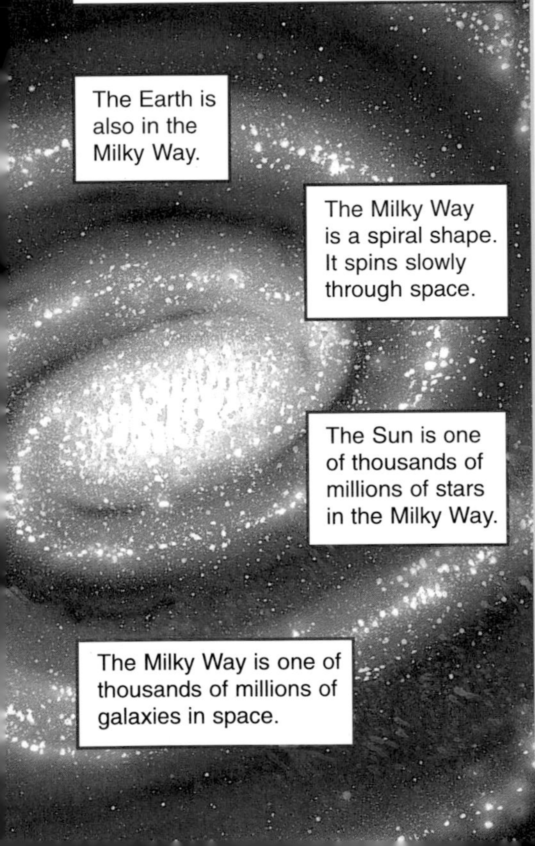

The Earth is also in the Milky Way.
The Milky Way is a spiral shape. It spins slowly through space.
The Sun is one of thousands of millions of stars in the Milky Way.
The Milky Way is one of thousands of millions of galaxies in space.

Star patterns

Long ago people saw patterns in the stars. These patterns are called constellations. You can see different ones from different parts of Earth.

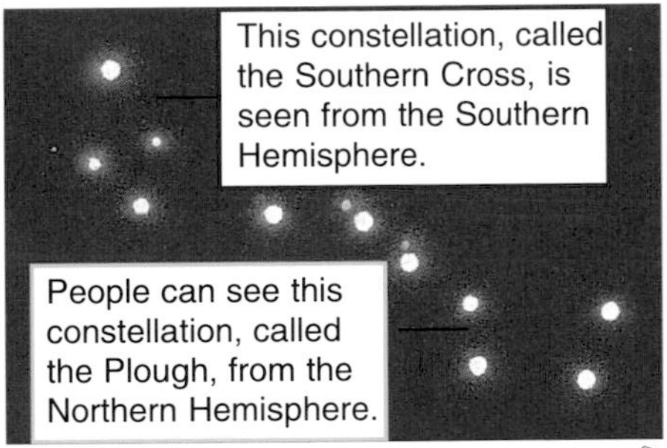

This constellation, called the Southern Cross, is seen from the Southern Hemisphere.
People can see this constellation, called the Plough, from the Northern Hemisphere.

Do you live in the Northern or Southern Hemisphere?

Sailing by the stars

The stars have always helped sailors find their way. The North Star shows which way is North, and two stars at the end of the Plough point to it.

The Solar System

Our part of the Milky Way is called the Solar System. The Sun is at the centre with nine planets and lots of moons and bits of rock going around it. You can see them in this picture.

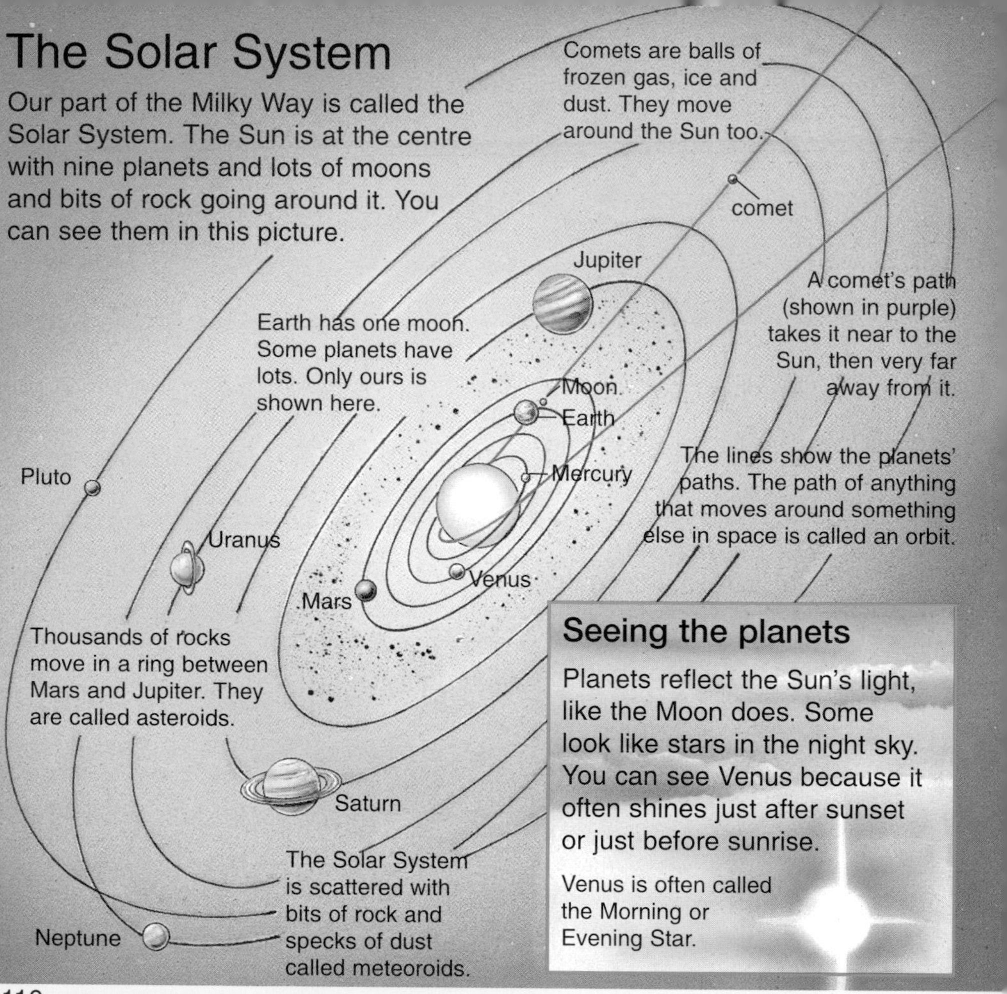

Comets are balls of frozen gas, ice and dust. They move around the Sun too.
comet
Jupiter
A comet's path (shown in purple) takes it near to the Sun, then very far away from it.
Earth has one moon. Some planets have lots. Only ours is shown here.
Moon
Earth
Mercury
The lines show the planets' paths. The path of anything that moves around something else in space is called an orbit.
Pluto
Uranus
Venus
Mars
Thousands of rocks move in a ring between Mars and Jupiter. They are called asteroids.
Saturn
The Solar System is scattered with bits of rock and specks of dust called meteoroids.
Neptune

Seeing the planets

Planets reflect the Sun's light, like the Moon does. Some look like stars in the night sky. You can see Venus because it often shines just after sunset or just before sunrise.

Venus is often called the Morning or Evening Star.

 Internet link *Go to* ***www.usborne-quicklinks.com*** *for a link to a Web site where you'll find photographs and fascinating facts about the planets in our Solar System.*

Night sights

Here are some other bright things you may see in the night sky. Some are natural and others are man-made.

As a comet gets near the Sun the gas and dust flow into a long, bright tail. You may very occasionally see one at night.

Sometimes meteoroids fall into the Earth's air. They burn up, making a bright streak called a meteor or shooting star.

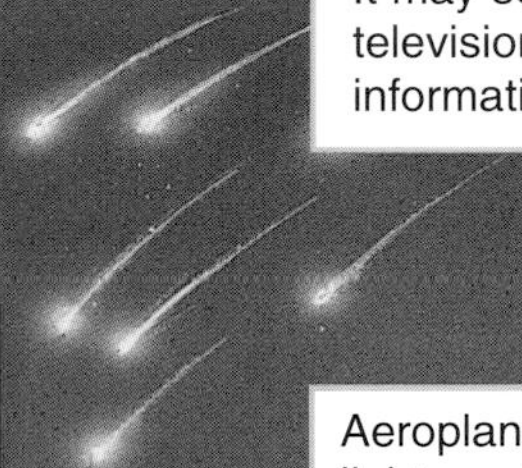

A satellite is a spacecraft. It may send telephone calls, television pictures and other information around the world.

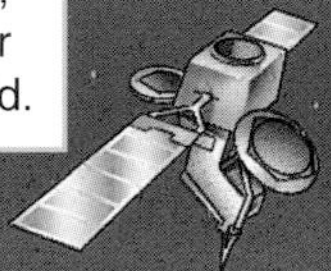

Satellites reflect sunlight and glint like slow-moving stars.

Aeroplanes use lights so they can be seen clearly in the dark.

Town lights reflect off clouds. They can make the sky glow.

People light fireworks at night as they show up best in the dark.

Glowing lights

This coloured light is called an aurora.

It begins at about 96 kilometres (60 miles) above the ground.

Sometimes the Sun gives out extra bursts of energy. These can make the sky near the poles glow with slowly changing colours.

Internet link *Go to* ***www.usborne-quicklinks.com*** *for a link to a Web site where you can find out what causes auroras, look at photographs and read lots of interesting information about them.*

Night life

Some animals come out at night. Most can see well in the dark, and have a good sense of hearing, smell or touch, too. These senses warn them of danger and help them to find food and mates in the dark.

Here you can see some animals that come out when it starts to get dark. These animals are nocturnal, which means “of the night”.

Most bats cannot see well. Some have a special kind of hearing to help them catch moths at night.

Badgers sniff the air for danger before leaving their burrows. The damp night air carries smells well.

Rabbits and deer go further afield at night. The dark helps to hide them from enemies.

Cats and foxes use their long whiskers to feel their way through small gaps.

Owls and cats have big eyes that open up in the dark to let in as much light as possible.

Hedgehogs use their snouts to smell and forage for grubs.

Internet link *Go to* ***www.usborne-quicklinks.com*** *for a link to a Web site you can find out facts about lots of different nocturnal animals.*

Noises at night

The dark hides friends as well as enemies. Some animals find mates by calling to them.

Frogs croak to let other frogs know where they are.

A male cricket makes a chirping call to a female by rubbing its wings together.

Bat squeaks

Bat squeaks make echoes as they bounce off things such as trees. Bats listen to the echoes to find out where things are.

Bats do not bump into things. They zigzag to avoid trees, or to catch insects.

Most bat noises are too high for people to hear.

Glowing in the night

Some insects have a special way of making light in their own bodies.

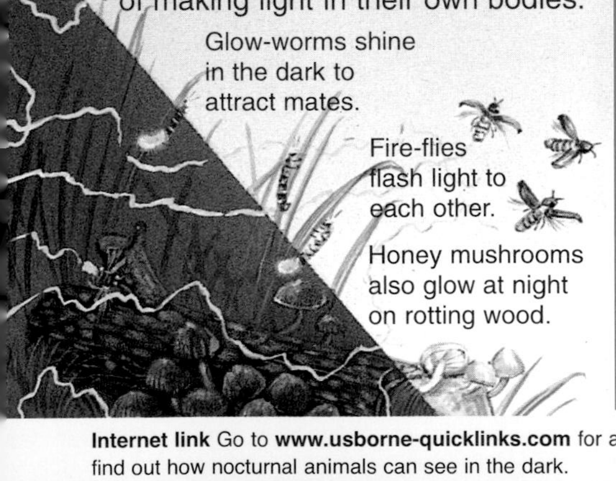

Glow-worms shine in the dark to attract mates.

Fire-flies flash light to each other.

Honey mushrooms also glow at night on rotting wood.

Flowers of the night

Some flowers are also nocturnal. They smell sweeter at night.

The scent attracts moths that get food from the flowers.

Moths also take pollen from one flower to another. This helps new flowers grow.

Night-flowering catchfly

Internet link Go to **www.usborne-quicklinks.com** for a link to a Web site where you can find out how nocturnal animals can see in the dark.

How light works

During the day, the Sun's light lets you see shapes and colours.

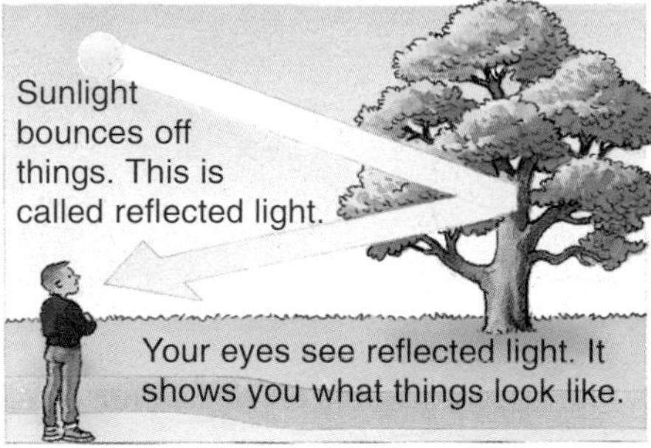

Sunlight bounces off things. This is called reflected light.
Your eyes see reflected light. It shows you what things look like.

At night there is not enough light to see things clearly.

People travelling at night use lights to see and be seen.

Light and colour

Sunlight looks clear but is really made up of many colours. You can see them when the Sun shines through raindrops and makes a rainbow.

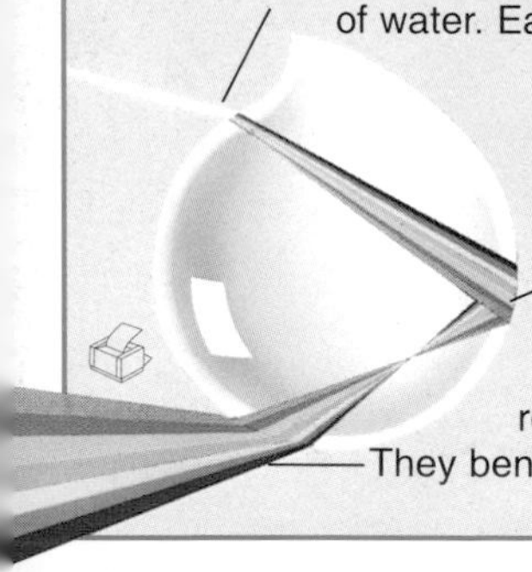

Light bends as it goes into a drop of water. Each colour bends a different amount, separating them.
The colours bounce off the back of the drop.
The drop reflects the colours. They bend on their way out.

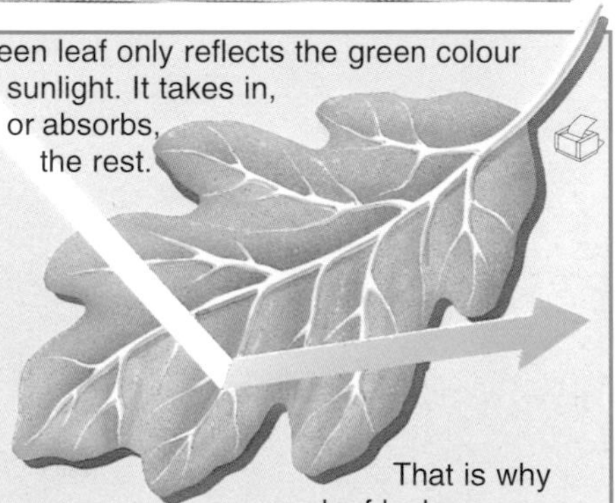

A green leaf only reflects the green colour in sunlight. It takes in, or absorbs, the rest.
That is why a leaf looks green.

Light gives all things their colour. When light hits things, some colours are reflected. The rest are taken in. You only see the reflected colours.

Make a colour mixer

You can see how lots of colours mix to make white. Cut out a card circle 10cm (4in) across. Lightly crayon in the rainbow colours.

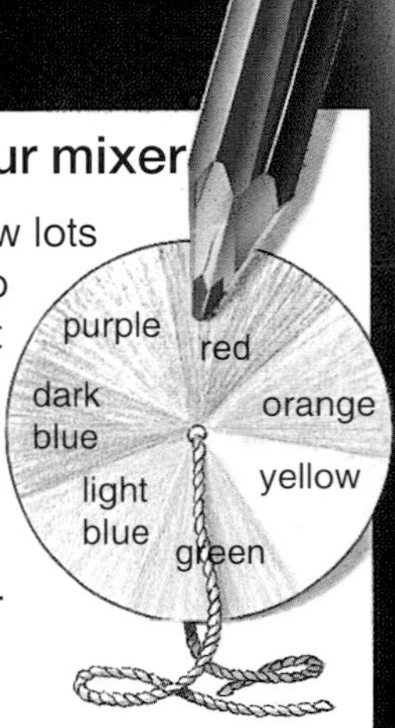

Thread some string through the centre.

Hold each end loosely. Swing the card around in big loops.

Pull both ends tight so the card spins fast. Look at the colours as the card spins.

The colours blend. If you spin the card very fast it looks almost white.

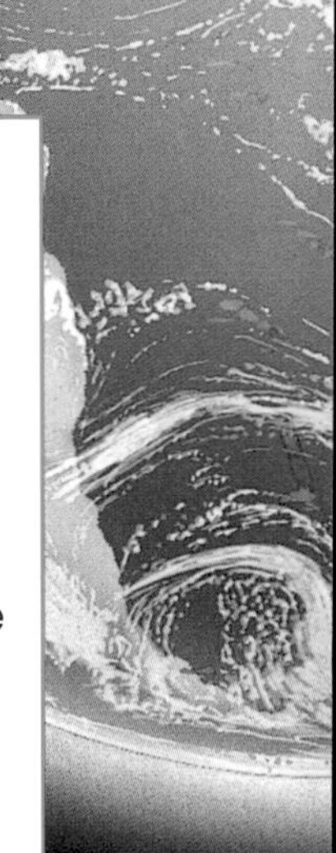

Why is sky blue?

In the day the sky is often blue, because there is a layer of air around the Earth.

This air is full of dust and drops of water. These scatter the blue colour in sunlight more than the other colours.

There is no air in space to scatter the Sun's light. This is why space is black.

A black sky

The sky above the Moon is black even during the day because there is no layer of air around it.

Internet link Go to **www.usborne-quicklinks.com** for a link to a Web site where you can find out more about white light, and see what happens to the colour of light when different colours are removed.

Shadows

Light only moves in straight lines. It leaves dark shadows behind things that stand in its way. That is why the Earth is always dark on one side. The Sun's light cannot bend around it.

Draw your shadow

On a sunny day, you stop some sunlight reaching the ground. This makes your shadow.

Ask a friend to draw around your shadow on a sunny morning.

Mark where you stood. Do it again at other times of the day.

Shadows always point away from the Sun.

See how your shadow moves and how long it gets, as the Sun moves across the sky.

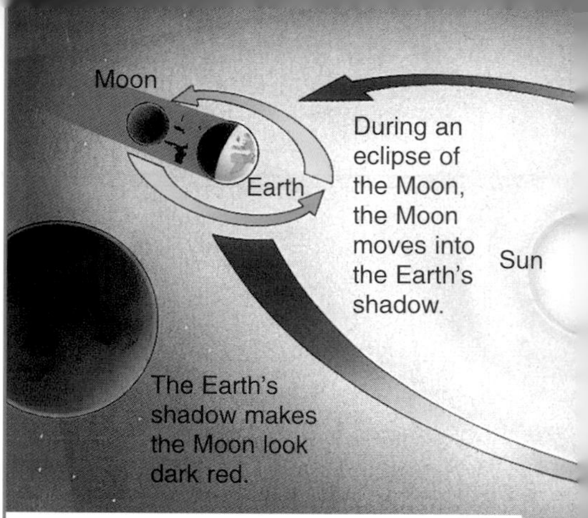

During an eclipse of the Moon, the Moon moves into the Earth's shadow.

The Earth's shadow makes the Moon look dark red.

The Earth's shadow

At times the Earth is directly between the Sun and the Moon. The Sun's rays cannot bend around to light the Moon. This is an eclipse of the Moon.

Day shadows

The Sun's rays reach the ground in a short, more direct path.

This makes short shadows.

Shadows are short at midday when the Sun is high in the sky.

 Internet link *Go to* ***www.usborne-quicklinks.com*** *for a link to a Web site where you can do a quiz and watch a short movie about different kinds of eclipses.*

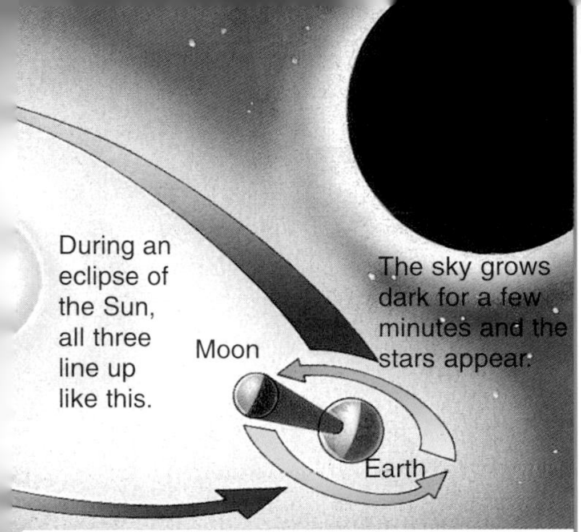

The sky grows dark for a few minutes and the stars appear.

The Moon's Shadow

Less often, the Moon moves directly between the Earth and Sun. It blocks out the Sun and casts a shadow on the Earth. This is an eclipse of the Sun.

The Sun's rays travel in a longer, slanting path to reach the ground.
Shadows are long and thin.

Shadows are long in the morning and evening, when the Sun is low.

Make a shadow clock

Fix a pencil upright on a piece of card, with Plasticine. Leave it in a sunny place in the morning.

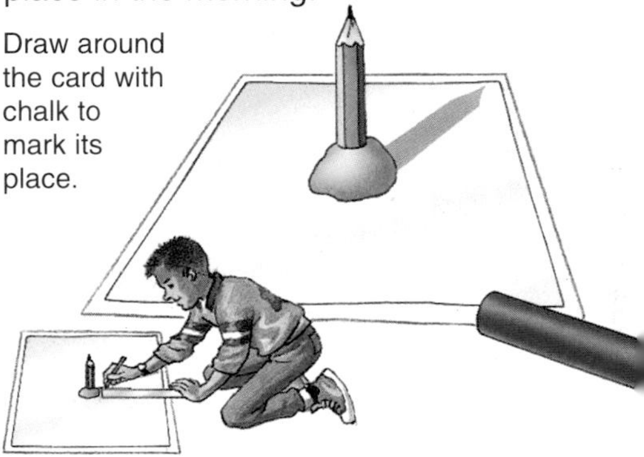

Draw around the card with chalk to mark its place.

Draw the pencil's shadow. Write the time by the shadow. Do this again every hour.

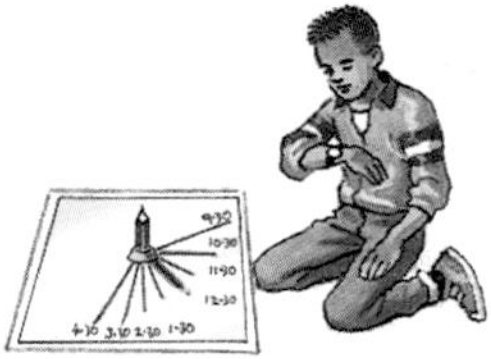

This clock will only be right for a few weeks. The shadows change as the Sun rises earlier or later during the year.

Put the card in the same position the next day. The shadow will show you roughly what time it is.

Electric lights

People have only used electric light bulbs for about 120 years. The first one was made by Thomas Edison in 1879. Here you see what happens when you turn on a light or torch.

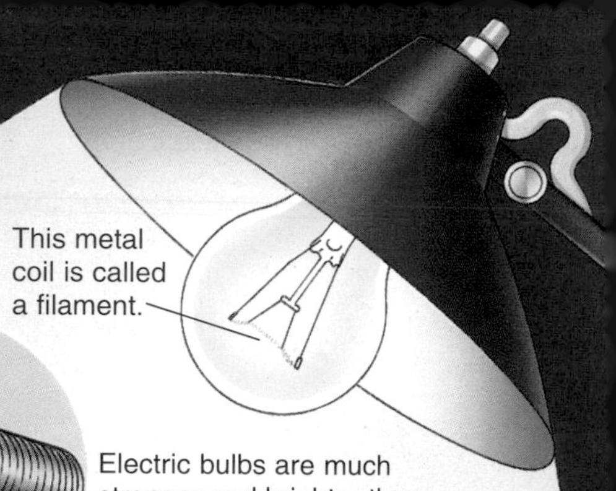
This metal
coil is called
a filament.

A torch makes a strong, steady beam.

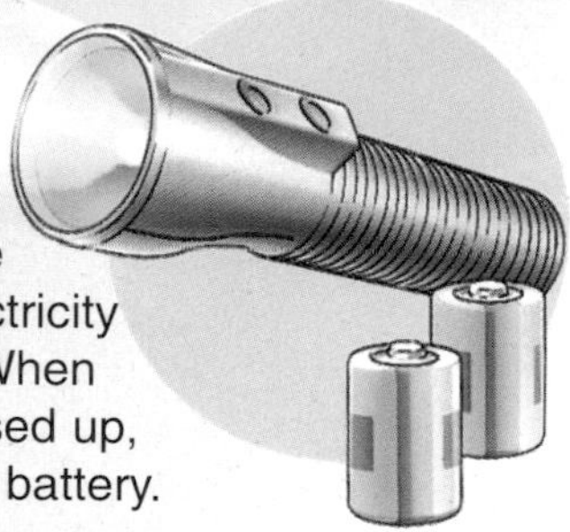

A battery inside the torch sends electricity to light up the bulb. When all the electricity is used up, you can put in a new battery.

Electric bulbs are much stronger and brighter than any light used before.

Electricity goes along hidden wires to the light bulb. It makes a metal coil inside the bulb glow white hot.

Guiding lights

At night, lighthouses warn ships of rocks with a strong, flashing light.

"Cat's-eyes" are
bits of glass set
in rubber blocks.

"Cat's-eyes" in roads reflect car lights back to the driver.

Bright lights on the runway help aeroplanes land when it is dark.

Internet links

Go to **www.usborne-quicklinks.com** and type in the keywords "pocket scientist 2" for links to these Web sites about the night.

Web site 1 Find out more about light by watching a fun, short movie. There is also a quiz to test your knowledge.

Web site 2 On this Web site you can find out about the phases of the Moon, and about NASA's search for water on the Moon using their Lunar Prospector. You can also compare what the Moon looks like from Earth and from space and play a game.

Web site 3 Go on a virtual tour of the Sun and see the latest amazing images of the Sun from space. There are also movies of the Sun, and lots of fascinating information about it.

Web site 4 Learn more about the seasons, what causes them, and which parts of the Earth have fewer than four seasons. There is also an interactive quiz to do.

Web site 5 This Web site is packed with information about the Earth, the Moon, stars and quasars. You can read more about the seasons and try out some online activities.

Web site 6 Find out about how we see light and colour and how our eyes work on this Web site. You can also take a virtual tour of an eyeball, discover more about rainbows and do some online experiments with colour.

For links to all these sites go to www.usborne-quicklinks.com and type in the keywords "pocket scientist 2".

More internet links

Here are some more Web sites to visit to find out about the night. For links to all these sites go to **www.usborne-quicklinks.com** and type in the keywords "pocket scientist 2".

Web site 1 On this Web site you can read about the science of light. There are also interactive activities to help you discover more about colour and shadows.

Web site 2 Learn about the night creatures of the Kalahari desert. Find out about these creatures' amazing eyes, which help them to see their next meal when people would only see darkness. You can also read about the surprising ways scientists study nocturnal animals.

Web site 3 This Web site is great for explaining how time zones work. You can also find out who invented daylight saving time and read more about the stars and the seasons.

Web site 4 Bats only come out at night and have an amazing way of using sound to find their way around. Find out more about how they do this, learn about where they live, what they eat, what they really look like and play bat games.

Web site 5 Explore the ancient stories behind the constellations, find out what's happening in the night sky this month and learn how to recognize the stars. You can also download and make a star-finder.

Web site 6 Find out more about different kinds of electricity and how it works on this fun Web site. There are safety tips and an experiment to try out.

For links to all these sites go to www.usborne-quicklinks.com and type in the keywords "pocket scientist 2".

WHAT'S THE EARTH MADE OF?

Susan Mayes

Designed by Lindy Dark
Illustrated by Stuart Trotter and Chris Shields

Consultant: Ben Spencer

CONTENTS

Planet Earth

The Earth is a planet which is made mostly of rock. It spins around the Sun in a part of space called the Solar System. There are nine planets in the Solar System altogether.

The Solar System

This picture shows the planets in the Solar System. Each one moves around the Sun on its own invisible path called an orbit.

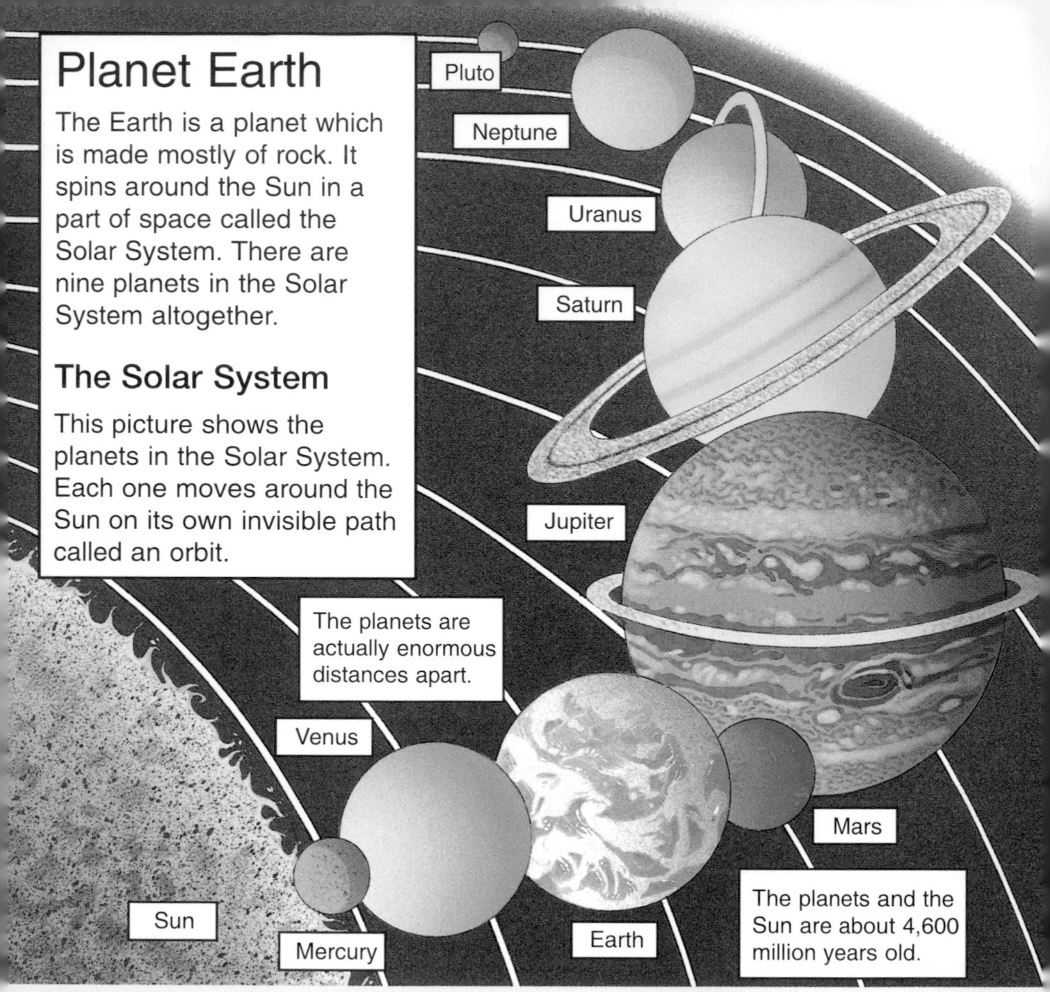

The planets are actually enormous distances apart.

The planets and the Sun are about 4,600 million years old.

The beginning

The Earth probably began as a huge, swirling cloud of dust and gases.

Then, the cloud started to shrink. It turned into a spinning ball of hot, runny rock.

The surface cooled and hardened into a rocky crust. Clouds formed and rain fell to make seas.

Inside and outside

The Earth is made up of layers. The thin outer layer is called the crust. It is solid rock. Underneath, there is a very thick, hot layer of rock, called the mantle.

The Earth's middle is called the core. It is hot, runny metal on the outside and solid metal on the inside. The inside is the hottest part of our planet.

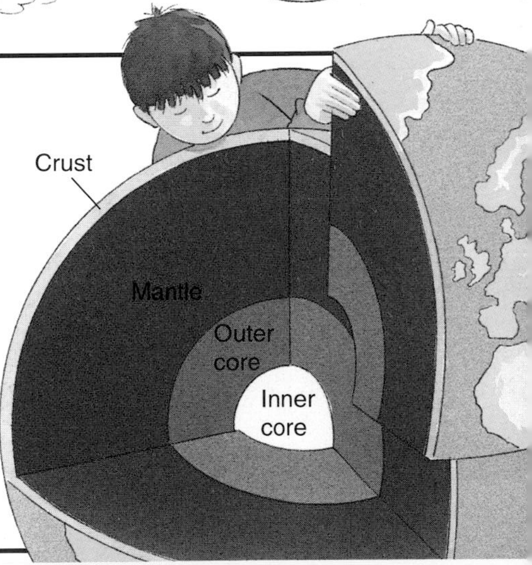

Internet link Go to ***www.usborne-quicklinks.com*** *for a link to a Web site where you can do a quiz and see a short movie about the Earth.*

The big jigsaw

The Earth's crust is not one whole piece, like the skin of an apple. It is made of separate pieces which fit together closely, like a giant jigsaw puzzle. These pieces are called plates.

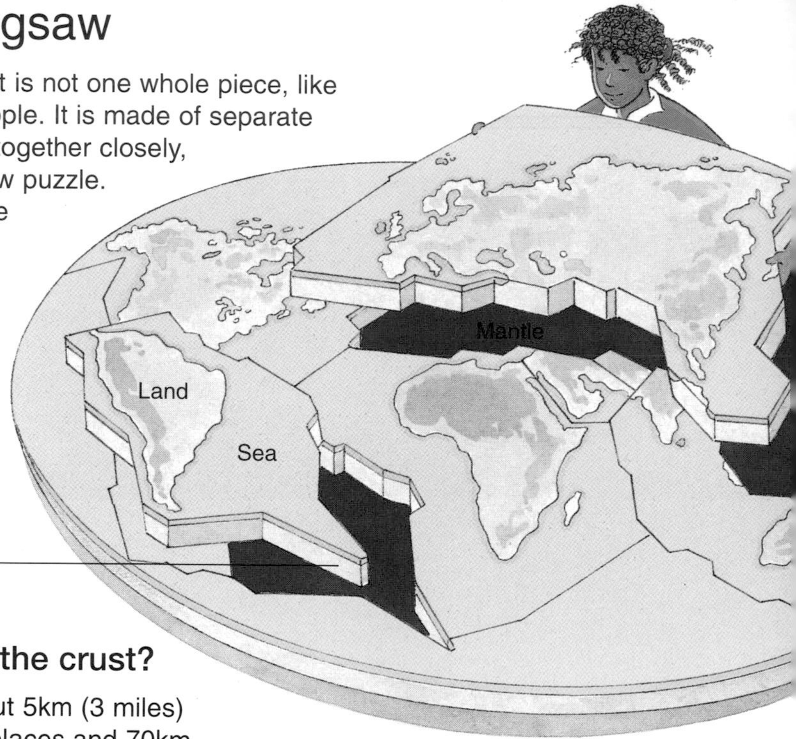

This flat model shows how the plates fit together.

Sea covers a lot of each plate. Land is the high part of a plate which sticks out of the water.

The edges of the plates are called plate boundaries.

How thick is the crust?

The crust is about 5km (3 miles) thick in some places and 70km (43 miles) thick in others. It is very thin compared with what is underneath. If the Earth was the size of a soccer ball, the crust would only be as thick as a piece of paper.

Floating plates

The plates float on the mantle. In the mantle there is hot, sticky liquid rock, called magma. The magma churns around and makes the plates move.

***Internet link** Go to **www.usborne-quicklinks.com** for a link to a Web site where you can discover how fossils are formed.*

Before and after

Some scientists think that 200 million years ago, the plates were joined so that the land was one huge piece. They call it Pangea.

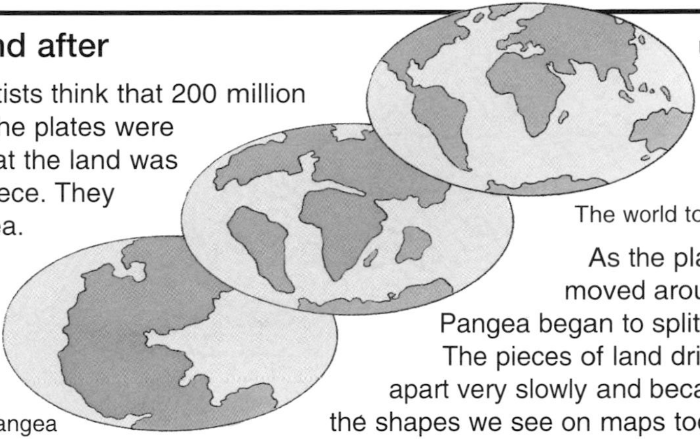

Pangea

The world today

As the plates moved around, Pangea began to split up. The pieces of land drifted apart very slowly and became the shapes we see on maps today.

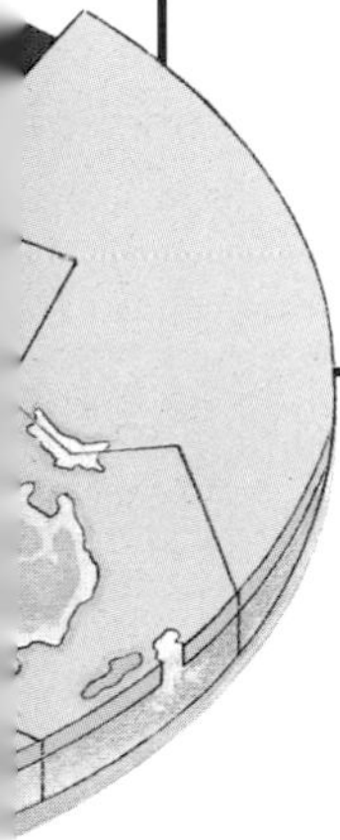

Fossil clues

Fossils are the remains of animals and plants that died long ago. The same kinds have been found far apart. This is probably because the land they once lived on separated.

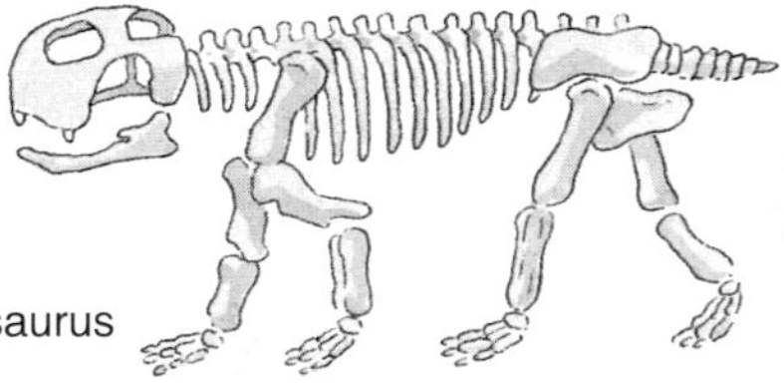

Lystrosaurus was a prehistoric animal. Its fossilized remains have been found in countries far apart.

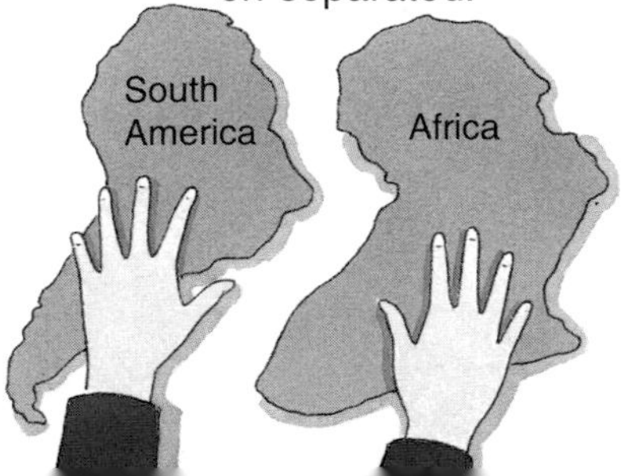

Fitting together

To see how the Earth's land used to fit together, trace the shapes of South America and Africa from a map of the world and cut them out. Can you tell where the countries used to join?

The changing crust

The Earth's plates move around very slowly. If one plate moves, the ones around it move, too. This makes the crust change in different ways.

Mountains

The world's highest mountain ranges are made when two plates crash into each other. The crust is pushed up into huge folds, called fold mountains.

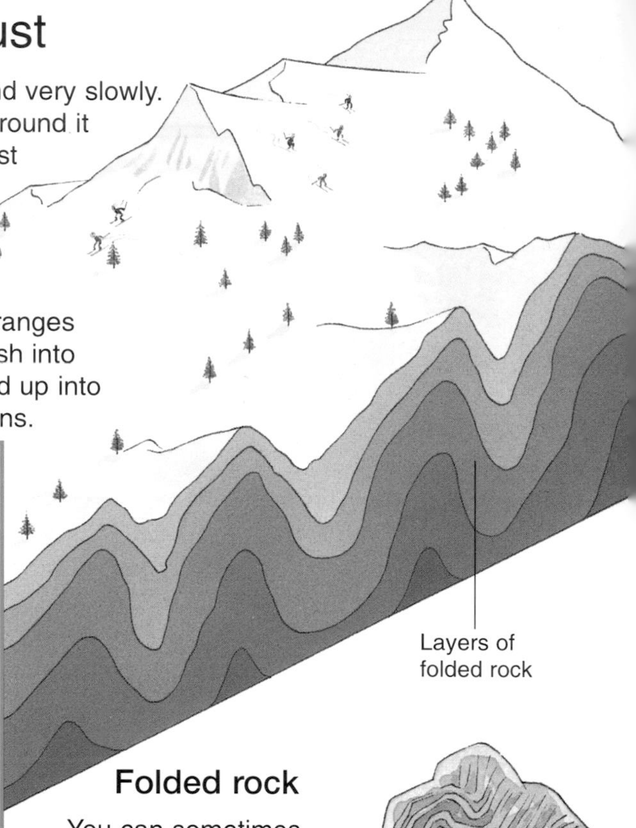

Make your own

To make a fold mountain, roll out three rectangles of Plasticine and sandwich them together. Push the ends inward and see how a fold appears.

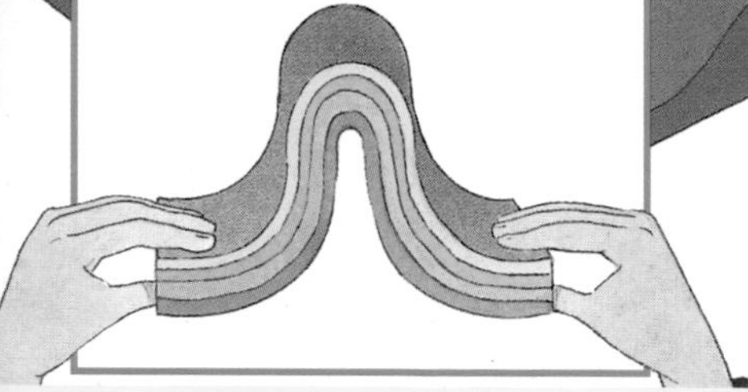

Folded rock

You can sometimes see rock with folds in it, in cliffs and mountain sides.

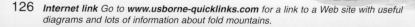

 Internet link *Go to* ***www.usborne-quicklinks.com*** *for a link to a Web site with useful diagrams and lots of information about fold mountains.*

Up and down

Plates often move apart under the sea. Magma comes up through the crack. It hardens into a ridge of new crust.

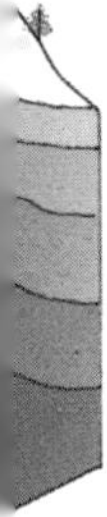

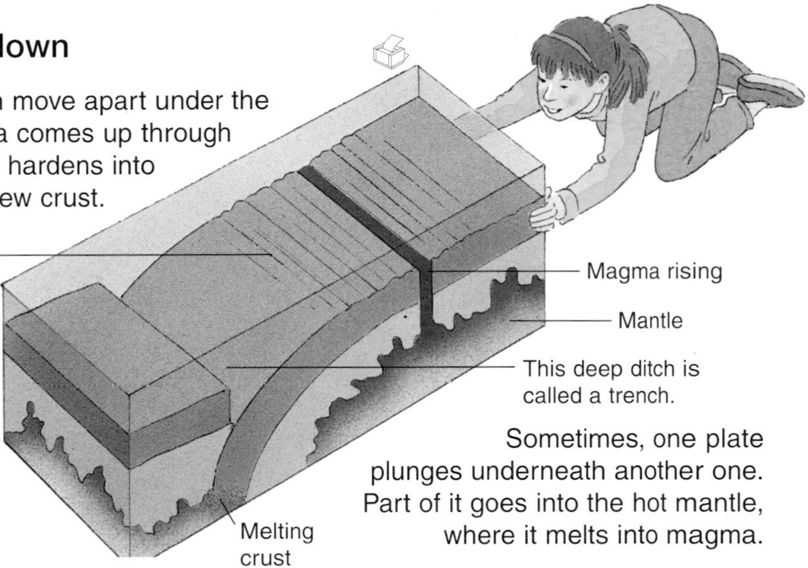

Sometimes, one plate plunges underneath another one. Part of it goes into the hot mantle, where it melts into magma.

Wearing away

Not all of the Earth's surface has been changed by movements in the crust. It has been shaped and worn away by water, wind and ice, too.

Wind throws grit and sand against rocks, wearing them away.

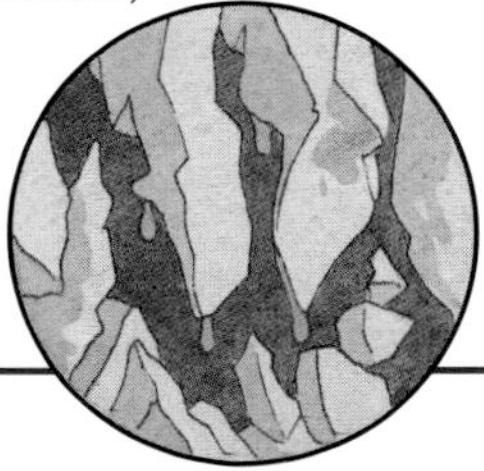

Rock breaks when water freezes in cracks and forces the rock apart.

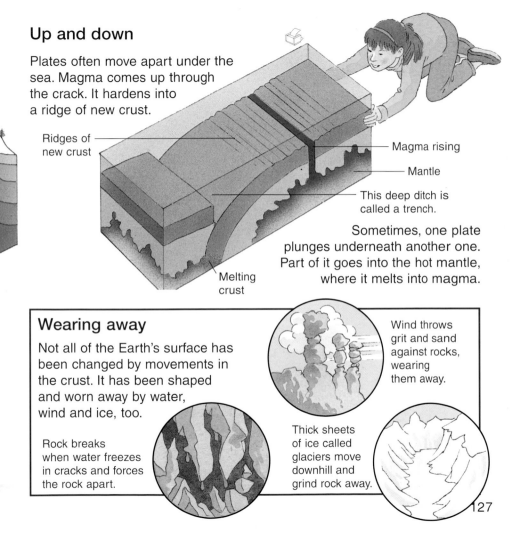

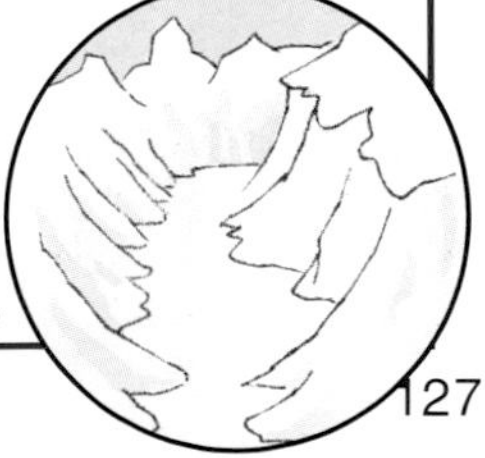

Thick sheets of ice called glaciers move downhill and grind rock away.

Earthquakes

An earthquake is when the Earth's crust shakes. Big earthquakes are violent and do lots of damage.

What happens?

Most earthquakes happen at plate boundaries. If the plates push against each other, the rocks get squeezed so hard that they sometimes slip or break. This makes vibrations, called shock waves, go through the rocks.

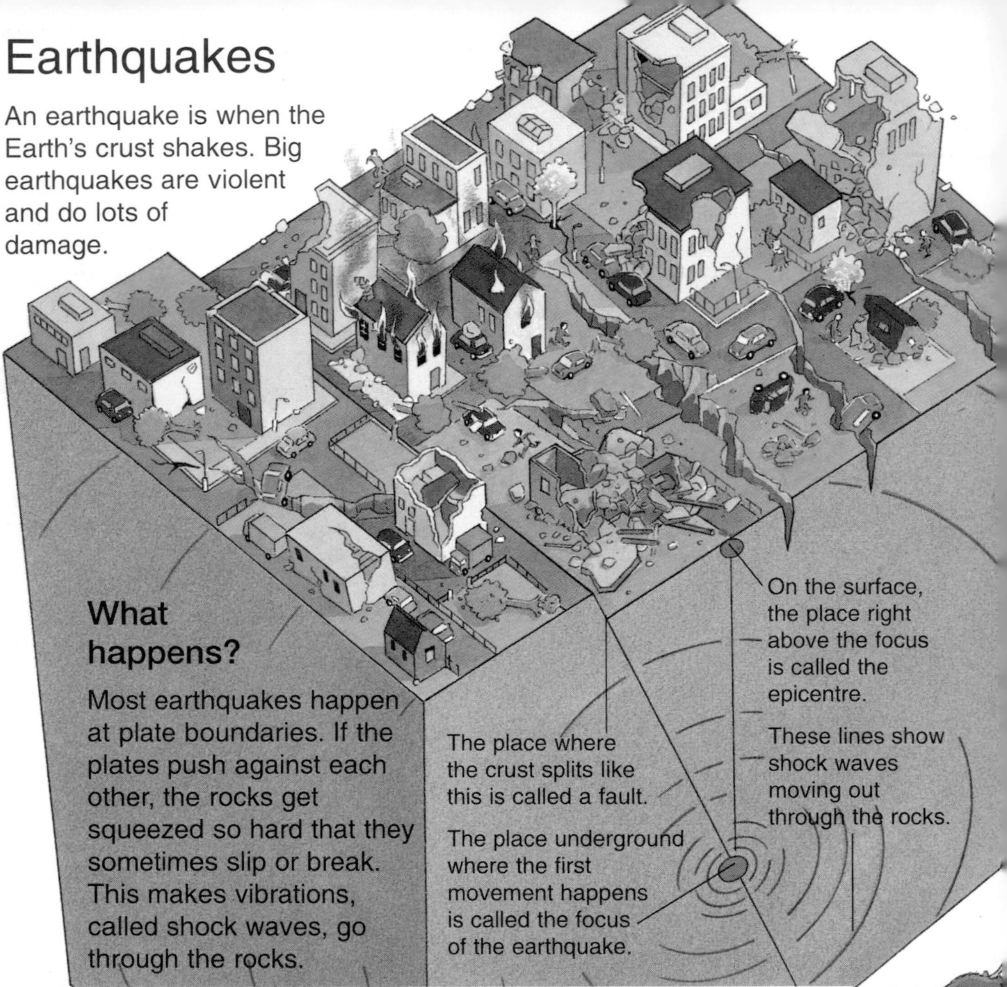

On the surface, the place right above the focus is called the epicentre.
These lines show shock waves moving out through the rocks.
The place where the crust splits like this is called a fault.
The place underground where the first movement happens is called the focus of the earthquake.

 Internet link *Go to **www.usborne-quicklinks.com** for a link to a Web site where you can create your own building and see what happens when an earthquake strikes.*

Measuring earthquakes

The Mercalli scale is a list of 12 things which scientists look for that tell them how strong an earthquake is. As the numbers get higher, the damage gets worse.

At number 3 on the scale, hanging objects swing.

At number 8, towers and chimneys collapse.

At number 12, nearly everything is damaged. Big areas of land slip and move.

Animal warnings

Animals have been known to behave strangely before some earthquakes. In China, mice left their holes and ran in all directions.

Making shock waves

Machines called seismometers can feel shock waves on the other side of the Earth. Try this experiment to make shock waves for yourself.

Place a piece of paper near the edge of a table and put a little salt in the middle.

Slip one end of a ruler under the paper. Hold the ruler gently, as shown in the picture.

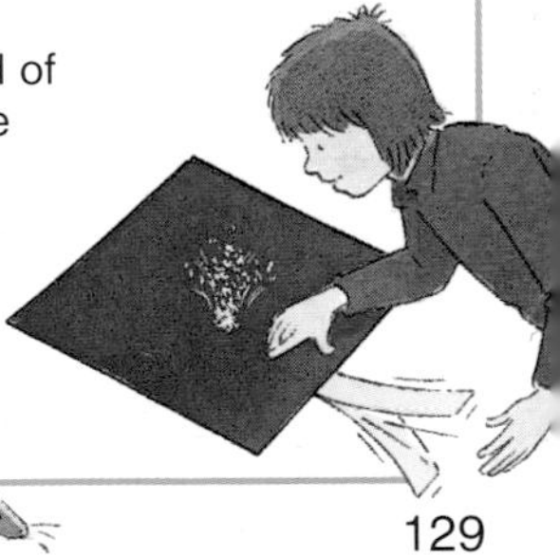

Hit the other end of the ruler to make shock waves go along it. See the salt jump.

Volcanoes

Sometimes, red hot magma from the Earth's mantle pushes its way up into weak places in the crust. Then, it bursts through to the surface. As it cools, it hardens and forms a volcano. You can see what is going on inside this erupting volcano.

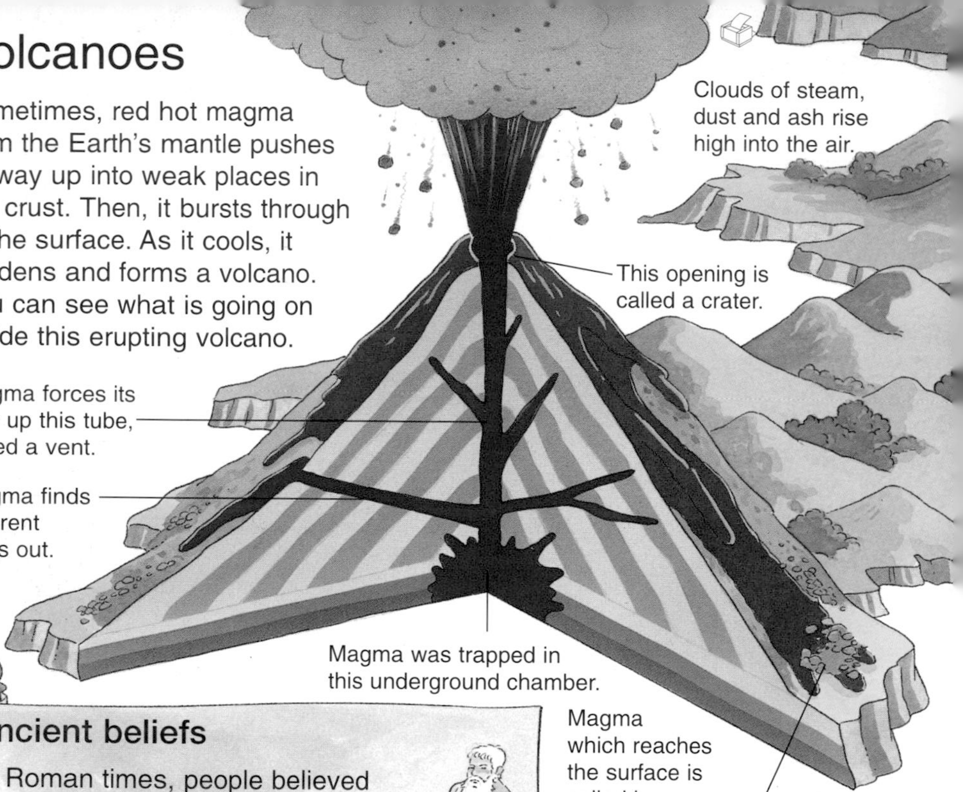

Clouds of steam, dust and ash rise high into the air.
This opening is called a crater.
Magma forces its way up this tube, called a vent.
Magma finds different ways out.
Magma was trapped in this underground chamber.
Magma which reaches the surface is called lava.
Lava cools and hardens into volcanic rock.
Layers of lava and ash build up each time the volcano erupts.

Ancient beliefs

In Roman times, people believed that volcanoes erupted because Vulcan, their god of fire, was making thunderbolts for the god Jupiter.

Internet link *Go to* ***www.usborne-quicklinks.com*** *for a link to a Web site where you can watch a short movie about volcanoes.*

Different shapes

Many volcanoes are tall cones. This is because their lava is thick and sticky. It does not flow far before it hardens.

Cone volcano

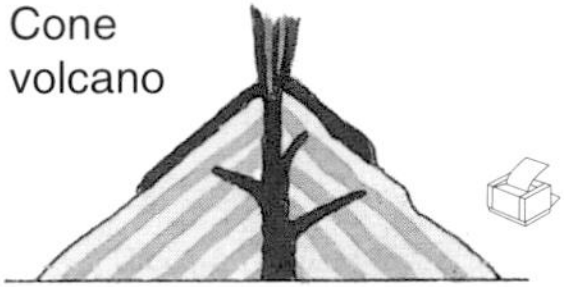

Some volcanoes are fairly flat. Their lava is runny and flows before it cools.

Shield volcano

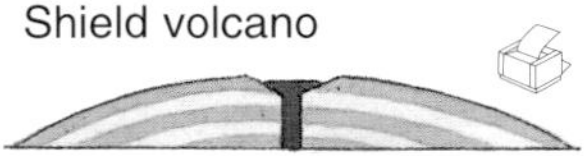

Volcanic rock

Pumice is a very light volcanic rock. It forms when lava hardens with gas bubbles trapped inside it.

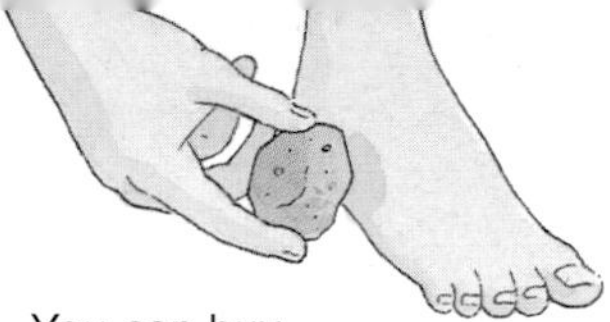

You can buy pumice in health shops, for rubbing away hard skin.

Underwater volcanoes

There are lots of volcanoes under the sea because that is where the Earth's crust is the most thin and weak. Some islands are huge volcanoes which poke out of the water.

Dead or alive?

A live, or active, volcano erupts fairly often. A sleeping, or dormant, one rests for a long time between eruptions. A dead, or extinct, volcano is one which will never erupt again.

Edinburgh Castle in Scotland is built on the remains of an extinct volcano.

Internet link *Go to* ***www.usborne-quicklinks.com*** *for a link to a Web site where you can do a quiz to find out how much you know about volcanoes.*

Heat and power

The Earth's crust gives us lots of the heat and power we use in our homes, schools, offices and factories. Here are some of the ways this happens.

Making hot water

In places with volcanoes, the rocks in the crust are very hot. They can make underground water boil and turn into steam.

Using hot water

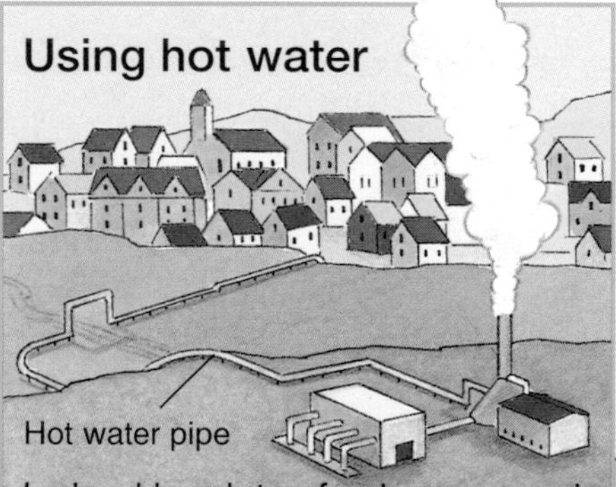

Iceland has lots of volcanoes and hot underground water. The water is pumped along pipes to heat many of the buildings there.

A geyser is a jet of hot water and steam which shoots out of the ground.

A hot spring is where heated water bubbles up through cracks, to the surface.

Steam power

Some countries make electricity using steam from the Earth's crust.

Steam is trapped in this rock.

The steam goes along pipes to a building called a power station.

In the power station, the steam pushes the blades of a machine around, to make electricity.

Underground fuel

Coal, oil and gas are called fossil fuels. They form very slowly in the crust. Coal is the remains of plants that died millions of years ago.

Oil and gas are made from the remains of tiny sea animals and plants. Fossil fuels are used in some power stations to make electricity.

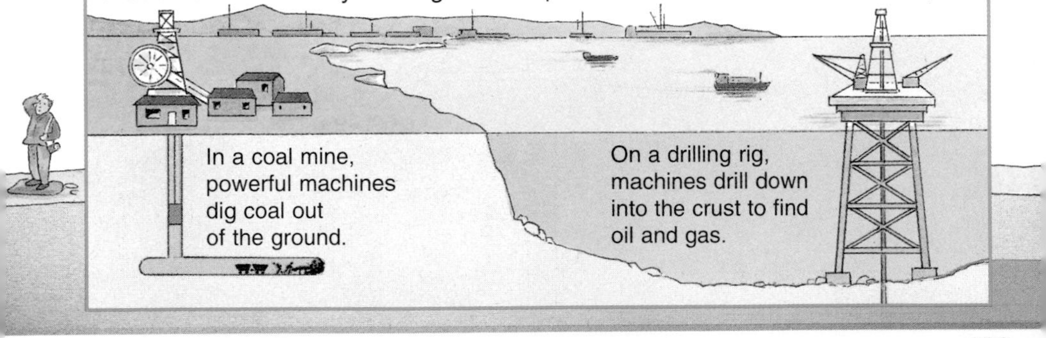

In a coal mine, powerful machines dig coal out of the ground.

On a drilling rig, machines drill down into the crust to find oil and gas.

Internet link *Go to* ***www.usborne-quicklinks.com*** *for a link to a Web site where you can watch a short movie about fossil fuels.*

Igneous rock

The Earth's crust is made up of three main kinds of rocks. Igneous rock is one of them. It is made when magma rises from the mantle, then cools and hardens. "Igneous" means fiery.

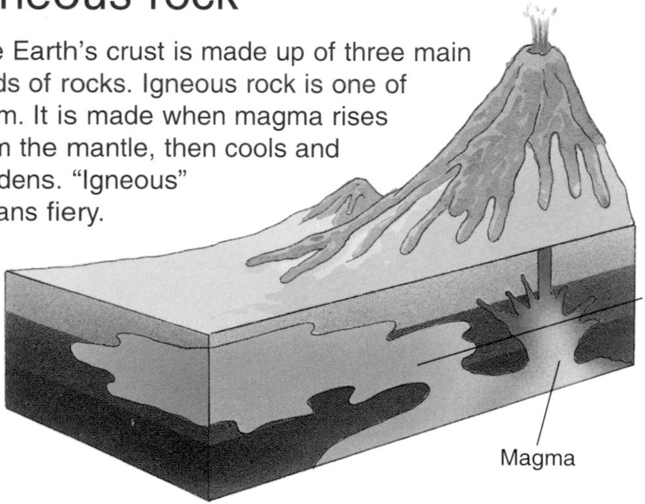

Volcanoes are made from igneous rock. They make more rock each time they erupt.

Sometimes, magma cools and hardens into a huge mass of igneous rock under the ground.

Granite

Granite is a very hard igneous rock which forms under the ground.

In some places, big lumps of granite stick out of the ground. They were buried once, but the soil and rock above wore away.

Granite is good for building because it is hard and strong.

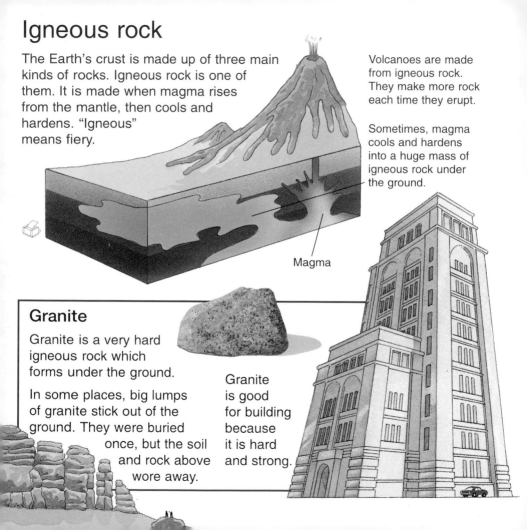

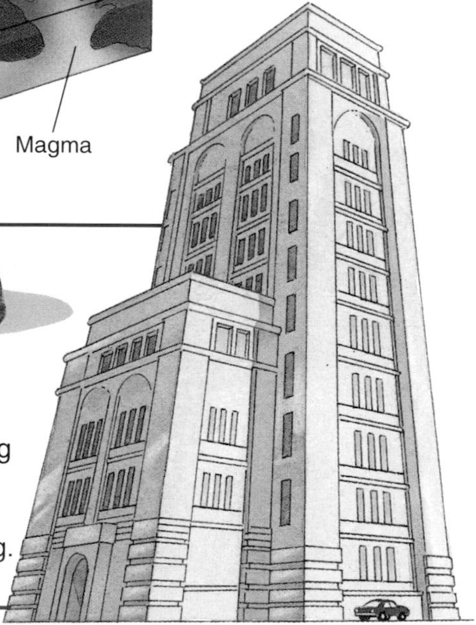

Sedimentary rock

The Earth's rocky crust is being worn away all the time. The tiny, worn fragments help to make new rock called sedimentary rock.

Fragments of rock can get washed into lakes, rivers and the sea. When they settle they are called sediment.

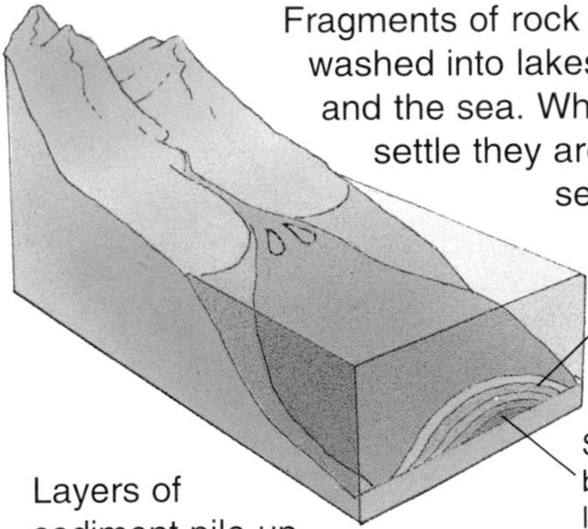

Layers of sediment pile up slowly. The bottom layers get squeezed together to form sedimentary rock.

Layer upon layer

There are lots of layers of sedimentary rock in the Grand Canyon, in Arizona, America.

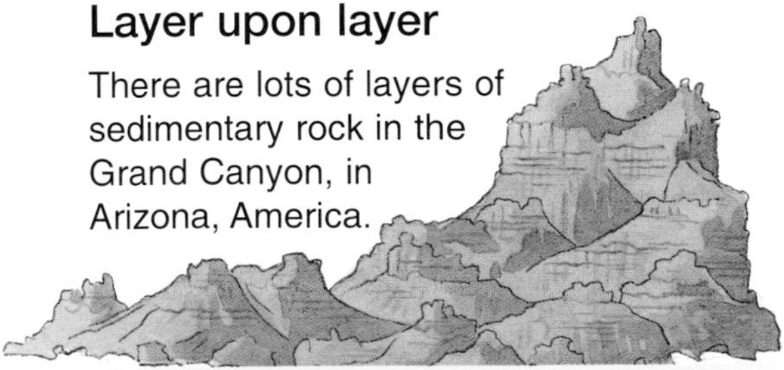

Sandstone

Sandstone is a sedimentary rock made from grains of sand from lakes, beaches or deserts.

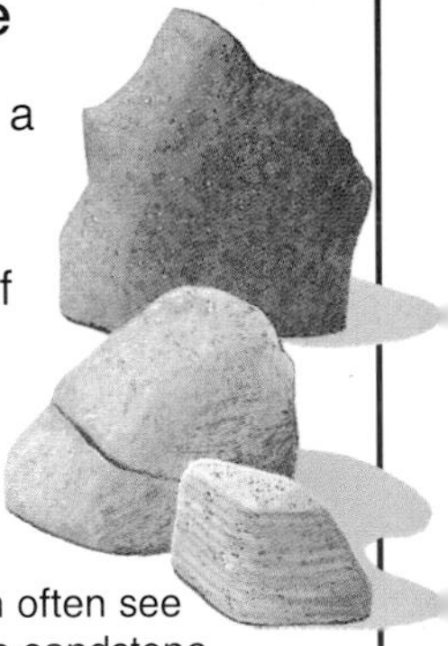

You can often see layers in sandstone.

Sandstone is used for building, but it can be worn away by the weather.

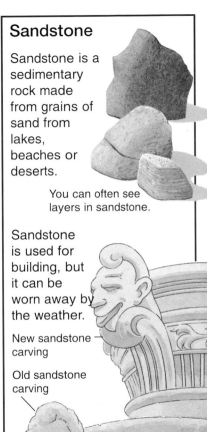

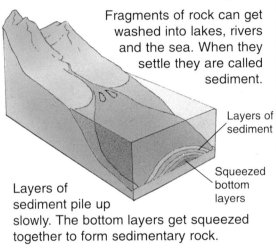

Internet link *Go to* ***www.usborne-quicklinks.com*** *for a link to a Web site where you can find out how different kinds of rock are made.*

Metamorphic rock

Metamorphic rock starts life as igneous or sedimentary rock. It is made when these kinds of rocks are squeezed or heated, or both.

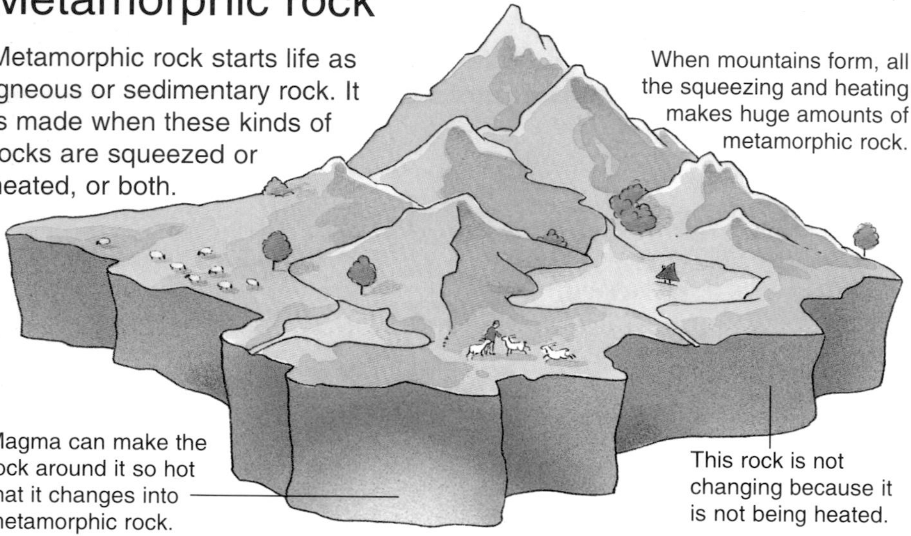
When mountains form, all the squeezing and heating makes huge amounts of metamorphic rock.
Magma can make the rock around it so hot that it changes into metamorphic rock.
This rock is not changing because it is not being heated.

Different kinds

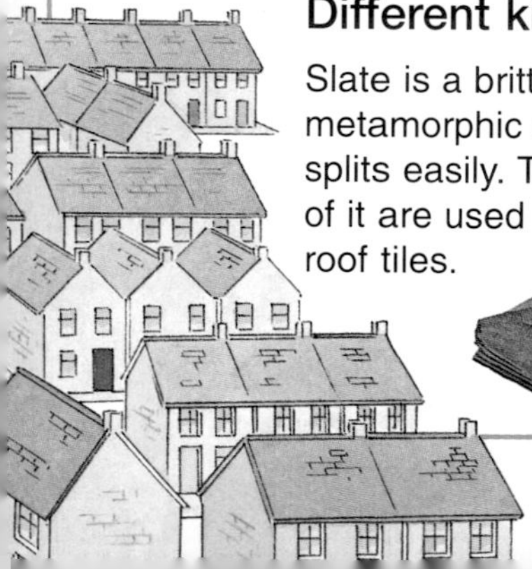

Slate is a brittle metamorphic rock which splits easily. Thin sheets of it are used to make roof tiles.

Marble is a metamorphic rock which is often carved to make works of art. It comes in different shades.

Rock spotting

You can find different kinds of rocks almost anywhere. Here are some good places to start looking.

Mountains and hills usually have lots of bare rock and loose stones.

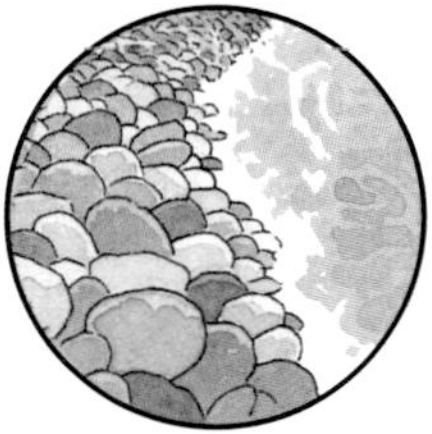

Many beaches are covered with pebbles. These are worn pieces of rock.

Buildings, statues and pavements are all made from different kinds of rocks.

Important notes

Never go alone.

Never go near dangerous places such as cliffs and deep water.

Always tell an adult where you are going.

Only collect loose rocks. Never break any off.

Things to take

These things will be useful when you go rock spotting.

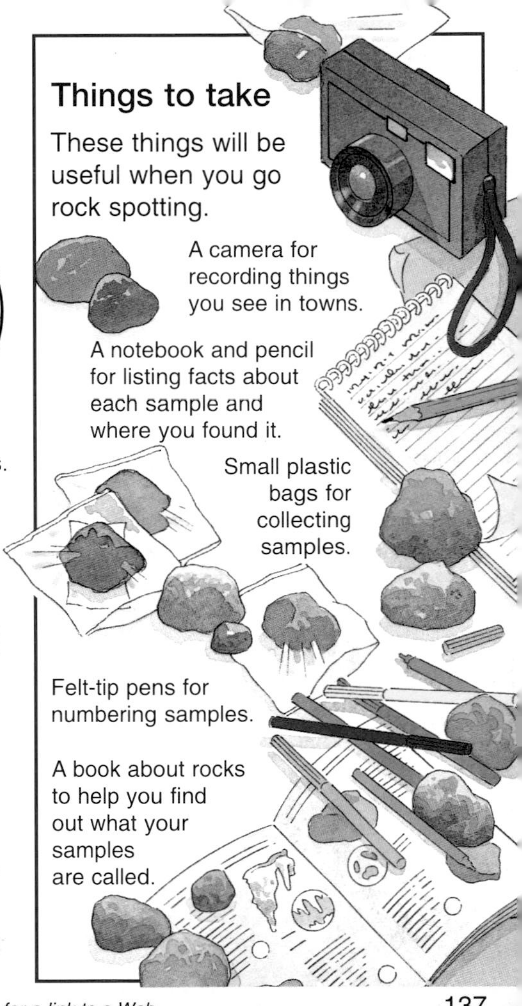

A camera for recording things you see in towns.

A notebook and pencil for listing facts about each sample and where you found it.

Small plastic bags for collecting samples.

Felt-tip pens for numbering samples.

A book about rocks to help you find out what your samples are called.

Internet link *Go to* ***www.usborne-quicklinks.com*** *for a link to a Web site you'll find words used to describe rocks.*

Minerals

All rocks are made up of building blocks, called minerals. Minerals come in different shapes, sizes and shades. They form crystals which grow packed tightly together.

This is rock seen through a powerful microscope. The shapes are mineral crystals.

Different mixtures

Most rocks are made from a mixture of minerals. Granite is made from three minerals, but it can have different amounts of each one in it. This is why there are different kinds of granite. Here are three of them.

Big crystals

If minerals have plenty of space to grow, they can become beautiful flat-sided crystals.

Amethyst

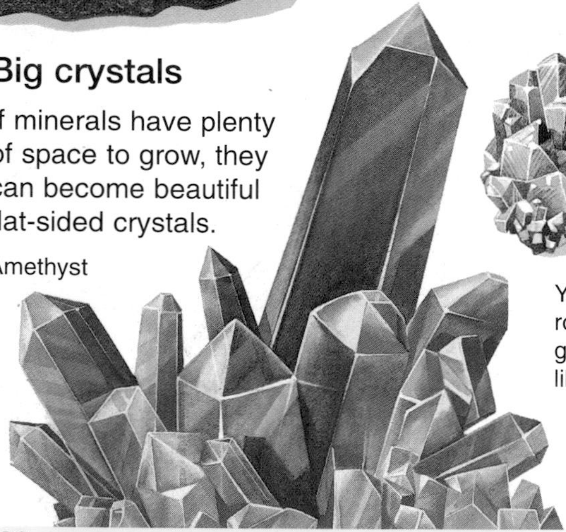

Pyrite

You can sometimes find rocks with crystals growing inside, like this.

 Internet link *Go to* ***www.usborne-quicklinks.com*** *for a link to a Web site with a quiz and a short movie about crystals.*

Minerals around us

Minerals are taken out of the ground and used to make all kinds of things that we use every day. Can you find any of these things in your home?

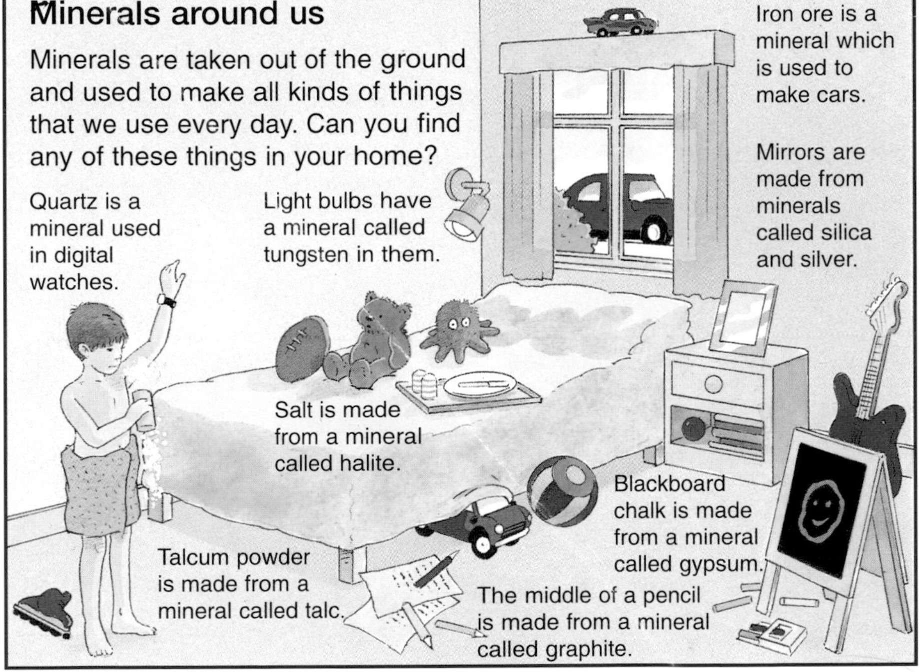

Iron ore is a mineral which is used to make cars.
Mirrors are made from minerals called silica and silver.
Quartz is a mineral used in digital watches.
Light bulbs have a mineral called tungsten in them.
Salt is made from a mineral called halite.
Blackboard chalk is made from a mineral called gypsum.
Talcum powder is made from a mineral called talc.
The middle of a pencil is made from a mineral called graphite.

Gemstones

Gemstones are mineral crystals which have been cut into special shapes and polished. They are very hard. They are also beautiful and expensive.

Caves

In some places, there are huge caves and tunnels under the ground. They have been carved out by water, which has soaked into the soil and rock, from the Earth's surface.

Rainwater and water from streams and rivers soak into the ground.

Soaking in

Rock which has tiny spaces or cracks in it lets water trickle through. Any rock which lets water through is called permeable rock.

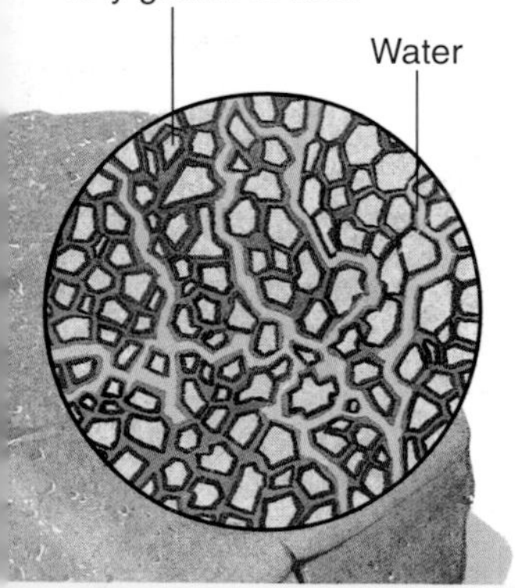

Sponge test

A bath sponge has spaces in it, rather like permeable rock. Try this experiment to see how water soaks through the spaces. It works best if you wet the sponge then squeeze it out first.

Put the sponge on a plate and pour water on slowly. Stop when the water starts trickling out.

To see how much water has soaked into the sponge's spaces, squeeze it over an empty jug.

Internet link *Go to* ***www.usborne-quicklinks.com*** *for a link to a Web site where you can go on a virtual tour of different kinds of caves and find out how they were formed.*

Carving out

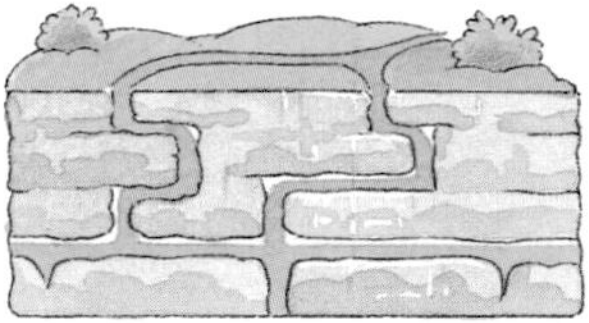

Limestone rock is made up of layers. Cracks between the layers let water trickle through.

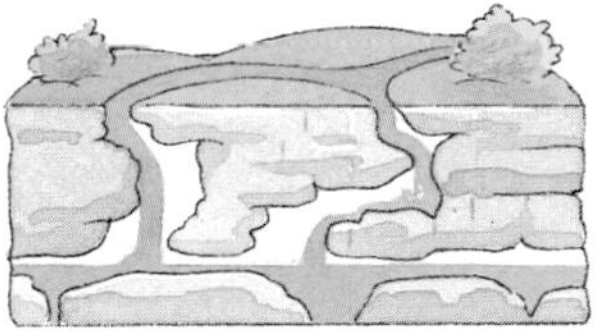

As the water trickles, it eats away at the rock. Very slowly the cracks become tunnels.

When water wears away big areas of rock, a cave is made.

Stalactites and stalagmites

Water drips from a cave roof and leaves behind tiny amounts of minerals. Very slowly, these form rocky icicles called stalactites. Drops hit the floor and towers called stalagmites form.

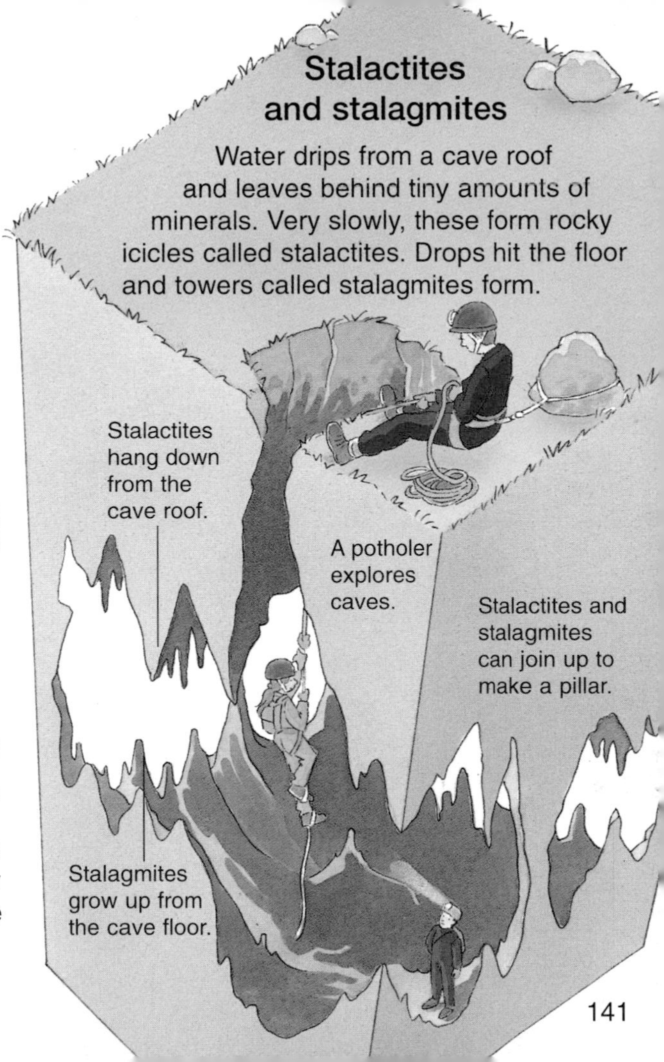

Stalactites hang down from the cave roof.
A potholer explores caves.
Stalactites and stalagmites can join up to make a pillar.
Stalagmites grow up from the cave floor.

Fossils

Scientists have found out what lived on Earth millions of years ago by studying fossils. Fossils are mostly found in sedimentary rock.

How fossils form

When an animal dies, its soft parts rot away but its hard skeleton is left. If it sinks into a muddy place, it gets covered with sediment.

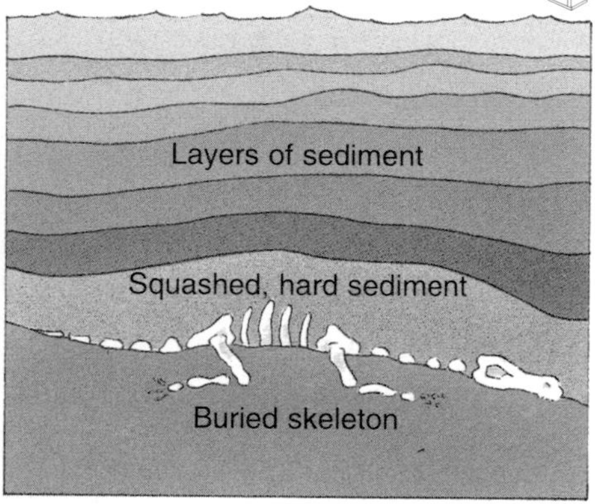

The bottom layers become squashed and harden into rock. Over time, minerals in the rock turn the skeleton to stone. This makes it into a fossil.

Finding fossils

People who study fossils are called palaeontologists. Take a close look next time you go to a rocky beach and you may find some fossils yourself.

Fossils are usually found when the rock around them gets worn away.

Pick up stones and turn them over to take a good look.

If you want to look at a really good fossil collection, contact your nearest museum to see what they have.

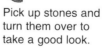

 Internet link *Go to* ***www.usborne-quicklinks.com*** *for a link to a Web site where you can play a game online, matching fossil pictures with the right description.*

Internet links

Go to **www.usborne-quicklinks.com** and type in the keywords "pocket scientist 2" for links to these Web sites about the Earth.

Web site 1 At this Web site there's an excellent guide to the different parts of the Solar system, including planets, asteroids, comets and moons. You can also read about the possibility of life on other planets.

Web site 2 Watch short, fun movies about science and other topics and test your knowledge with quizzes.

Web site 3 There is lots of information about rocks on this Web site, as well as some amazing pictures to look at. Become an expert and then take the rock quiz.

Web site 4 On this site you will find lots of links to pages with fascinating facts and spectacular images of volcanoes.

Web site 5 This Web site is packed with interesting information about the nine planets in our Solar system. You can look at close-up photos of the planets, read about how they got their names and find out how much you would weigh on each planet.

Web site 6 An online magazine with tips on identifying and collecting rocks, minerals and fossils and lots of information about how our world works.

For links to all these sites go to www.usborne-quicklinks.com and type in the keywords "pocket scientist 2".

More internet links

Here are some more Web sites to visit to find out about the Earth. For links to all these sites go to **www.usborne-quicklinks.com** and type in the keywords "pocket scientist 2".

Web site 1 What are earthquakes? Why do they occur? Why can't we predict them? Find out the answers to these questions on this Web site, which also has great animated diagrams and pictures.

Web site 2 See amazing photographs of stalactites and stalagmites and read about how they were formed.

Web site 3 Watch animations that show the four different layers of the Earth and how the Earth's crust, its outermost layer, continually changes as continental plates collide and create mountains, trigger earthquakes and cause volcanoes to erupt.

Web site 4 Try some fun puzzles and online quizzes from NASA where you can test your knowledge about Earth Science, see how much you know about earthquakes and plate tectonics, and identify the continents on a map showing the Earth 250 million years ago.

Web site 5 Watch a geyser shoot out a jet of hot water, travel to the depths of the Earth and find out about hot springs, mud pots and steam coming out of the ground.

Web site 6 Solve mysteries about a floating rock, look at a geological timeline and find fast and fun answers to common questions about rocks and fossils.

For links to all these sites go to www.usborne-quicklinks.com and type in the keywords "pocket scientist 2".

WHAT'S OUT IN SPACE?

Susan Mayes

Designed by Steve Page
Illustrated by Martin Newton, Chris Lyon and Joseph McEwan

Consultant: Sue Becklake

CONTENTS

Space watching

At night, when the sky is clear, you can see hundreds of stars far out in space. On most nights you can see the Moon as well.

If you want a better look at the Moon, you can use binoculars to make it look bigger and closer.

The Solar System

The things you can see in the sky at night only make up a little of what's out in space. Our planet, Earth, is in one tiny part of space called the Solar System.

The Solar System is made up of nine planets, lots of moons and lumps of rock called asteroids. There are also balls of ice and rock called comets. Everything moves around the Sun.

Astronomers

An astronomer is someone who looks at things in space. People have been doing this for thousands of years.

A modern astronomer uses a telescope to see things further away than you could ever imagine.

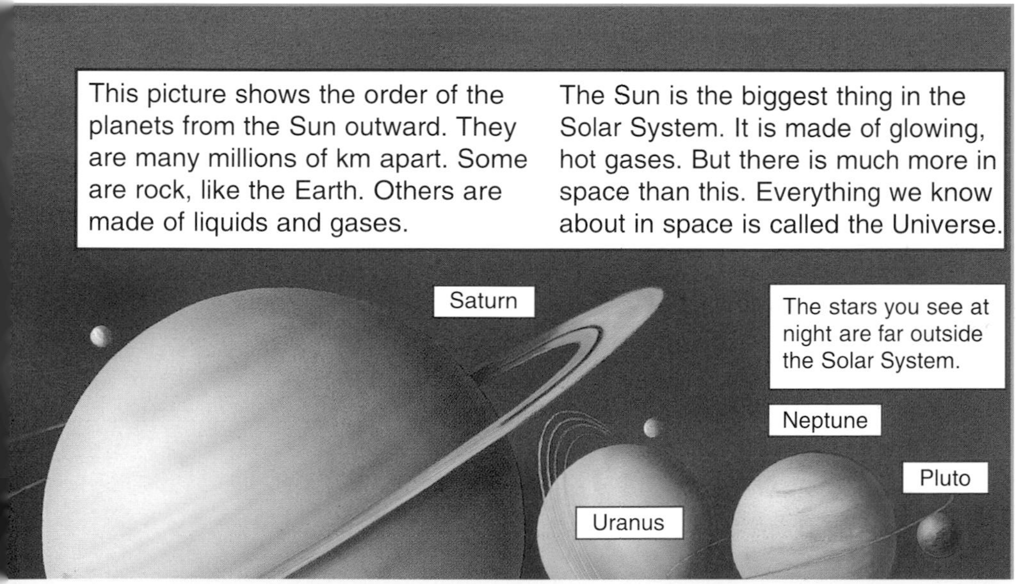

This picture shows the order of the planets from the Sun outward. They are many millions of km apart. Some are rock, like the Earth. Others are made of liquids and gases.

The Sun is the biggest thing in the Solar System. It is made of glowing, hot gases. But there is much more in space than this. Everything we know about in space is called the Universe.

The stars you see at night are far outside the Solar System.

***Internet link** Go to **www.usborne-quicklinks.com** for a link to a Web site where you can find fascinating facts about the planets in our Solar System.*

Light and dark

The Sun is the only thing in the Solar System which makes light. Nothing else has light of its own.

Astronomers can only see planets and moons because the Sun shines on them and makes them show up.

Moving around

Each planet goes around the Sun on its own invisible path called an orbit.

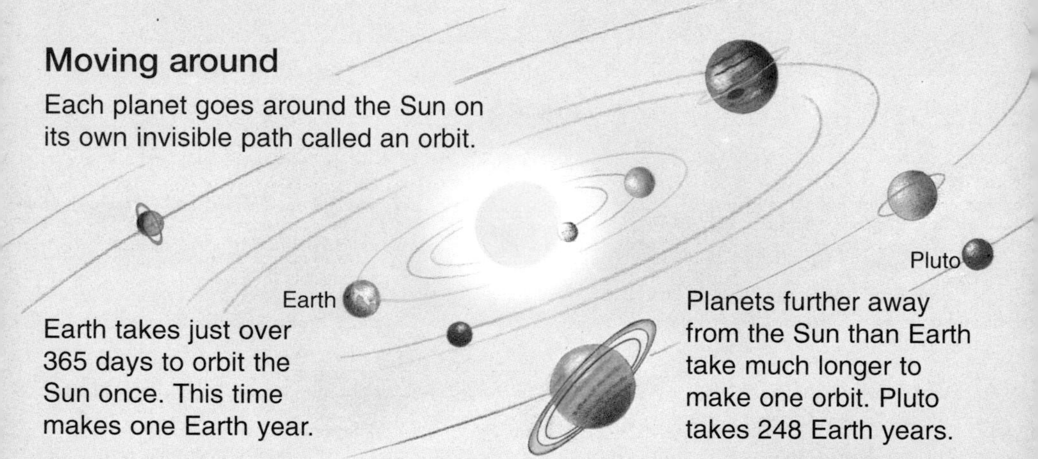

Earth takes just over 365 days to orbit the Sun once. This time makes one Earth year.

Planets further away from the Sun than Earth take much longer to make one orbit. Pluto takes 248 Earth years.

Day and night

As the Earth makes its long journey around the Sun, it turns all the time. It makes one turn every 24 hours.

When your side of Earth faces the Sun, you have day. When you are turned away from the Sun, it is night.

You cannot always see the Sun, but it shines in space all the time.

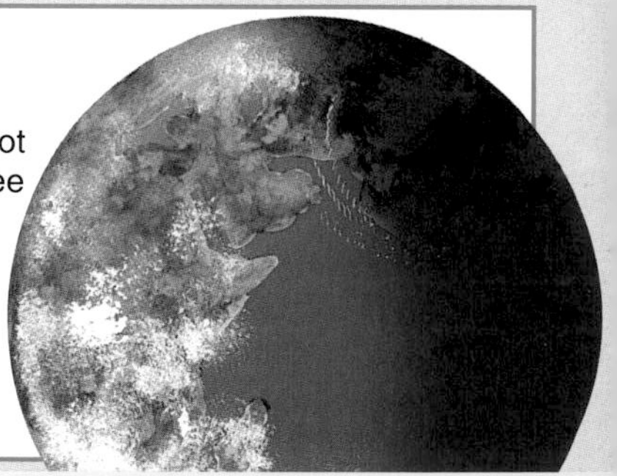

Watching the Moon

At night, the Moon seems to shine brightly, but the light you see is really from the Sun. It shines on half of the Moon all the time and lights it up.

Use binoculars to take a closer look at the Moon. The big dark patches are mainly flat areas called seas, but there is no water in them. The dark rings are craters. They were made by space rocks which crashed into the Moon.

The Moon's shape

The Moon moves around the Earth all the time. Each night you can see a different amount of the bright side. Sometimes you can see more of it and sometimes you can see less. The Moon's shape does not really change.

You cannot see a New Moon. The Sun shines on the other side.

This is a Crescent Moon. You can only see part of the side lit by the Sun.

This is a Full Moon. You can see all of the bright side lit by the Sun.

***Internet link** Go to **www.usborne-quicklinks.com** for a link to a Web site where you can see some amazing pictures of the Moon.*

Going to the Moon

The hardest part of going into space is getting off the ground. This is because of something invisible called gravity. Gravity pulls everything near the Earth back to the ground.

If you throw a ball up in the air, it comes down again. It is gravity which pulls the ball back. Without gravity, the ball would go up into space.

Breaking away

A spacecraft going to the Moon has to break away from Earth's gravity. A powerful rocket blasts it into space to escape the strong pull. The spacecraft gets to the Moon in about three days.

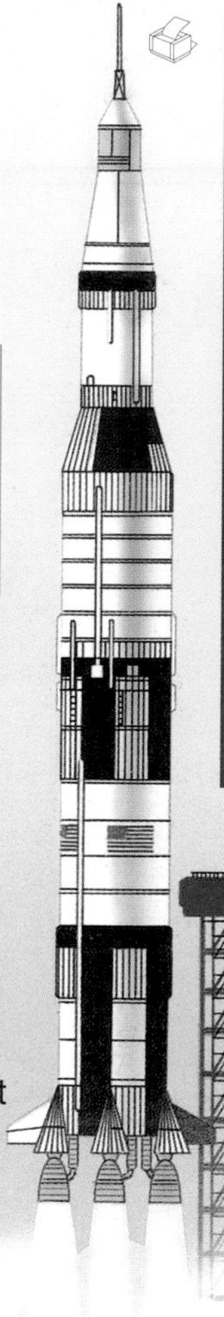

The spacecraft is only the small part near the top. The other parts carry the fuel needed to power the rocket.

Gravity in space

There is gravity around planets and moons, but there is less gravity out in space.

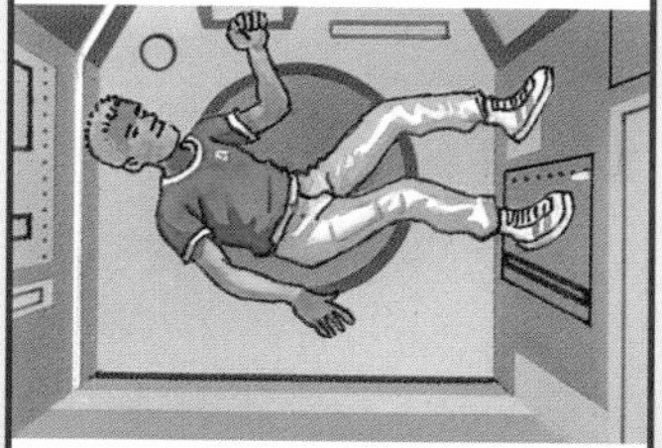

Astronauts in space feel weightless because there is less gravity to hold them down.

The first Moon-walk

The Moon is the only place in space where people have landed. On 20th July 1969, American astronauts were the first people to land there. They went in the Apollo 11 spacecraft.

When the astronauts walked on the Moon, they seemed to float with each step. This is because the Moon's gravity is weaker than Earth's, so it did not pull them down so strongly.

Neil Armstrong was the first person to walk on the Moon.

The astronauts left scientific instruments on the Moon. They also collected rock and dust to take back to Earth.

The Lunar Module took the astronauts down to the Moon while Apollo 11 stayed in space.

It was very hot in the sunlight but very cold at night. The astronauts had to take their own air supply in tanks because there is no air on the Moon.

The Moon's surface is dry and dusty. There is no wind to blow the soil around or rain to wash it away. Footprints will stay there forever.

Internet link *Go to* ***www.usborne-quicklinks.com*** *for a link to a Web site where you can look at photographs from Apollo 11's voyage to the Moon.*

About the Sun

The Sun is the most important thing in the Solar System. It gives the planets their light and heat. Its gravity stops the planets from flying off into space.

The Sun is really a medium-sized star. Many stars you see at night are bigger and brighter than it is. They look small because they are so far away.

Where the Sun came from

Scientists think that the Sun and the planets may have formed inside a huge cloud of gas and dust in space.

The gas and dust were squashed together in the middle of the cloud and this part became very hot. This is where the Sun began. The planets formed at about the same time.

DANGER!

Never look directly at the Sun, or with binoculars or a telescope. The strong light will seriously damage your eyes.

What the Sun is like

The Sun is not a ball of rock like the Earth. It is made of hot glowing gases which make it look like a fiery ball. Huge amounts of light and heat come from the surface.

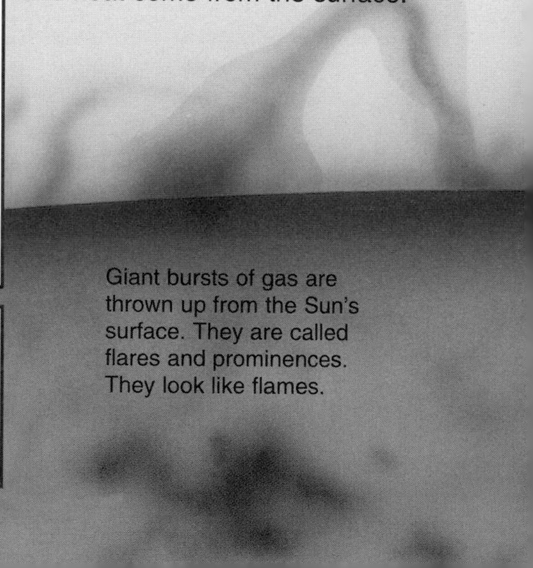

Giant bursts of gas are thrown up from the Sun's surface. They are called flares and prominences. They look like flames.

Hiding the Sun

Sometimes the Moon comes between the Sun and the Earth and covers up the Sun. This is an eclipse of the Sun.

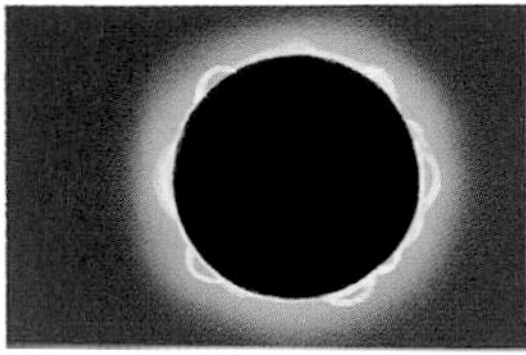

This glow is called the corona. It only shows during an eclipse.

The Moon is much smaller than the Sun but it can hide the Sun from our view. This happens because the Moon is much closer to us.

How it works

You can blot out a ceiling light by holding a coin in front of your eye. Cover the other eye with your hand.

Because the coin is close to your eye, it can easily blot out the light, which is further away. The Moon can blot out the Sun in the same way.

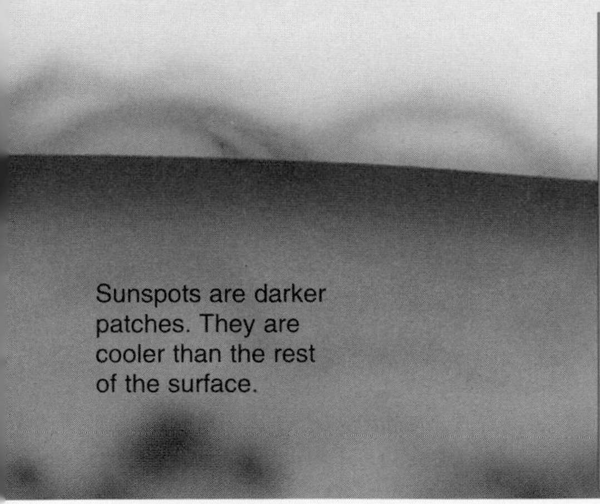

Sunspots are darker patches. They are cooler than the rest of the surface.

Life on Earth

Nothing would live or grow on Earth without the Sun's light and heat. The Earth's atmosphere only lets through the light and heat we need to live, keeping out the Sun's harmful rays.

Internet link *Go to* ***www.usborne-quicklinks.com*** *for a link to a Web site where you can see how an eclipse happens and then create your own.*

Exploring the planets

Scientists can find out more about the planets by sending machines called probes out into space. These do not carry people, only special equipment.

Next to the Sun

Mercury is the closest planet to the Sun. It has mountains and craters like our Moon, but it is much hotter.

The American probe, Mariner 10, passed Mercury three times. It sent back pictures.

Our closest planet

Venus is Earth's closest planet. Its rocky surface is very hot and its air is thick and poisonous.

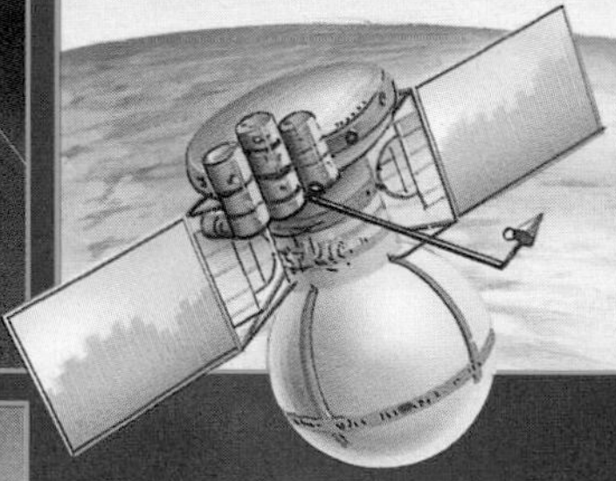

This Russian probe, Venera 9, sent back the first pictures from the surface.

The red planet

This is the American probe, Viking 2.

Mars is the planet which is most like Earth. It has mountains, valleys and volcanoes, but it has a pink sky. Mars is covered with red dust.

Going further

It takes a probe many years to reach planets far away from the Sun.

The American probes, Pioneers 10 and 11, have been to the edge of the Solar System, exploring planets on the way.

 Internet link *Go to* ***www.usborne-quicklinks.com*** *for a link to a Web site where you can find out about the history of space missions by clicking on an interactive timeline.*

The giants

Jupiter and Saturn are the biggest planets in the Solar System. They are made of gases and liquids. The American probes Voyager 2 and Pioneer 11 have been to take a look at them. Pioneer 10 also went to look at Jupiter.

Saturn has many thin rings made up of small pieces of ice. They form bright bands.

Jupiter is the largest of all the planets. It has a patch called the Great Red Spot. This is a huge long-lasting storm.

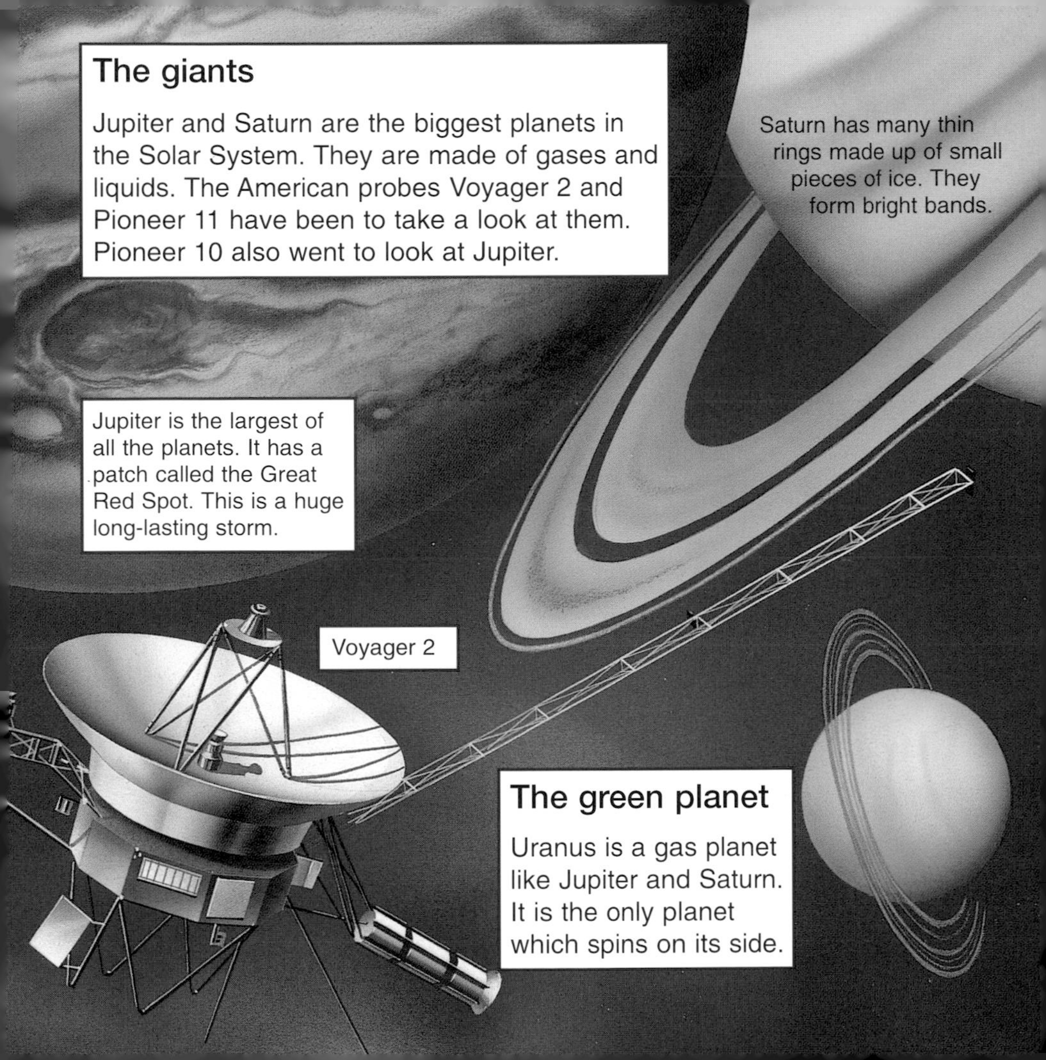

Voyager 2

The green planet

Uranus is a gas planet like Jupiter and Saturn. It is the only planet which spins on its side.

Voyager's last visit

The probe, Voyager 2, was sent into space in 1977. It had to travel for 12 years before it reached the planet Neptune.

The smallest planet

Pluto is the smallest planet in the Solar System. It is dark and icy. Its moon, Charon, is about half its size.

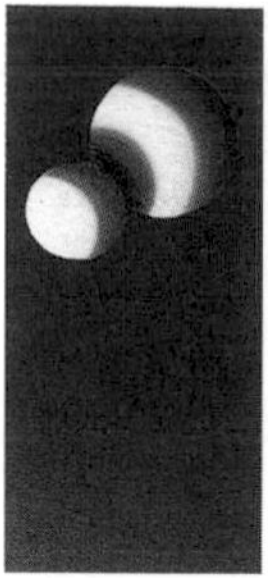

Voyager 2 did not visit Pluto, so there is still a lot to find out.

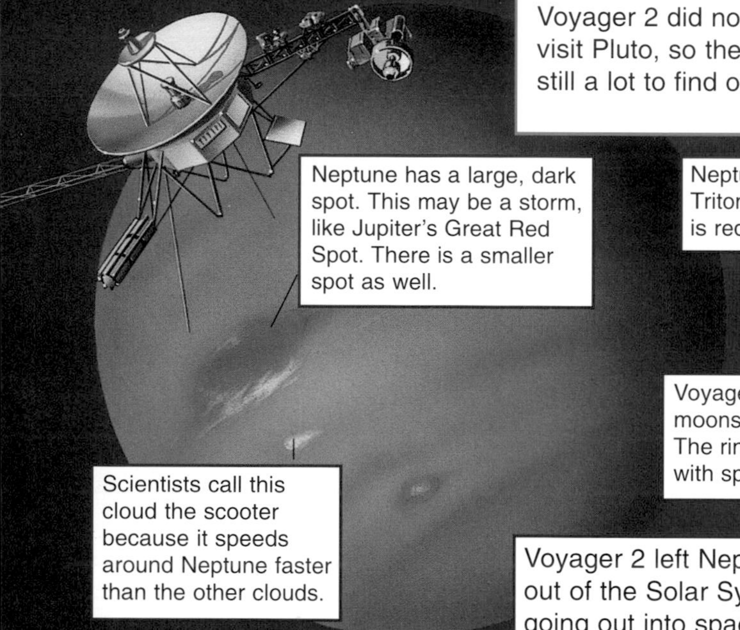

Neptune has a large, dark spot. This may be a storm, like Jupiter's Great Red Spot. There is a smaller spot as well.

Neptune's biggest moon, Triton, is cold and icy. It is reddish-pink.

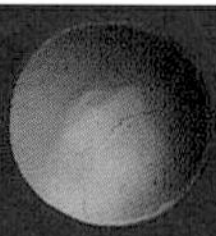

Voyager found six new moons and three faint rings. The rings can only be seen with special instruments.

Scientists call this cloud the scooter because it speeds around Neptune faster than the other clouds.

Voyager 2 left Neptune and moved out of the Solar System. It will keep going out into space, even when all its machines stop working.

Internet link *Go to* ***www.usborne-quicklinks.com*** *for a link to a Web site where you can look at photographs and read fascinating facts about the Voyager mission.*

Visitors from space

Comets are balls of ice and rock which move in huge orbits around the Sun. A comet sometimes comes into our part of the Solar System from beyond Pluto.

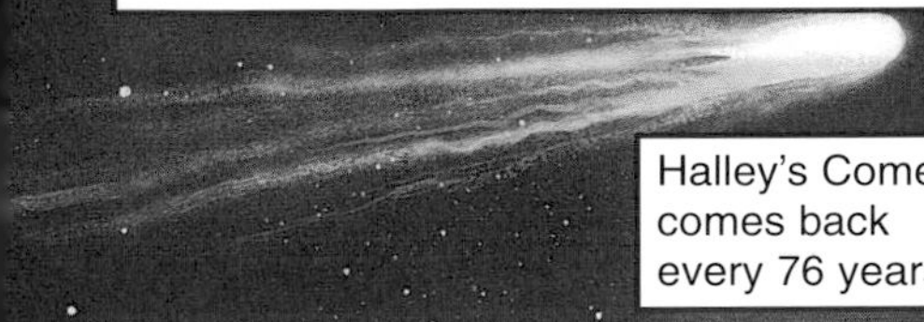

Halley's Comet comes back every 76 years.

The hard icy middle of the comet is called a nucleus. When the comet gets near the Sun, the ice boils away and makes a tail of gas and dust.

Asteroids

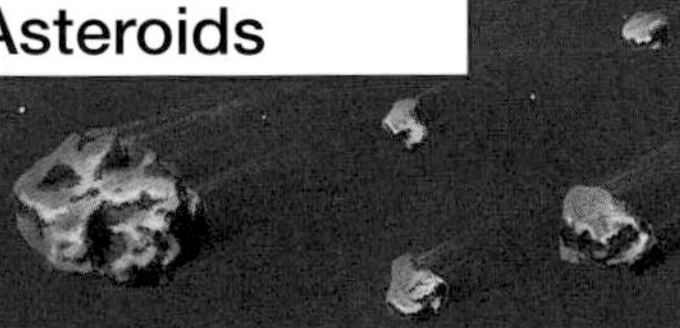

Between Mars and Jupiter there are thousands of rocks called asteroids. They orbit the Sun in a ring called the asteroid belt. Some asteroids are hundreds of miles across.

Meteors

Sometimes a space rock or a speck of dust speeds into the Earth's air. It burns up making a streak of light called a meteor or a shooting star. You can sometimes see one at night.

Making craters

Big space rocks which crash into planets or moons are called meteorites. Most of our Moon's craters were made by meteorites billions of years ago.

This crater is in Arizona, America.

There used to be craters on Earth, but they have been worn away over thousands of years. The crater in this picture is over 1 km (0.6 mile) across.

Looking at stars

If you could count all the stars you see in the night sky, there would be over a thousand. Astronomers can see millions more with telescopes.

What a star is

A star is a ball of glowing gases just like the Sun, our closest star. Light from nearly all stars takes thousands of years to reach us on Earth.

Most stars move around each other in groups of two or more. From Earth these groups usually look like a single star. Our Sun is unusual because it is on its own.

Why stars twinkle

Starlight has to pass through the Earth's air before it reaches us. The air moves and changes all the time. It makes a star's light look brighter, then dimmer, so it seems to twinkle.

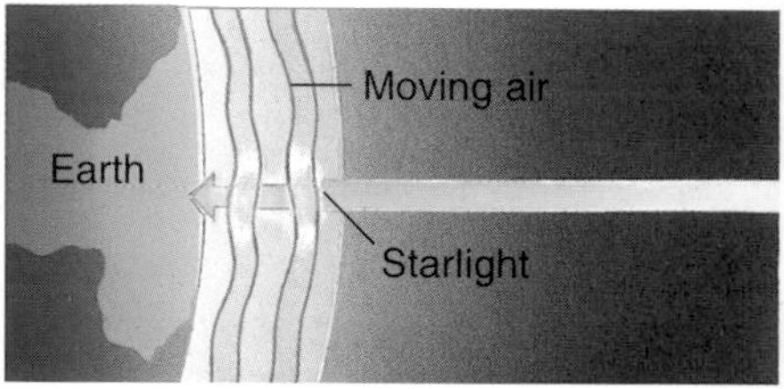

Galaxies

Stars belong to spinning groups called galaxies. There are millions of galaxies and each one has millions of stars. Our Solar System is in a spiral-shaped galaxy called the Milky Way.

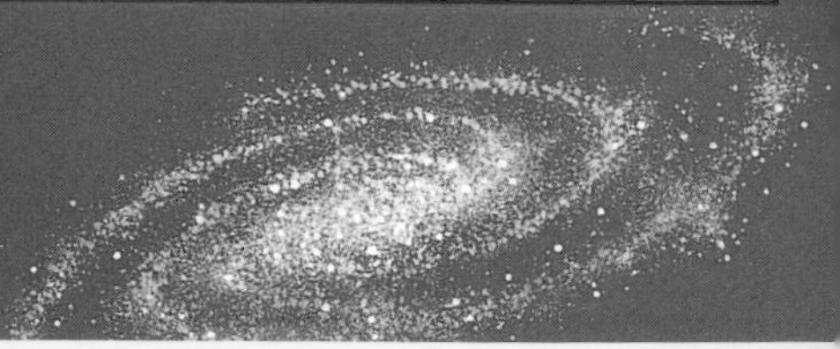

 Internet link *Go to* ***www.usborne-quicklinks.com*** *for a link to a Web site where you can do a quiz and watch a short movie about the life cycle of stars.*

The life of a star

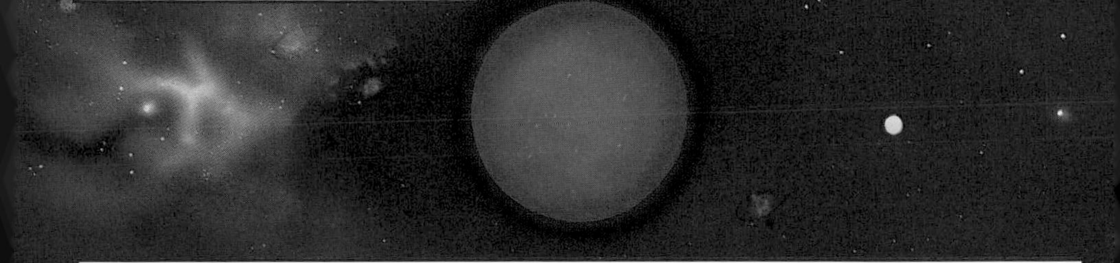

A star begins in a gas cloud called a nebula. The cloud collapses and squashes together. Its middle gets so hot that it glows as a new star.

The star shines brightly for many millions of years, then it swells up and becomes much cooler. This huge star is called a red giant.

The outer layers of the red giant disappear into space. A piece called a core is left behind. It shrinks to a small star called a white dwarf.

Exploding stars

Some big, heavy stars grow into enormous supergiant stars which can explode into space. An exploding star is called a supernova.

Black holes

When some stars explode they leave a big core. It shrinks and becomes small but very heavy. Its strong gravity sucks everything in, even light. It is called a black hole.

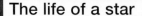

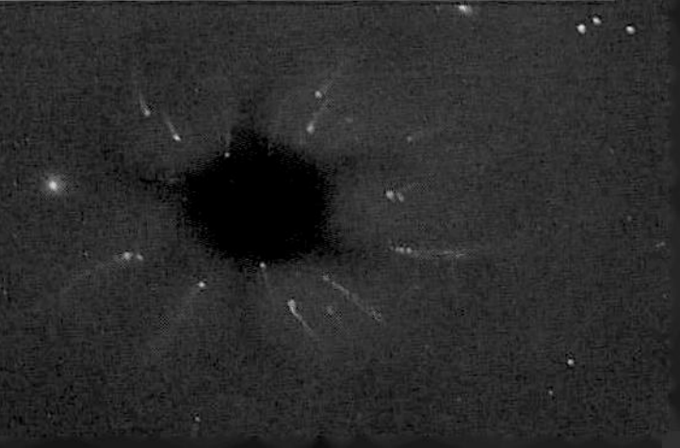

Space shuttles

The Americans have built a kind of spacecraft called a space shuttle. The first American shuttle flew in 1981. A shuttle is a launch vehicle that blasts into space like a rocket, but it comes back to land on a runway like a glider. It can travel into space again and again.

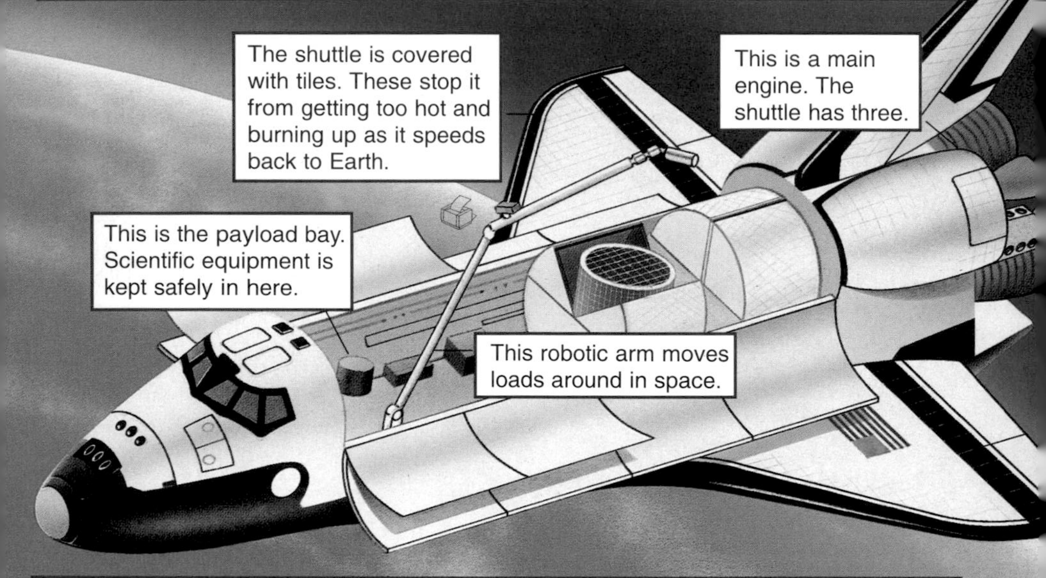

The shuttle is covered with tiles. These stop it from getting too hot and burning up as it speeds back to Earth.
This is a main engine. The shuttle has three.
This is the payload bay. Scientific equipment is kept safely in here.
This robotic arm moves loads around in space.

Inside the American shuttle the astronauts can launch machines called satellites into space from the payload bay.

On some flights, a special room called Spacelab is put inside the payload bay. Scientists do all kinds of experiments in here.

 Internet link *Go to **www.usborne-quicklinks.com** for a link to a Web site where you can find out all about space shuttles, including how they are moved around when they are on Earth.*

The "flying armchair"

Sometimes, astronauts leave the shuttle to work out in space. They are often strapped into a machine known as the "flying armchair".

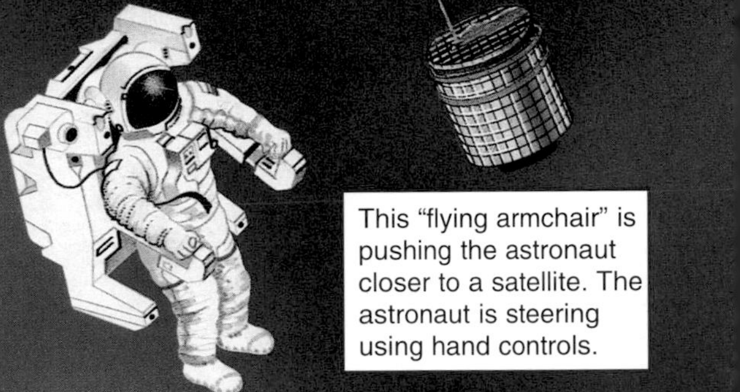

This "flying armchair" is pushing the astronaut closer to a satellite. The astronaut is steering using hand controls.

Space journey

The shuttle is blasted into space by its own engines and two large booster rockets.

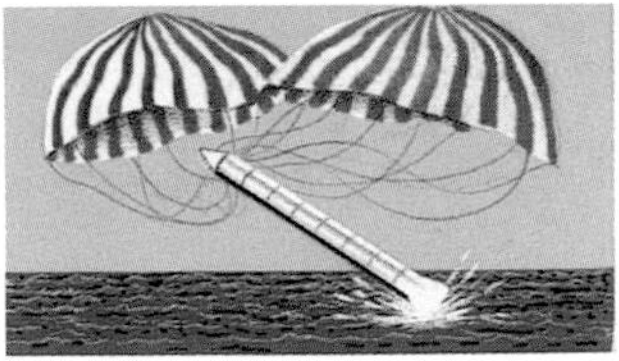

The rockets parachute into the sea when their fuel is used up. They will be used again.

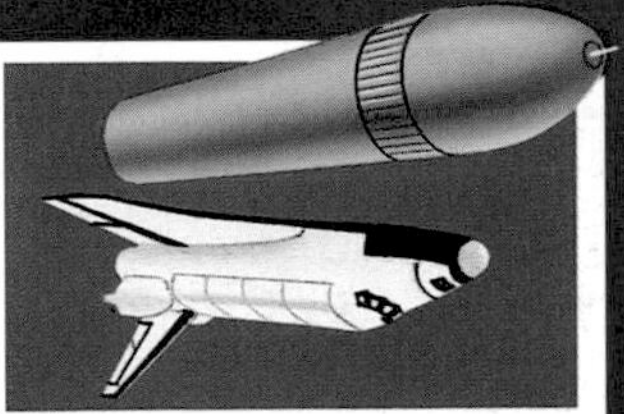

When the shuttle has used all the fuel in the huge tank, the tank falls away.

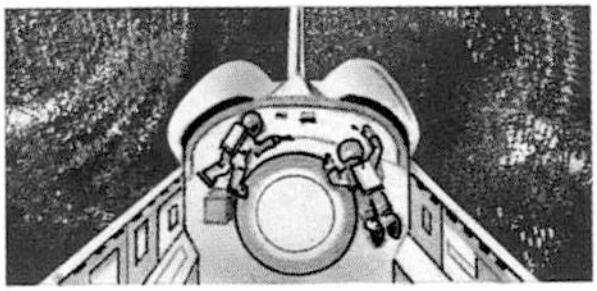

In orbit, the payload bay doors open. The astronauts begin to work and do experiments.

When the shuttle comes back to Earth it gets red hot because it is going so fast.

The shuttle does not use engines to land. It glides down onto a long runway.

About satellites

A satellite is a thing which moves around something bigger than itself in space. There are natural satellites such as moons. They orbit planets.

The satellites on these pages are machines. They are launched into orbit by a rocket or space shuttle. They carry equipment to do their work.

High above the world

Different kinds of satellites are put into different orbits. Some move in high orbits, around the middle of the Earth. They move in time with Earth so they stay above the same place.

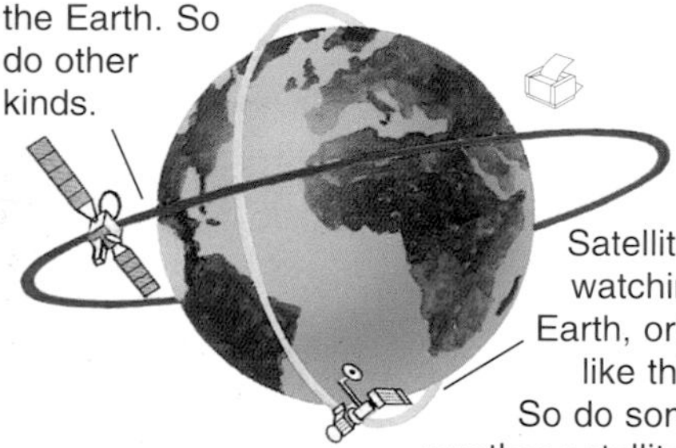

Television satellites orbit the Earth. So do other kinds.
Satellites watching Earth, orbit like this. So do some weather satellites.

Other satellites make low orbits over the top of the Earth. They go around it several times a day. The Earth turns below them, so they pass over a different part on each orbit.

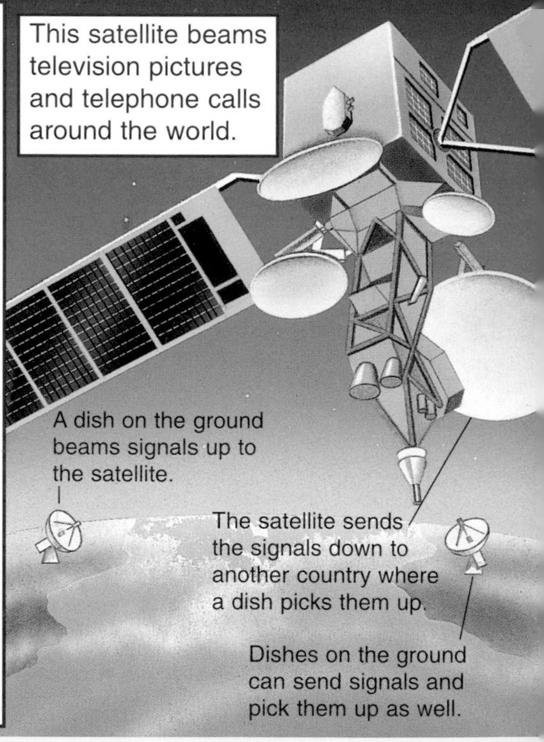

This satellite beams television pictures and telephone calls around the world.
A dish on the ground beams signals up to the satellite.
The satellite sends the signals down to another country where a dish picks them up.
Dishes on the ground can send signals and pick them up as well.

 Internet link *Go to **www.usborne-quicklinks.com** for a link to a Web site where you can find out lots more about satellites and build your own virtual satellite online.*

The small squares on the panels are solar cells. They change sunlight into electricity to power the satellite.

There are hundreds of satellites orbiting the Earth. In the night sky they look like slowly moving stars.

Small satellite dishes on many houses pick up television signals.

Watching the weather

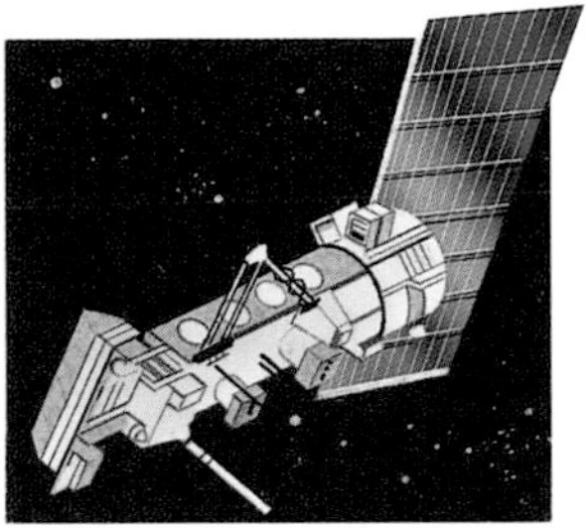

This satellite takes pictures of clouds moving around the Earth and measures the temperature of the air.

The information is beamed down to Earth. Scientists use it to work out what the weather may be like.

Watching space

This astronomy satellite looks out into space. It can see things that scientists cannot see from Earth.

The information from satellites can help scientists find out about things such as black holes or galaxies.

Space stations

A space station is a kind of satellite. It is big enough for people to live and work inside. Astronauts travel to the station once it is in orbit.

The first space stations

America and Russia have both launched space stations. The Russians sent up their first Salyut station in 1971. The Americans launched Skylab in 1973.

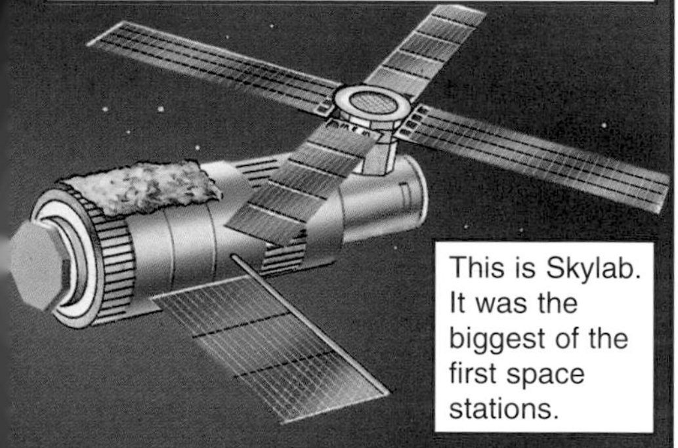

This is Skylab. It was the biggest of the first space stations.

The space stations were launched using rockets. Astronauts visited them for a few weeks at a time and sometimes worked outside in space.

Living in space

Astronauts have to learn new ways to do ordinary things like washing and eating. These are more difficult to do in space as everything floats around.

This special shower is in a bag. It stops water drops from floating about.

Most space food is dried. Astronauts have to add water before they eat it.

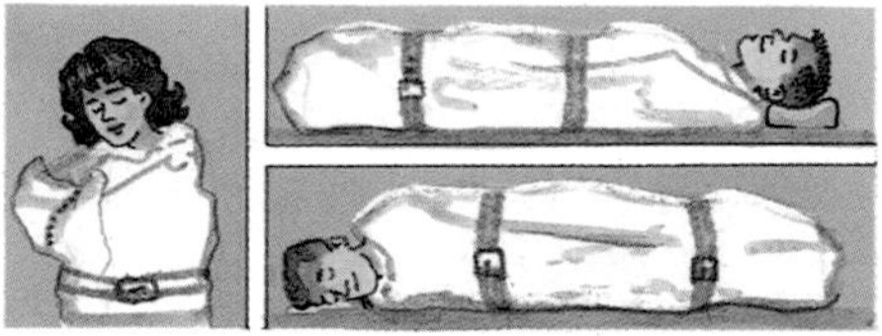

Astronauts can sleep any way up in space. They don't float around because they are strapped into sleeping bags.

 Internet link *Go to* ***www.usborne-quicklinks.com*** *for a link to a Web site where you can find out more about living in space.*

Staying in Mir

In 1986 the Russians launched a space station called Mir, which stayed in space for 15 years. Extra parts called modules were added. In March 2001, Mir was brought back to Earth, and landed in the sea.

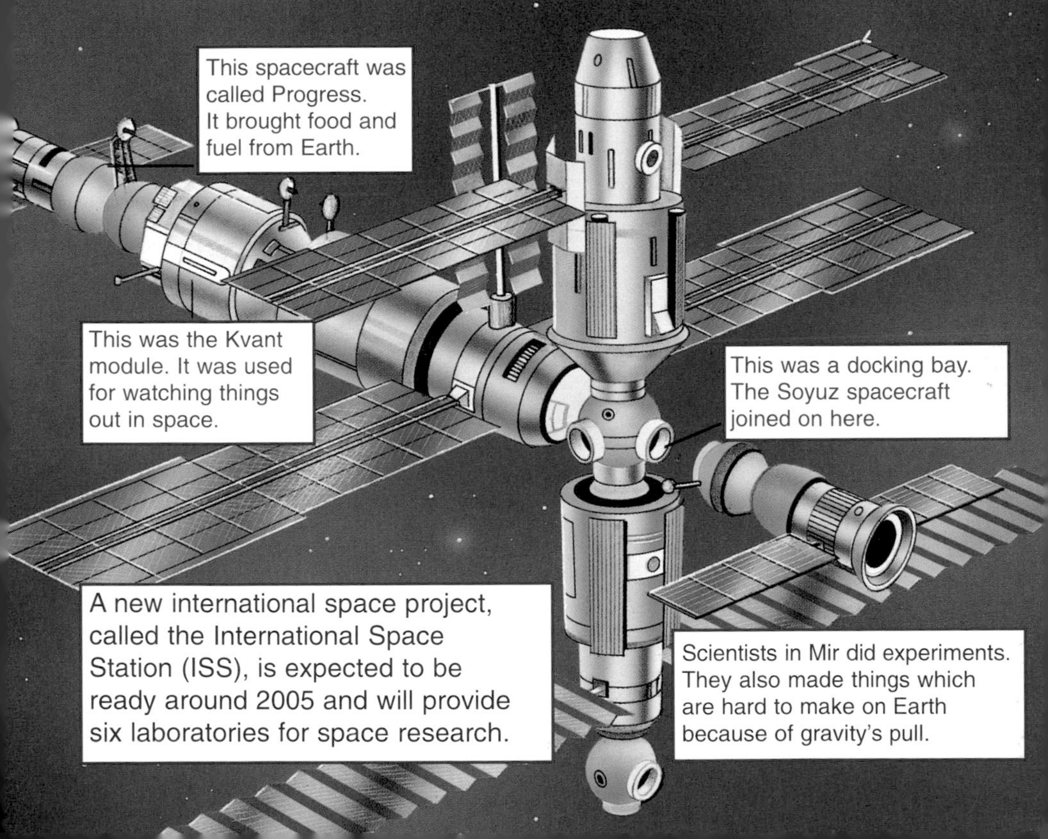

This spacecraft was called Progress. It brought food and fuel from Earth.
This was the Kvant module. It was used for watching things out in space.
This was a docking bay. The Soyuz spacecraft joined on here.
Scientists in Mir did experiments. They also made things which are hard to make on Earth because of gravity's pull.

A new international space project, called the International Space Station (ISS), is expected to be ready around 2005 and will provide six laboratories for space research.

The future in space

Scientists have made many amazing discoveries in space. Now they are making new plans and inventing new machines to help them learn more.

Telescope in space

The Hubble Space Telescope orbits high above Earth. It sees much further into space than astronomers can from the ground. It may discover far off planets with signs of life on them.

More about probes

Probes have been sent to Jupiter and Saturn. One called Galileo has orbited Jupiter. Another, called Cassini, is going to orbit Saturn.

Galileo has sent a smaller probe down into Jupiter's clouds.

The probes can also visit some of the moons circling the planets. They can send pictures and information back to Earth over several years.

Space planes

There may soon be a plane which can fly into space and then speed to anywhere on Earth in an hour.

Space planes would also be able to carry satellites out into space and visit space stations.

Internet links

Go to **www.usborne-quicklinks.com** and type in the keywords "pocket scientist 2" for links to these Web sites about space.

Web site 1 At this Web site you can find out all about space, including black holes, galaxies and what astronauts wear. There's also a glossary, which explains lots of space words.

Web site 2 Find out lots of fascinating facts about the planets in our Solar System and look at photographs of each one.

Web site 3 This Web site is packed with information about space and space travel. You can read myths from all over the world about the planets, find out about famous astronomers through the ages, e-mail space postcards and play space games.

Web site 4 Read about the race to reach the Moon, Apollo 11's voyage, and what we learned about the moon from the voyage. There are also lots of photographs to look at.

Web site 5 At this Web site, you can watch fun, short movies about space and test your knowledge with quizzes.

Web site 6 This Web site has lots of fascinating photographs of space. These include photographs of comets, asteroids, the nine planets in the Solar System and the Sun. There are also some amazing pictures of deep space and some great artwork.

For links to all these sites go to www.usborne-quicklinks.com and type in the keywords "pocket scientist 2".

More internet links

Here are some more Web sites to visit to find out about space. For links to all these sites go to **www.usborne-quicklinks.com** and type in the keywords "pocket scientist 2".

Web site 1 Read fascinating space facts, find interesting ideas to download and print, and play interactive games and activities. For example, find out how NASA's satellite dishes listen for signals from space or see if you can choose the best items to take on a mission to Mars.

Web site 2 Try building the Milky Way online, sort out the Hubble Space Telescope's mission in space and find out the truth about black holes.

Web site 3 Design your own space station, find out about astronomers through the ages and read about all the different kinds of spacecraft.

Web site 4 Here you'll find answers to the most puzzling questions about the Universe and some brilliant space games. Try and navigate your lunar lander onto the landing pads, control the Mars rover and save planet Earth from invading aliens.

Web site 5 On this Web site you can travel to the nine planets of the Solar System, find out about the changing seasons and discover what meteor showers are. There are also lots of games to play and fun activities to try out.

Web site 6 Look at a slide show and read about the International Space Station.

For links to all these sites go to www.usborne-quicklinks.com and type in the keywords "pocket scientist 2".

WHAT MAKES A CAR GO?

Sophy Tahta

Designed by Lindy Dark
Illustrated by Stuart Trotter

Consultant: Derek Sansom

CONTENTS

Parts of a car

Cars are made up of many different parts which all work together to make the car go. You can see some of these parts here and find out how they work later in this section.

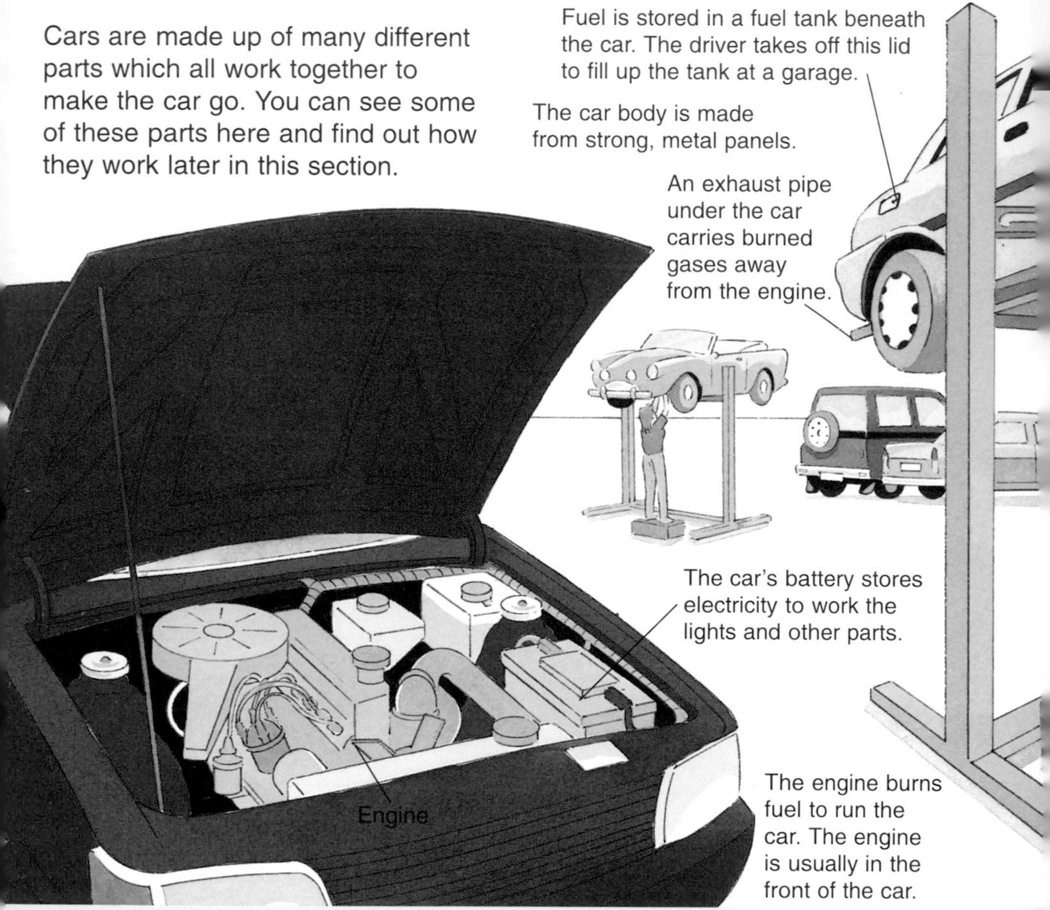

Fuel is stored in a fuel tank beneath the car. The driver takes off this lid to fill up the tank at a garage.
The car body is made from strong, metal panels.
An exhaust pipe under the car carries burned gases away from the engine.
The car's battery stores electricity to work the lights and other parts.
The engine burns fuel to run the car. The engine is usually in the front of the car.
Engine

 Pictures with the symbol [symbol] *can be downloaded from* ***www.usborne-quicklinks.com***

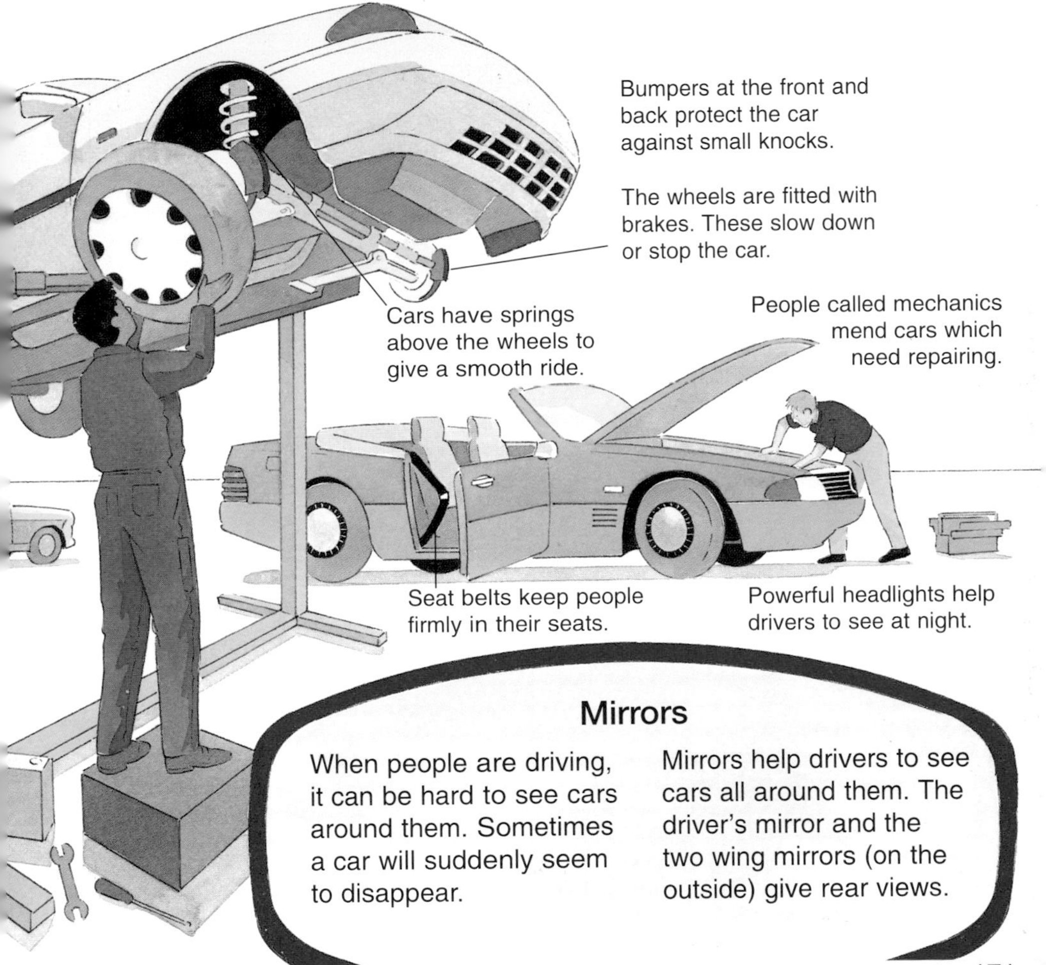

Bumpers at the front and back protect the car against small knocks.
The wheels are fitted with brakes. These slow down or stop the car.
Cars have springs above the wheels to give a smooth ride.
People called mechanics mend cars which need repairing.
Seat belts keep people firmly in their seats.
Powerful headlights help drivers to see at night.

Mirrors

When people are driving, it can be hard to see cars around them. Sometimes a car will suddenly seem to disappear.

Mirrors help drivers to see cars all around them. The driver's mirror and the two wing mirrors (on the outside) give rear views.

***Internet link** Go to **www.usborne-quicklinks.com** for a link to a Web site where you can learn the basics about how cars work and test yourself with a quiz.*

Inside the engine

Cars need energy to go. The engine produces energy. It does this by burning fuel and air inside tubes called cylinders. Here you can see how this energy turns the wheels.

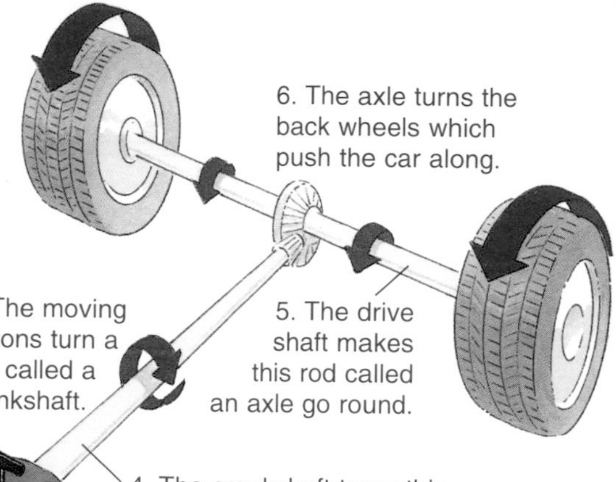

1. The fuel is lit by an electric spark from a spark plug.

2. The burning fuel forces drums, called pistons, to move up and down inside the cylinders.

3. The moving pistons turn a rod called a crankshaft.

4. The crankshaft turns this rod called the drive shaft.

5. The drive shaft makes this rod called an axle go round.

6. The axle turns the back wheels which push the car along.

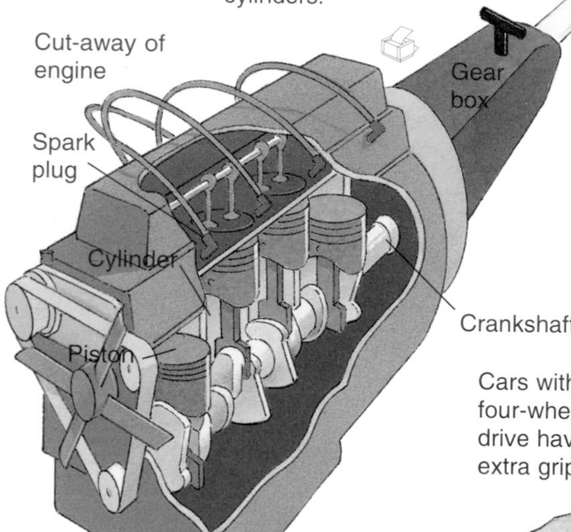

Different drives

Power from the engine can go to the back wheels, the front wheels or to all four wheels. Whichever system a car uses, is called its drive.

Cars with four-wheel drive have extra grip.

How a piston works

Each piston does four movements, or strokes, as it goes up and down twice.

Pistons move quickly in turn to keep the crankshaft spinning all the time.

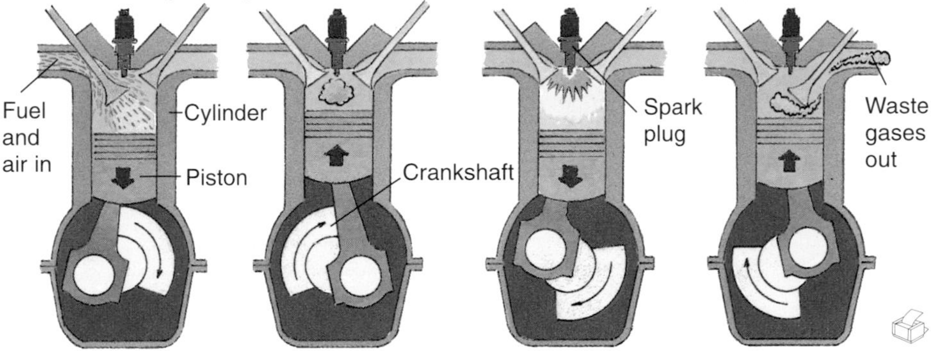

On the first stroke, the piston moves down. It sucks fuel and air into the cylinder.

On the second stroke, the piston goes up. It pushes the fuel to the top of the cylinder.

On the third stroke, the fuel is lit by the spark plug. The explosion forces the piston down.

On the fourth stroke, the piston moves back up. It pushes waste gases out into the exhaust pipe.

Piston power

When a car is going along at 80km (50 miles) an hour, a piston in the engine may move up and down about 2,500 times each minute.

Try counting roughly how many times you can tap a pencil on a table in one minute, and then imagine how fast a piston moves.

Internet link *Go to* ***www.usborne-quicklinks.com*** *for a link to a Web site where you can watch a short movie about how an engine works.*

Fuel and energy

Some of a car's energy is used to turn the wheels and some of it is used to make electricity.

Electricity is stored in the battery. It runs parts such as the lights and horn and also lights up the dashboard.

Dashboard
Clock
This dial shows how fast the car is going.
These dials show how much fuel, oil and water are left.
Indicator
Steering wheel
The car heater and radio run on electricity, too.
These switches turn the lights on and off.
This button beeps the horn.

Where fuel comes from

Fuel for cars is made from oil. Oil is found under the ground or the bottom of the sea. It was formed millions of years ago from the rotten remains of tiny sea animals.

People use giant drills to find oil and pump it up.

All lit up

Drivers use lights to see at night and to let other cars know what they are doing. See if you can tell which lights cars are using next time you are out.

Two red brake lights come on at the back of the car when the driver presses the brake pedal. Most new cars also have a third brake light in the middle of the rear windscreen.

Using energy

Cars burn fuel to make energy, just as you eat food to keep you going. The more energy cars use, the more fuel they burn.

Big, heavy cars and trucks use more fuel than smaller ones.

Cars burn more fuel to go fast or uphill.

An uphill climb

Cars use more energy when they go uphill because they are driving against gravity. Gravity is a force which pulls everything down.

Cars need more energy to go uphill as the force of gravity pulls them back.

Gravity makes it easier for cars, and you, to go downhill.

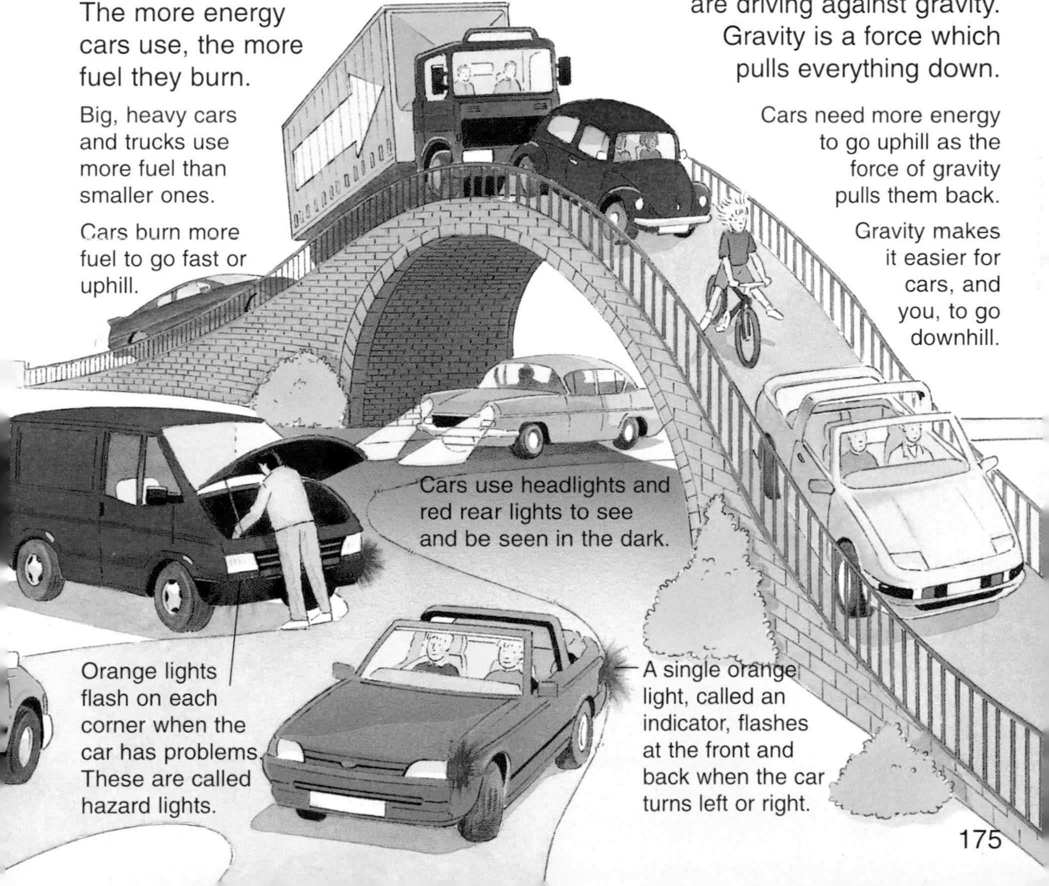

Cars use headlights and red rear lights to see and be seen in the dark.

Orange lights flash on each corner when the car has problems. These are called hazard lights.

A single orange light, called an indicator, flashes at the front and back when the car turns left or right.

Gears and steering

Gears make cars go at different speeds. Most cars have four or five gears to go forward and one gear to make them go back.

Cars start off in first gear. This gives extra force to move the wheels.

Second and third gears help cars to pick up speed and climb uphill.

What are gears?

Car gears are tiny, toothed wheels in the gear box. They make the drive shaft turn at different speeds.

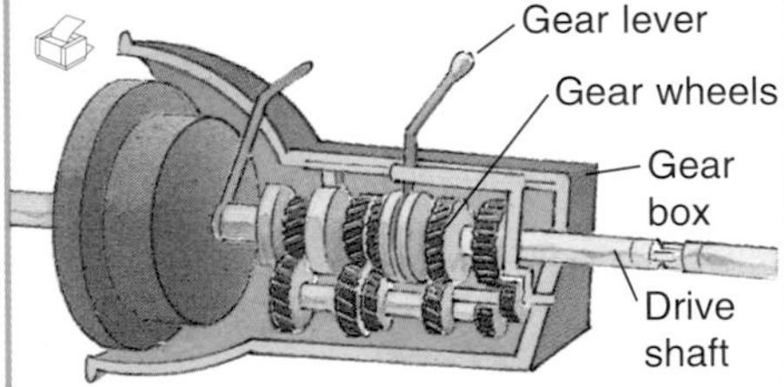

In some cars, the gears change on their own. In other cars, the driver moves a gear lever to choose which gear will turn the drive shaft.

Did you know?

In 1930, a Model A Ford car drove 5375 km (3340 miles) in reverse gear, from New York to Los Angeles in the USA. It drove back to New York in reverse gear, too.

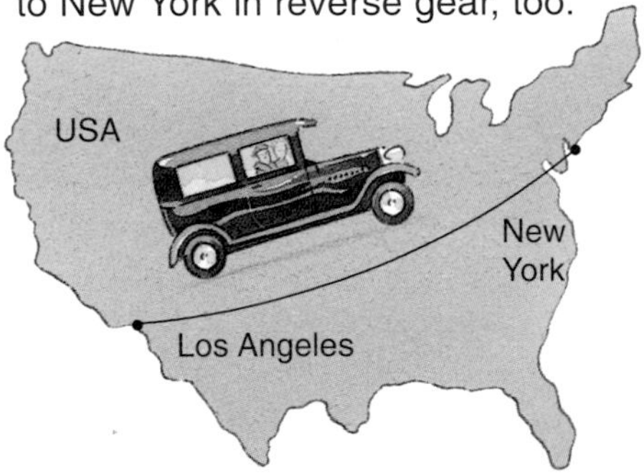

 Internet link *Go to* ***www.usborne-quicklinks.com*** *for a link to a Web site where you can find out how gears work.*

Fourth and fifth gears are used to drive fast on flat roads.

The reverse gear makes the wheels turn the other way.

Steering a car

The steering wheel is joined to the front wheels. The driver turns the steering wheel to point the wheels the correct way.

A smooth ride

Springs and shock absorbers help cars drive smoothly on bumpy roads. They are called the car's suspension.

Shock absorbers are tubes of gas which stop the springs from bouncing too much.

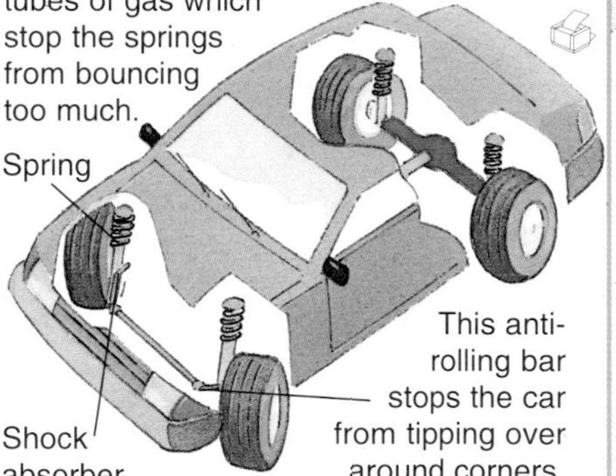

This anti-rolling bar stops the car from tipping over around corners.

A rough ride

Early cars had bad suspension and thin wheels. They bumped up and down a lot and were not at all comfortable to ride in.

Slowing down

The driver presses the brake pedal to slow down or stop the car. Here you can see how it works.

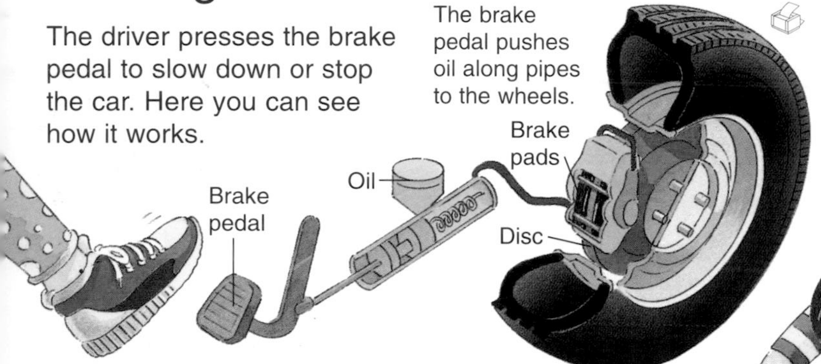

The brake pedal pushes oil along pipes to the wheels.

The oil pushes brake pads against a metal disc in the wheels to stop the wheels from turning.

Friction

Brakes use a force called friction to work. Some forces make things start or stop. Friction tries to stop things from moving when they rub together.

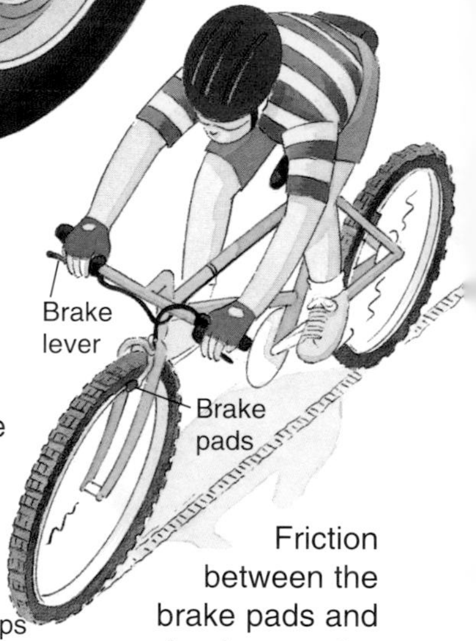

You can see how friction works on a bike. Press the brake lever and see how the brake pads rub against the wheel.

Friction between the brakes and wheel stops the wheel from spinning.

Friction between your shoe and the road also helps you to stop.

Friction between the brake pads and wheel wears the pads down. When they are very worn they need to be changed.

***Internet link** Go to **www.usborne-quicklinks.com** for a link to a Web site where you can find out more about friction.*

Getting a grip

Wheels have grooves called tread. Tread helps wheels to grip the road when the car brakes or turns. It is like the tread on your shoes, which gives you better grip, too.

The pattern of tread helps to push water away on wet roads.

Chains can be hooked onto wheels to grip snowy roads.

Racing cars do not use tread on dry tracks. They only use tread when it rains.

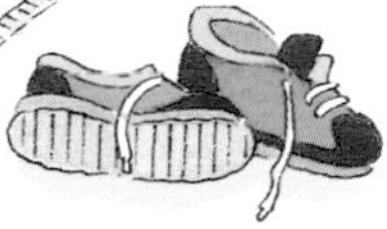

Friction in the air

There is also friction between moving things and air. Air pushes against moving things to slow them down. This sort of friction is called drag.

Cars have rounded smooth shapes which move through the air more easily. These are called streamlined shapes.

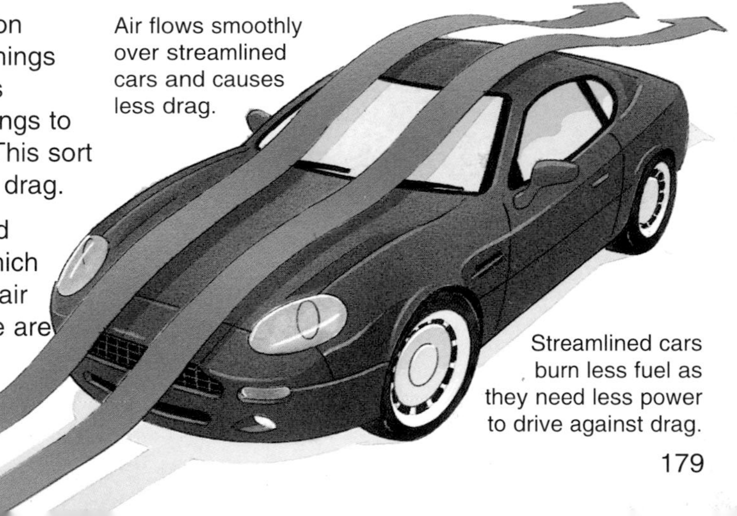

Air flows smoothly over streamlined cars and causes less drag.

Streamlined cars burn less fuel as they need less power to drive against drag.

Making a car

Millions of cars are made each year in car factories all over the world. Each car is made from thousands of parts.

Here you can see how a car is put together, step by step, on a moving track called an assembly line.

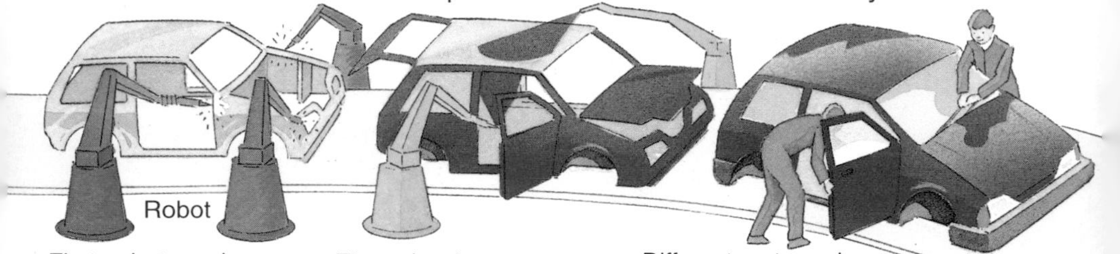

First, robots make the car body from sheets of metal.

Then, the doors are put on and the car is sprayed with paint.

Different parts such as the windows and lights are fitted next.

Crash testing

Every few years, car makers design a new model of car. They crash it to test how safe it is and then look at the damage to see how it can be made safer.

Some cars have air bags. These inflate in a crash to protect people in front.

The front and back of the car are made to take the shock of the crash and crumple.

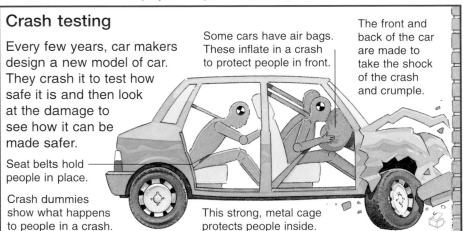

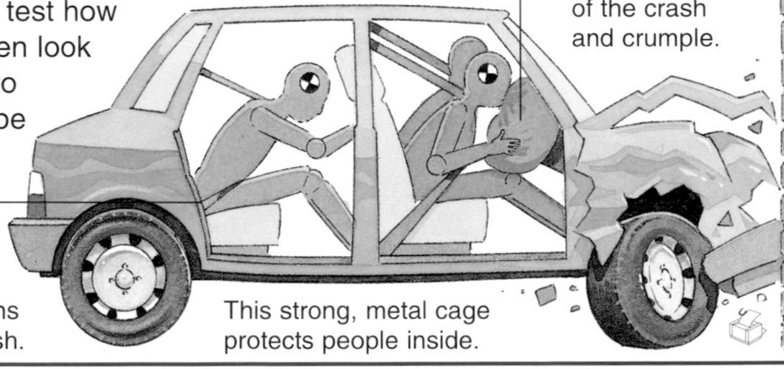

Seat belts hold people in place.

Crash dummies show what happens to people in a crash.

This strong, metal cage protects people inside.

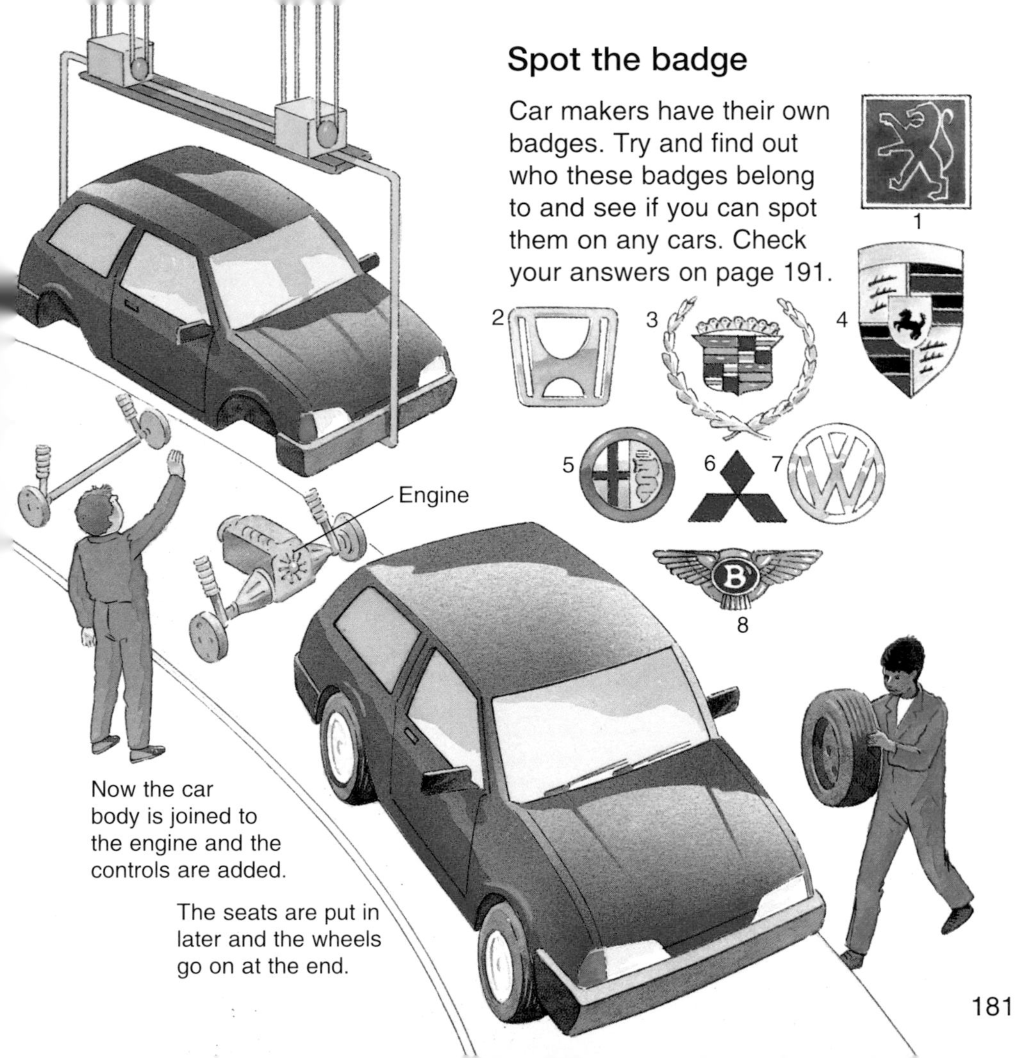

Spot the badge

Car makers have their own badges. Try and find out who these badges belong to and see if you can spot them on any cars. Check your answers on page 191.

Now the car body is joined to the engine and the controls are added.

The seats are put in later and the wheels go on at the end.

Cars and pollution

Cars send out waste gases called fumes from their exhaust pipes. These are unhealthy to breathe and cause dirt, or pollution, in the air.

Clean-up

A filter called a catalytic converter can be put on car exhausts. It cleans some of the fumes, but not others.

Heat-up

A layer of gases called the atmosphere surrounds the Earth. It traps the Sun's heat like glass in a greenhouse. Extra car fumes in the atmosphere trap more heat. This is known as global warming.

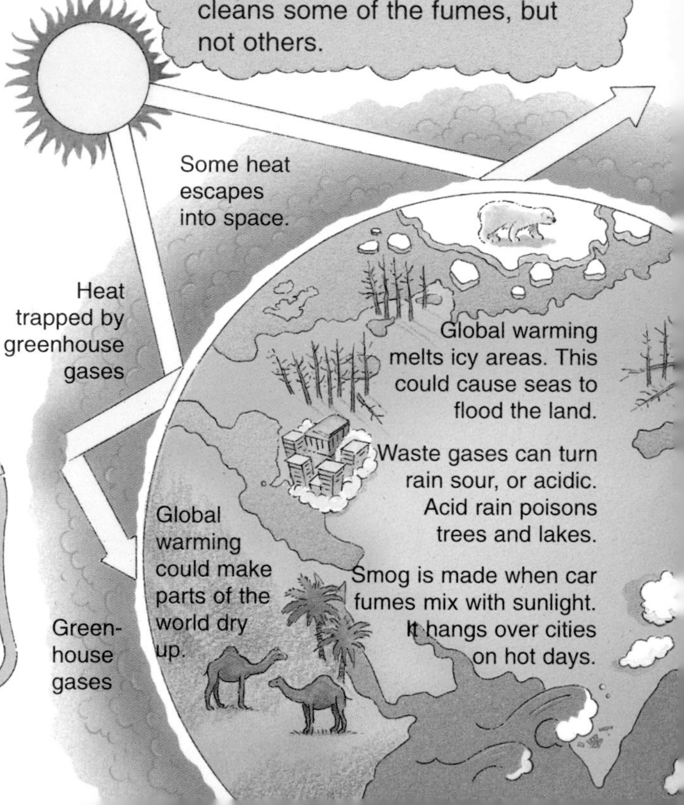

Some heat escapes into space.
Heat trapped by greenhouse gases
Green-house gases
Global warming melts icy areas. This could cause seas to flood the land.
Waste gases can turn rain sour, or acidic. Acid rain poisons trees and lakes.
Global warming could make parts of the world dry up.
Smog is made when car fumes mix with sunlight. It hangs over cities on hot days.

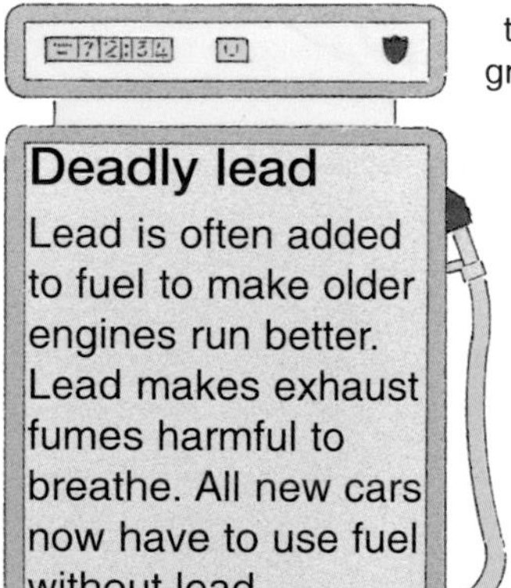

Deadly lead

Lead is often added to fuel to make older engines run better. Lead makes exhaust fumes harmful to breathe. All new cars now have to use fuel without lead.

New kinds of fuel

Car fumes are caused by burning fuel. The oil that makes car fuel will one day run out. People are looking for cleaner ways to run cars which use less oil.

Fuel from plants

Fuel can be made from plants such as sugar cane. It causes less pollution and will not run out.

Sugar cane is grown to make fuel in Brazil.

Electric cars

Electric cars run on batteries. They make no pollution, but soon run out of power. People are trying to make better ones.

Sun-powered cars

A few cars use energy from the Sun. They have special panels which change sunlight into electricity, but they are not powerful enough to use everyday yet.

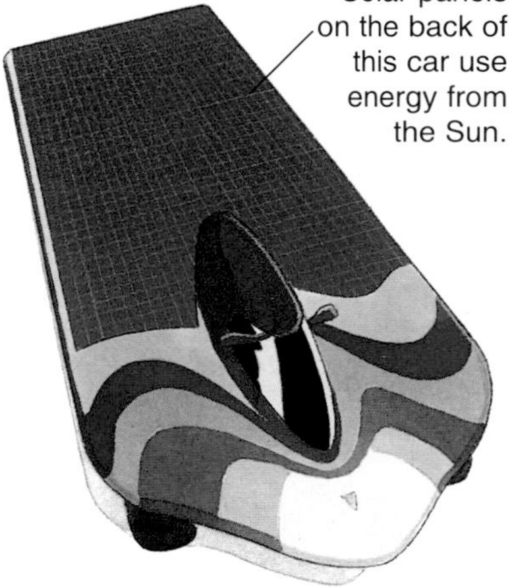

Solar panels on the back of this car use energy from the Sun.

Internet link Go to **www.usborne-quicklinks.com** for a link to a Web site where there is lots of interesting information about global warming.

Cars and traffic

Cars can cause traffic jams, as well as pollution. Here are some ways that people can cut down on traffic and pollution.

In some towns it is easier and cheaper to use trains and buses. Trains carry hundreds of people who might otherwise go by car.

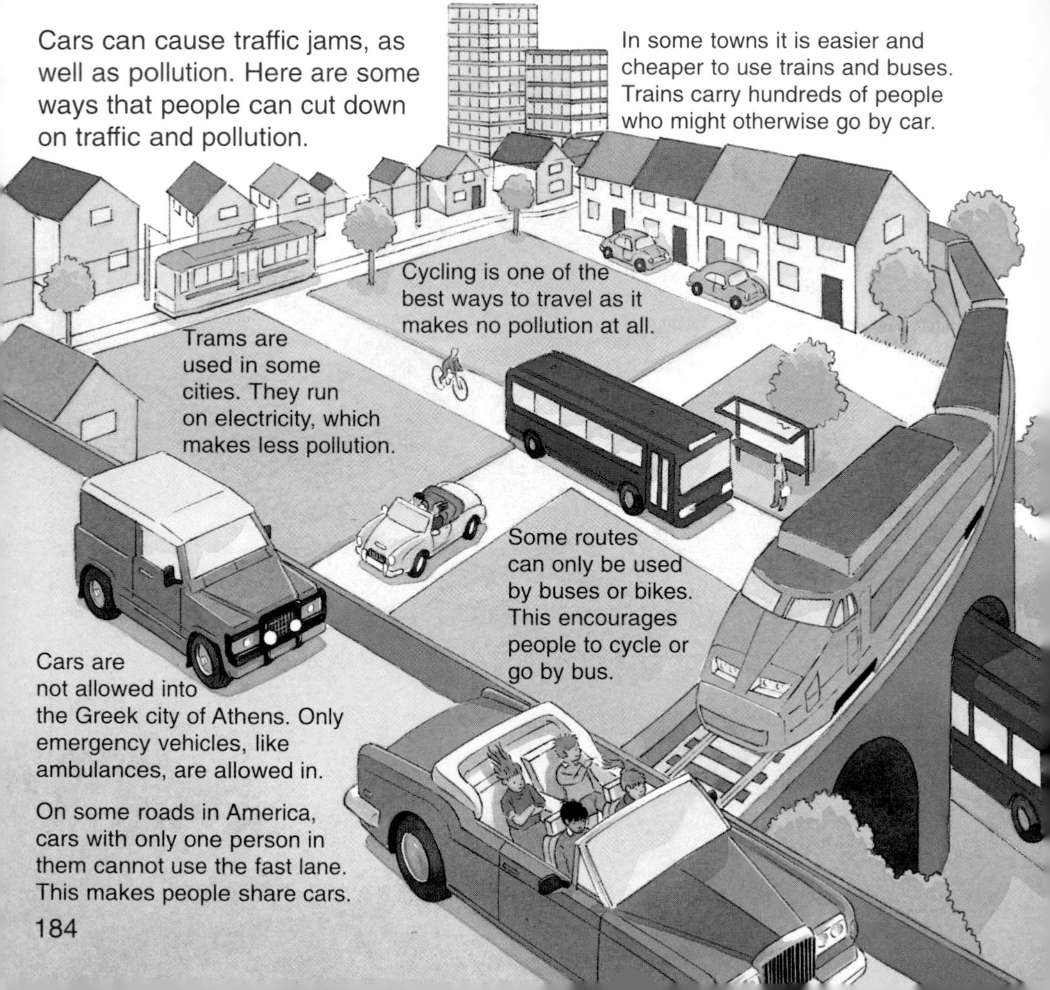

Cycling is one of the best ways to travel as it makes no pollution at all.

Trams are used in some cities. They run on electricity, which makes less pollution.

Some routes can only be used by buses or bikes. This encourages people to cycle or go by bus.

Cars are not allowed into the Greek city of Athens. Only emergency vehicles, like ambulances, are allowed in.

On some roads in America, cars with only one person in them cannot use the fast lane. This makes people share cars.

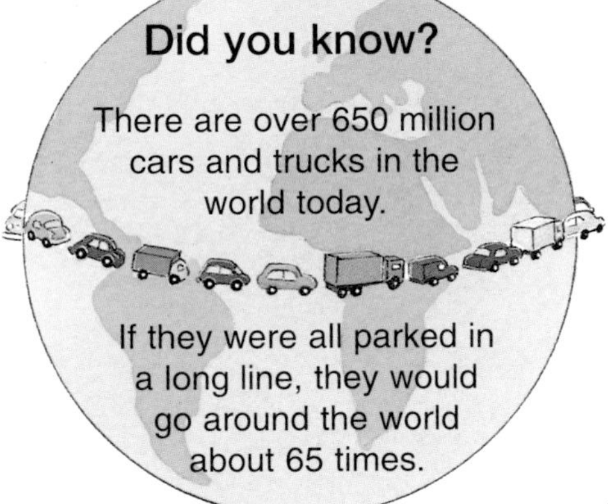

Did you know?

There are over 650 million cars and trucks in the world today.

If they were all parked in a long line, they would go around the world about 65 times.

Bumper to bumper

In 1980, a traffic jam stretched north for 176 km (109 miles) from the south coast of France. It was the longest ever recorded.

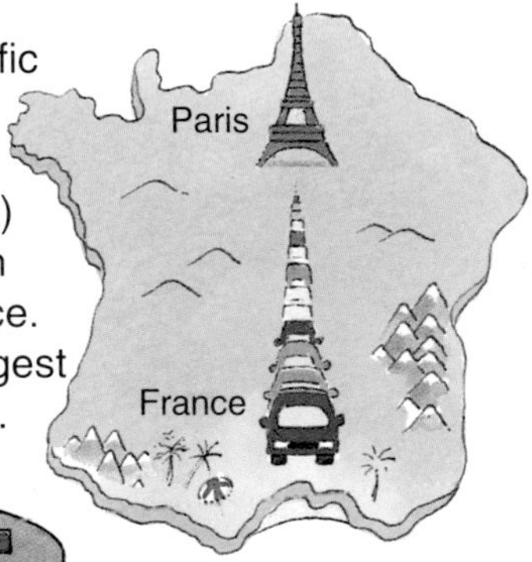

Driving with computers

Computers are now used in some cars to avoid accidents and traffic jams. Car makers have already tested the ideas below.

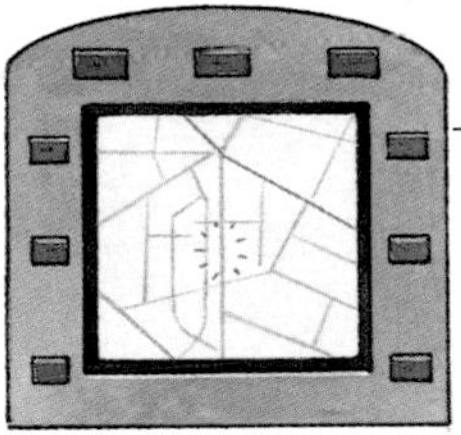

Some cars have a computer screen on the dashboard. It shows the driver which roads to take to avoid accidents.

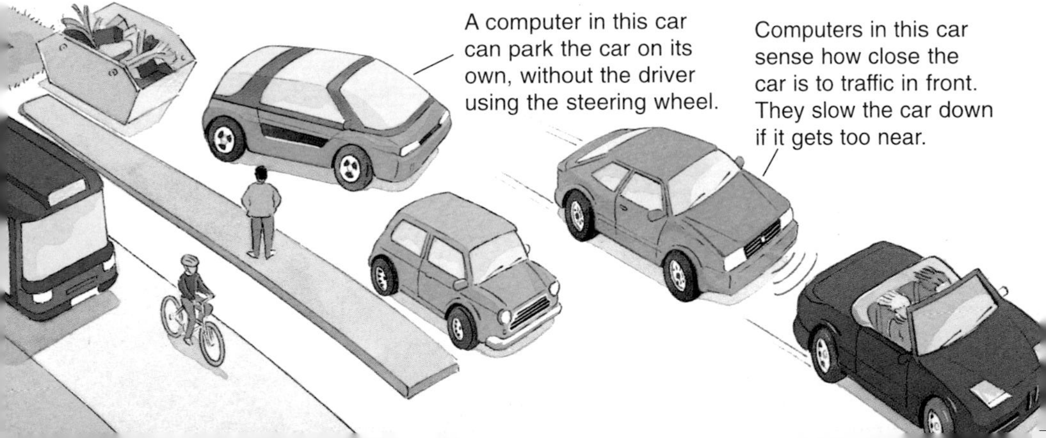

A computer in this car can park the car on its own, without the driver using the steering wheel.

Computers in this car sense how close the car is to traffic in front. They slow the car down if it gets too near.

Cars in the past

The first cars were made over 100 years ago. They were slow and unreliable to begin with, but people soon learned how to make them faster and better.

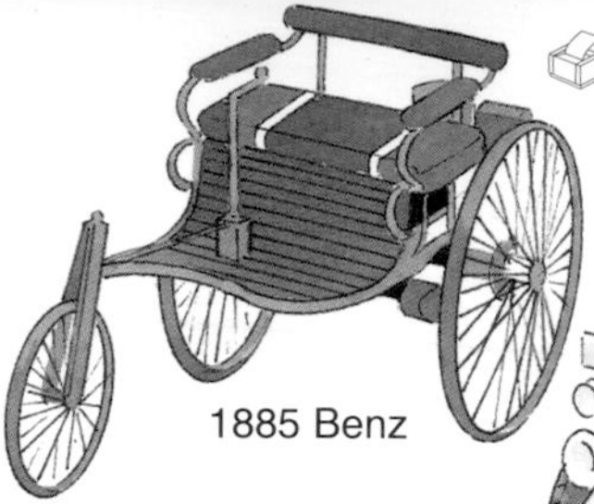

1885 Benz

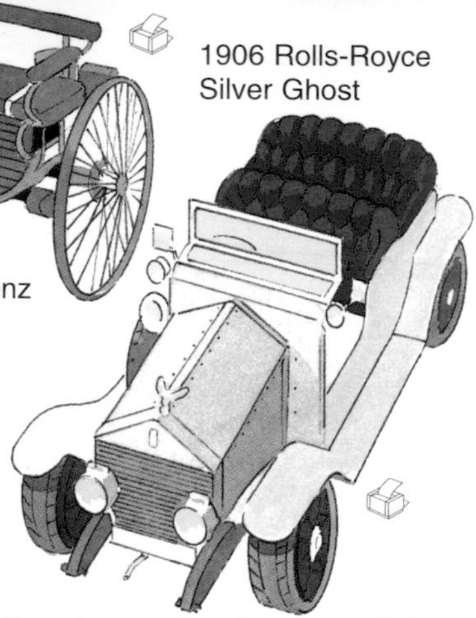

1906 Rolls-Royce Silver Ghost

The first car

The first car to be sold to the public was made by Karl Benz in Germany in 1885.

"Best car in the world"

Many early cars were very grand. The Rolls-Royce Silver Ghost was called "the best car in the world" because it was so splendid to drive.

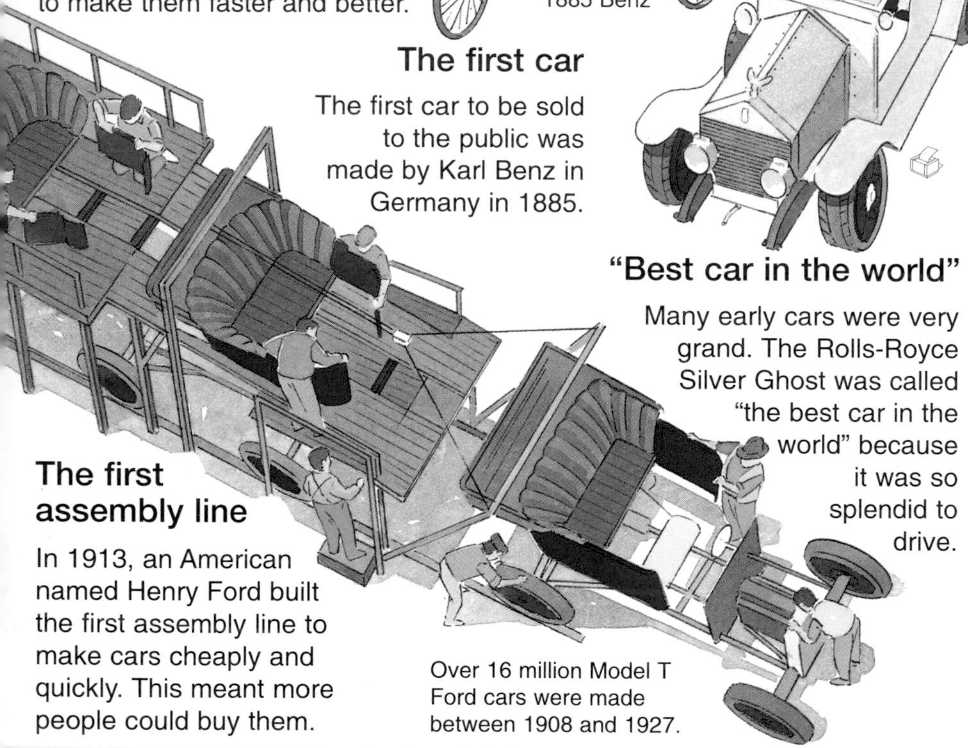

The first assembly line

In 1913, an American named Henry Ford built the first assembly line to make cars cheaply and quickly. This meant more people could buy them.

Over 16 million Model T Ford cars were made between 1908 and 1927.

 Internet link *Go to* ***www.usborne-quicklinks.com*** *for a link to a Web site where you can find out more about Henry Ford and the Model T.*

Cars for everyone

All kinds of cars were made in the 1920s and 1930s, from racy sports cars and luxury cars to big, family cars.

"Gas guzzlers"

Big, flashy cars were popular in America in the 1950s and 1960s. They were called "gas guzzlers" because they burned so much fuel.

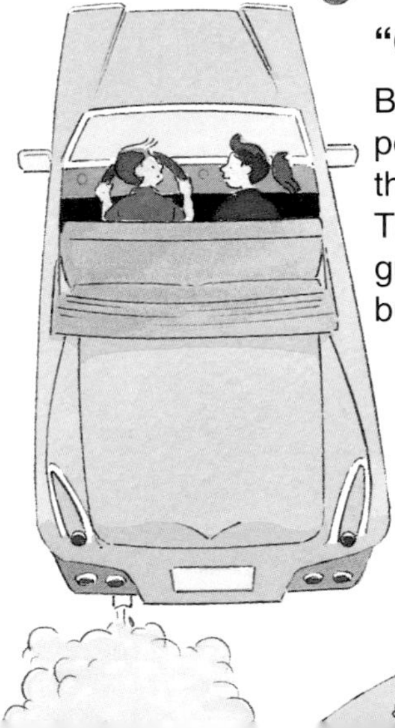

This 1957 Cadillac had high, pointed tail fins.

Small and friendly

Smaller cars which burned less fuel were made in Europe. Today, car makers around the world are making smaller cars to save fuel.

Racing cars

Racing cars have much more powerful engines than ordinary cars and go a lot faster. Different kinds of racing cars drive on different tracks.

Formula One cars

Formula One cars take part in Grand Prix races. Grand Prix means big prize in French. Drivers win points for their finishing place in each race. The driver with the most points in the year is the World Champion.

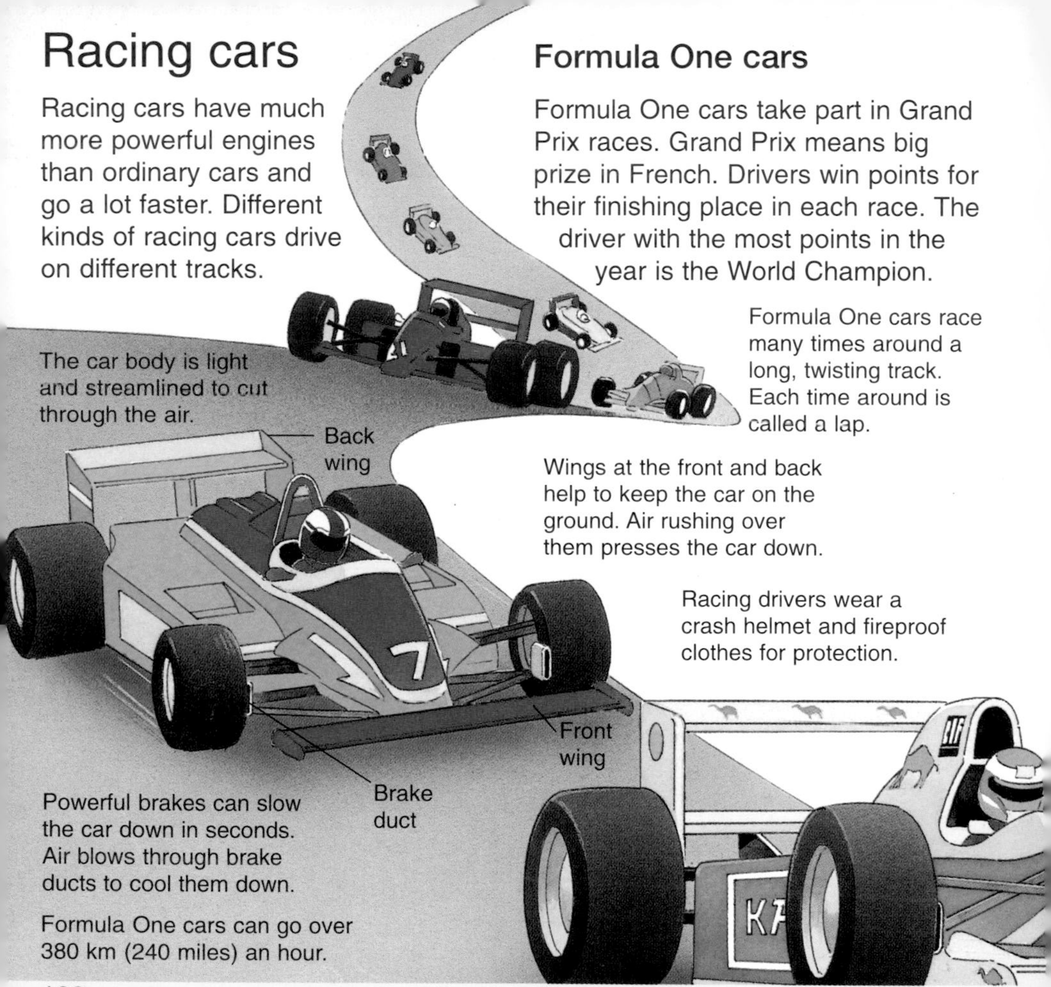

Formula One cars race many times around a long, twisting track. Each time around is called a lap.

The car body is light and streamlined to cut through the air.

Wings at the front and back help to keep the car on the ground. Air rushing over them presses the car down.

Racing drivers wear a crash helmet and fireproof clothes for protection.

Powerful brakes can slow the car down in seconds. Air blows through brake ducts to cool them down.

Formula One cars can go over 380 km (240 miles) an hour.

 Internet link *Go to* ***www.usborne-quicklinks.com*** *for a link to a Web site where you can build your own racing car online.*

Dragsters

Dragsters race each other in pairs down a short, straight track. The whole race only lasts about six seconds.

Dragsters can drive at up to 480 km (300 miles) an hour.

Parachutes slow down dragsters at the end of a drag race.

Rally cars

Rally cars take part in races called rallies over mountain, country and desert tracks. Rallies are split into stages. The driver who finishes all of the stages in the best overall time wins.

These extra lights are for driving in the dark.

Rally cars have extra strong suspension to drive over bumpy ground.

A co-driver next to the driver reads the map and gives directions.

Unusual cars

All these cars are unusual in different ways. Some are built to do special things and others are made to look as amazing as possible.

Orange car

This orange car was built in the 1970s by a fruit company. The company used it as an advertisement.

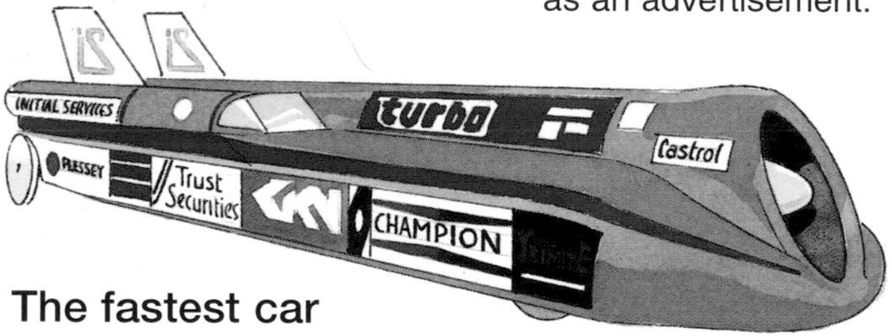

This is Thrust 2. It broke the land speed record in 1983.

The fastest car

A car called Thrust SSC broke the land speed record in 1997 when it sped across the Nevada Desert in America at 1228 km (763 miles) an hour.

The moon buggy helped the astronauts to explore where they had landed.

On the Moon

This electric moon buggy was the first car in space. Astronauts drove it on the Moon in 1971 and left it there when they returned.

Internet links

Go to **www.usborne-quicklinks.com** and type in the keywords "pocket scientist 2" for links to these Web sites about cars.

Web site 1 Discover more about the history of cars, and find out about cars that have appeared in films, including James Bond cars and The Batmobile. You'll find lots of interesting information and some amazing photographs.

Web site 2 On this Web site you can click on lots of different car parts, to see detailed descriptions and clear diagrams that show you how they work.

Web site 3 Take a virtual tour of a Mercedes-Benz car museum, test-drive a racing car and build your own car online. You can also find out more about racing cars and the cars of the future.

Web site 4 Find out how different parts of a car work by looking at amazing animated diagrams. These include pistons moving, fuel being put into a car and a steering wheel turning wheels.

For links to all these sites go to www.usborne-quicklinks.com and type in the keywords "pocket scientist 2".

Answers to page 181

1. Peugeot
2. Honda
3. Cadillac
4. Porsche
5. Alfa Romeo
6. Mitsubishi
7. Volkswagen
8. Bentley

More internet links

Here are some more Web sites to visit to find out about cars. For links to all these sites go to **www.usborne-quicklinks.com** and type in the keywords "pocket scientist 2".

Web site 1 On this Web site you can look at some great photos of different models of Porsches, and even build your own Porsche online. After you've built your Porsche, you can click to see a 3-D view of it.

Web site 2 Find out about the history of motoring and browse a car museum's collection spanning from the unusual first cars built in the 1880's to mass-produced cars of today, and see other vehicles from the last century, including vans and motorcycles.

Web site 3 Look at photographs of Beetle cars and VW Kombi vans, find out about their history and see how they look today. You can also discover how they work, play a game and read some fun facts about them.

Web site 4 Read about the fascinating role of engineers in the process of designing and building new cars and in the development of special parts for older cars. You can also find out how to become an engineer, then try some online games for fun.

For links to all these sites go to www.usborne-quicklinks.com and type in the keywords "pocket scientist 2".

SCIENCE EXPERIMENTS WITH MAGNETS

Helen Edom

Designed by Radhi Parekh and Diane Thistlethwaite
Illustrated by Simone Abel

Consultants: Joan and Maurice Martin

CONTENTS

What can a magnet do?

The experiments and games in this section will help you find out what magnets can do. You can use any magnet for most of the activities but you will need bar magnets for some of them.

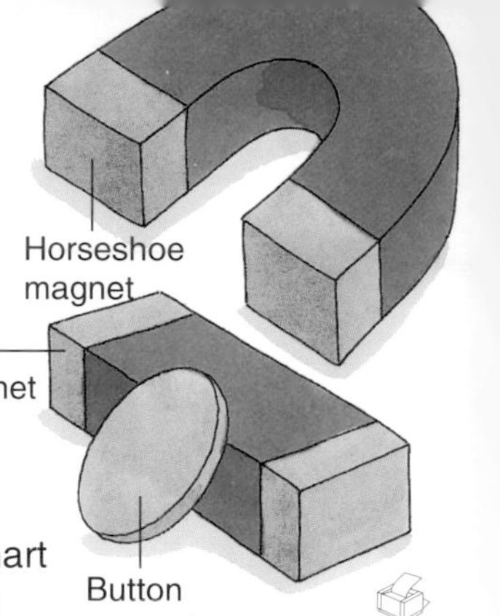

Sticking test

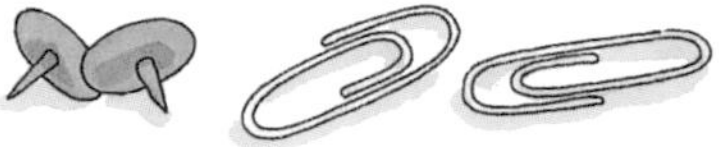

Magnets stick to some things but not to others. Find different things to test with your magnet.

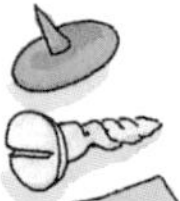

Here are some things you can try. Make a chart to show what happens with each one.

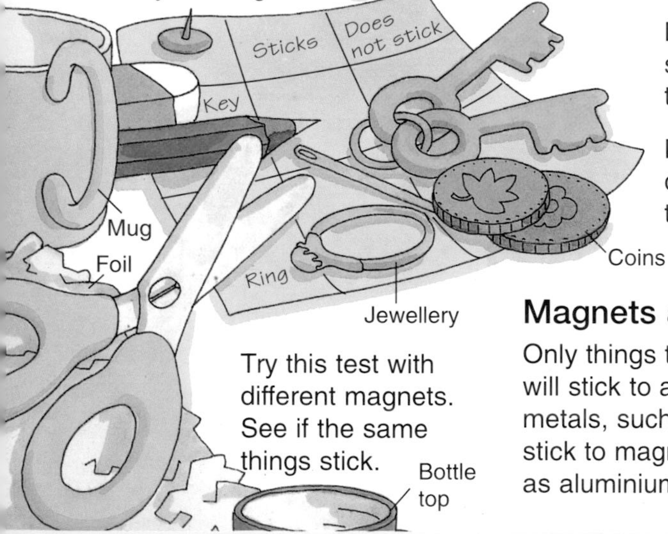

Look at the things that stick to the magnet. Are they all metal?

Look at the things that do not stick. Are any of them metal?

Try this test with different magnets. See if the same things stick.

Magnets and metals

Only things that are made of metal will stick to a magnet. Only some metals, such as iron, steel and nickel stick to magnets. Other metals, such as aluminium, do not stick at all.

Useful magnets

Look around your home to see if you can find magnets being used.

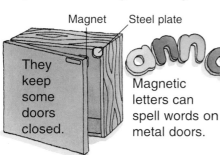

They keep some doors closed.

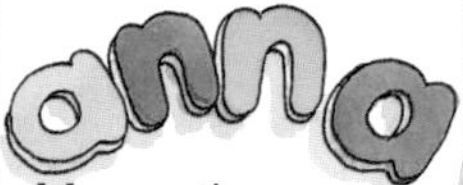

Magnetic letters can spell words on metal doors.

Sorting cans

Cans are usually made from aluminium or steel. Try a magnet out on lots of different ones. The ones that do not stick are aluminium.

Old cans are melted so that their metal can be used again. Magnets are used to sort the cans so the aluminium ones can be melted separately.

Matching socks game

Use the sticking power of your magnets to make a game.

You need: 2 magnets, thread, paper, paints, sticky tape, scissors, paperclips, large box

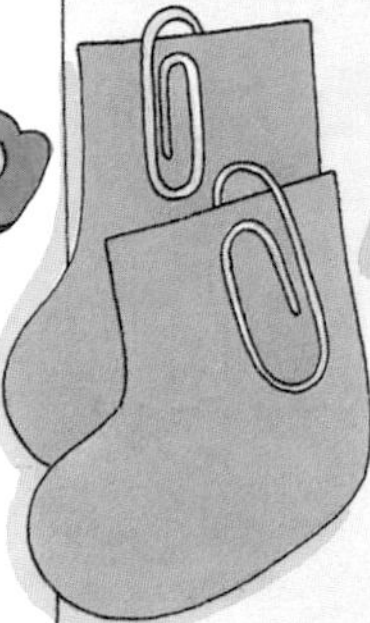

Cut the paper into sock shapes. Colour them in twos so they look like different pairs. Put a paperclip on each sock.

Throw the socks into the box. Tape a thread to each magnet. Take turns with a friend to dip a magnet into the box and pull out a sock.

See who can get the most pairs.

Pulling power

Magnets can pull, or attract, some metal things towards them.

Pulling test

See how far your magnet can pull a pin.

Put a ruler flat on a table.

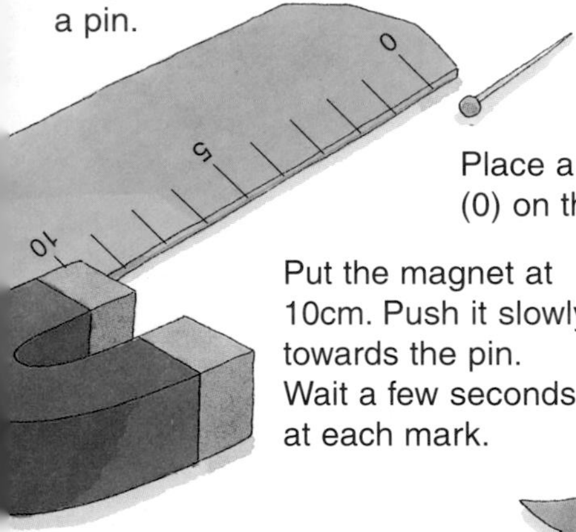

Place a pin at zero (0) on the ruler.

Put the magnet at 10cm. Push it slowly towards the pin. Wait a few seconds at each mark.

When the pin jumps to the magnet, look at the number beside the magnet. This shows how far the pin has jumped.

Try the same test with as many magnets as you can. See which one can pull the pin furthest.

You could write down your results on a chart like this.

Using pulling power

Workers who build things out of steel can get tiny splinters of steel in their eyes. Doctors use a special magnet to pull the splinters out.

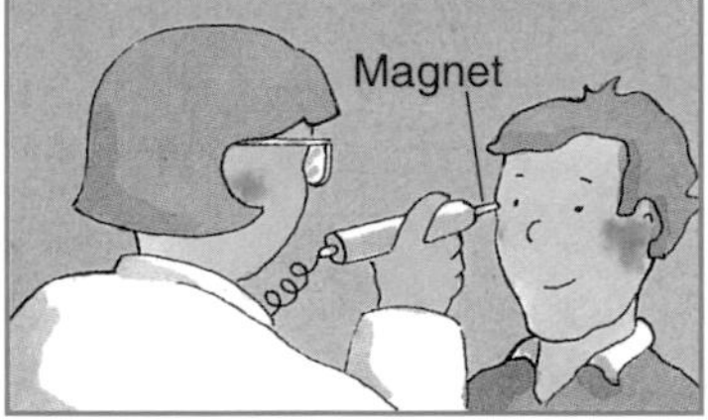

 Internet link *Go to* ***www.usborne-quicklinks.com*** *for a link to a Web site where there's an activity to find out more about magnets and a quiz to test your knowledge.*

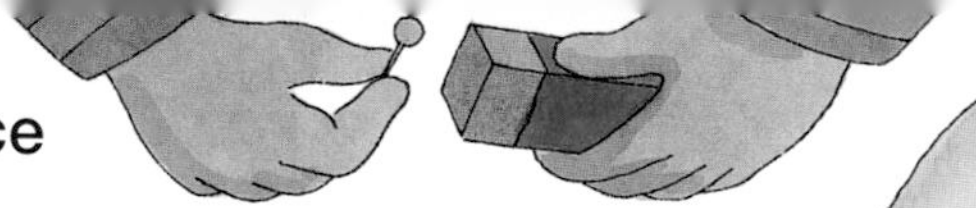

Force

Magnets make things move with an invisible pull called magnetic force.

Try pulling a pin off a magnet. Feel the magnetic force pulling against you. You have to pull more strongly than the magnet.

Gravity

The Earth tries to pull everything down towards its centre. This pull is called the force of gravity. You have to pull against it when you lift things up.

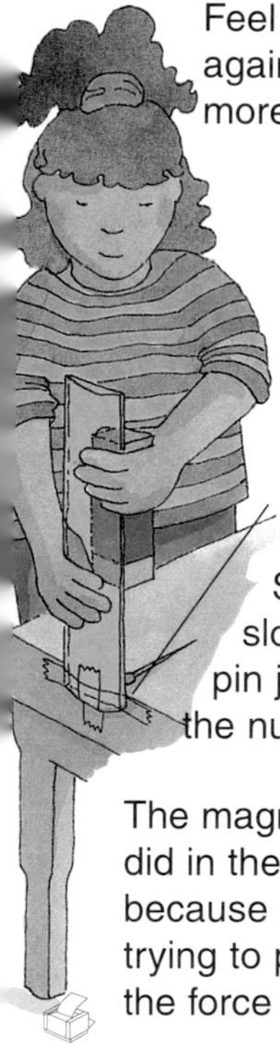

Pulling upwards

Hold the ruler up against the edge of a table so zero is level with the table-top. Put a pin at zero.

Use sticky tape to help to keep the ruler upright.

Slide your strongest magnet slowly down the ruler until the pin jumps up. Stop and look at the number beside the magnet.

The magnet cannot pull the pin as it did in the last test you did. This is because another kind of force is trying to pull the pin down. This is the force of gravity (see above right).

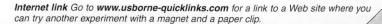

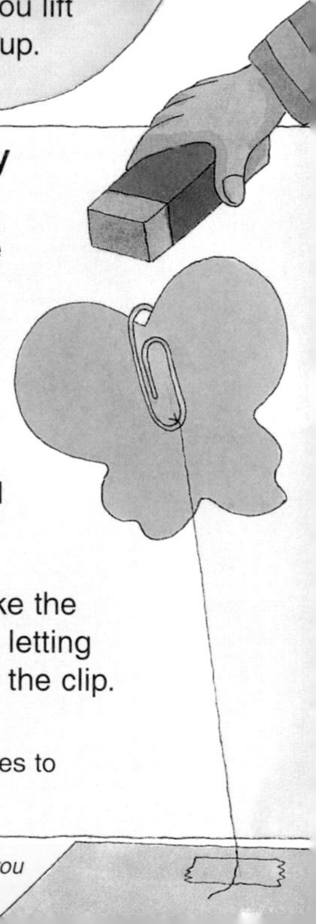

Flying butterfly

Cut a butterfly shape out of some tissue. Slide a paperclip on to it.

Tie one end of a thread to the clip. Tape the other end to a table.

See if you can make the butterfly fly without letting your magnet touch the clip.

The force of gravity tries to pull the clip down.

Internet link *Go to* ***www.usborne-quicklinks.com*** *for a link to a Web site where you can try another experiment with a magnet and a paper clip.*

Pulling through things

Try these experiments to see if you can stop a magnet working.

Blocking test

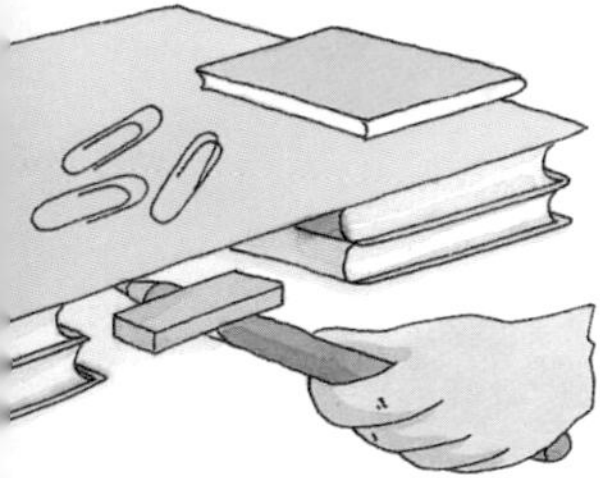

Rest a sheet of paper across two piles of books. Put paper clips on top.

You could tape the magnet onto a pencil.

Rest more books on top to keep the paper still.

Hold a magnet underneath. Can you make it move the paperclips?

The magnet works through the paper. See if it can work through other things.

Here are some you could try.

Sticky metal

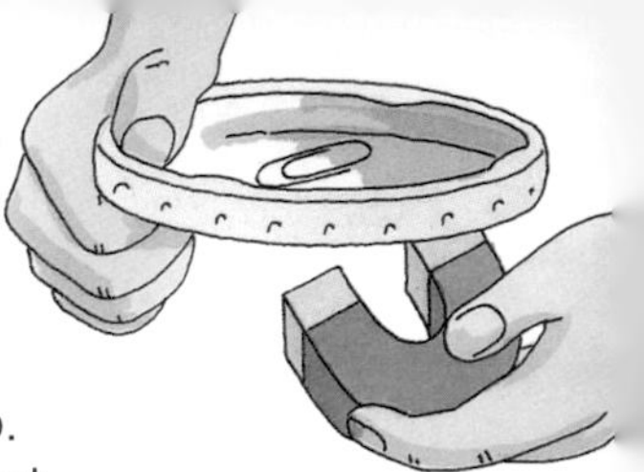

Find a metal lid that sticks to a magnet. Put a paperclip on top. See if the magnet can move the clip from under the lid.

You could use a baking tray instead.

The paperclip is hard to move or may not move at all. This is because the iron or steel in the lid traps the magnet's force.

Keepers

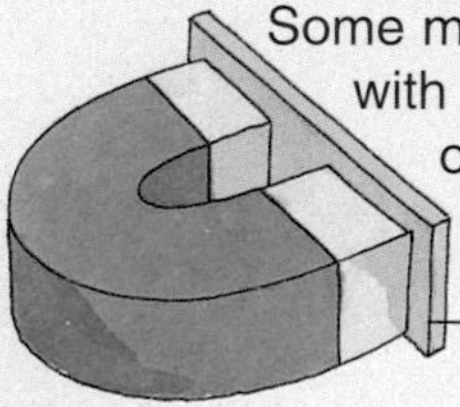

Some magnets are sold with a piece of iron on them, called a keeper.

Keeper on a horseshoe magnet.

The keeper stops the magnet attracting things when it is not being used.

Bar magnets are stored in pairs with two keepers.

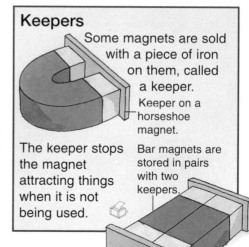

Fun with water

You need:
magnet,
plastic tray
or carton,
magazines,
corks,
drawing pins,
water

Rest the tray across two piles of magazines. Pour water inside. Push a pin into each cork and put them in the water.

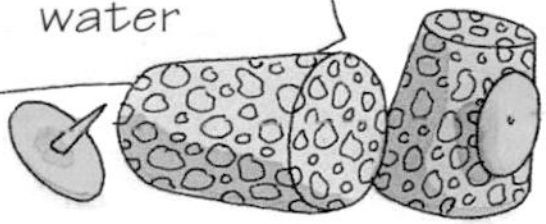

Push the pin in here.

Hold the magnet underwater. Can you make the corks move?

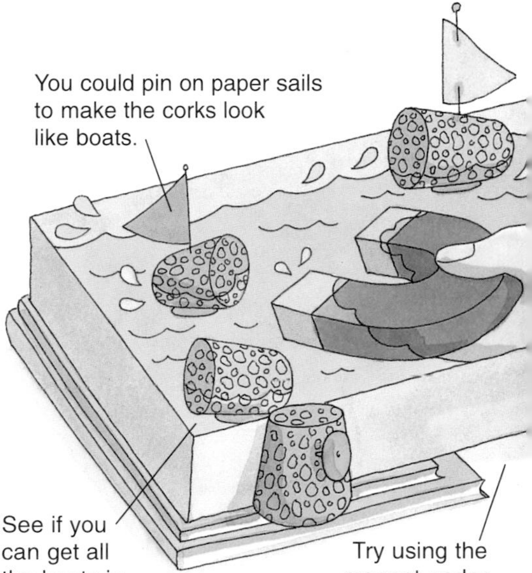

You could pin on paper sails to make the corks look like boats.

See if you can get all the boats in one corner.

Try using the magnet under the tray as well.

Magnetic holders

Because magnets can work through paper and paint, they can be used to hold up notices on a refrigerator's metal door.

Magnetic puzzle

Put a sheet of paper and a nail on a table. How can you use your magnet to pick up the paper? The experiments on this page should give you a clue.

If you get stuck, turn to the answer on page 216.

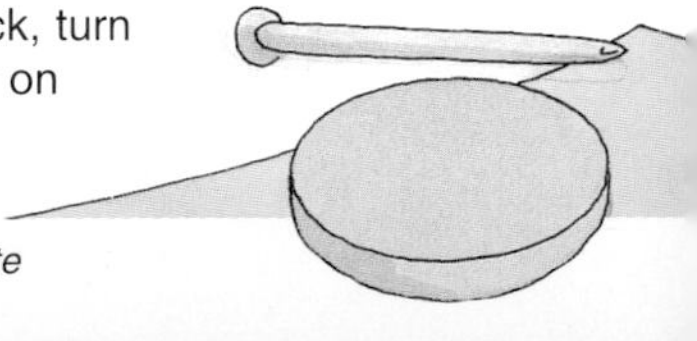

Internet link *Go to* ***www.usborne-quicklinks.com*** *for a link to a Web site where you can make a magnetic charmer.*

Pushing and pulling

These experiments will help you find out more about a magnet's force.

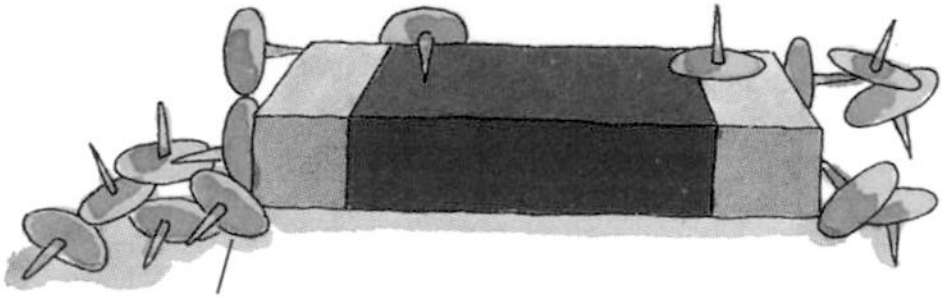

A bar magnet has most pins at the ends.

This round magnet is strongest on each flat side.

Where is a magnet strongest?

Put a magnet into a box of drawing pins. Lift it out carefully. Where are there most pins? Try this experiment with all sorts of magnets.

A horseshoe magnet has lots of pins at both ends.

Every magnet has two strong places. These are called poles. They are at opposite ends.

About poles

Both poles pick up pins in the same way. Try this experiment to see if the poles are the same in other ways.

1. Put two bar magnets 20cm apart, so that the ends face each other. Push one towards the other. Watch what happens.

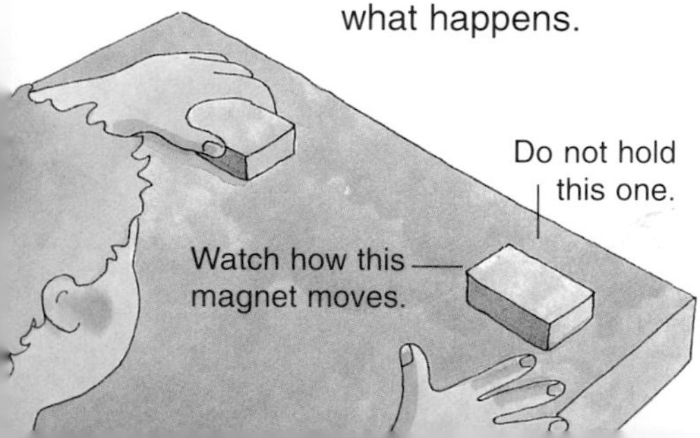

Do not hold this one.
Watch how this magnet moves.

2. Tape coloured paper on to the poles (ends) that stick. Use two different colours.

3. Turn both magnets around. Do the other poles also stick? Mark them so each magnet has its poles in different colours, as shown.

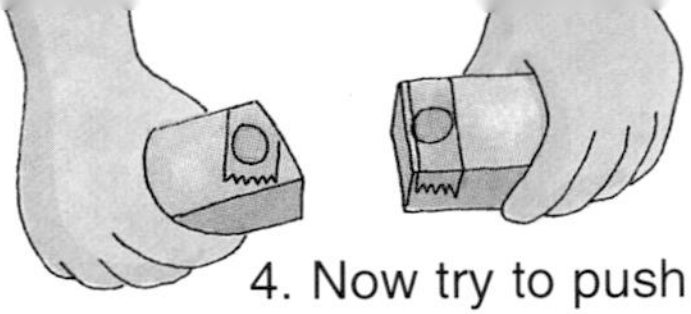

4. Now try to push two of the same-coloured poles together. Can you feel them pushing back?

Each magnet has two sorts of pole. One is called north, the other south. Poles of the same kind push each other away but different poles pull towards each other.

North pole ⇇ ⇉ North pole

North poles push away, or repel, each other.

South pole ⇇ ⇉ South pole

South poles repel each other.

North pole | South pole

A north pole and a south pole pull together, or attract.

Try putting different-shaped magnets together. Can you find which poles are the same?

Pushing game

Tape one magnet onto a toy car. Use one pole of another magnet to push the car along.

How fast can you make the car go?

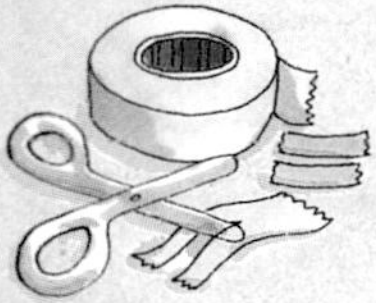

Floating magnets

Use the marked magnets for this trick. First cut some thin strips of sticky tape.

Put a pencil on one magnet. Put the other magnet on top so the same colours are together. Tape the magnets together.

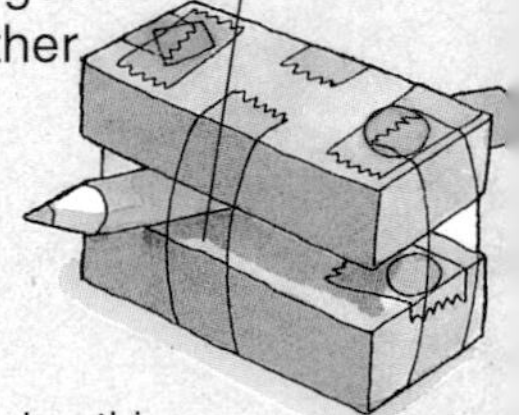

Keep the tape loose like this.

Now take the pencil away. The top magnet floats above the bottom magnet.

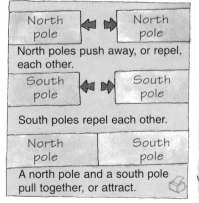

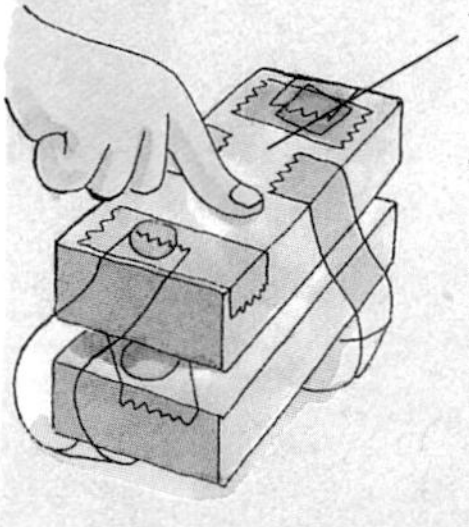

Try pressing this magnet.

The same-coloured poles try to push each other away. This keeps the magnet in the air.

Finding your way

Magnets help sailors, explorers and hikers to find their way. Here you can find out how.

Pointing magnet

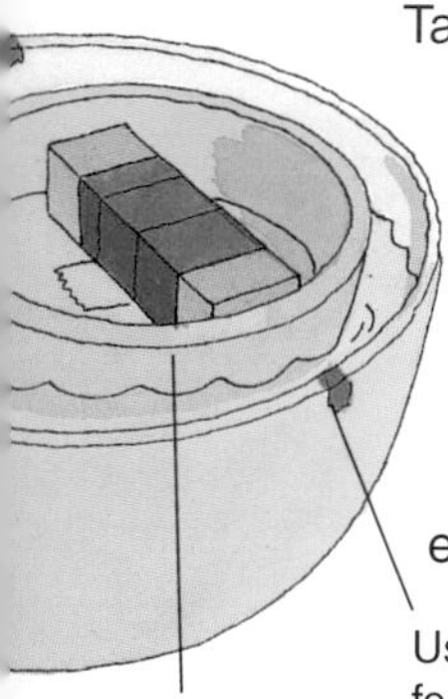

Tape a bar magnet into a plastic pot. Float the pot in a bowl of water. Let the pot settle.

Mark the bowl opposite the two ends of the magnet.

Use a felt-tip pen for the marks.

The magnet turns back to face the same way.

Turn the pot, then let go. What happens?

A magnet always turns to point the same way, if it can swing easily. Its north pole (see page 201) points north. Its south pole points south.

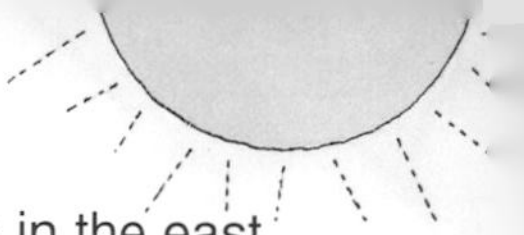

Finding north

The Sun always rises in the east and sets in the west. If you get up early and face the sun, north is on your left.

Never look straight at the sun. It can hurt your eyes badly.

Mark the north end of the magnet in the pot with a blob of Plasticine or paint.

Make a compass

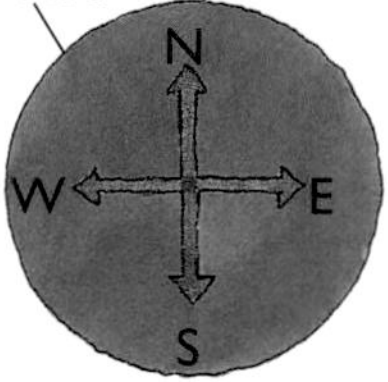

Cut a circle of card to fit in the pot. Mark east, west, north and south.

Just use the first letters.

When the compass is finished it always shows the right directions.

Put the card in the pot so 'N' is over the north end of the magnet. Then all the arrows will point the right way.

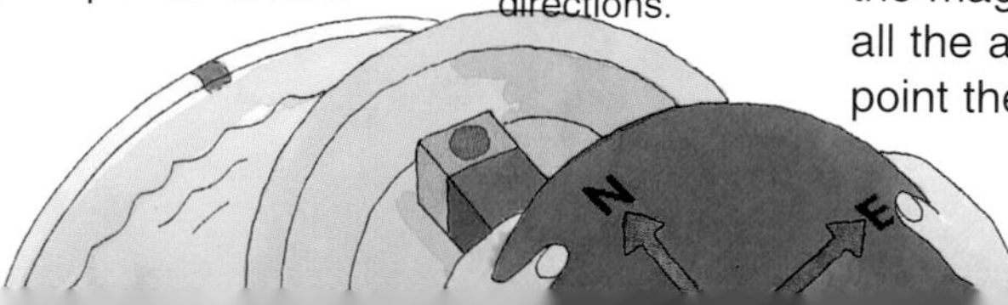

Chinese inventors

The Chinese invented the first compasses. This one had a magnet inside the turtle shape.

The magnet made the turtle turn so its head pointed north.

How a hiker's compass works

A hiker's compass has a magnetic needle. It always points north.

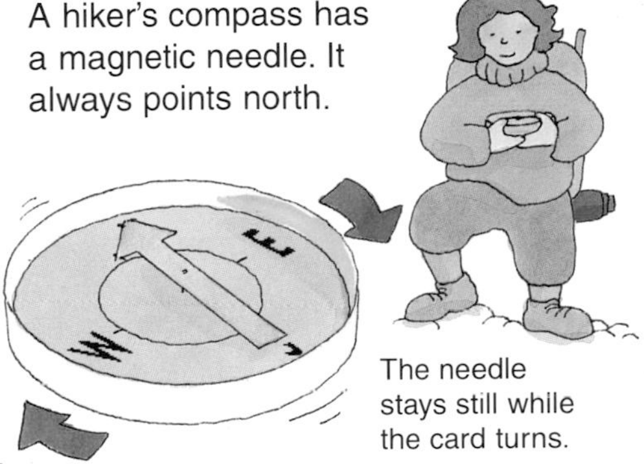

The needle stays still while the card turns.

To find other directions, the hiker turns a card beneath. When N (north) is under the needle all the arrows point the right way.

Another north pole

The north poles of all magnets point to one place. This place is called the Earth's magnetic North Pole. It is in the icy, northern Arctic.

Explorers have found that compasses do not work at the Earth's North Pole. The magnet inside just spins around.

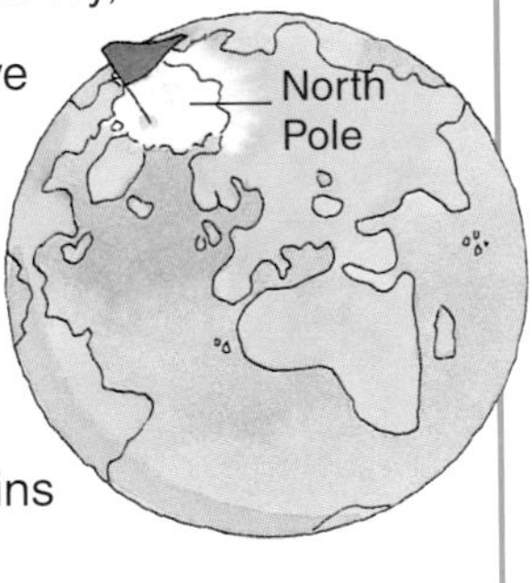

Compass puzzle

Which way does this hiker have to go to get to the mountains?

Remember the hiker has to turn the compass so 'N' is under the needle.

Answer on page 216.

Internet link *Go to* ***www.usborne-quicklinks.com*** *for a link to a Web site where you can find out how to make another simple compass.*

Making magnets

You can use one magnet to make another. Here are some ways to try this.

Hanging magnets

Hang a nail from the end of a magnet. Try hanging another nail onto the first one. Do they stick together?

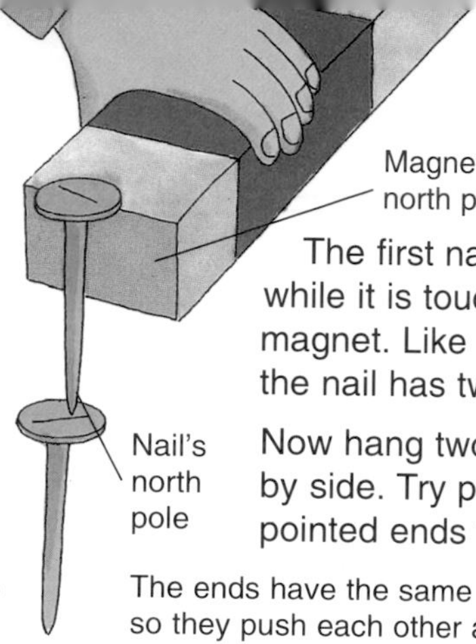

You can use pins instead of nails.

The first nail is a magnet while it is touching the big magnet. Like all magnets the nail has two poles.

Now hang two nails side by side. Try pushing the pointed ends together.

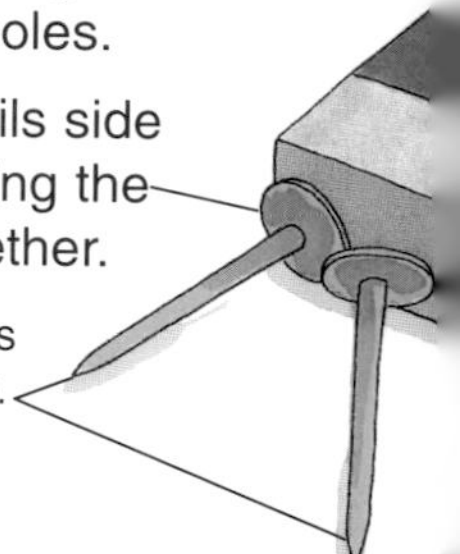

The ends have the same poles so they push each other away.

A lasting magnet

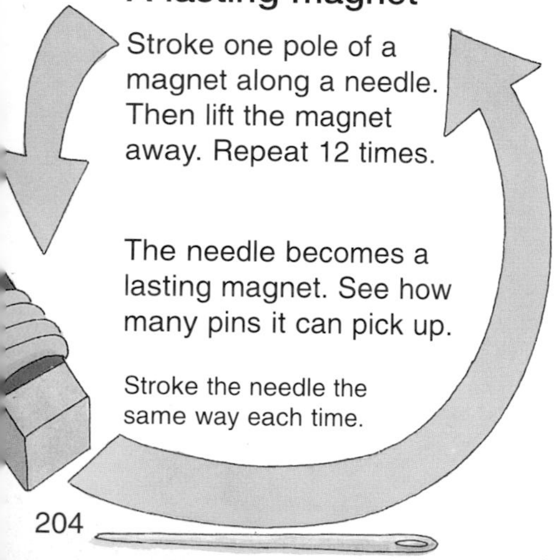

Stroke one pole of a magnet along a needle. Then lift the magnet away. Repeat 12 times.

The needle becomes a lasting magnet. See how many pins it can pick up.

Stroke the needle the same way each time.

Inside a magnet

A magnet is made up of many tiny parts called domains. Each one is like a mini-magnet. They all line up and point the same way.

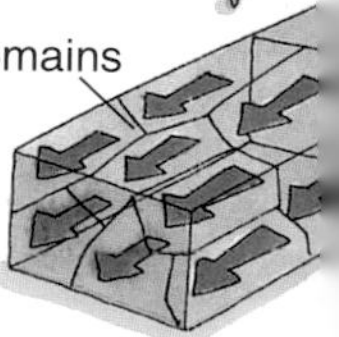

Any metal that sticks to a magnet also has domains. These are jumbled up. A magnet can make them line up. Then the metal becomes a magnet.

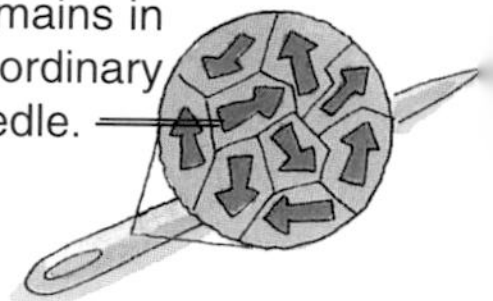

Domains in an ordinary needle.

Domains in a magnetised needle.

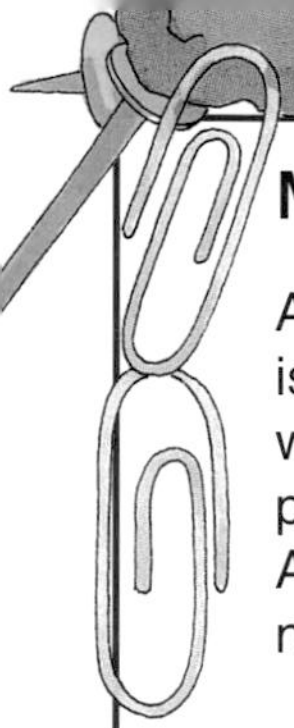

Magnetic rock

A rock called magnetite is a natural magnet. It was first found at a place called Magnesia. All magnets get their name from this place.

Can you spoil a magnet?

Drop a magnetised needle to a table. Do this a few times. Then see if the needle can still pick up pins.

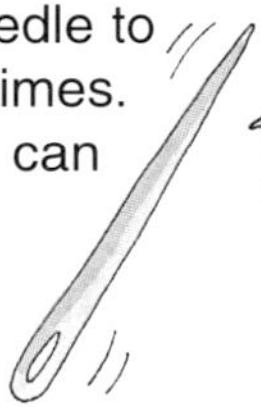

What happens

The domains are shaken out of line so the needle stops being a magnet. Take care not to hit or drop your magnets in case they get spoiled in the same way.

Swimming ducks

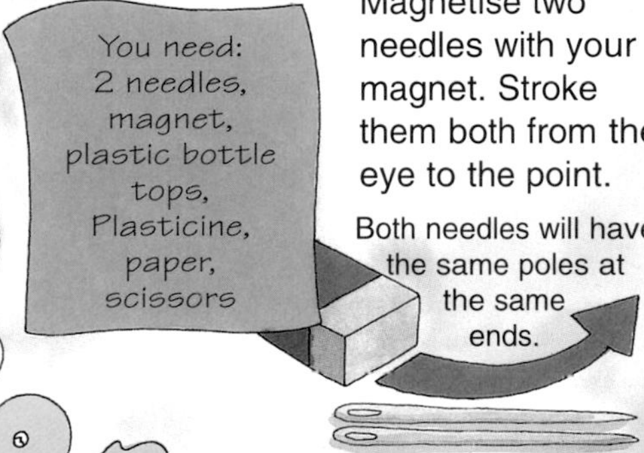

Magnetise two needles with your magnet. Stroke them both from the eye to the point.

Use Plasticine to stick each one to a bottle top. Cut out duck shapes and stick them on top.

Stick one duck so its beak is over the needle's eye. Stick the other so its beak is over the point.

Float the bottle tops in water. The ducks seem to swim towards each other.

These ends have different poles so they attract each other.

Around your magnet

Try these experiments so you can find out more about the forces around your magnet.

Magnetic field

Magnetic force works above and below a magnet as well as at its sides.

Magnet patterns

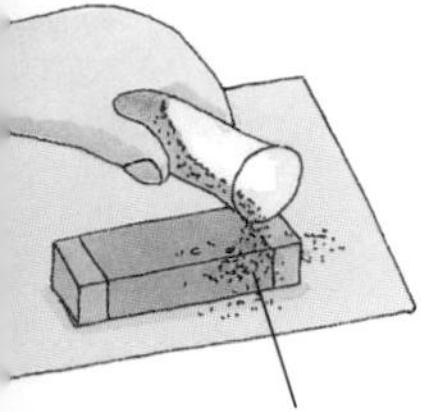

Sprinkle the filings evenly.

Put a magnet under some card. Sprinkle iron filings (see below) on top. Tap the card lightly. What happens?

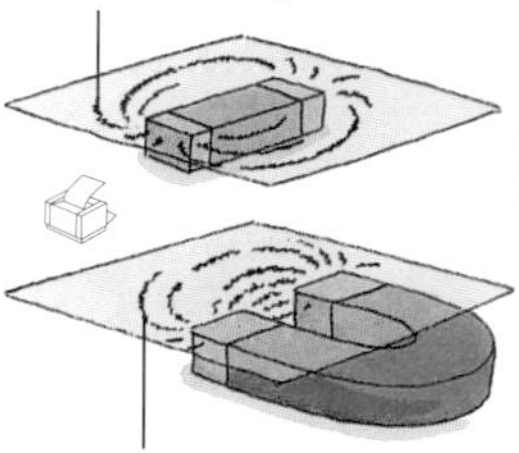

Pattern made by a bar magnet.

Pattern made by a horseshoe magnet.

The magnet pulls the filings into a pattern around it. This shows that a magnet's force works all round, although it is strongest at the poles.

Using iron filings

Iron filings are tiny pieces of iron. Ask an adult to make some by filing an iron nail.

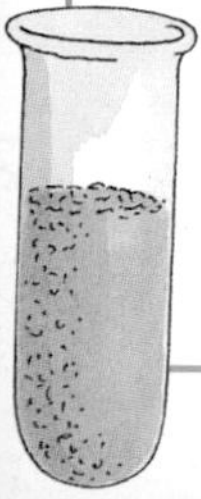

Chemistry sets often have iron filings in tubes like this.

Travelling needle

You need:
needle,
slice of cork,
bar magnet,
Plasticine,
bowl of water,
sticky tape

1. Magnetise a needle by stroking it with the south pole of a magnet. Stroke the needle 12 times from the eye to the point.

The point will have a north pole.

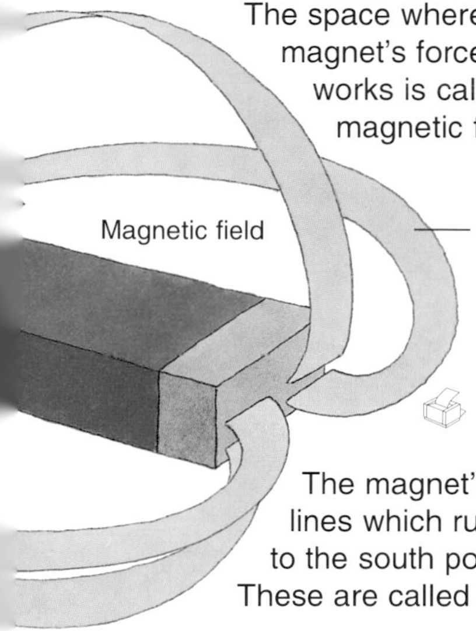
The space where a magnet's force works is called its magnetic field.
Magnetic field
Line of force
The magnet's force goes in lines which run from the north to the south pole of a magnet. These are called lines of force.

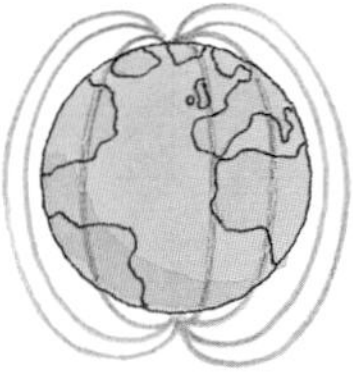

The Earth's magnetic field

The planet Earth behaves as if it has a huge magnet inside. It has a magnetic field like other magnets.

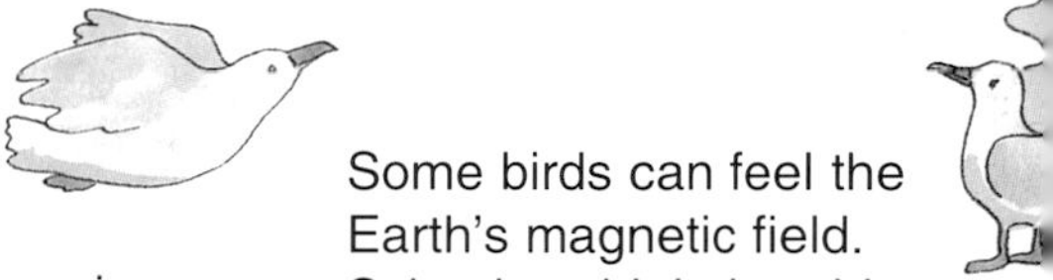

Some birds can feel the Earth's magnetic field. Scientists think that this helps them find their way when they fly. No one really knows how.

2. Push the needle through the cork. Float it in water so the point is on top.

Be careful with sharp ends.

Stick Plasticine under the cork so it floats upright.

3. Tape the magnet inside the bowl. Move the needle near to the magnet's north pole. Then let go.

The needle floats round to the south pole. It follows a line of force in the magnetic field.

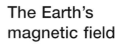

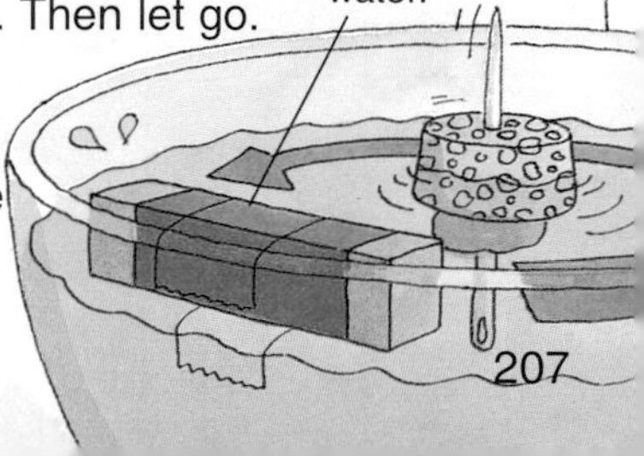
Tape the magnet well above the water.

Electricity and magnets

Electricity can act like a magnet. Here you can find out how.

What is electricity?

Electricity is caused by tiny invisible things called electrons. These move easily through metal. Their flow is called an electric current.

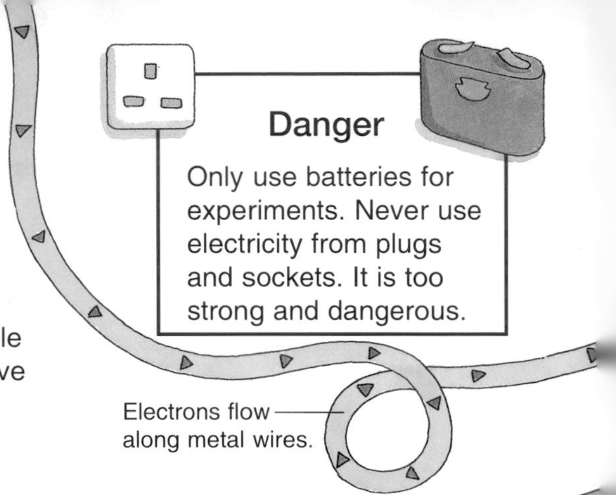
Electrons flow along metal wires.

Danger

Only use batteries for experiments. Never use electricity from plugs and sockets. It is too strong and dangerous.

Electric surprise

You need: a 4.5 volt battery, a 5cm piece of straw, needle, sticky tape, scissors, 150cm of plastic coated wire

1. Ask an adult to help you cut off the plastic at each end of the wire. Tape one end on to a terminal on the battery.

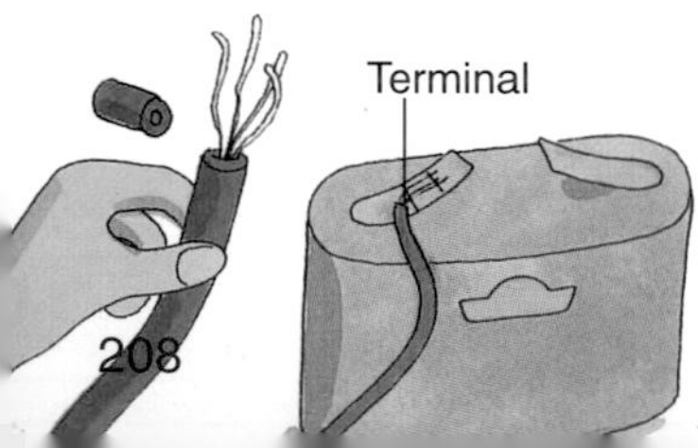
Terminal

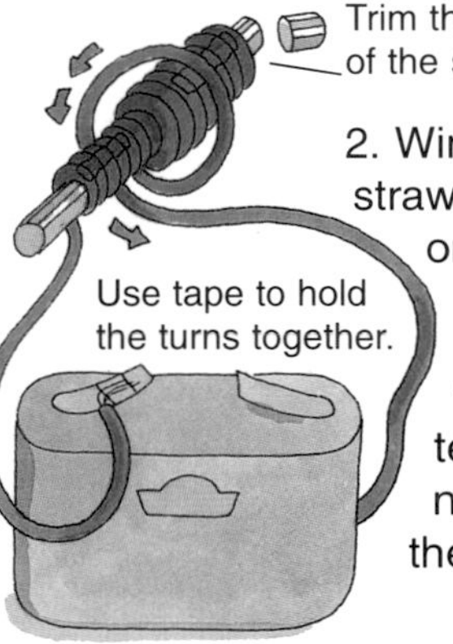
Trim the ends of the straw.
Use tape to hold the turns together.

2. Wind the wire onto the straw to make a coil. Wind on three layers of wire.

3. Tape the free end of the wire to the second terminal. Hold the needle lightly just inside the coil. What happens?

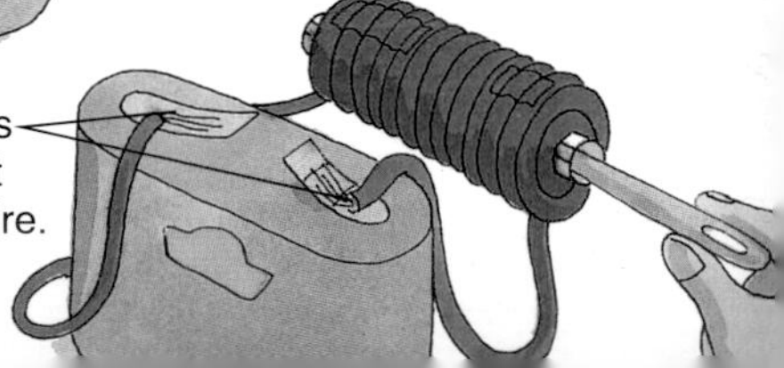
When both terminals are joined, a current flows through the wire.

4. The needle is pulled inside the coil. This is because an electric current has a magnetic field. The coil makes the field strong enough to attract the needle.

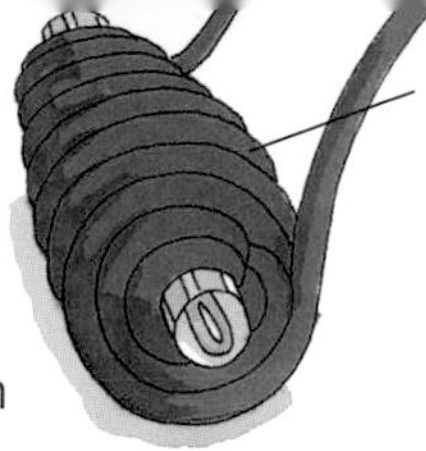

This coil is called a solenoid.

Your battery will quickly run down if you leave the solenoid on for long. Switch it off by taking one wire off a terminal.

Railway signal

Use your solenoid to make a model signal.

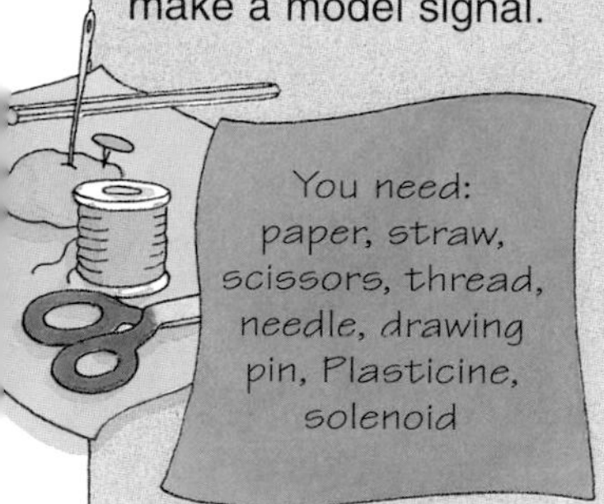

You need:
paper, straw, scissors, thread, needle, drawing pin, Plasticine, solenoid

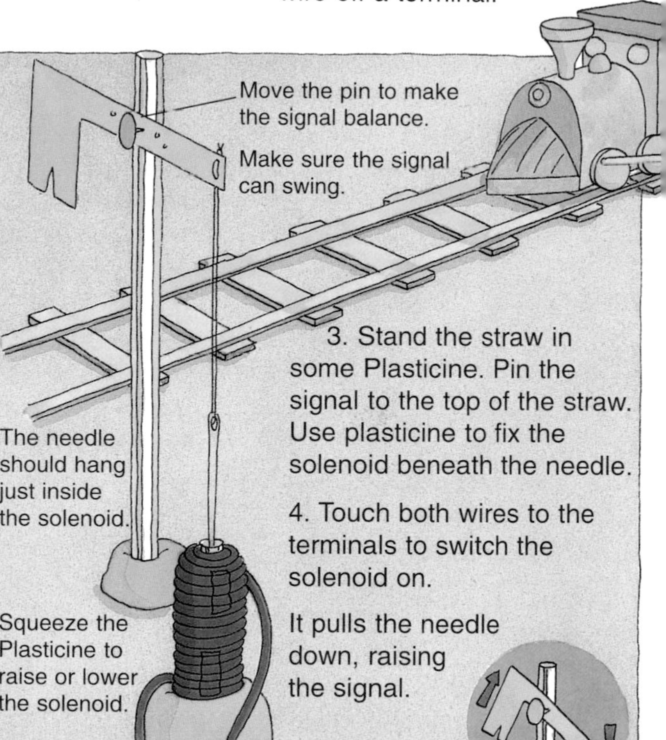

Move the pin to make the signal balance.

Make sure the signal can swing.

The needle should hang just inside the solenoid.

Squeeze the Plasticine to raise or lower the solenoid.

1. Cut the paper into this signal shape. Thread the needle and sew it onto the thin end.

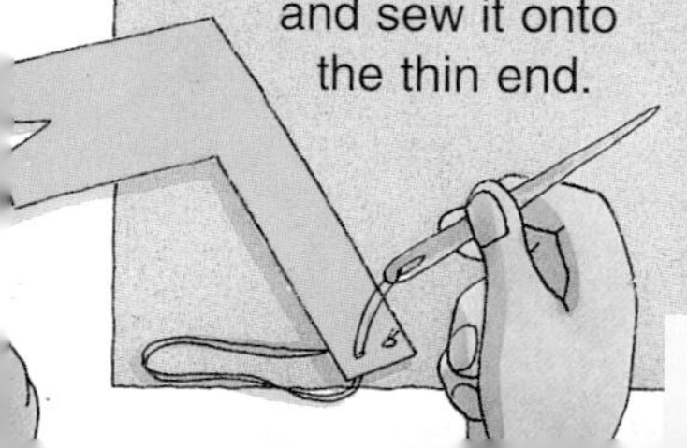

3. Stand the straw in some Plasticine. Pin the signal to the top of the straw. Use plasticine to fix the solenoid beneath the needle.

4. Touch both wires to the terminals to switch the solenoid on.

It pulls the needle down, raising the signal.

Internet link *Go to* ***www.usborne-quicklinks.com*** *for a link to a Web site with a movie about magnets.*

Electromagnets

Some magnets use electricity to make them work. These are called electromagnets.

Making an electromagnet

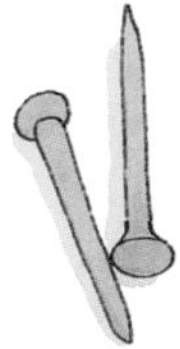

You can turn the solenoid on page 208 into an electromagnet. Just put a long iron or steel nail inside the straw. Then tape both wires to the battery.

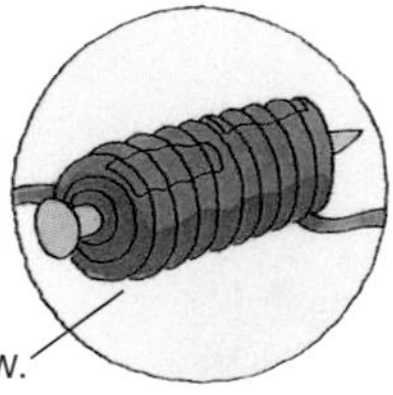

You can rewind the wire around the nail if the nail does not fit in the straw.

Now see if your electromagnet picks up the same things as other magnets.

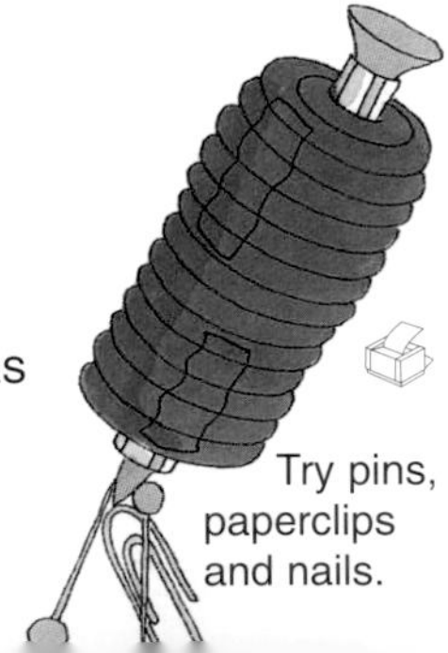

Try pins, paperclips and nails.

Magnetic cranes

Some cranes use electromagnets to pick up iron and steel. These magnets are very strong.

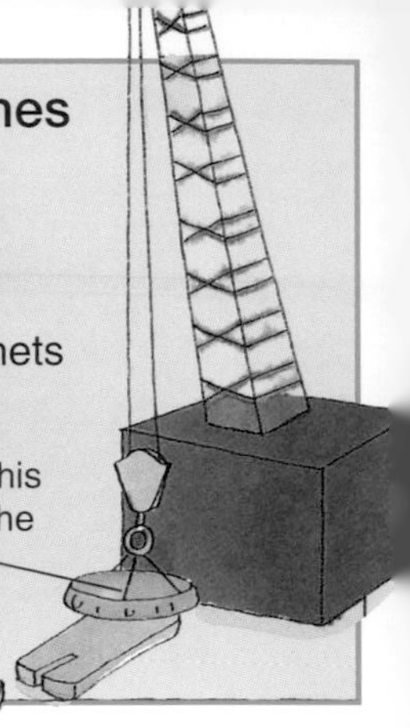

The driver switches this magnet off to make the crane drop its load.

Why electromagnets work

The metal inside the solenoid strengthens its magnetic field. This makes a strong magnet.

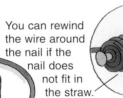

Switching off

Now take one end of the wire away from the battery to stop the current. See if paperclips still stick.

The electromagnet stops working because the magnetic field leaves the wire when the current stops flowing.*

* If the nail inside is still magnetic, turn to page 215 to find out why.

Making a toy crane

You can use an electromagnet to make a crane.

You also need: a cotton reel, short piece of straw, short pencil, scissors, short ruler, small box, sticky tape, Plasticine, 50cm of thread

1. Tape the ruler inside the box, as shown. Stick the cotton reel behind it with Plasticine. Push the pencil into the reel, point downwards.

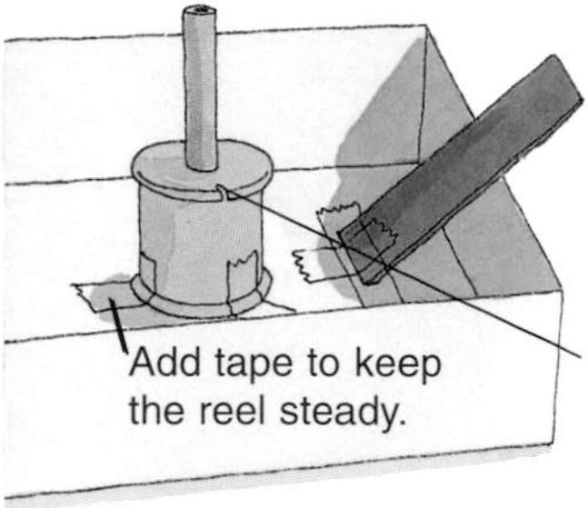

Add tape to keep the reel steady.
One end of a reel has a notch. This goes on top.

2. Tape the straw onto the ruler. Push the thread through the straw. Tie one end to the electromagnet. Tape the other end to the pencil, leaving a tail.

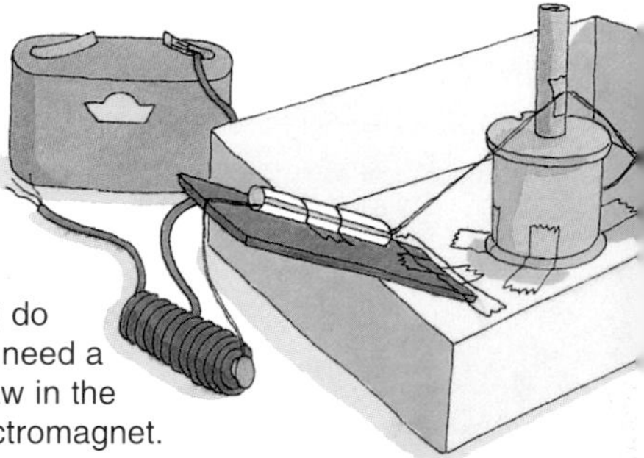

You do not need a straw in the electromagnet.

3. Put the battery inside the box. Tape both wires to the terminals when you want to pick up a load. Turn the pencil to wind the electromagnet up.

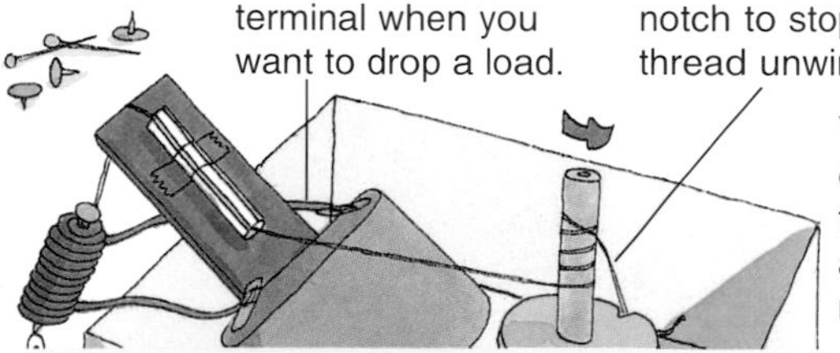

Pull one wire off the terminal when you want to drop a load.
Push the tail into the notch to stop the thread unwinding.

You could stick everything into a truck, instead of a box, to make a mobile crane.

Internet link *Go to* ***www.usborne-quicklinks.com*** *for a link to a Web site where you can find out more about electromagnets.*

Magnets and machines

Magnets help to make many electric machines work. Here you can find out about some of them.

Making electricity

A machine called an electric generator is used to make electricity. The generator has a coil of wire with magnets around it.

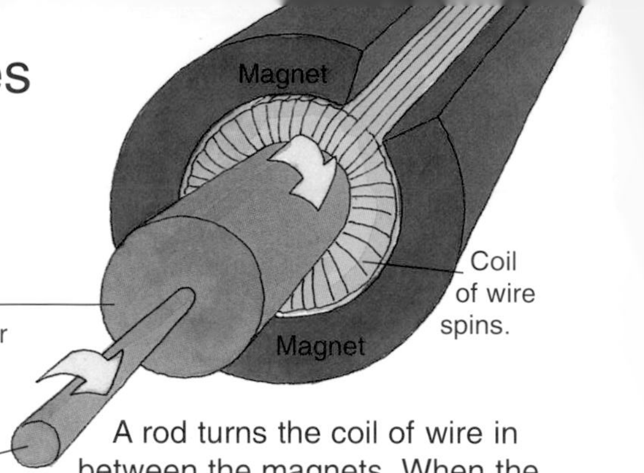

A rod turns the coil of wire in between the magnets. When the coil turns in the magnetic field, electricity flows through the wire.

An electric motor

An electric motor has a coil of wire and magnets like a generator, but works the other way round. The coil is still until electricity flows into it from a battery. The flow of electricity in between the magnets makes the coil spin.

Here you can see how an electric motor turns the wheels in a toy car.

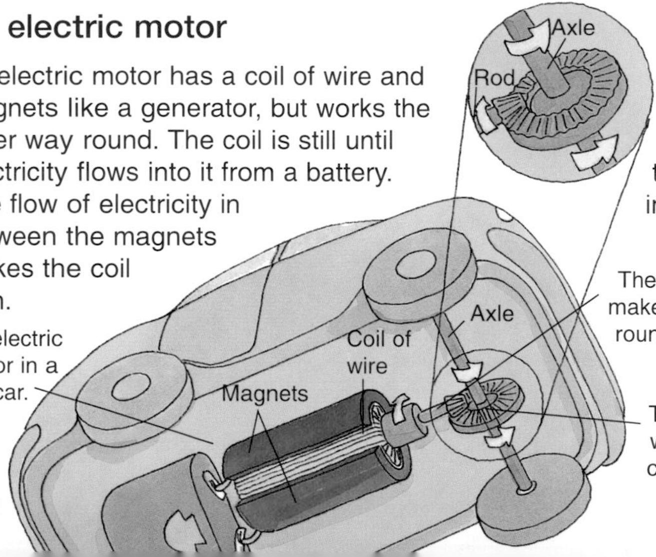

Axle
Rod
An electric motor in a toy car.
Magnets
Coil of wire
Axle
The spinning coil makes this rod turn round and round.
The rod makes the wheels turn, so the car moves along.

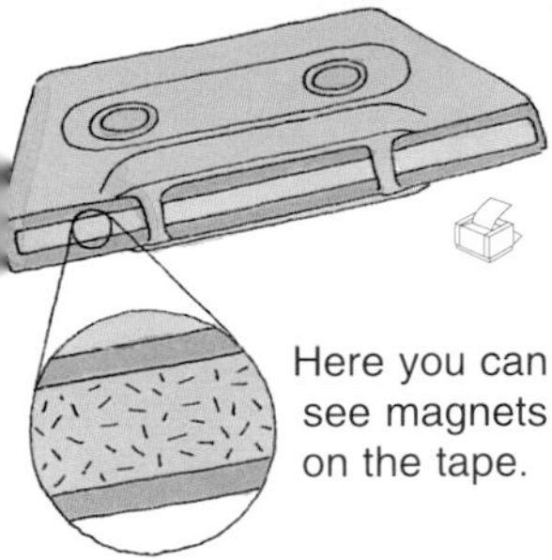

Tape recorders

A tape is covered in tiny magnets. These are used to record sounds in a tape recorder.

When someone speaks into a microphone, it changes the sound into electrical signals.

The signals go to an electromagnet. This arranges the magnets on the tape in a pattern to match the signals.

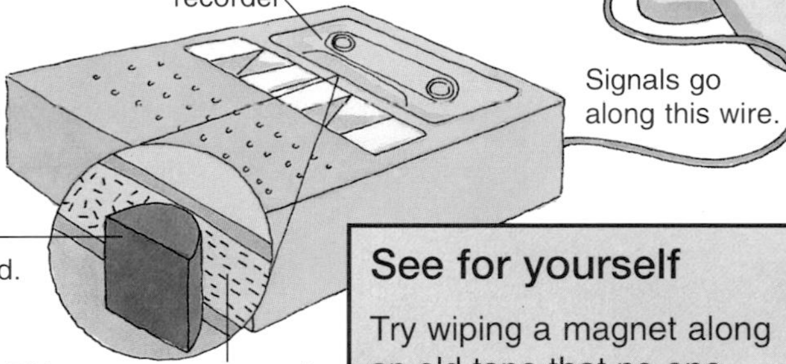

Tape recorder
Signals go along this wire.
The electromagnet is called a recording head.
This pattern stays on the tape to record the sound.

When you play the tape it moves past a different electromagnet, called a playback head. The pattern makes this head give off electric signals.

These are the same as the signals made when the sound was recorded. They go to a loudspeaker which uses them to make the sound again.

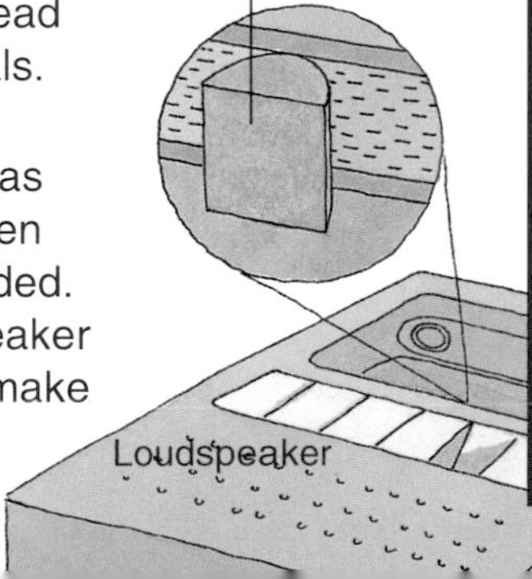

See for yourself

Try wiping a magnet along an old tape that no one wants. Then play the tape.

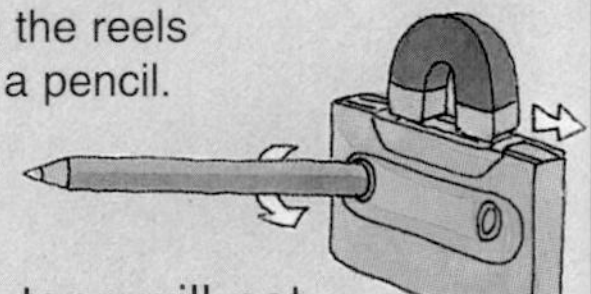

Turn the reels with a pencil.

The tape will not work properly. This is because the magnet has destroyed the pattern that recorded the sound.

How the experiments work

These pages give more detailed explanations of how some of the experiments in this section work. To find out even more about the experiments, visit the Web sites recommended. For links to all these Web sites, go to **www.usborne-quicklinks.com**

Pulling power (pages 196-197)

A strong magnet can affect an object at a greater distance than a weaker one. It is said to have a stronger magnetic field (see page 206).

Internet link *Go to* ***www.usborne-quicklinks.com*** *for a link to a Web site where you can print out a page to do another experiment about magnetic fields. You will need a bar magnet and a compass.*

Gravity

All planets pull things towards their centre. This pull, or gravitational force, makes things feel heavy when you lift them. If it did not act, everything on the planet would become weightless and float around.

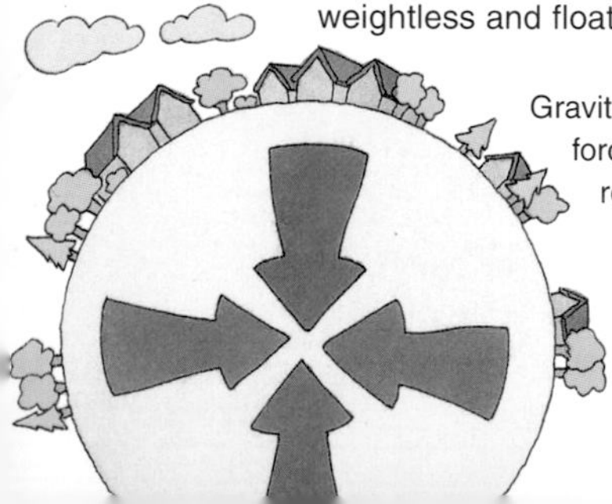

Gravitational force acts all round the planet.

Blocking tests (pages 198-199)

Magnetic force is almost unaffected by things a magnet does not attract. It works as well through a sheet of paper as it does through air. A thick wad of paper may seem to stop a magnet working. But this is simply because the depth of paper keeps objects out of the magnet's field. However, even a thin sheet of iron, steel or nickel does interfere with a magnet's field.

Keepers

Iron keepers trap the magnetic field so there are no free poles (see page 200) to attract other objects. This closed circuit helps to keep the field strong.

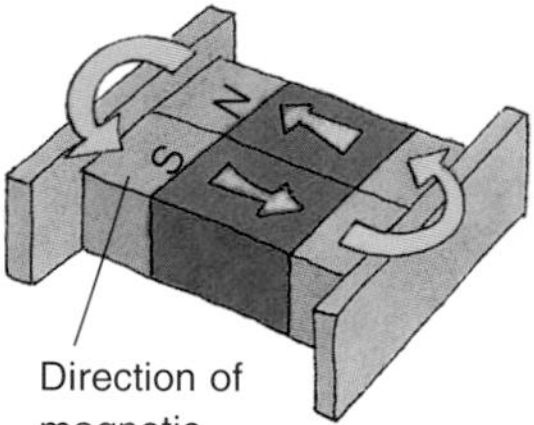

Direction of magnetic field.

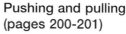

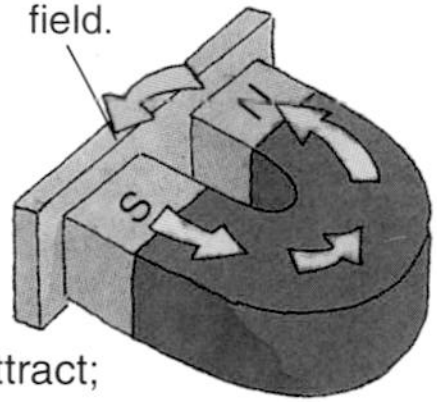

Pushing and pulling (pages 200-201)

Every type and shape of magnet has two kinds of pole; north and south. In every case, unlike poles attract; like ones repel each other.

Internet link *Go to* ***www.usborne-quicklinks.com*** *for a link to a Web site where you can do an interactive experiment about attraction and repulsion.*

Finding your way (pages 202-203)

The Earth's magnetic field (see page 207) acts as if it has a south pole in the Arctic. This attracts the north poles of all magnets. The place where they point is confusingly known as the magnetic north pole.

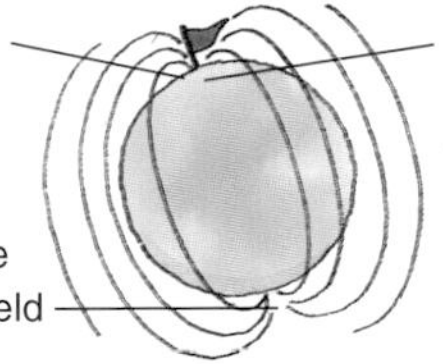

***Internet link** Go to **www.usborne-quicklinks.com** for a link to a Web site where you can find out more about the Earth's magnetic north pole.*

Making magnets (pages 204-205)

Different magnetic metals have different qualities. Soft iron is easy to magnetise but also loses its magnetism easily. Steel is harder to magnetise but keeps its magnetism unless hammered or heated.

Electricity and magnets (pages 208-209)

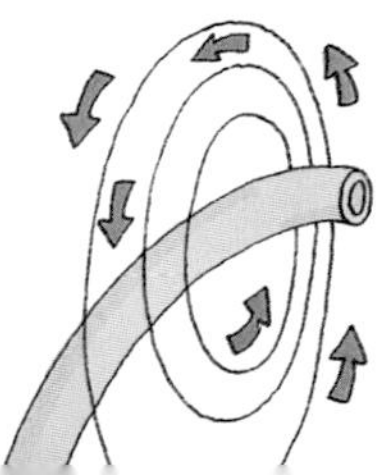

A current flowing in a wire produces a magnetic field in a pattern of concentric circles. A large current has a strong field.

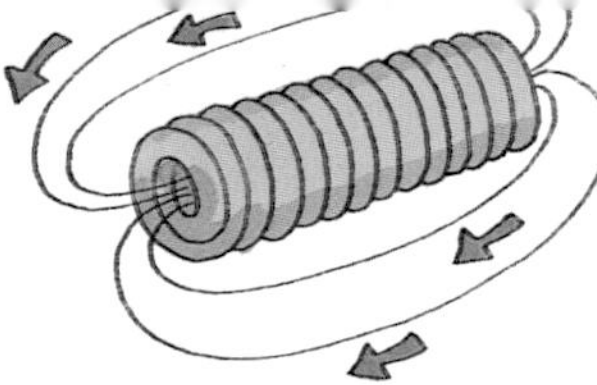

Coiling the wire into a solenoid increases the amount of current-carrying wire. It also creates a magnetic field like that of a bar magnet.

Plastic-coated wire works well and can be bought from any electrical shop. Glazed copper wire gives even better results but is more difficult to find.

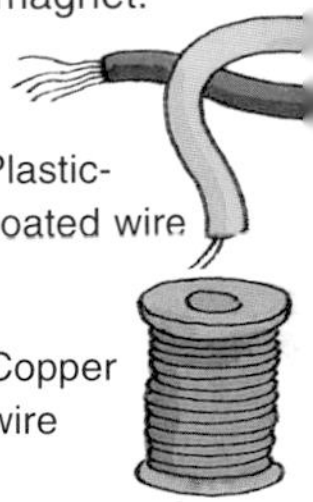

Electromagnets (pages 210-211)

An iron or steel core strengthens the magnetic field of a solenoid. This makes a strong magnet. An electromagnet can be made even stronger by making more turns of the wire.

The core may stay magnetic even when the current is turned off. This depends on the type of metal. Industrial electromagnets use soft iron which does not stay magnetic.

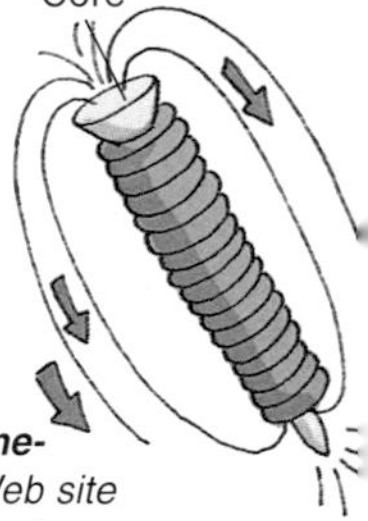

***Internet link** Go to **www.usborne-quicklinks.com** for a link to a Web site where you can find out more about electromagnetic forces.*

More internet links

Here are some more Web sites to visit to find out about magnets. For links to all these sites go to **www.usborne-quicklinks.com** and type in the keywords "pocket scientist 2".

Web site 1 This Web site is packed with experiments to do with magnets. You can make a magnetic field that's stronger than the Earth's, find out how magnetism makes doorbells work and try out a fun experiment with iron filings.

Web site 2 On this site you can discover more about permanent magnets, temporary magnets and electromagnets. You can also find out who discovered magnetism and how it was discovered. There are activities to try out and pictures to colour in.

Web site 3 Read about magnetism and then test your knowledge with an interactive quiz at the end.

Web site 4 Try out lots more experiments with magnets and read more about them on this Web site. You can also learn about magnetism in space and read some fun facts about magnets.

Answers to puzzles

Page 199 - Put the nail under the paper. Then put your magnet on top. The magnet sticks to the nail through the paper.

The paper is now squashed between the nail and the magnet so you can lift it up by raising the magnet.

Page 203 - The hiker has to go north to get to the mountains.

For links to all these sites go to www.usborne-quicklinks.com and type in the keywords "pocket scientist 2".

SCIENCE EXPERIMENTS WITH LIGHT & MIRRORS

Kate Woodward

Designed by Radhi Parekh
Illustrated by Simone Abel
Additional designs: Mary Forster

Consultant: John Baker

CONTENTS

Light all around

Light is all around you. Try the experiments in this section to find out more about light and the different ways it behaves.

Sunlight

The Sun is a ball of burning hot gases. It gives off a very bright light. This light travels a distance of 150 million km (93.2 million miles) to reach the Earth.

Moving light

You need a torch for some of the experiments. Switch one on in a dark room.

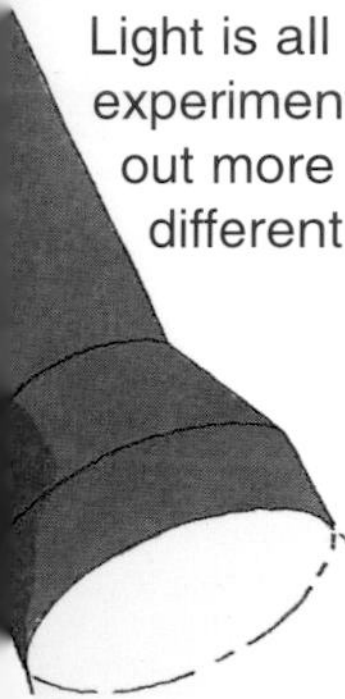

The light travels away from the torch.

See how the torch lights up things on the other side of the room.

Anything that makes light is called a light source. Light travels from its source to light things up far away.

Making light

How many things can you think of that make light? Here are some to start you off.

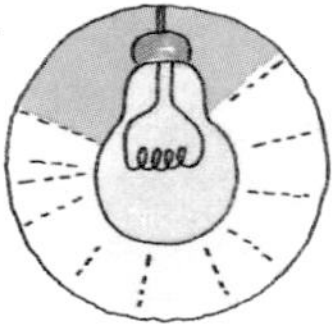

Light moves away from a light bulb to light up a room.

Car headlights can light up the road for a long way ahead.

Speedy light

Light is the fastest thing in the universe. It moves at 300,000 km (186,451 miles) a second. It takes only eight and a half minutes to reach Earth from the Sun.

Passing through

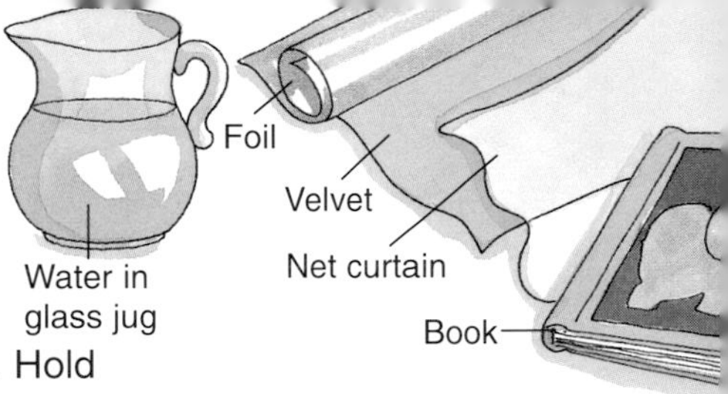

Collect some things to test whether light can travel through them or not. Here are some you can try.

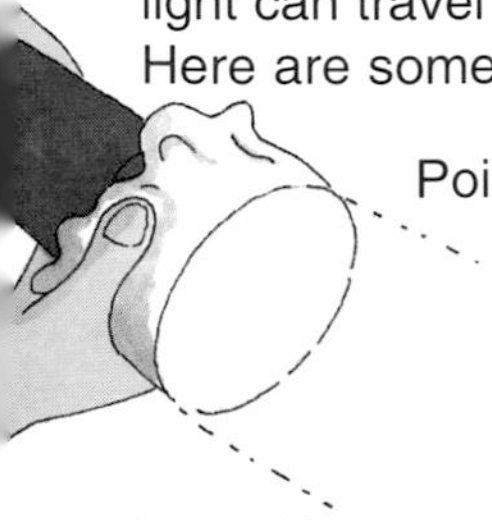

Point a torch at some paper. Hold each thing in front of the torch. Try to guess if it will let light through on to the paper.

Switch on the torch to see if you are right. Make a chart to show what happens with the different things.

You could make your chart like this.

Different names

Clear things that let light through are called transparent. Things that stop light are called opaque. Some things let light through even though you cannot see through them. These are called translucent.

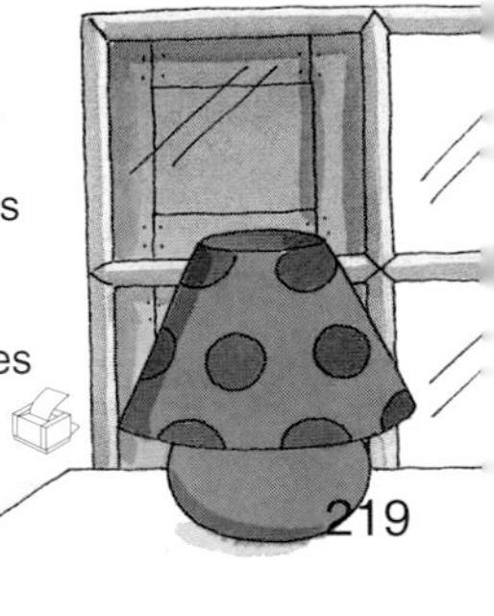

Glass windows are transparent.

Wooden shutters are opaque.

Most lampshades are translucent.

Which comes first?

Thunderclouds make lightning and a rumble of thunder at the same time.

You see lightning before you hear thunder because light travels faster than sound.

Internet link *Go to* ***www.usborne-quicklinks.com*** *for a link to a Web site where you can watch a short movie all about light.*

Travelling light

Although you cannot see it, light is always moving. Here you can find out more about how it travels.

Aiming light

Cover the end of a torch with foil. Make a hole with a pencil so a thin beam of light can shine through.

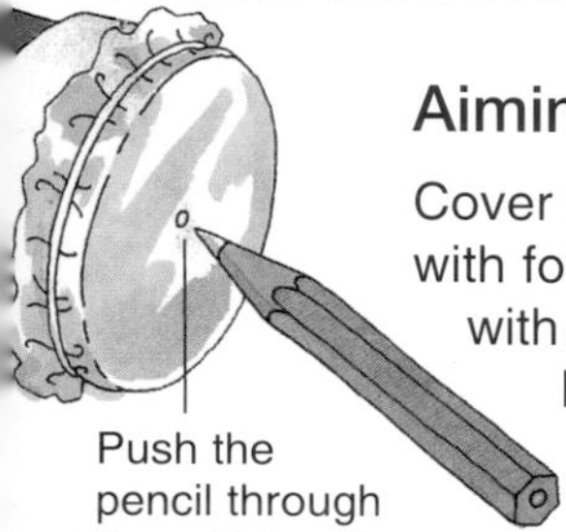

Push the pencil through the middle of the foil.

Move the torch around. Can you make the beam hit anything you want?

It is easy to aim the beam because the light goes in a straight line.

In the spotlight

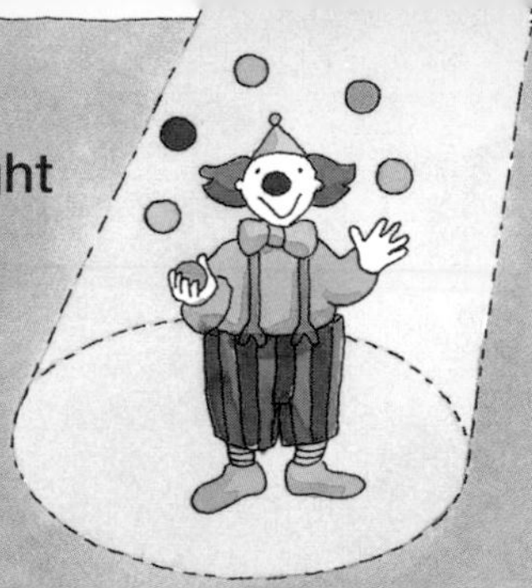

Because light travels in straight lines, strong light from theatre spotlights can be aimed at the actors on a stage.

Rays

Each tiny part of light goes along a straight line. These lines are called rays.

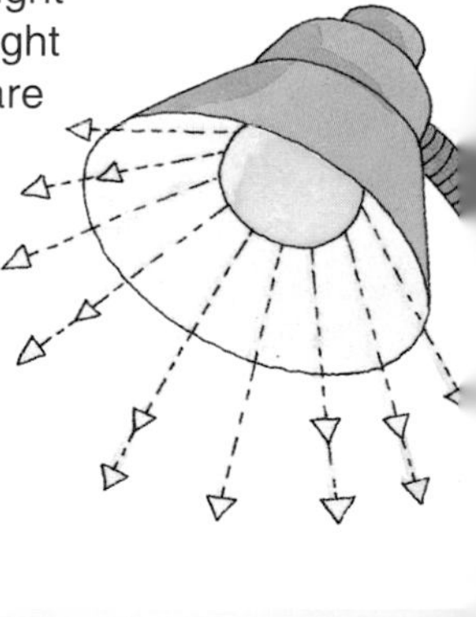

This picture shows how rays travel away from a light source.

 Internet link *Go to* ***www.usborne-quicklinks.com*** *for a link to a Web site with an activity and an interactive quiz about light.*

Bouncing light

Put the foil-covered torch on a table in a dark room. Hold a mirror in front of it. What happens to the beam of light?

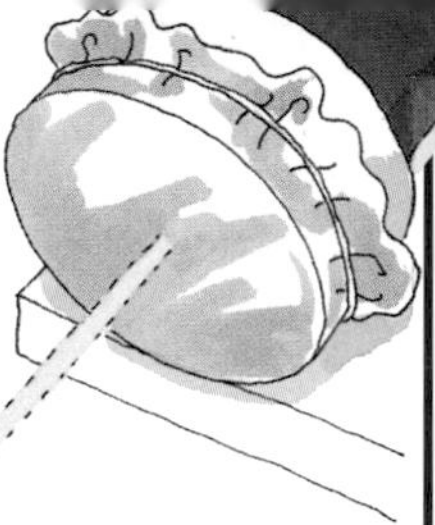

Look out for the light spot at the end of the beam. Is it where you expected?

When light hits things, it can bounce off them and travel in a different direction.

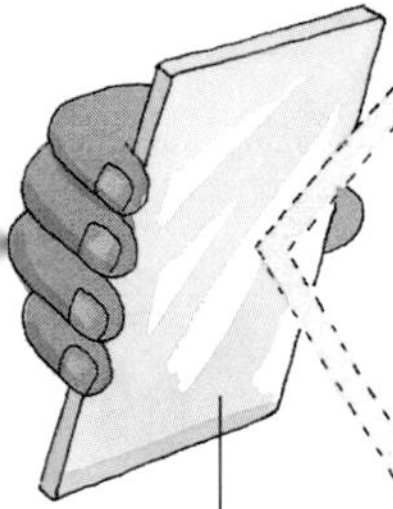

You could try using foil or a shiny tin lid instead of a mirror.

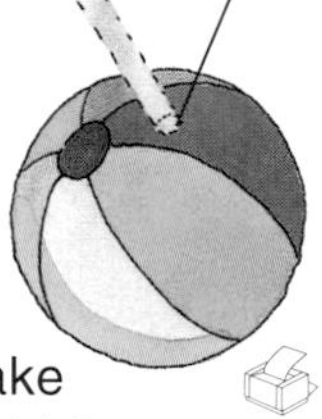

Light spot

Try moving the mirror. Can you make the light spot hit different things in the room?

Why is night dark?

The Earth is like a huge ball. It spins around once every 24 hours. For some of the time your part of the Earth faces the Sun and so it is light.

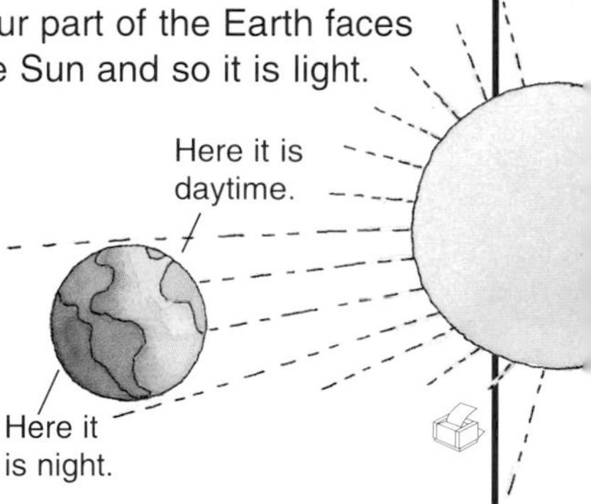

Here it is daytime.
Here it is night.

The sunlight cannot bend around the Earth, so the other side is dark.

How you see

Some light bounces off all the things you see. The light carries a picture of each thing to your eyes.

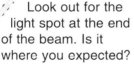

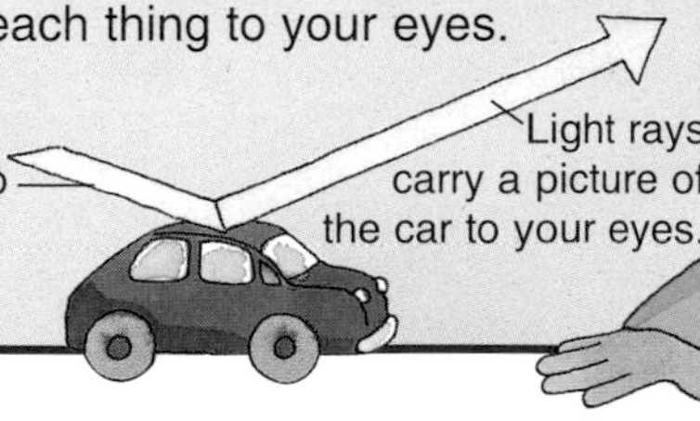

Light goes to this toy car.
Light rays carry a picture of the car to your eyes.

Looking in mirrors

When you look in a mirror you see your own face. The picture in the mirror is called a reflection.

Finding reflections

Look for different things that you can see your face in. What do you notice about them?

Feel each one to find out if it is rough or smooth. Do all the things look shiny?

See if your reflection looks the same in all of them. Is it always the same shape?

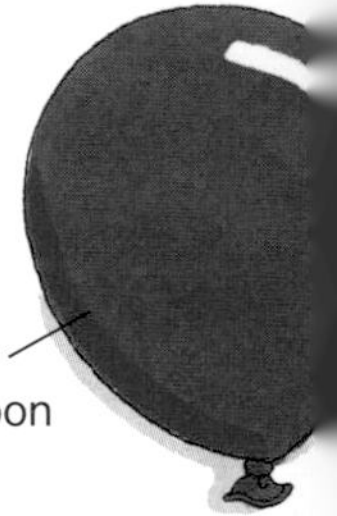

Seeing a reflection

You see a reflection when light rays bounce off something and on to a mirror.

The light rays bounce off the mirror and into your eyes. This makes you see the reflection.

You see the best reflections in things that are flat, shiny and smooth. These make good mirrors.

 Internet link *Go to* ***www.usborne-quicklinks.com*** *for a link to a Web site where you can find out more about mirrors and reflection.*

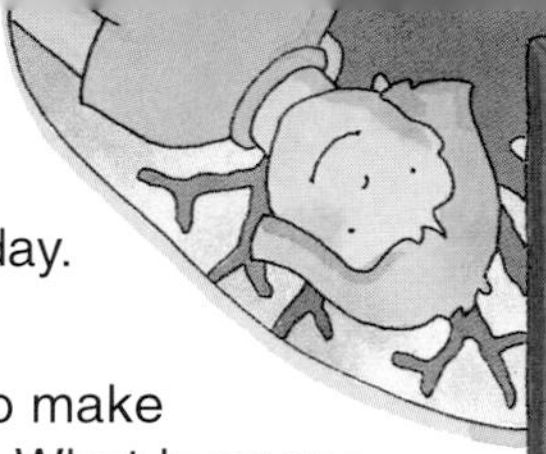

Reflections in water

Look at a puddle on a calm day. It gives a good reflection.

Drop a small pebble in to make ripples in the water. What happens to the reflection?

The light bounces off the ripples in all directions. This makes the reflection disappear.

Glass mirrors

Many mirrors are made of glass. They have a thin layer of silver or aluminium under the glass.

Lots of light bounces off this shiny layer so the mirror gives off a good reflection.

Make an unbreakable mirror

You can use this unbreakable mirror for many of the experiments in this book.

You need:
stiff clear plastic*,
aluminium foil,
stiff cardboard,
scissors,
sticky tape

1. Cut out rectangles from the foil, the plastic and the cardboard.

Make the rectangles all the same size.

2. Put the foil on the cardboard, shiniest side up. Then, put the plastic on top.

3. Put a thin band of tape around the edges to finish it.

*You could use a clear plastic lid from a food container.

Reflections

You do not always see what you expect to see when you look in a mirror. Reflections often look different from real things.

You and your reflection

Look at your reflection in a large mirror. Hold up your left hand.

Watch what happens in the mirror. It's easier if you stand slightly sideways.

Your reflection holds up its right hand. Reflections are always the wrong way around like this. Try other movements to see what happens in the mirror.

Mirror magic

Draw half a circle. Put a mirror along the straight edge.

The mirror shows the half circle back-to-front so it looks like the other half of the circle.

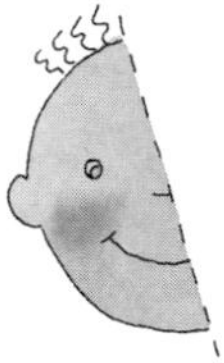

Place your mirror on the dotted lines to complete these three pictures.

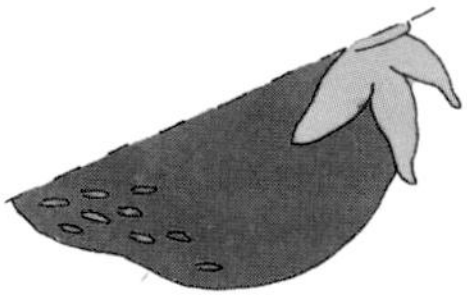

Can you draw halves of other things that you can complete with a mirror?

This only works with things that split into two halves exactly the same. Things like this are called symmetrical.

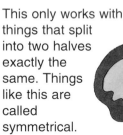

A butterfly is symmetrical.

 Internet link *Go to* ***www.usborne-quicklinks.com*** *for a link to a Web site where you can find out more about mirrors and test yourself as you go along.*

Funny reflections

Find a large, shiny spoon that can act like a mirror. Look at your face in the back of it.

Mirrors that curve outwards like this are called convex.

Is the reflection the same shape as in a flat mirror?

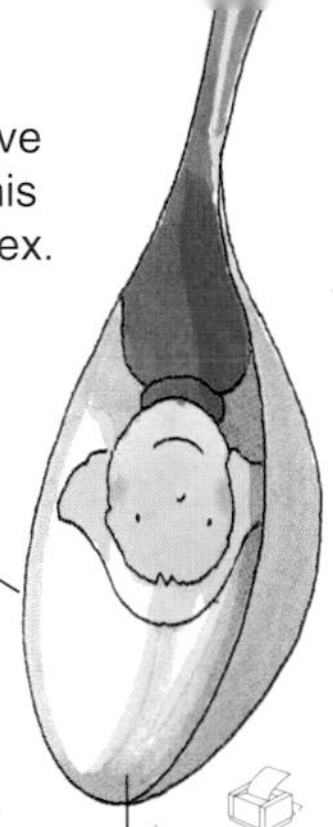

Mirrors that curve inwards like this are called concave.

Now turn the spoon over. What happens to your reflection? Does it change if you bring the spoon closer to your face?

Is the reflection always the same way up?

Curved mirrors even change a reflection's shape. Some can even turn a reflection upside-down.

Trick mirrors

Funfairs often use curved mirrors to make people look a funny shape.

Secret code writing

This secret code can only be read in a mirror.

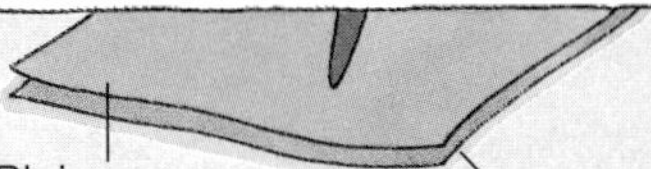

Plain paper

Carbon paper

You need: a mirror, carbon paper, paper, a knitting needle

1. Lay the carbon paper inky side up. Put plain paper over it. 'Write' on top with the knitting needle.

2. The message appears back-to-front on the other side of the plain paper.

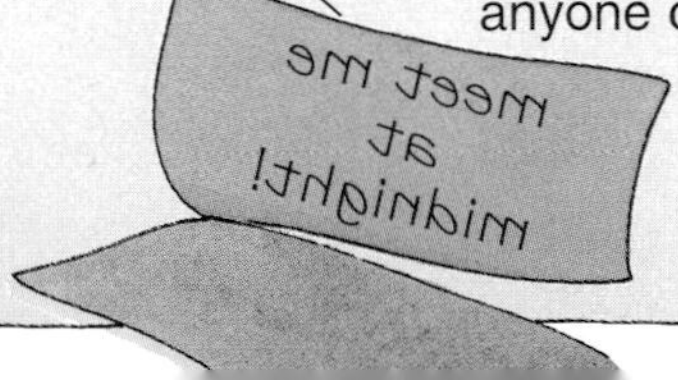

3. Use a mirror to turn the message around so anyone can read it.

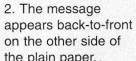

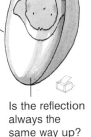

Changing reflections

See what happens to the reflections if you use more than one mirror.

Endless reflections

Put tape down one edge only.

1. Put two mirrors face to face and tape them together.

2. Stand the mirrors up and put something small in between. How many reflections can you see?

3. Now move the mirrors closer together. Watch the reflections.

Count the reflections now.

As the mirrors get closer together, the light bounces from one to the other and back again. You see reflections of reflections.

You see most reflections if you untape the mirrors and hold them face to face either side of the object.

Making shapes

Tape the mirrors together again. Put a pencil in front of them. Can you make its reflection form different shapes?

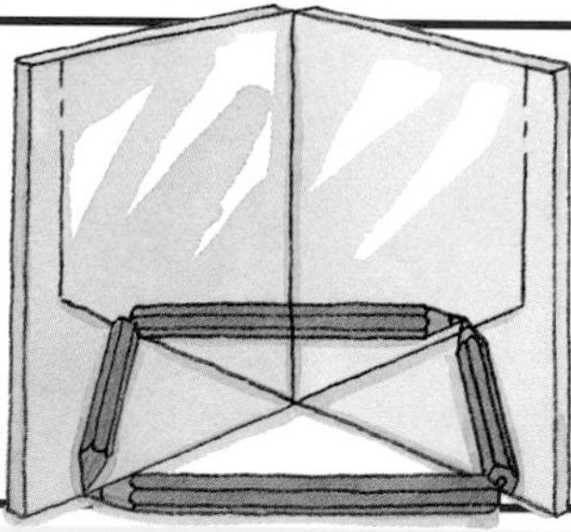

Open or close the mirrors to make these shapes.

Triangle Pentagon Hexagon

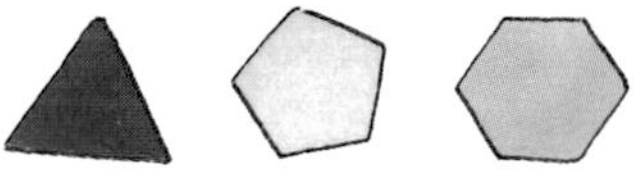

(3 sides) (5 sides) (6 sides)

 Internet link *Go to* ***www.usborne-quicklinks.com*** *for a link to a Web site where you will find games all about mirrors and light.*

Make a kaleidoscope

Kaleidoscopes use reflections to make colourful patterns.

You will need:
3 rectangular mirrors the same size,
coloured paper cut into tiny shapes,
clear plastic, cardboard,
tracing paper, scissors,
sticky tape, a coloured pencil

1. Tape the long sides of the mirrors together.

The mirrors face each other.

2. Stand the mirrors up on some cardboard. Draw around them and cut out the shape.

3. Tape the cardboard to the mirrors. Push a pencil in the middle to make a hole.

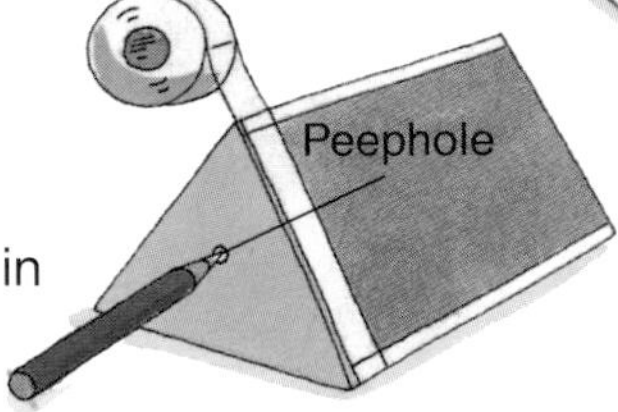

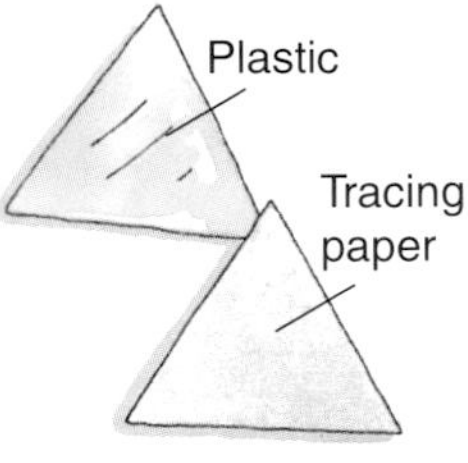

4. Draw around the mirrors on the plastic and tracing paper. Cut out the shapes.

5. Tape two sides of these together to make an envelope. Put the coloured paper inside.

You only need a few pieces.

6. Tape up the third side and stick the envelope to the open end of the mirrors.

The tracing paper goes on the outside.

7. Point this end to the light and look through the peephole.

The mirrors reflect the shapes in a pattern. It changes when you shake the kaleidoscope.

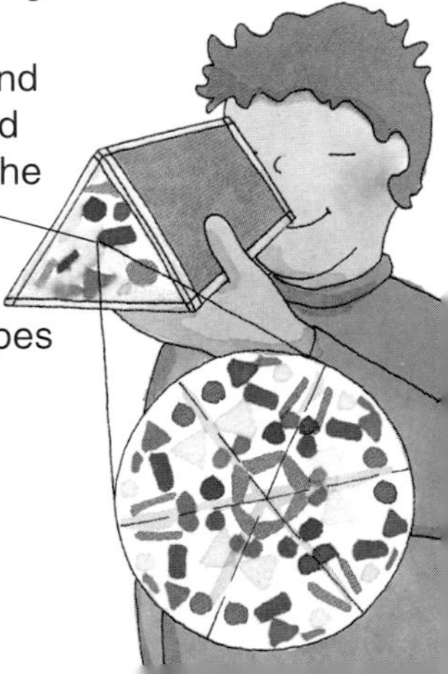

Looking around

Mirrors can help you see around corners and in awkward places. Here you can find out how.

Looking behind

Hold a mirror in front of you. Can you see anything else besides your reflection?

Try moving the mirror slightly to one side.

You can see things behind you because light bounces off them and on to the mirror.

Ask a friend to move around behind you. Can you always see her reflection in the mirror?

You have to tilt the mirror to see your friend in different places.

Make a periscope

This shows you how to use mirrors to make a periscope.

You will need:
a long, thin cardboard box,
2 small mirrors the same size,
scissors,
sticky tape

1. Ask an adult to cut matching slits in two opposite sides of the box, as shown. Do this near the top and the bottom.

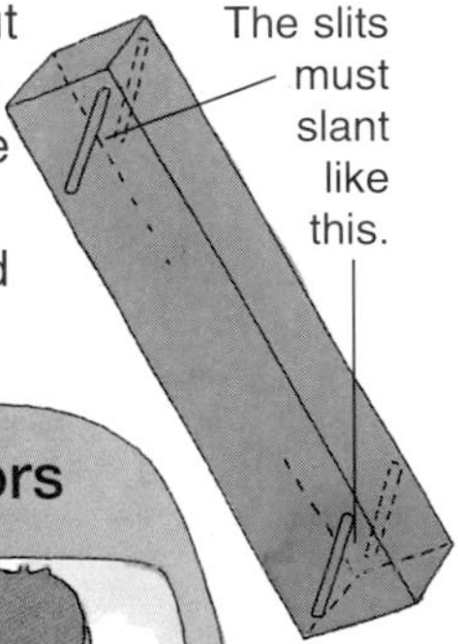

The slits must slant like this.

Useful mirrors

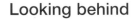

Drivers use mirrors to help them see other traffic on the road behind them.

***Internet link** Go to **www.usborne-quicklinks.com** for a link to a Web site where you can play a simple mirror game.*

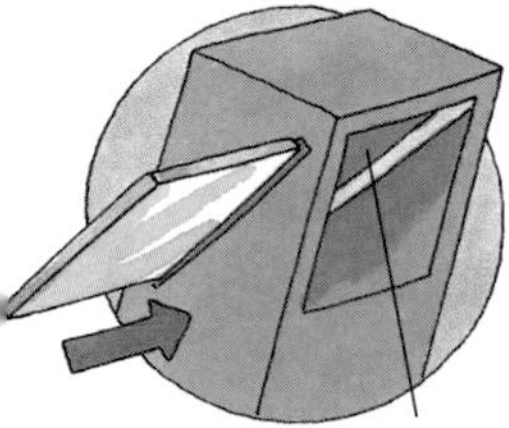

Cut the window in the side nearest the top of the slits.

2. Cut a window level with the top slits. Slide a mirror though the slits so the shiny side faces the window. Tape it in place.

3. Cut another window, this time level with the bottom slits on the opposite side of the box. Slide a second mirror through the slits and fasten it with tape.

The shiny side of the mirror faces the window.

4. Point the periscope over a wall. Look through the bottom window. What can you see?

How it works

You can see things over the wall because light from them travels to the top mirror.

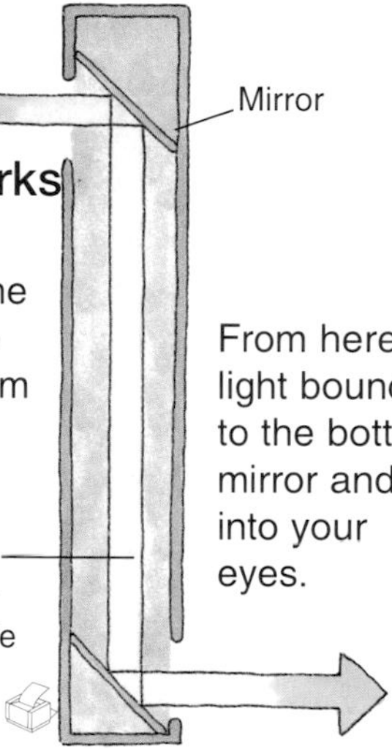
Mirror
Light bounces from one mirror to another inside the box.

From here, light bounces to the bottom mirror and into your eyes.

Up periscope

The crew of a submarine can see what is happening above the surface by raising a periscope out of the water.

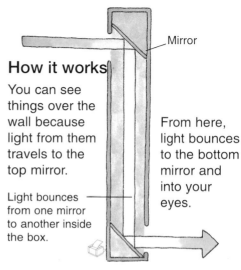

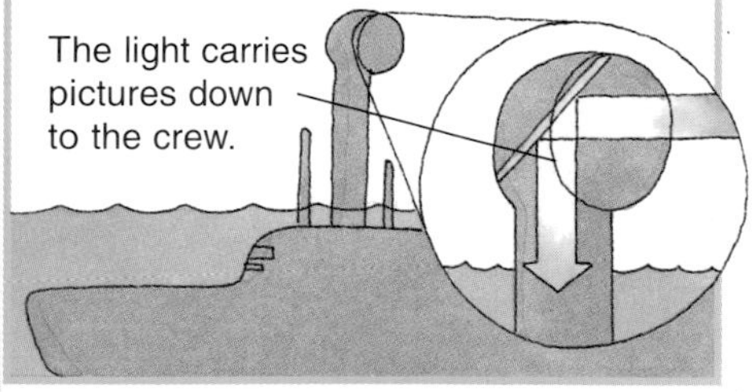
The light carries pictures down to the crew.

Tricks of light

Light can play some surprising tricks on your eyes. You cannot always believe what you see.

Straight or bent?

Put a straw in a glass of water. Look down on it from above. What happens to the straw?

The straw looks bent at the surface of the water.

Try other straight things to see if they look bent too.

Light travels more slowly through water than through air. As it slows down, it changes direction. This can make things in water look bent when they are really straight.

Appearing coin

Stick a coin to the bottom of a bowl with tape. Look over the edge of the bowl, then move back until you just cannot see the coin anymore.

Keep still and ask a friend to pour water into the bowl. What happens?

When the bowl is empty, the edge of the bowl stops you seeing the coin.

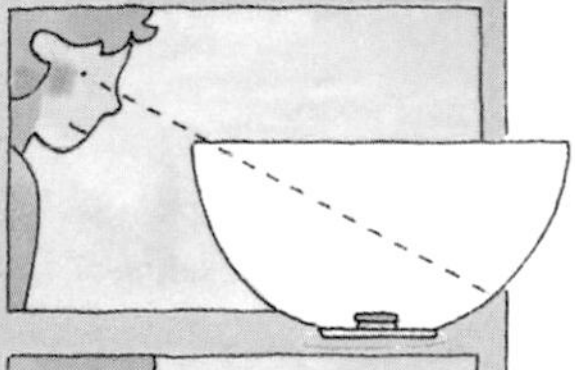

When the bowl is full, the light bends over the edge, so you can see the coin.

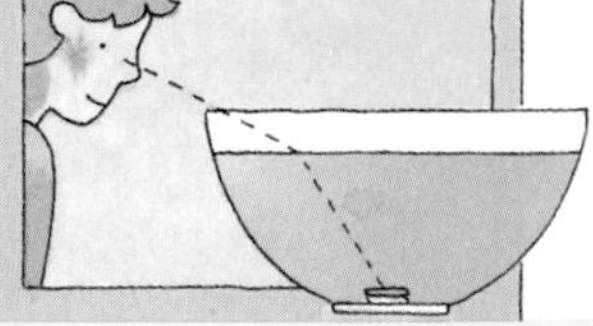

 Internet link *Go to* ***www.usborne-quicklinks.com*** *for a link to a Web site where you can try an optical illusion experiment.*

Changing shape

Collect some things that you can see through. Hold them in front of a book. What happens to the words?

Try some of these things.

The words look a different shape because light bends when it passes through any clear object.

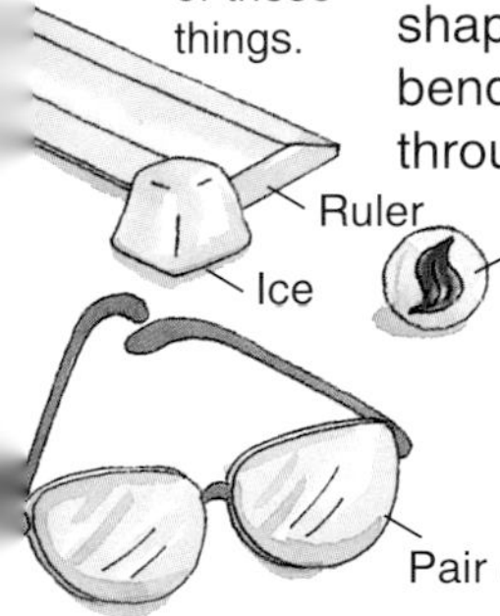

The amount it bends depends on the shape of the object.

Fill a clean glass jar with water and stand it in front of the page. The jar and the water make a solid curved shape.This shape bends the light to make the words look bigger. This is called magnification.

The words look bigger through the jar.

In the pool

A swimming pool looks shallower than it really is because of the way light is bent through water. This also makes your legs look short and fat.

Magnifying glass

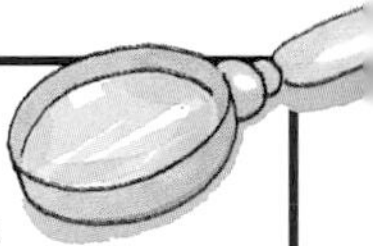

A magnifier is made of a piece of solid curved glass called a lens. The lens makes light bend just as a jar of water does.

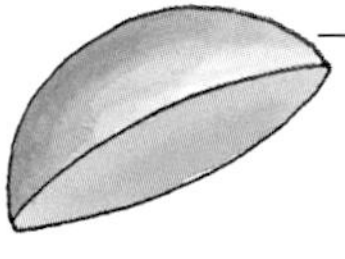

This lens has been cut in half so you can see how it is curved.

Lenses are used in microscopes to make tiny things look many times bigger.

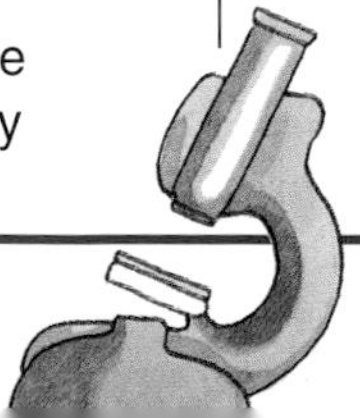

Making pictures

Photographs are pictures made by light rays. Here you can find out how light can make pictures and how light helps you to see pictures too.

Make a pinhole camera

Light can make pictures appear for a moment inside this camera.

1. Cut out the top of the box, then paint the inside black. Let the paint dry. Tape tracing paper over the opening.

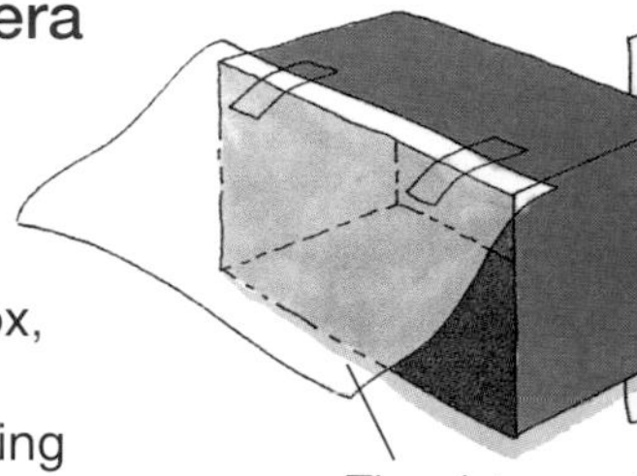

You need:
a cardboard box,
black paint and
paintbrush, tracing
paper, sticky tape,
scissors, a pin,
a dark cloth

The pictures will appear on this tracing paper screen.

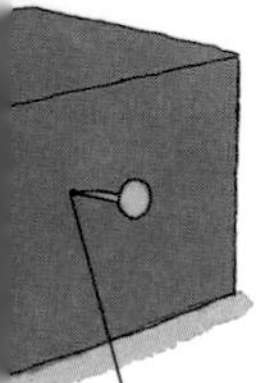

2. Use a pin to push a tiny hole in the box, opposite the tracing paper screen.

3. Go outside. Hold the screen up to your eyes. Ask a friend to put a cloth over your head and around the sides of the box.

Point the hole at different things to get a picture on the screen. Do you see anything surprising?

How the pictures appear

Light rays bounce off things and carry a picture through the pinhole on to the screen.

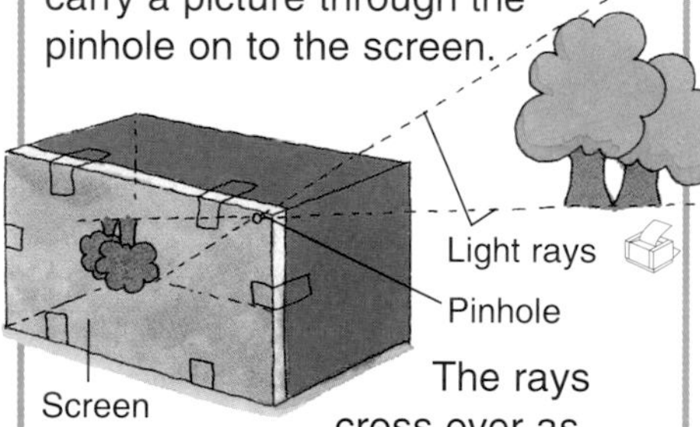

The rays cross over as they pass through the pinhole, so the pictures appear upside-down.

 Internet link *Go to* ***www.usborne-quicklinks.com*** *for a link to a Web site where you can watch a short movie about how you see.*

Taking photographs

Real cameras have film at the back instead of a screen.

When you press a button, a shutter lets light in. The light marks a picture on the film. This can be printed on to paper to make a photograph.

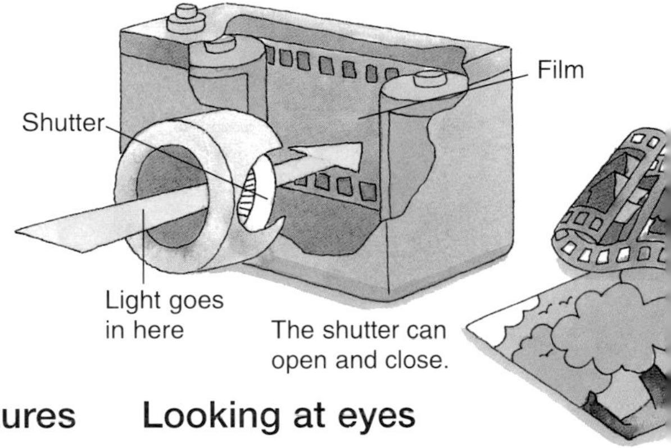

How your eyes see pictures

Your eye works a little like a pinhole camera. A hole at the front, called the pupil, lets light in.

The light carries a picture to the back of the eye. This part is called the retina.

This shows the inside of the eye.

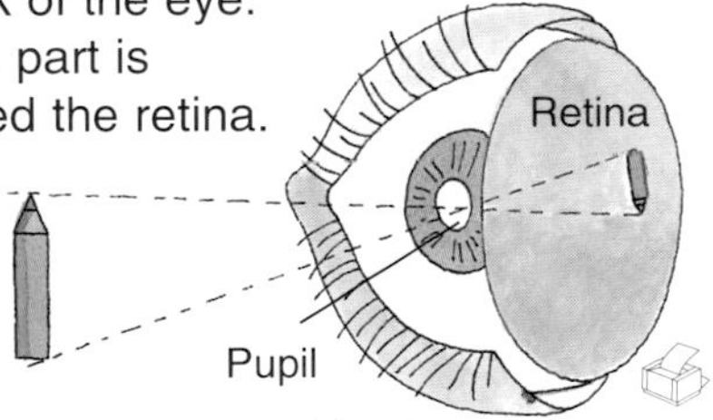

This picture is upside-down. Your brain turns it around so that you see things the right way up.

Looking at eyes

Stand in a dim room for a few minutes and look at your eyes in a mirror. Look closely at your pupils. Then put the light on. See how your pupils change size.

In dim light pupils open up to let more light in so you can see more.

In bright light pupils close up to stop too much light damaging your eyes.

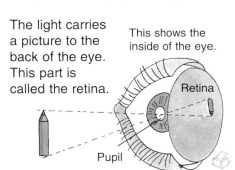

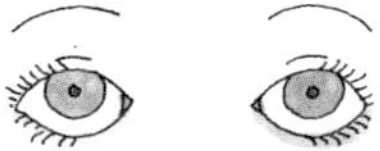

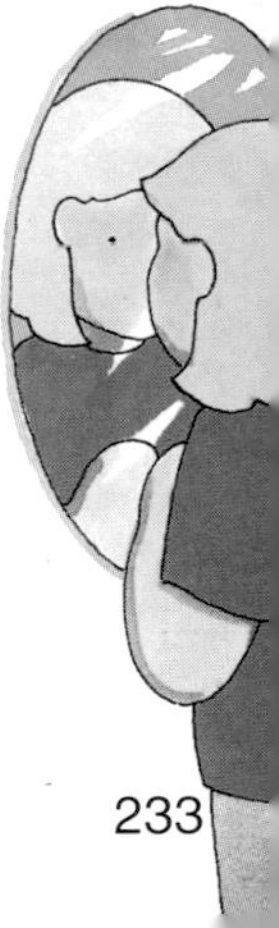

The colour of light

Most light looks clear or white, but it is really a mixture of different colours.

Make your own rainbow

You can make the different colours appear like this.

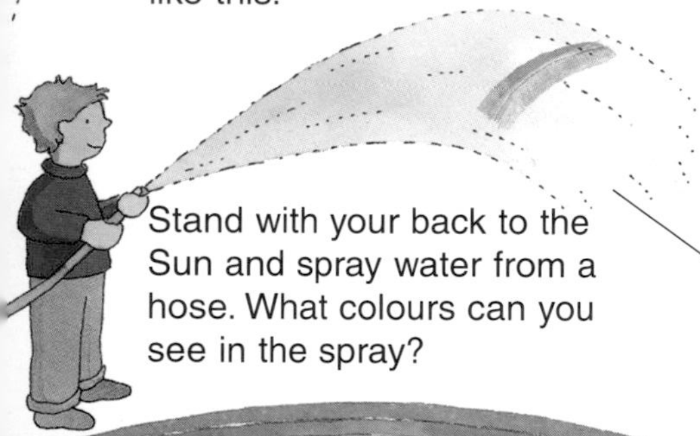

Stand with your back to the Sun and spray water from a hose. What colours can you see in the spray?

Look into the spray against a dark wall or hedge.

Colour wheel

You need: cardboard, a jar, coloured crayons, scissors, a pencil, a ruler

You can make colours change with this spinning colour wheel.

1. Draw around the bottom of a jar to make a circle. Cut the circle out.

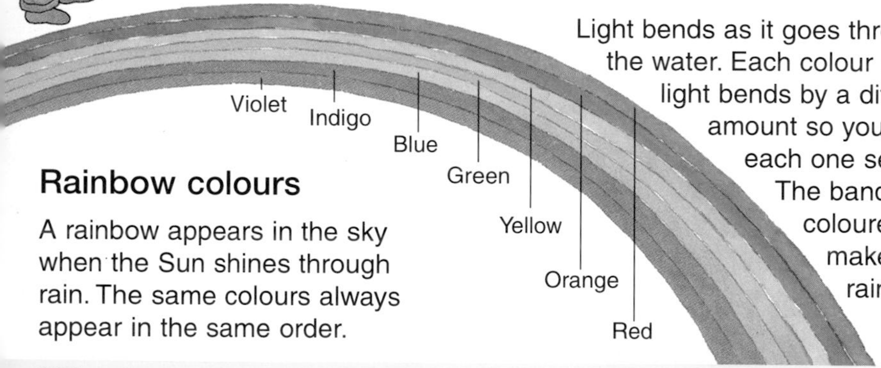

Light bends as it goes through the water. Each colour of light bends by a different amount so you see each one separately. The bands of coloured light make a rainbow.

Rainbow colours

A rainbow appears in the sky when the Sun shines through rain. The same colours always appear in the same order.

 Internet link *Go to* ***www.usborne-quicklinks.com*** *for a link to a Web site where you can find out how to make an indoor rainbow.*

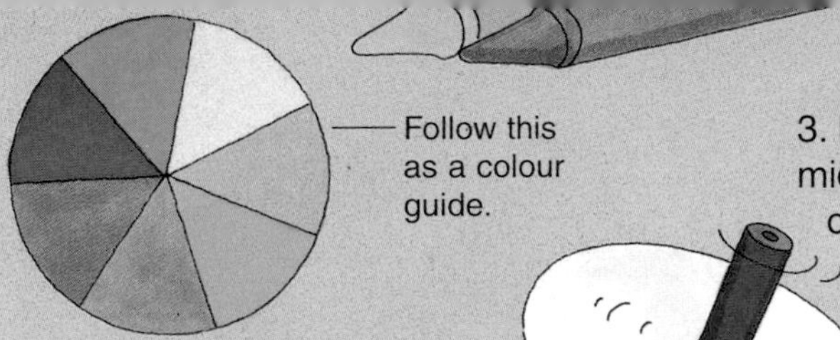

Follow this as a colour guide.

3. Push a sharp pencil through the middle of the circle. Spin it quickly on a table. Watch what happens to the colours on the card.

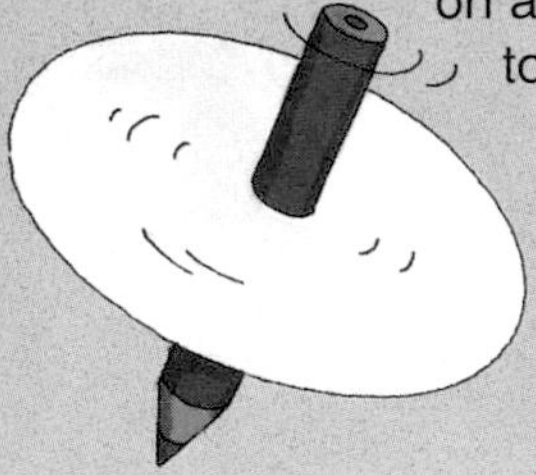

2. Divide the circle into seven roughly equal parts. Colour each part a different rainbow colour.

Different colours of light bounce off each part of the wheel. As the wheel spins, these merge to make one very pale colour.

Coloured things

Most things only let some colours of light bounce off them. You can see the colours as they bounce off.

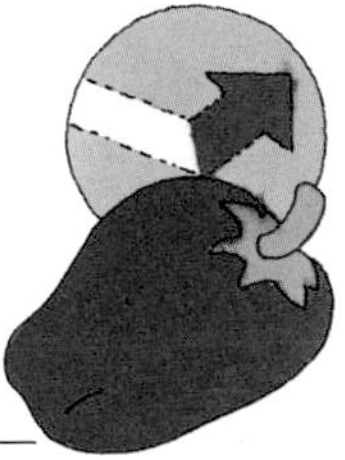

This red pepper looks red because only red light bounces off it.

If all the colours bounce off something, you see them mixed together. This mixture looks white.

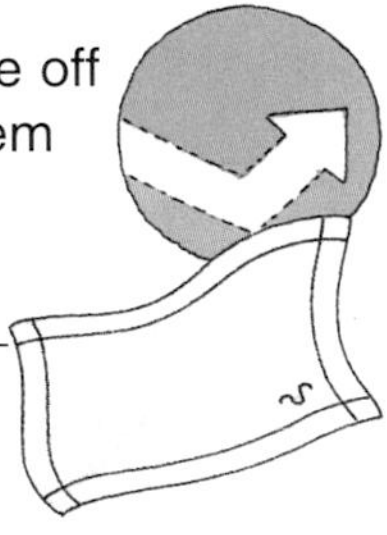

This hanky looks white because all the colours bounce off it.

Changing colour

Collect some see-through sweet wrappers in different colours. Look at some white paper through each one. Does the paper always look white?

All the colours of light bounce off the paper, but each wrapper only lets its own colour through. This makes the paper look the same colour as the wrapper.

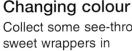

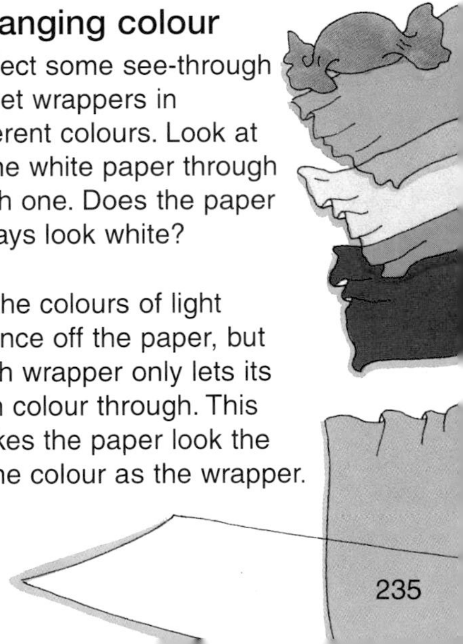

Light and shadow

Whenever there is light, things have shadows. Here you can find out how shadows happen.

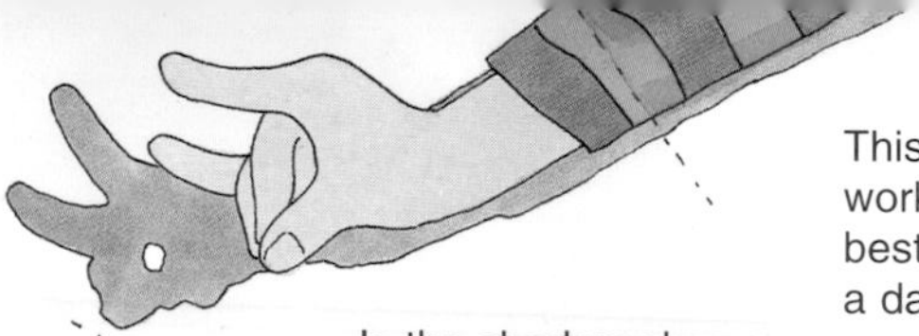

This works best in a dark room.

Is the shadow always the same shape and size as your hand?

Making shadows

Put a torch on a chair and shine it at a wall. Put your hand in front. What do you see on the wall?

A shadow shows where your hand blocks the light and stops it reaching the wall.

Make different shapes with your hand. See what happens to the shadow.

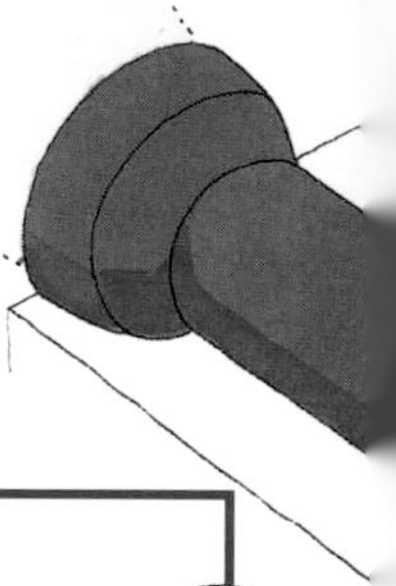

Sun shadows

Things outside have shadows because they keep sunlight from reaching the ground.

Go outside with a friend on a sunny day. Measure each other's shadows at different times. Does your shadow stay the same length?

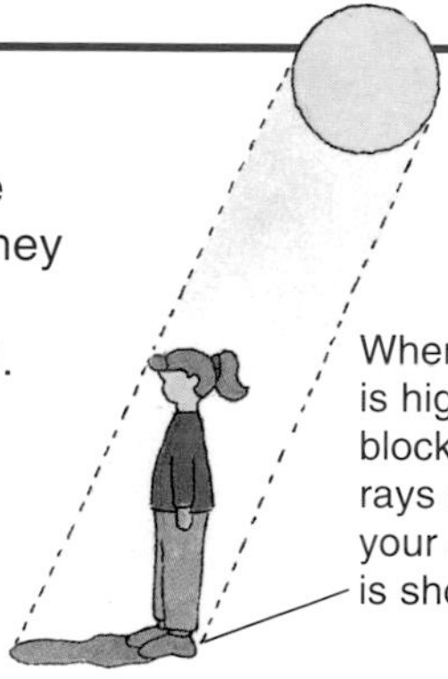

When the Sun is high you only block out a few rays of light so your shadow is short.

All shadows are short at midday, when the Sun is high in the sky.

When the Sun is low you block out more rays of light and so your shadow is long.

Shadows are longer in the morning and evening, when the Sun is low.

 Internet link *Go to* ***www.usborne-quicklinks.com*** *for a link to a Web site where you can find out how to use shadows for measuring.*

Make a shadow theatre

1. Cut the top and bottom out of a cardboard box. Cut a slot in each side, as shown.

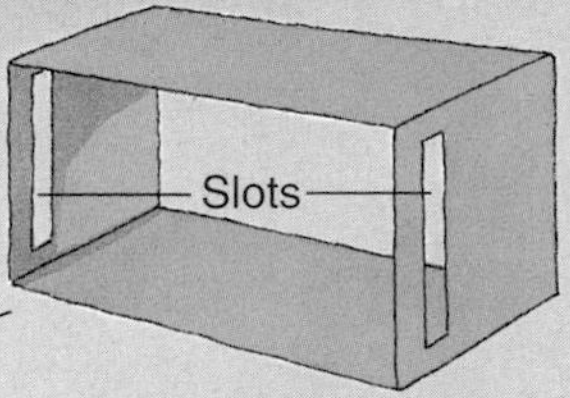

2. Cut out cardboard shapes for puppets. Tape each one to a ruler.

Give your shadow show in a dark room.

Move the puppets to make the shadows act out a story.

3. Tape tracing paper over one end of the box. Push the puppets through the slots. Shine a light behind the puppets to make their shadows appear.

Shadow clock

Early on a sunny morning, push a stick firmly into the ground. Put a stone at the end of the stick's shadow.

Write the time on the stone with chalk.

See where the shadow is after an hour. Mark the shadow again with another stone. Do this every hour until late afternoon.

The shadow moves because the Sun moves across the sky. The shadow always falls on the side of the stick which is away from the Sun.

The next day you can tell the time by seeing which stone the shadow is on.

The stones show how the shadow moves.

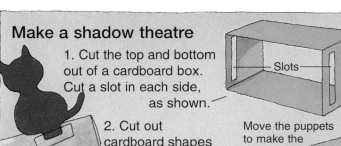

How the experiments work

These pages give more detailed explanations of how the experiments in this section work. To find out even more about the experiments, visit the Web sites recommended. For links to all these Web sites, go to **www.usborne-quicklinks.com**

Travelling light (pages 220-221)

Light rays are given off from all light sources. They spread out as they go. Objects further away from a source are less brightly lit than those close to it because fewer rays hit the same surface area.

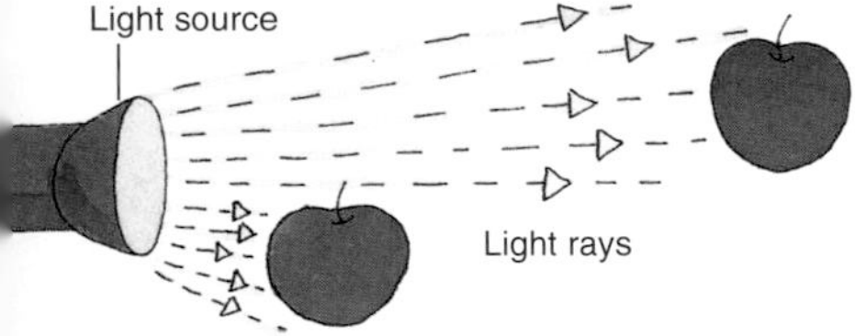

***Internet link** Go to **www.usborne-quicklinks.com** for a link to a Web site where you can find out more about how light travels.*

Safety with mirrors

It is safer to put tape around the edges and across the back of a glass mirror. This stops pieces of glass from scattering if the mirror breaks.

Reflections (pages 224-225)

The way light rays bounce off a mirror affects the way you see the image, or reflection, in the mirror.

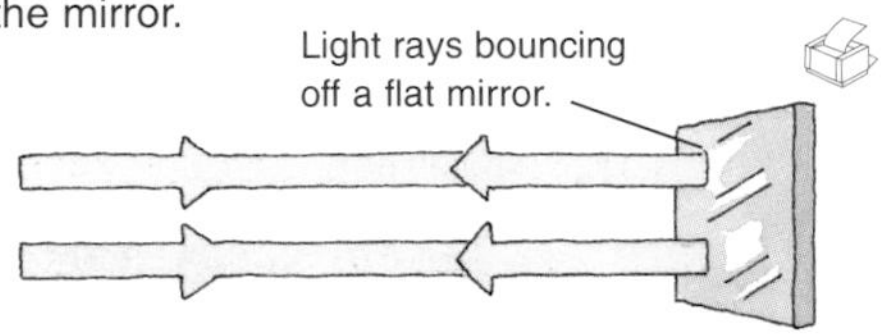

When light rays hit a flat mirror head on, they bounce straight back. The image looks the same size as the object.

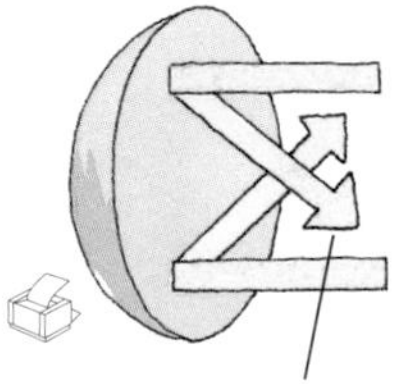

When light rays hit a concave mirror they bounce inwards so they cross. This makes the image look upside-down, unless you are very close to the mirror.

Light rays bouncing off a concave mirror.

A convex mirror makes light rays bounce outward. This makes the image look smaller than the real object.

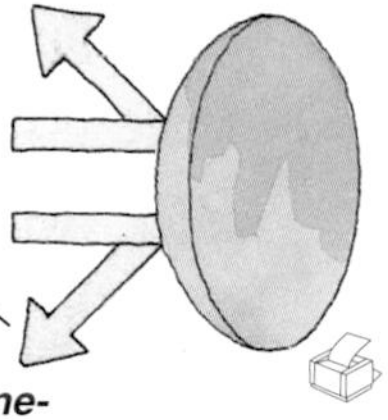

Light rays bouncing off a convex mirror.

***Internet link** Go to **www.usborne-quicklink.com** for a link to a Web site where you can discover how light reflects off smooth and rough surfaces.*

Endless reflections (pages 226-227)

The smaller the angle between two mirrors, the more light can bounce between them. This results in more reflections. In theory, you can see an infinite number of reflections from a point between two parallel mirrors. In real life, this is impossible because you cannot stand between the mirrors without getting in the way of the reflected light.

Tricks of light (pages 230-231)

The way light rays change direction as they travel from one material (such as air or water) to another is known as refraction.

Magnifiers

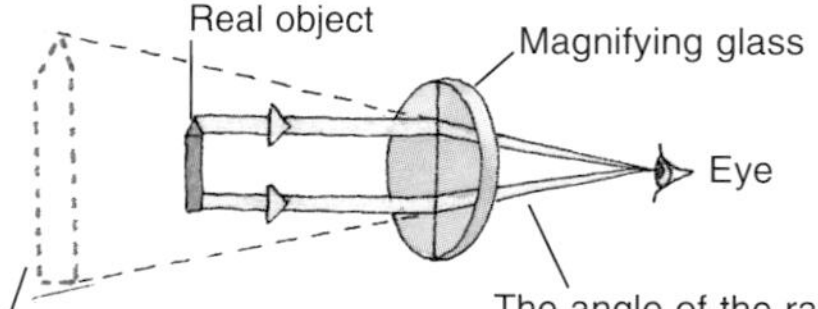

Rays of light reflected from an object are bent inward as they go through a magnifying lens. The angle of the rays travelling into your eye causes the image you see to look bigger than the object.

Making pictures (pages 232-233)

The picture inside the pinhole camera may be blurred because the rays from a particular point of an object do not hit the screen at the same place. In modern cameras (and in the human eye) a lens bends so that rays coming from any one point on the object meet to form a clear image.

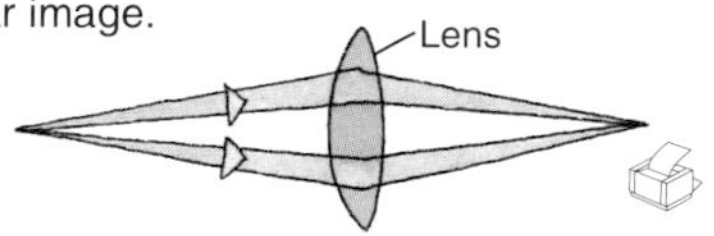

The colour of light (pages 234-235)

Different colours of light bounce off different parts of the spinner. As it turns, they mix into one colour. This looks near-white, not pure white, because the colours of the crayon on the spinner are not exactly the same as those of light.

Internet link *Go to* ***www.usborne-quicklinks.com*** *for a link to a Web site where you can discover what happens when you mix coloured light.*

Light and shadow (pages 236-237)

The shadow clock only tells the time accurately for a few days. This is because the relative positions of the Earth and the Sun slowly change throughout the year. This gradually changes the place where the shadow falls at a given time.

More internet links

Here are some more Web sites to visit to find out about light and mirrors. For links to all these sites go to **www.usborne-quicklinks.com** and type in the keywords "pocket scientist 2".

Web site 1 Discover how different materials can change the speed of light. You can also read fun facts about what might happen if you could travel at the speed of light, and play a time travel game.

Web site 2 On this Web site you can find out some great facts about coloured light and then test your knowledge with a interactive quiz.

Web site 3 Try out an interactive experiment about light detectors. There are also two experiments to try out at home - one to play tricks on your eyes and one to reflect light with a mirror.

Web site 4 On this Web site you can try out an experiment with shadows to find out more about the way light travels.

For links to all these sites go to www.usborne-quicklinks.com and type in the keywords "pocket scientist 2".

SCIENCE EXPERIMENTS WITH WATER

Helen Edom

Designed by Jane Felstead
Illustrated by Simone Abel
Edited by Cheryl Evans

Consultant: Frances Nagy (Primary Science Adviser)

CONTENTS

Experimenting with water

Water behaves in some surprising ways. The experiments in this section will help you find out about them.

Things you need

You can do all the experiments with everyday things. Here are some useful things to collect.

Being a scientist

Read what you have to do carefully. See if you can guess what might happen before you try an experiment.

Watch closely to see if you were right. Write or draw everything you notice in a notebook.

Changing shape

Try doing these things to start finding out about water.

Pour water onto some hard ground outside. Pour more water into a small jar. Does the water make the same shape?

Looking at the top

Try gently shaking a half-full bottle of water. What happens to the top, or surface, of the water? Let the bottle stand. What happens to the top now?

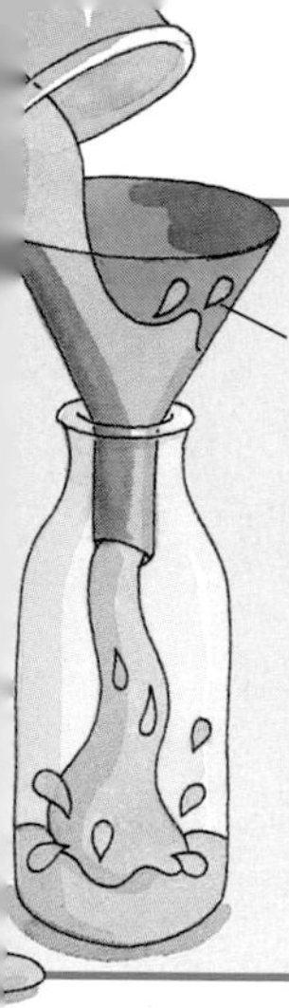

Use a funnel so you don't spill any.

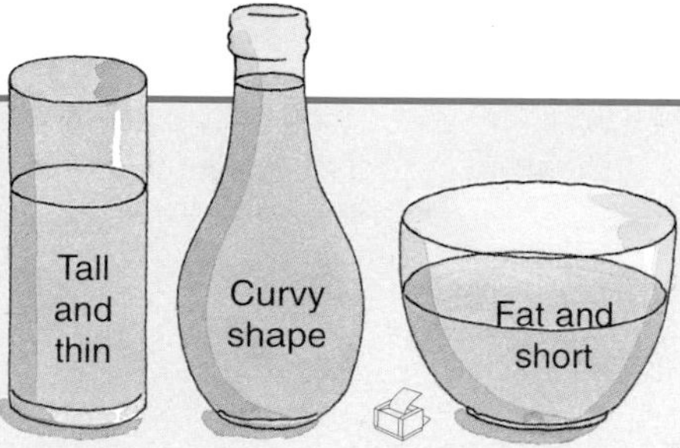

Show they all hold the same amount by emptying them back into the jar, one at a time.

Collect all sorts of glasses and bottles. Pour a full jar of water into each one. Can the water change to any shape?

The water looks different in each thing. Ask a friend to guess which has the most water inside.

Rest the bottle on books to keep it steady.

What do you think will happen if you tilt the bottle? Can you make the top of the water slope? Try it and see. Check the top against a level table.

Now bend a clear plastic tube* into a U-shape. Hold it under a tap to get water inside. Is the top of the water at the same height (level) on both sides?

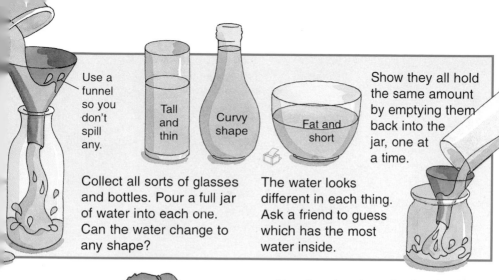

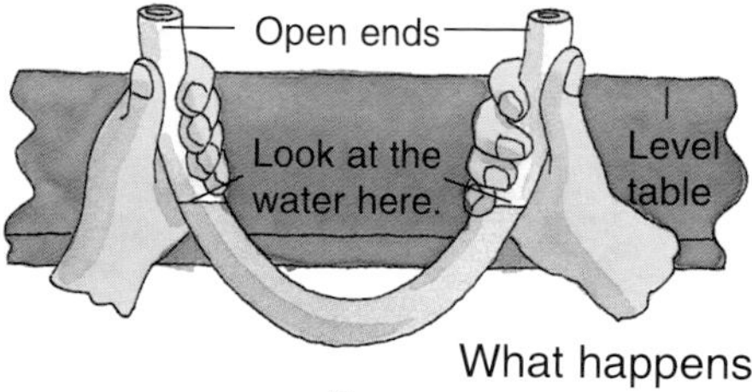

What happens if you raise one end? Watch very carefully.

*You can buy this cheaply from a hardware shop.

Floating

Some things float on water while others sink.

Which things float?

Collect some things to test for floating. Can you guess which ones float before you put them in water?

Make a chart to show your results.

Look at the things that float. Are they all light? Are any of them big? Do they all float in the same way?

Guess what happens if you attach a thing that floats to one that sinks.

Underwater floating

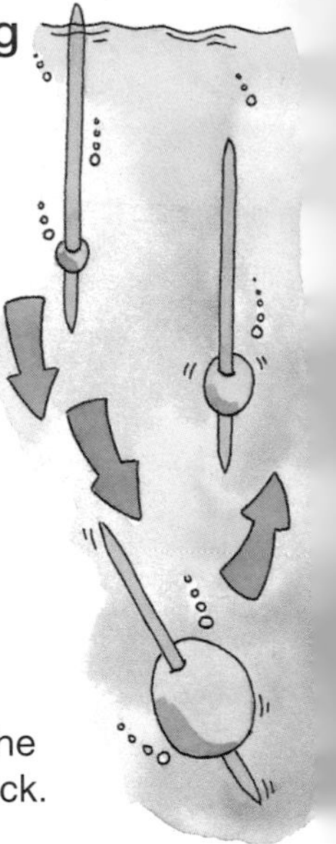

Attach some Plasticine to a toothpick to make it float upright. Add more until it sinks.

Take off a little at a time. Can you make the stick float just under the surface?

Pushing power

Try pushing a blown-up balloon into a bucket of water. It is hard to do. The water seems to push back.

What happens if you let go?

See how the water rises up the side of the bucket as the balloon pushes it aside.

 Internet link *Go to* ***www.usborne-quicklinks.com*** *for a link to a Web site where you can find out why some things float and some things sink.*

Changing shape

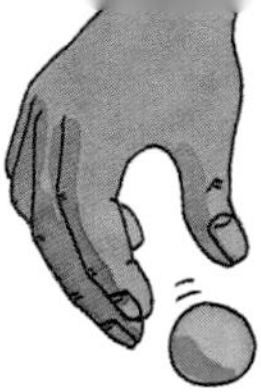

Drop a ball of Plasticine in some water. Does it float?

Flatten the ball and shape it like a boat with high sides. Does it float now?

Make the sides higher if it sinks.

Testing shapes

Why does the Plasticine float when you change its shape? Try this to help you find out.

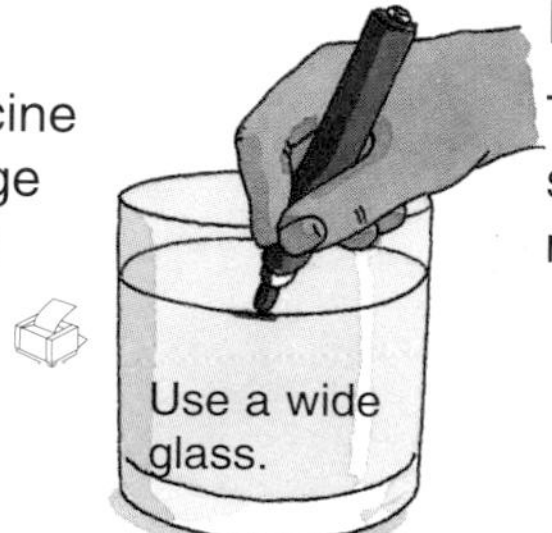

Use a wide glass.

Use a felt-tip pen to mark the water-level in a glass of water.

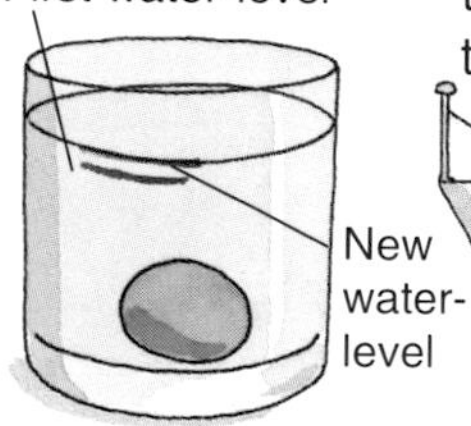

Drop in a ball of Plasticine. The water rises a little as the ball pushes it aside. Mark the new level.

Shape the ball into a boat and float it on the water. Why does the level rise higher?

How it works

The boat-shape takes up a bigger space than the ball so it pushes more water aside.

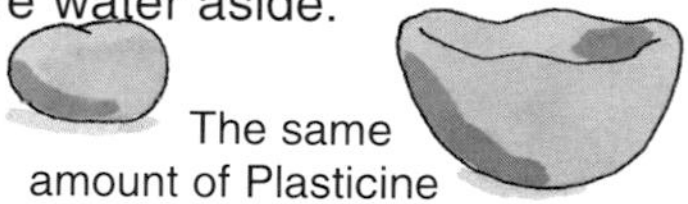

The same amount of Plasticine takes up more space.

The more water is pushed aside, the more it pushes back. It pushes the boat so hard that it floats.

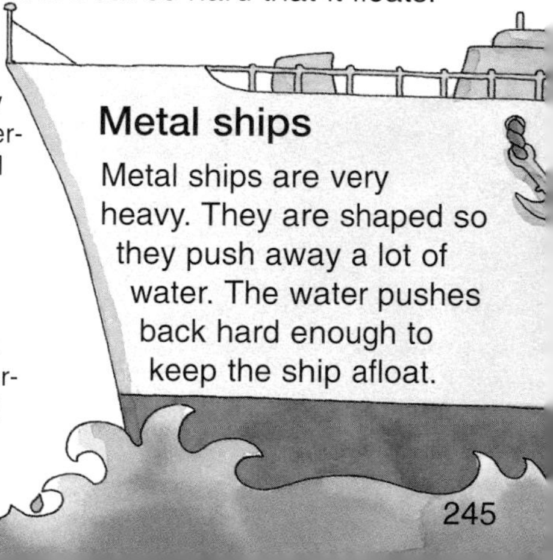

Metal ships

Metal ships are very heavy. They are shaped so they push away a lot of water. The water pushes back hard enough to keep the ship afloat.

Fun with boats

Boats float so well that they can carry heavy things across water.

Everything that a boat carries is called its cargo.

Loading boats

Think of some things which might make good boats. You can see some here. Try them out on water.

Load your boats with a cargo of stones or marbles. Can some carry more than others?

Is it easier to push a boatload of cargo along the ground or on the water? Try it to see.

Try loading a plastic tray with marbles. What happens?

Load some marbles into a plastic egg box. What happens if you put them all at one end?

Try putting one marble into each cup-shape. Does it float better like this?

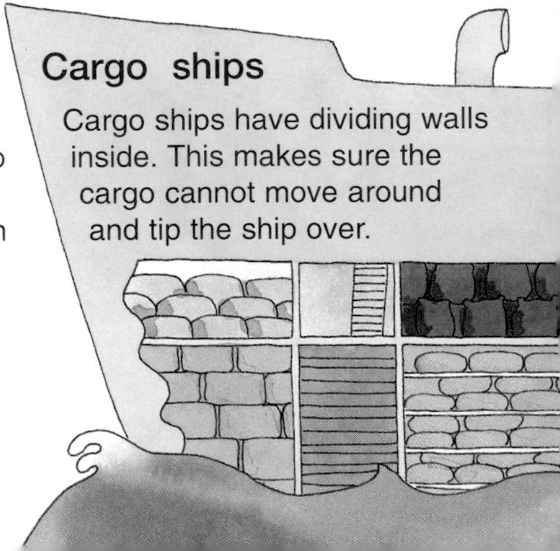

Cargo ships

Cargo ships have dividing walls inside. This makes sure the cargo cannot move around and tip the ship over.

Sinking boat

Stick Plasticine under a jar so that it floats upright. Put a mark at the waterline. Load marbles gently into this boat. What happens to the mark?

Mark inside the jar.

See how many marbles you can get in the jar.

Put lots of salt in the water. Float the jar now. Does the water come up to the same mark? Can the jar carry more marbles?

Plimsoll line

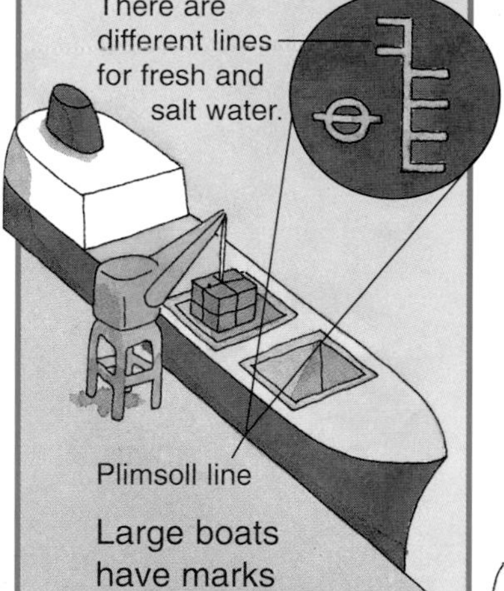

Large boats have marks called Plimsoll lines. People stop loading a boat when the water comes up to this mark.

Submarine can

Push an empty drink can underwater so that it fills with water and sinks.

Poke one end of a plastic tube into the can. Blow into the other end. What happens?

The air you blow into the can pushes out the water. This makes the can lighter so it rises to the surface.

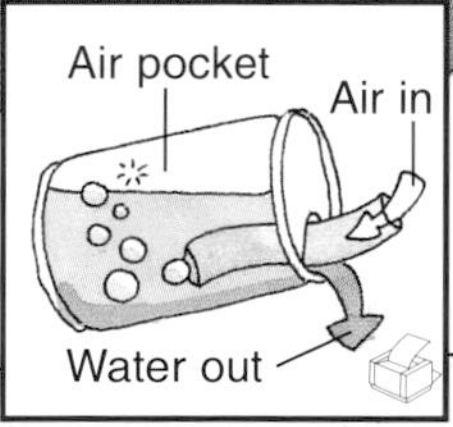

Submarines

Tanks inside a submarine can be filled with water to make it sink. Air is pumped into the tanks to make the submarine rise again.

Internet link *Go to* ***www.usborne-quicklinks.com*** *for a link to a Web site where you can find out how to make different kinds of boats.*

Water's 'skin'

Here are some surprises about the top, or surface, of water.

Bulging glass

Fill a glass to the brim with water. Look closely at the top of the water. Gently slide in some coins, one at a time.

Can you see the top rise above the glass?

How many coins can you put in before the water overflows?

Pond skaters

Insects called pond skaters can walk across the top of ponds. They are so light they do not break the water's 'skin'.

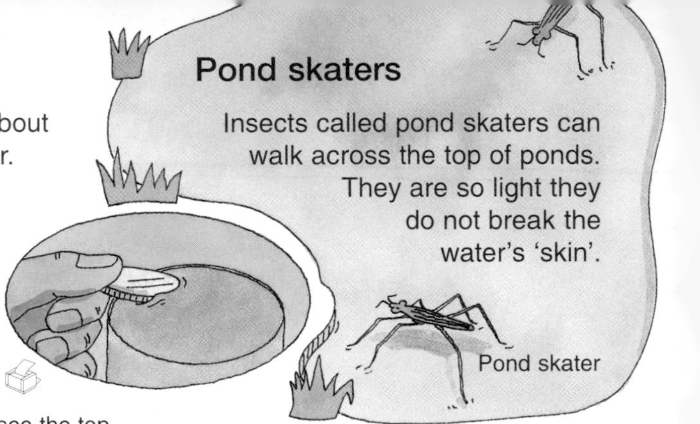

When you put the coins in the glass the top of the water seems to bulge as if it is held by a thin skin. The surface of water often behaves like a skin.

Floating a needle

You can float a needle by placing it carefully on the 'skin' like this.

Put a needle on a spoon. Slide the spoon into the water.

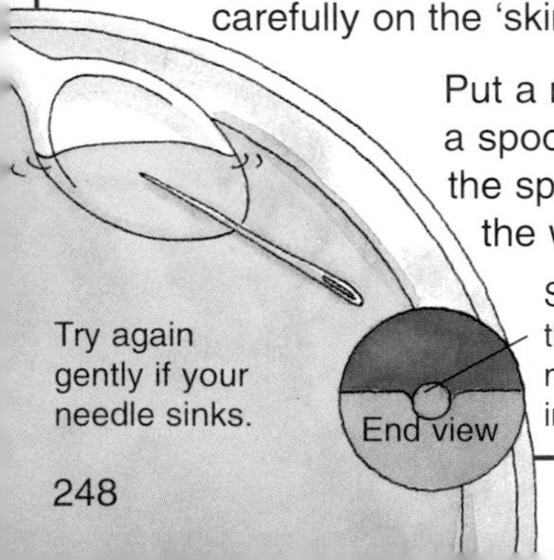

Try again gently if your needle sinks.

See how the needle makes a dip in the 'skin'.

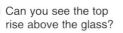

What happens if you touch the water with a straw dipped in washing-up liquid?

The washing-up liquid makes the skin weaker so it stretches. It gets too stretchy to hold up the needle.

Drips and drops

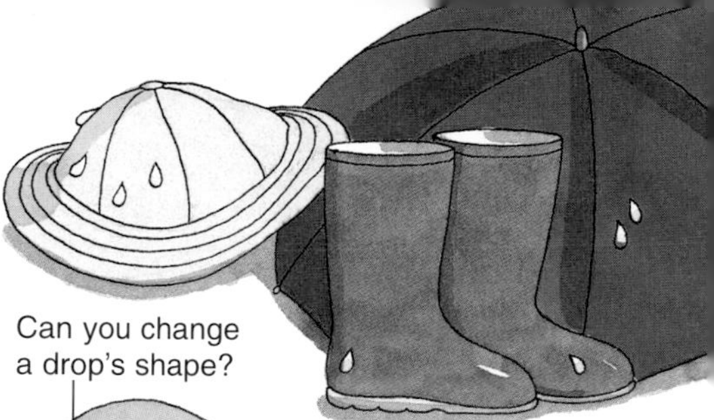

Look out for drops left behind after a rainstorm. Can you guess why water stays in drop shapes?

Try catching a drop from a dripping tap.

Now roll it gently between your finger and thumb.

What shape are drops as they fall?

Can you change a drop's shape?

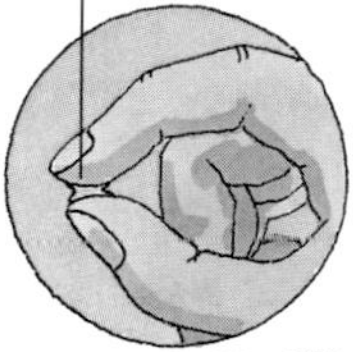

All drops are held by water's skin. This holds them even when they change shape.

Flattening drops

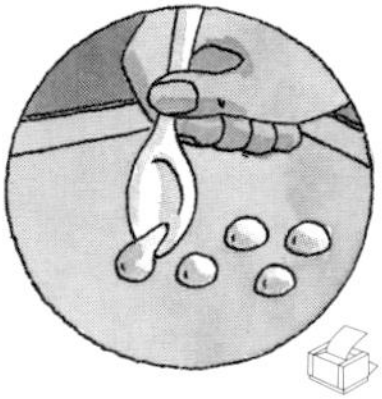

Spoon some drops onto a clean plastic tray. Can you think of a way to make the drops flatter?

Try touching them with a straw dipped in washing-up liquid.

The washing-up liquid makes the skin stretch so the drops spread out.

Blowing bubbles

Stir a spoonful of water into three spoonfulls of washing-up liquid. This mixture has a very stretchy skin.

Bend some wire into a loop. Dip it in the mixture.

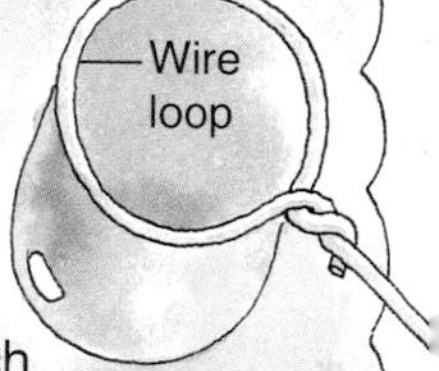

Look at the skin across the loop. Blow gently. Watch how the skin stretches to make a bubble.

Internet link *Go to* ***www.usborne-quicklinks.com*** *for a link to a Web site where you can find out more about water's skin.*

Vanishing water

You may have noticed how puddles dry up after rain. Have you ever wondered where the water goes?

Finding out

You might think the water just soaks into the ground or runs away. Try an experiment to see if this is true.

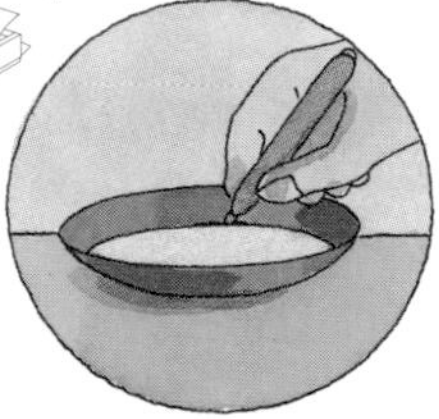

Pour some water into a saucer. Use a felt-tip pen to mark a line just above the water.

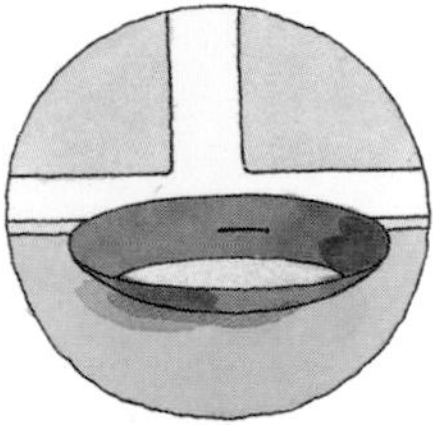

Leave the saucer on a table for a few days. Look at your mark and the water-level every day.

The water slowly vanishes. It cannot run out or soak through the saucer. It must get out another way.

How water 'vanishes'

The water escapes into the air in tiny drops called water vapour. They are too small to see.

This shows water vapour evaporating from a saucer.

This is how a puddle dries up.

Which dries fastest?

Fill three more saucers. Leave one in a cool, shady place, one in a warm place and one in a draughty place. Do they all dry out just as quickly?

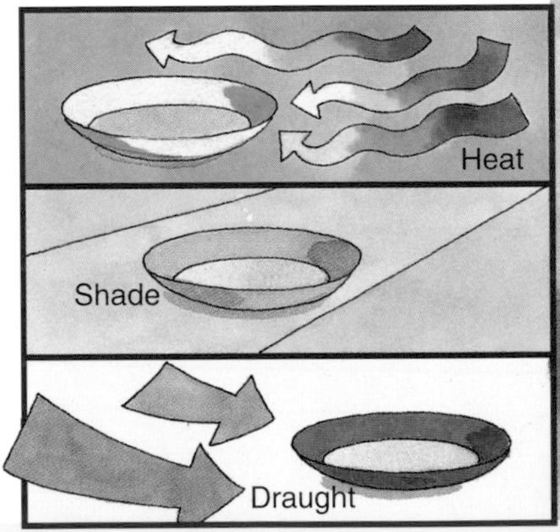

 Internet link *Go to* ***www.usborne-quicklinks.com*** *for a link to a Web site where you can find out how to do another evaporation experiment.*

Water in the air

The way water escapes into the air is called evaporation. Water evaporates all the time from rivers and seas so the air is full of invisible water vapour.

Getting it back

Fill a jar with ice-cubes to make it cold. Does anything happen to the outside of the jar?

Wipe the jar with a dry tissue. Does it get damp?

Water drops form on the jar because the cold jar cools the air nearby. When water vapour in the air cools, its drops get big enough to see. This is called condensation.

Steam

Sometimes condensation happens in mid-air. Then the drops look like mist. This happens when water boils.

The water gives off hot water vapour. This cools as it meets colder air and turns to drops you see as steam.

Never touch steam as it can burn you badly.

Clouds and rain

Clouds are also made up of condensation drops. These form when water vapour rises from the ground and meets cold air above.

Drops in the cloud join up and get heavier. Then they fall as rain.

Everlasting seas

Although water evaporates from seas they never dry up. Enough rainwater runs into them to keep them full.

Mixing

Water mixes well with many different things. To find out more about the way water mixes first collect some jars.

Pour some water into each jar. Add a different thing to each one.

You could try:
soap powder,
sand, salt, flour,
sugar, shampoo,
cooking oil,
powder paint,
orange juice,
jelly

Guess what might happen to each thing before you put it in.

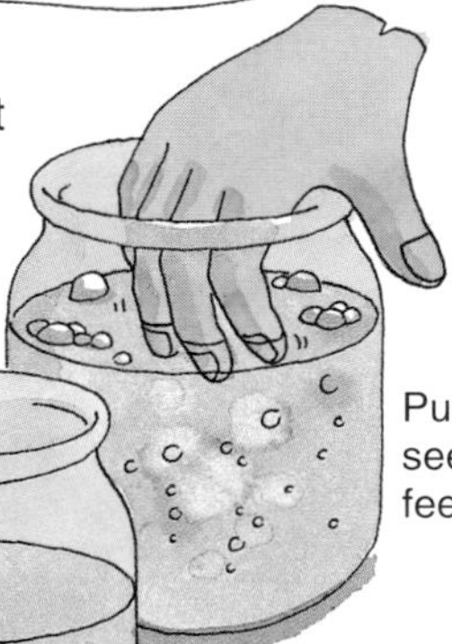

Does anything change if you put the same things into warm water?

Does the colour change?

Do any of the things you put in disappear?

Put your fingers in to see if the mixtures feel like plain water.

Does the water get cloudy or look clear?

Write everything that does happen in your notebook.

Does it make a difference if you stir the mixtures? Watch what happens.

 Internet link *Go to* ***www.usborne-quicklinks.com*** *for a link to a Web site where you can find out if oil is heavier than water.*

Separating mixtures

Try to think of ways to separate mixtures.

Oil floats so you can scoop it out with a spoon.

Does this work with any other mixtures?

You could use a paper towel like a fine sieve. First fold the kitchen paper in four. Pull open one side to make a cone.

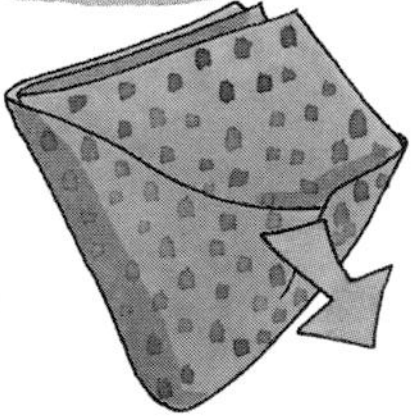

Put the cone into a funnel. Try pouring a sand mixture into it.

Bits of sand are trapped.

Water passes through tiny holes in the paper.

Can you separate other mixtures like this?

Solutions

Some things mix so well that you cannot separate them by scooping or sieving. A mixture like this is called a solution.

Separating solutions

Salt water is a solution. Put a drop on a saucer. Leave it until the water evaporates (see pages 250-251).

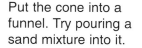

What is left behind? Taste it and see.*

Can you separate other solutions like this?

Instant food

Many foods are partly made of water. Soup, milk and potatoes are often dried and stored as powder.

When people want to eat them they just mix them with water again.

*Never taste things unless you know that they are things you can eat.

Water power

Water nearly always flows downhill. Its flow is strong enough to push things.

Make a model water wheel

You will need:
2 plastic egg boxes,
2 small cardboard plates,
a stapler, some scissors,
2 empty cotton reels,
a pencil, 2 long rulers or
flat sticks, Plasticine
and sticky tape

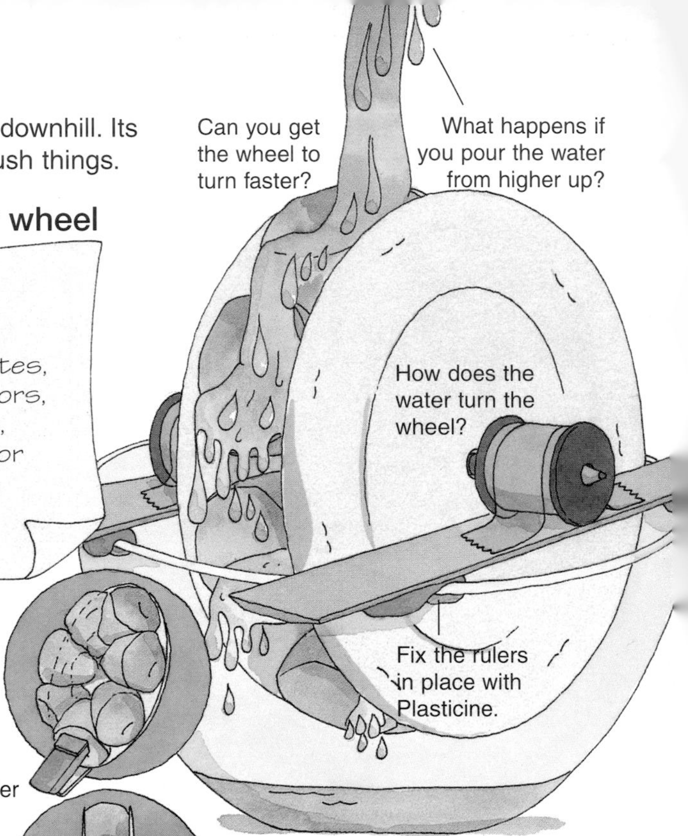

Can you get the wheel to turn faster?
What happens if you pour the water from higher up?
How does the water turn the wheel?
Fix the rulers in place with Plasticine.
Stapler

Cut the cup-shapes* out of the egg boxes. Staple them on to one plate as shown. Staple the second plate on to the other side of each cup.

Push the pencil through the centre of the plates. Then, push the cotton reels on to the ends of the pencil.

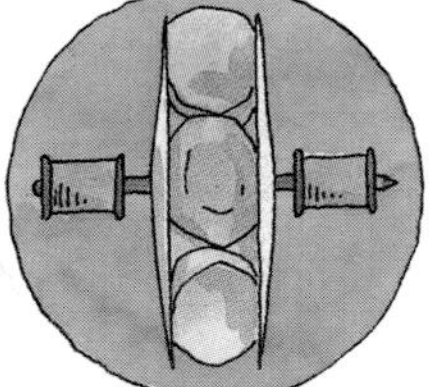

Tape a ruler below each reel. Place the rulers across a bowl. Pour water on the wheel and watch what happens.

*You may not need all of the cup-shapes.

Powering machinery

Long ago people used water wheels to turn machinery for grinding wheat into flour.

Today water is used to power machines that make electricity. The water spins huge wheels called turbines to make these machines work.

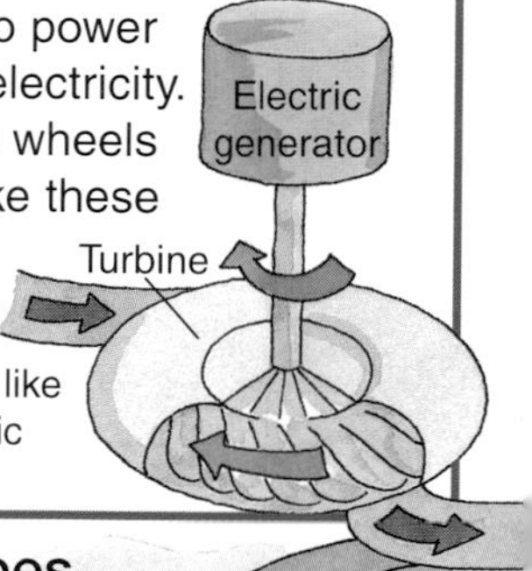

Electricity is made like this in hydro-electric power stations.

Getting stronger

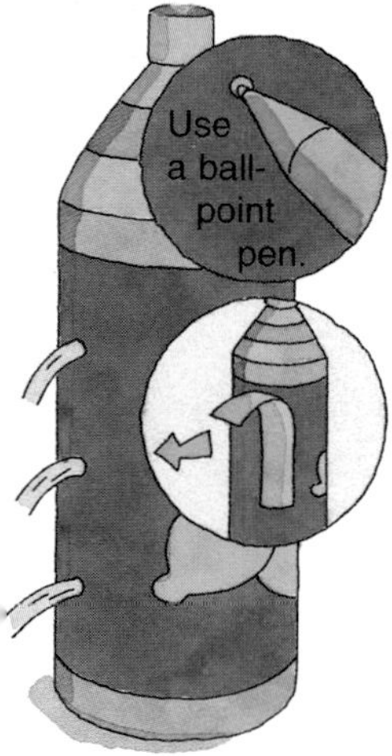

Take the top off an empty squeezy bottle.* Make three holes in the bottle, one above the other.

Tape over the holes. Fill the bottle with water. Then, rip the tape off quickly.

Watch how jets of water spurt out. Which goes furthest?

The lowest jet should go furthest as water above it helps to push it out.

*Get an adult to help you take the top off.

Powerful pipes

Pipes to hydro-electric power stations take water from the bottom of lakes or reservoirs. The deeper the pipes are, the faster the water flows along them.

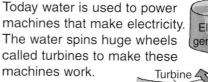

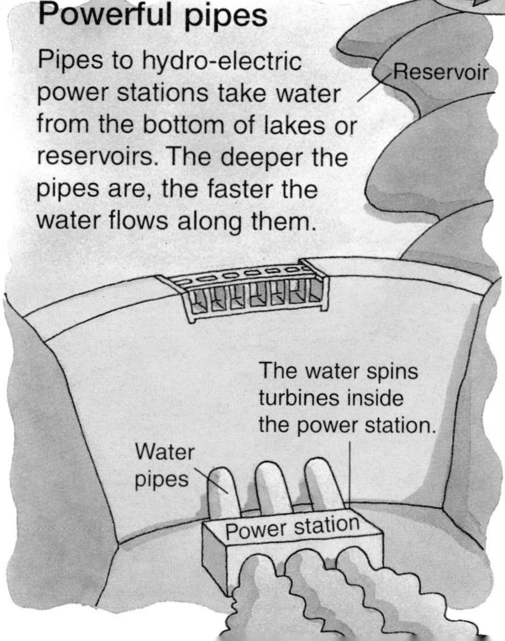

Air and water tricks

Most things that look empty are really full of air. Water has to push the air out before it can get in them.

Tissue trick

Do you think you can keep a tissue dry underwater? Try this.

First, stuff the tissue tightly into a glass so it cannot fall out.

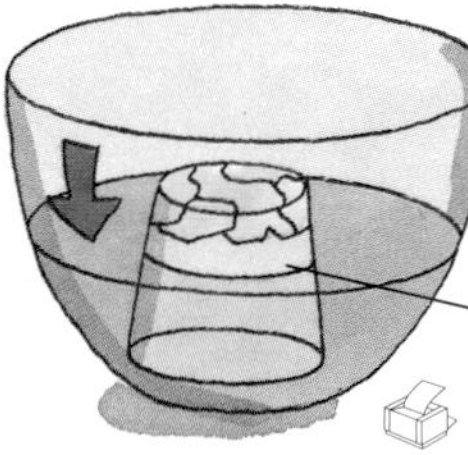

Turn the glass over and push it straight down into some water.

Does the water fill the glass?

Take the glass out. Is the tissue wet?

Keep the glass straight.

This works because the glass is full of air. The water cannot push the air out so the tissue stays dry. What happens if you tilt the glass?

Magic pot

Find an empty plastic pot with a tight lid. Use a drawing pin to make holes in its base.

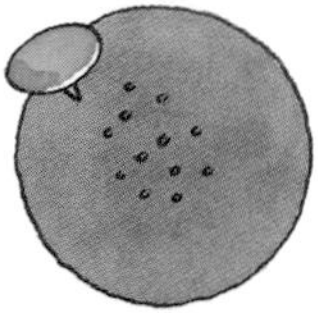

Take off the lid and push the pot underwater. Now put the lid on.

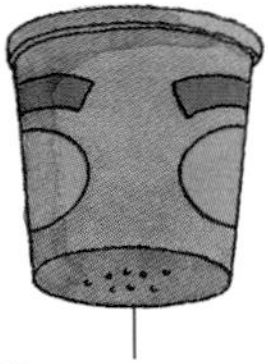

Does any water fall out?

What happens when you lift the pot up out of the water?

Air tries to get in the holes. It pushes so hard the water cannot get out.

Now push a ballpoint pen through the lid to make another hole. This lets air in at the top. The air helps to push the water out below.

What happens if you put your finger over the hole?

Internet link *Go to* ***www.usborne-quicklinks.com*** *for a link to a Web site where you can do an experiment which makes water mysteriously rise.*

Flowing upwards

Can you make water flow upwards?

1. Stand a glass in the kitchen sink. Put one end of a plastic tube in the glass. Put the other end under a tap to fill the glass.

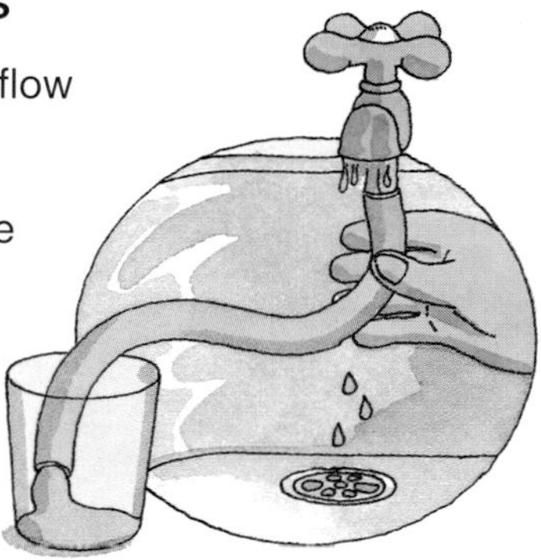

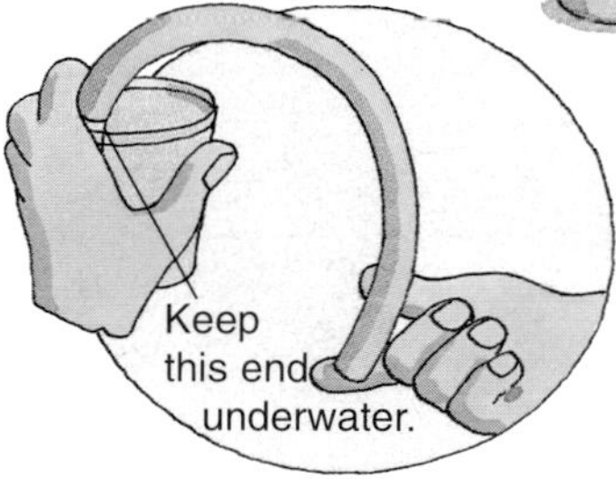
Keep
this end
underwater.

2. Put your finger over the top of the tube to keep the water in. Lift the glass up on to the draining board with your other hand.

3. Bend the tube until your finger is lower than the glass. Take your finger off.

The water should run up out of the glass through the tube. Can you think why?

Keep trying if this does not work the first time.

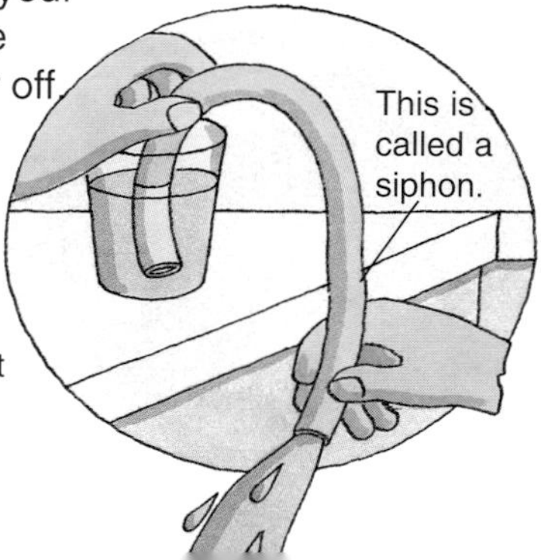
This is
called a
siphon.

How the siphon works

As water runs down the tube it pulls up more water behind it. Air helps to push the water into the tube so the siphon keeps flowing.

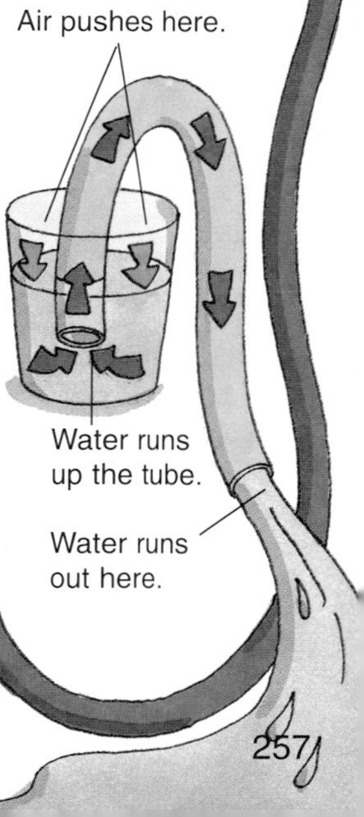
Air pushes here.
Water runs
up the tube.
Water runs
out here.

Taking in water

Some things soak up water while others keep water out.

Wetting different things

Do you think water will soak into any of these things?

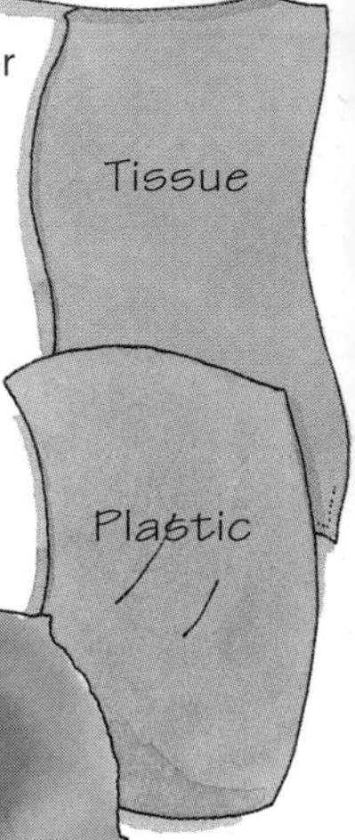

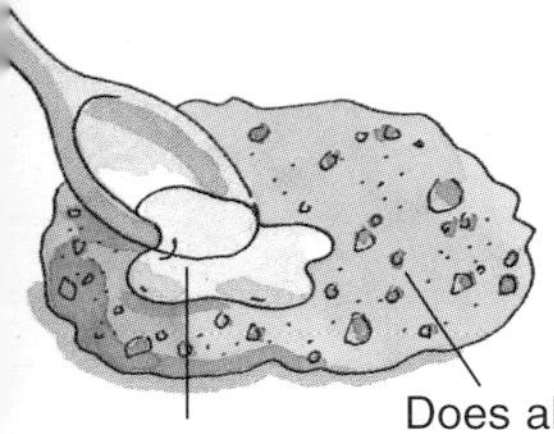

Put a spoonful of water on a dry sponge. What happens to the water?

Does all the water disappear?

Does all the sponge get wet?

Spoon water on to other things. Make a chart to show what happens to each one.

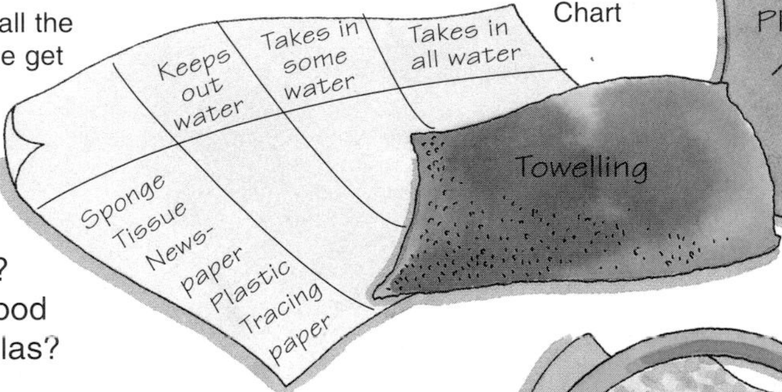

Chart

Which things could you use for mopping up spills? Which might be good for making umbrellas?

Looking closely

Look at things that take in water through a magnifying glass.

Can you see tiny gaps? The water gets in through these gaps.

Tissue seen through a magnifying glass.

 Internet link *Go to* ***www.usborne-quicklinks.com*** *for a link to a Web site where you can do another experiment to see how plants take up water.*

Rising water

Do you think water can climb upwards?

Dip a strip of paper towel into water. Watch what happens.

Climbing through celery

Pour a few drops of ink into a glass of water. Cut the end off a stalk of celery. Look at the cut edge closely.

Put the stalk in the water. Leave it for three days. Does anything happen?

Cut the stalk into slices. Look for inky spots inside. These show where water has risen up the stalk.

How plants drink

A plant has roots under the earth. These have tiny holes in them.

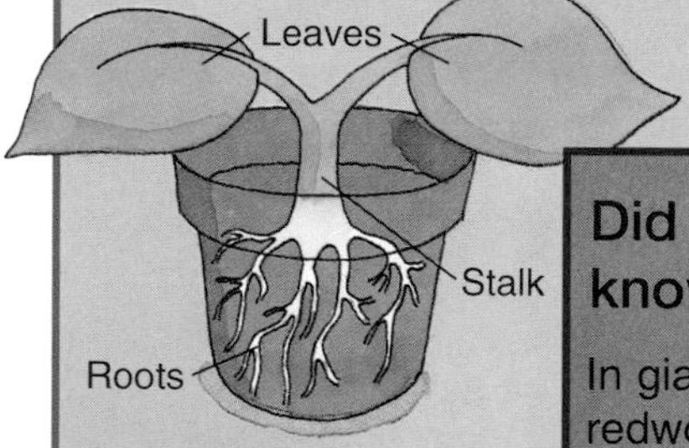

Water in the earth goes into the roots. It is sucked up to the leaves through thin tubes in the stalk.

Did you know?

In giant redwood trees, water has to climb 100m (300ft) to reach the highest leaf.

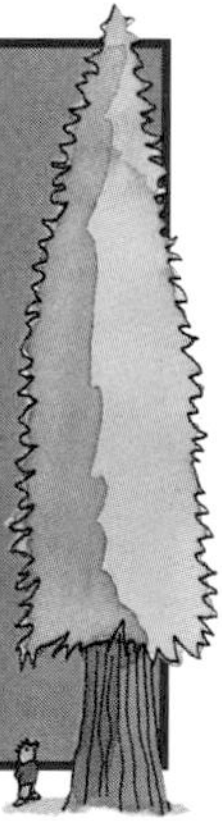

Frozen water

When water gets very cold it freezes hard and turns to ice.

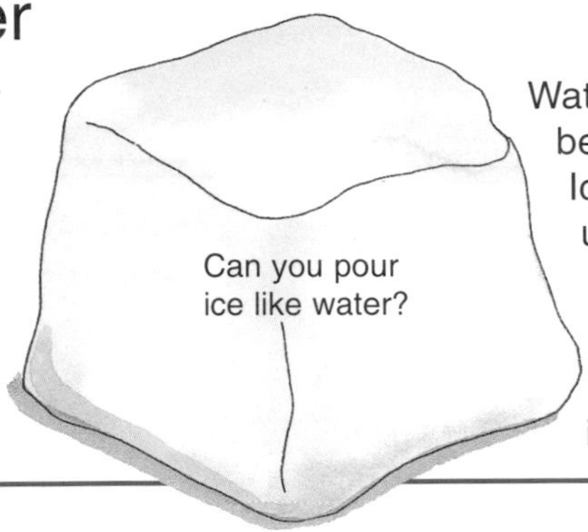

Can you pour ice like water?

Water can change shape because it is a liquid. Ice keeps one shape unless it melts and turns back to water.

Anything that keeps its shape, like ice, is called a solid.

Differences

Look at an ice-cube. How is it different from water?

Taking up space

Fill up to the brim.

Find a plastic pot with a lid. Fill it with water and put on the lid. Ask if you can put the pot in the freezer. What happens when all the water turns to ice?

Ice takes up more space than water. It pushes the lid up when it gets too big for the pot.

Does ice float?

Put some ice in a bowl of water to see if it floats.

How much floats above the surface?

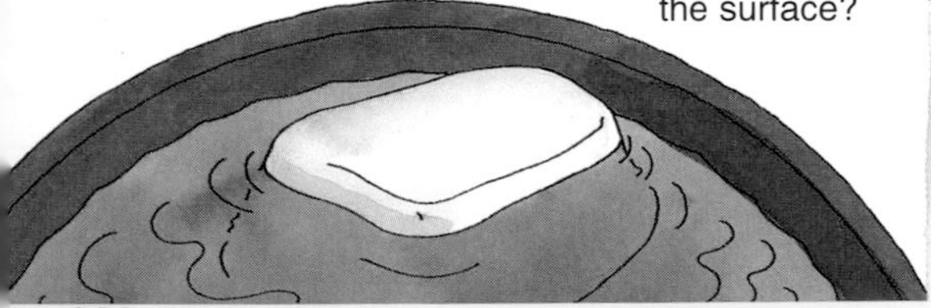

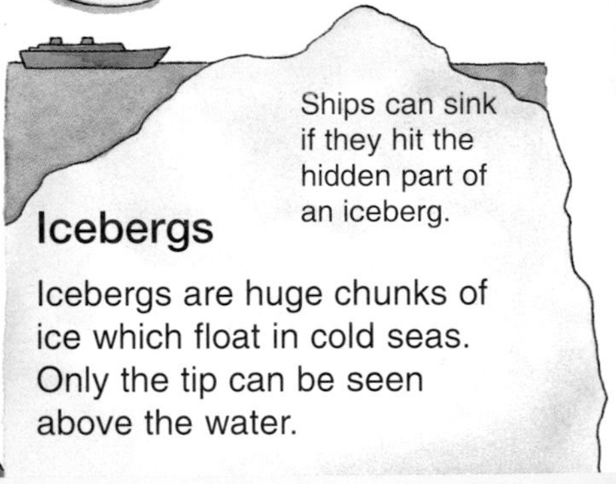

Ships can sink if they hit the hidden part of an iceberg.

Icebergs

Icebergs are huge chunks of ice which float in cold seas. Only the tip can be seen above the water.

 Internet link *Go to* ***www.usborne-quicklinks.com*** *for a link to a Web site with another ice experiment.*

Melting ice

Ice melts when it gets warmer.

What happens if you put one ice-cube in cold water, one in hot water and one on a plate?

Try this out to see if you are right.

Use a watch to time how fast they melt.

Melting without heating

Try sprinkling an ice-cube with salt.

What happens to the salt?

The salt mixes with the ice. Salty ice melts quickly because it melts at cooler temperatures than plain ice.

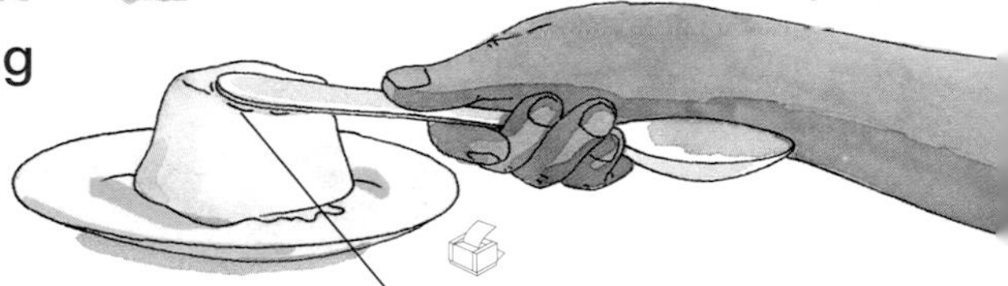

Try pressing an ice-cube with a spoon-handle.

What happens to the ice here?

Ice always melts when it is pressed.

Why ice is slippery

Ice melts when your feet press on it. A thin layer of water forms under your shoes. This stops them from gripping so you slide around.

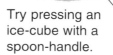

How the experiments work

These pages give more detailed explanations of how the experiments in this section work. To find out even more about the experiments, visit the Web sites recommended. For links to all these Web sites, go to **www.usborne-quicklinks.com**

Experimenting (pages 242-243)

Like all liquids, water flows, changes shape to fit any container, keeps the same volume and finds its own level.

Floating (pages 244-245)

When an object is dropped in water, its bulk pushes some of the water aside. The water pushes back, exerting a force called upthrust. If an object is heavy its weight may overcome the upthrust so it sinks. If it is light enough, it floats. It is possible to make something push aside more water by changing its shape, as shown by the Plasticine boat experiment.

Internet link *Go to* ***www.usborne-quicklinks.com*** *for a link to a Web site where you can watch a movie about buoyancy.*

Fun with boats (pages 246-247)

A boat sinks into water until it displaces the same weight of water as its own weight. When loaded, the boat sinks lower into the water until it displaces the weight of its cargo too.

Salt water weighs more than fresh water. A boat has to displace less salt water to equal its own weight. This makes it float higher in salt water. It can also carry more.

Internet link *Go to* ***www.usborne-quicklinks.com*** *for a link to a Web site where you can find out more about how boats float.*

Water's 'skin' (pages 248-249)

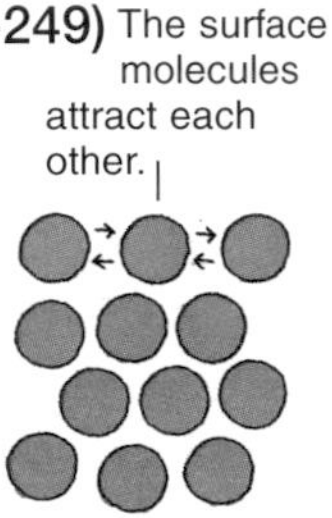
The surface molecules attract each other.

Like all substances, water is made up of tiny particles called molecules. Water molecules hold together most strongly at the surface. This makes it able to resist slight pressure, just like a skin. This effect is known as surface tension.

Internet link *Go to* ***www.usborne-quicklinks.com*** *for a link to a Web site where you can find out more about surface tension.*

Vanishing water (pages 250-251)

Molecules move constantly in a liquid. They often break free and escape as gas (evaporation). Heat gives molecules more energy so they move faster and break free more easily.

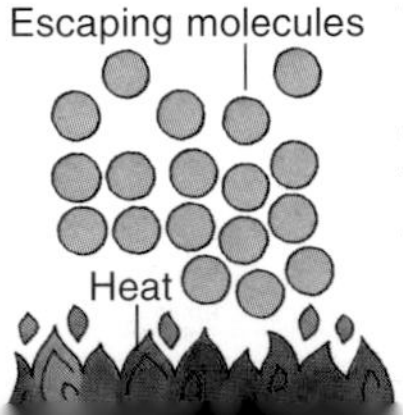
Escaping molecules
Heat

When a gas cools, its molecules lose energy and can form a liquid again. That is what happens when water vapour condenses.

Mixing (pages 252-253)

Water forms different substances with various other substances:

Solutions

A solution is formed when a substance, such as salt, dissolves in water. Its molecules spread out among the water molecules so they are thoroughly mixed.

Suspensions and emulsions

A suspension is formed when a powdery substance, such as fine sand, does not dissolve. Its particles stay large enough to see. They can be easily filtered out. A liquid, such as oil, that refuses to mix with water can form an emulsion. It stays in droplets suspended in water.

Internet link *Go to* ***www.usborne-quicklinks.com*** *for a link to a Web site where you can do some simple solution experiments at home.*

Water power (pages 254-255)

Water flows downwards due to gravity (Earth's pull). The force of its flow is useful for powering machinery. Its flow is also affected by its depth. The deepest parts of any volume of water are under the most pressure because of the weight above.

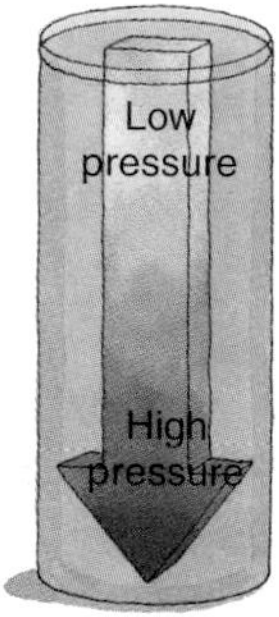

Air and water tricks (page 256-257)

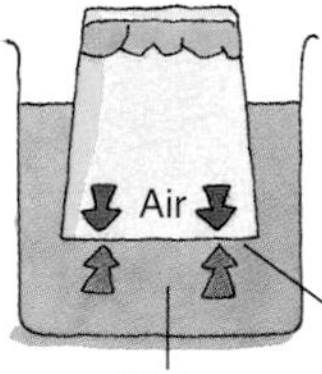

When a glass is pushed underwater, air is trapped inside. The air pressure balances the water pressure outside.

The water compresses the air but cannot push past it.

Taking in water (pages 258-259)

Water molecules can be more attracted to other substances than they are to each other. The attraction enables water to travel a long way into some substances. This is called capillary action.

Capillary action encourages water to climb up plants. Plants allow water to evaporate from their leaves which also helps to 'suck up' the water.

Frozen water (pages 260-261)

When water becomes very cold the molecules lock together to form a solid (ice). Heat gives the molecules energy so they can break free and change to liquid. This also happens if pressure is applied.

Internet link *Go to* ***www.usborne-quicklinks.com*** *for a link to a Web site where you can find out more about ice by doing an experiment.*

More internet links

Here are some more Web sites to visit to find out about water. For links to all these sites go to **www.usborne-quicklinks.com** and type in the keywords "pocket scientist 2".

Web site 1 This Web site has lots of information and activities about water. Watch an animated diagram showing how the water cycle works and read fascinating facts about water. You can also try out some more water experiments and find out about water quality and the environment.

Web site 2 Test your knowledge with a quiz on water at this Web site. You can also find out about the water in you, how much water there is on Earth and try out some challenge questions about water.

Web site 3 Read some water basics and then learn about water as a solid, liquid and gas. There are diagrams to look at and an activity to try out to see how water can change from a gas into a liquid. You can also do a mixing experiment and an experiment to see if ice can grow.

Web site 4 This Web site is packed with experiments about water. Find out how to float a cork in the middle of a glass, use water to magnify small pictures, create a mini water cycle and much more.

For links to all these sites go to www.usborne-quicklinks.com and type in the keywords "pocket scientist 2".

SCIENCE EXPERIMENTS WITH AIR

Helen Edom and Moira Butterfield

Designed by Sandy Wegener
Illustrated by Kate Davies

Consultant: Geoffrey Puplett

CONTENTS

Air all around

Although you cannot see it, air is all around you. Try the experiments in this section to find out some of the things that air can do.

Things you need

The things you need for the experiments are easy to find. Here are some to collect.

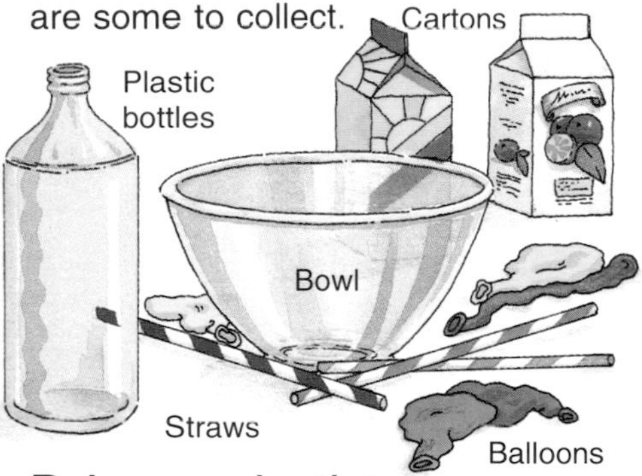

Being a scientist

Before you do an experiment, guess what will happen. Watch to see if you are right and write down what you find out.

Feeling air

How can you tell that air is all around you? Try flapping some cardboard next to your face.

The cardboard makes the air move. You can feel the air moving against your cheek.

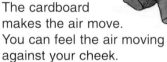

The atmosphere

All around the earth there is a thick blanket of air called the atmosphere. Outside in space, above the atmosphere, there is no air at all.

 Pictures with the symbol can be downloaded from **www.usborne-quicklinks.com**

A paper race

Moving air can push things around. You can use it to make this game work.

You need a piece of cardboard and a strip of paper for each player. Fold up one end of each strip.

You could add a face.

See who can cross the finish line first.

Mark a finish line with thread. Flap the cardboard behind the strips to make the air blow them along.

Testing for air

Find an empty, clear plastic bottle. Try this experiment to see if it is really as empty as it looks.

Push the bottle into a bowl of water so it begins to fill up. Watch what happens to the water.

You see bubbles as the water pushes out air from inside the bottle. Most things that look empty are really full of air.

Internet link *Go to* ***www.usborne-quicklinks.com*** *for a link to a Web site where you can watch a short movie about the Earth's atmosphere.*

Air that pushes

Air pushes against things all the time. You are so used to it pushing against you that you do not notice it.

Heavy newspaper

Tear a sheet of newspaper in half and smooth it out on a table. Put a ruler under the paper so that it sticks out over the edge of the table.

Use a new newspaper.

Stand to one side so the ruler cannot hit you.

Press down on the ruler to see if you can flick it off the table.

This is surprisingly hard to do because air presses down on the newspaper, keeping it in place.

Upside-down trick

This trick can be messy so try it over a bowl.

Fill a plastic cup full of water so the water bulges up above the top.

Put some cardboard on top and turn the cup upside-down, holding the cardboard in place.

Make sure there are no gaps between the cardboard and the cup.

Let go of the cardboard and see what happens.

Air pushes on the cardboard and keeps it in place. This makes the water stay in the cup.

 Internet link *Go to* ***www.usborne-quicklinks.com*** *for a link to a Web site where you can read a short article to get you thinking about air.*

Collapsing carton

Sip all the drink out of a juice carton. Keep on sipping so you empty out the air. Watch what happens.

Use a cardboard carton with a hole for a straw.

When the carton is completely empty, the air outside pushes in the carton's sides.

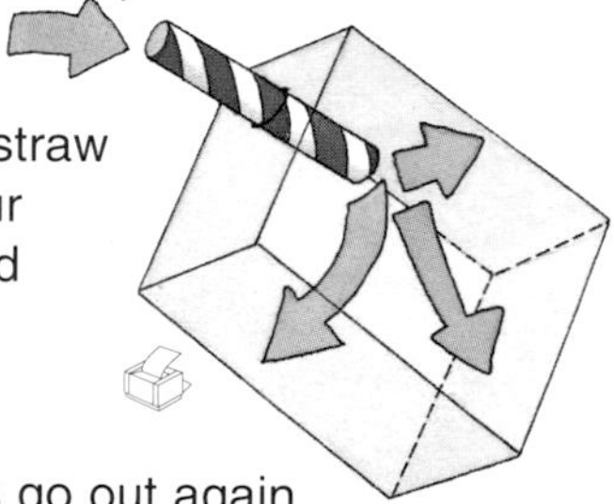

Take the straw out of your mouth and watch the carton.

The sides go out again because air rushes into the carton and pushes them out.

See what happens to the carton if you blow even more air into it.

Pumping up

Try pumping up a bicycle tyre. Keep feeling the tyre with your fingers to see how hard it is.

Air pushes harder when it is squeezed together. The more air you put inside the tyre, the harder the tyre feels.

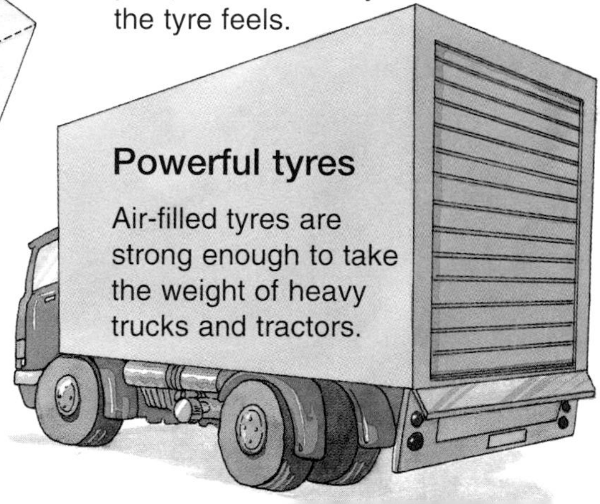

Powerful tyres

Air-filled tyres are strong enough to take the weight of heavy trucks and tractors.

Changing size

When air gets warmer it expands, which means that it spreads out.

Disappearing dent

Watch what happens if you warm up the air inside a ping-pong ball.

Cover the glass with a plate for example, to keep the ball down.

Watch the dent carefully.

First, push a dent in the ball. Then, put it in a glass full of warm water.

The water heats up the air in the ball, so the air expands. The expanding air pushes out the dent.

A jumping coin

You can use expanding air to make a coin jump.

Stand a long-necked bottle in a deep bowl. Wet the rim of the bottle and set a large coin on top. Then, pour warm water into the bowl.

The coin must cover the hole completely.

Hold the bottle to keep it from falling over.

The warm water heats up the air inside the bottle. The air spreads out and pushes the coin upward.

Getting colder

Try this experiment to find out what happens when air becomes colder.

You could use an empty fizzy drink bottle.

1. Put some ice-cubes into a plastic bag and crush them with a rolling pin. Then, put the ice in a plastic bottle. Screw on the lid.

2. Shake the bottle, then put it down. Watch what happens to the bottle as the ice cools the air inside.

3. When air cools, it shrinks. The bottle's sides go inward so no empty space is left inside.

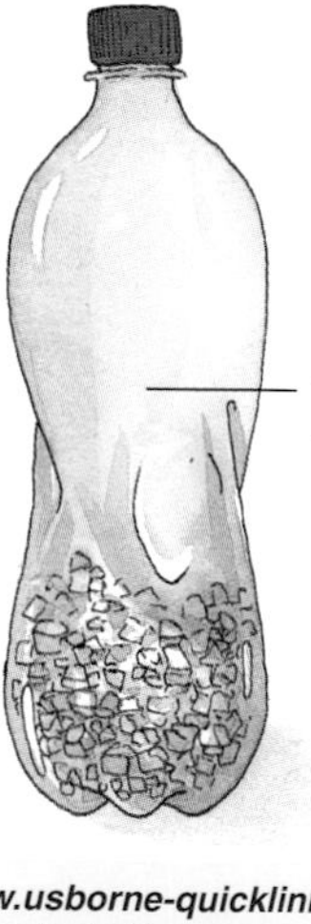

The cold air takes up less space.

Thunderstorms

In thunderstorms, lightning heats the air around it. The air expands so quickly that it makes a loud noise. You hear this noise as thunder.

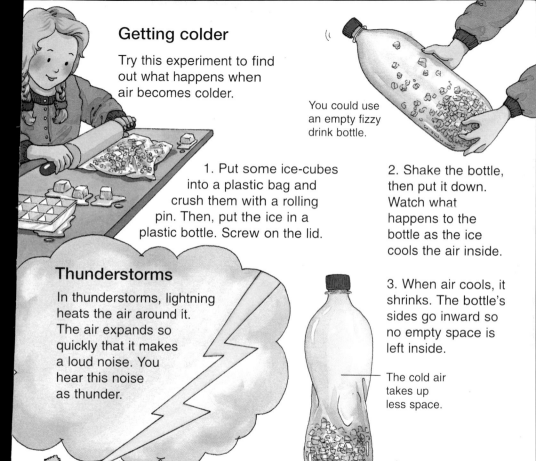

Internet link *Go to* ***www.usborne-quicklinks.com*** *for a link to a Web site where you can find out what happens when lightning strikes.*

Rising air

When air gets warmer it becomes lighter, so it moves upward.

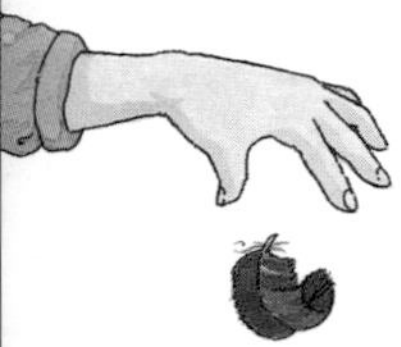

Flying feather

Drop a small pillow feather above a warm radiator. See which way the feather floats.

Do not try this experiment above a fire.

The radiator heats up the air above it. The warm air rises and pushes the feather upwards.

Hot air balloons

Huge balloons can carry people underneath them. Burners heat the air in the balloon to make it rise. When the people want to land, they let the air cool again so the balloon sinks to the ground.

Wriggly snake

You can use warm air to make this snake wriggle.

1. Draw around a plate to make a circle on paper. Cut out the circle.

2. Draw a line around and around inside the circle to make a spiral. Colour the spiral like a snake, then cut it out.

3. Use a needle to push a thread through the snake's head.

 ***Internet link** Go to **www.usborne-quicklinks.com** for a link to a Web site where you can do an interactive experiment on how hot air balloons fly.*

Flowing air

In cold weather, go into a room with its heating on and close the door.

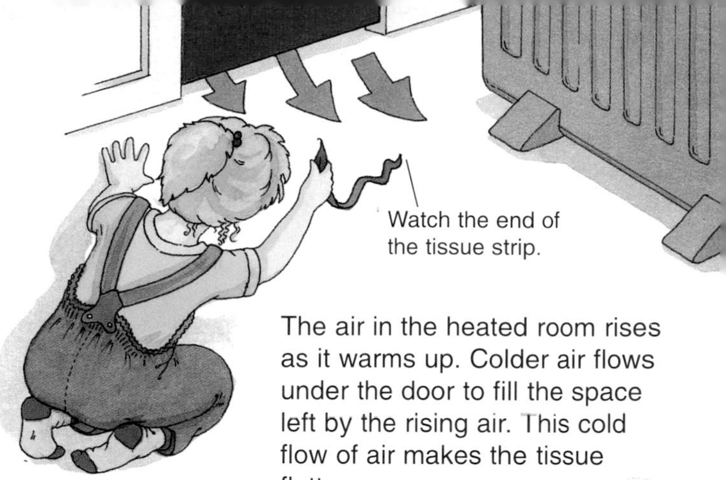
Watch the end of the tissue strip.

Hold a strip of tissue by the bottom of the door. See if the tissue moves.

The air in the heated room rises as it warms up. Colder air flows under the door to fill the space left by the rising air. This cold flow of air makes the tissue flutter.

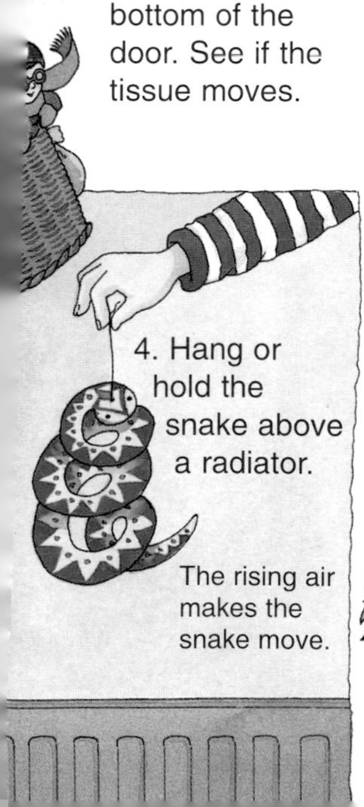

4. Hang or hold the snake above a radiator.

The rising air makes the snake move.

Why there is wind

Wind happens because the Sun warms up parts of the land and sea. These warm parts heat up the air above them, like a radiator.

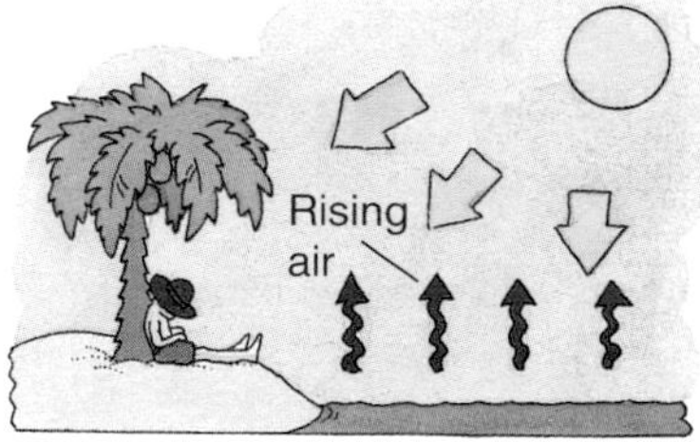
Rising air

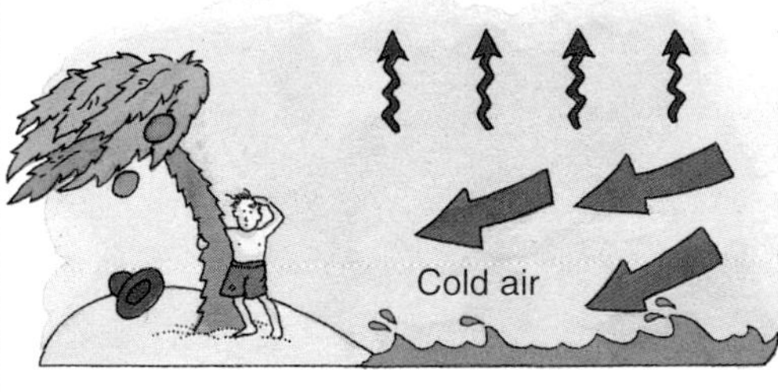
Cold air

The warm air rises and cold air flows into the space beneath. The flow of air is the wind.

Wind

The wind is moving air. You can feel it push against you and see it blowing things around.

Strong and gentle

Look out for things that move in the wind.

A gentle wind, called a breeze, can make smoke drift, flags flutter and leaves rustle.

A very strong wind, called a gale, can make whole trees sway and branches break.

Wind and rain

Look out for moving clouds in the sky. The wind moves clouds around from place to place, bringing the rain with them.

Dangerous winds

The strongest winds of all are called hurricanes. Hurricanes can travel at 320 kilometres per hour (200 mph) and blow away trees and buildings.

Changing wind

See if you can tell which way the wind is blowing. These tests will help.

Wet your finger and hold it up. It feels coldest on the side the wind is coming from.

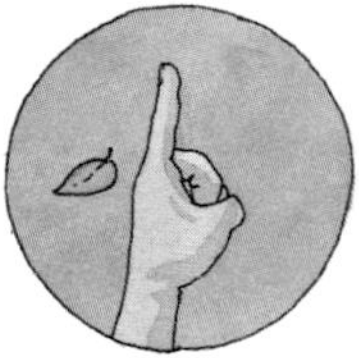

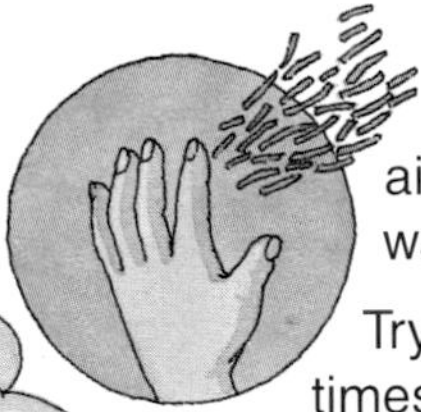

Throw grass in the air and watch which way the wind blows it.

Try the tests at different times to see how often the wind changes direction.

Make a weather vane

You can make a weather vane to help find out where the wind comes from.

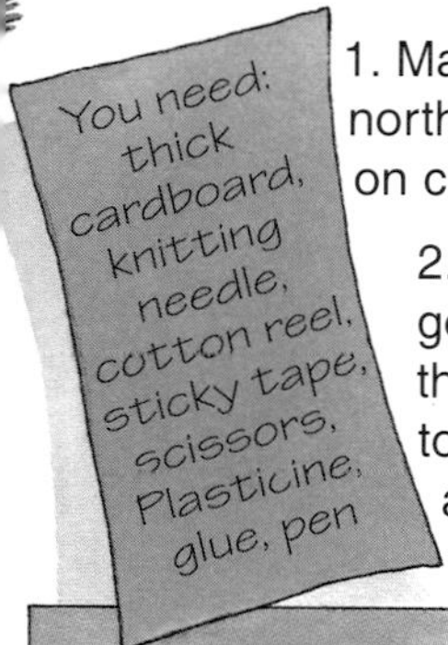

1. Mark the directions, north, south, east and west on cardboard. (see below).

2. Early in the morning, go outside and place the card so east points towards the Sun*. Now all the directions are in the right place.

In the early morning, the Sun is always in the east.

3. Cut an arrow out of cardboard. Tape it to the cotton reel. Glue a circle of cardboard on top.

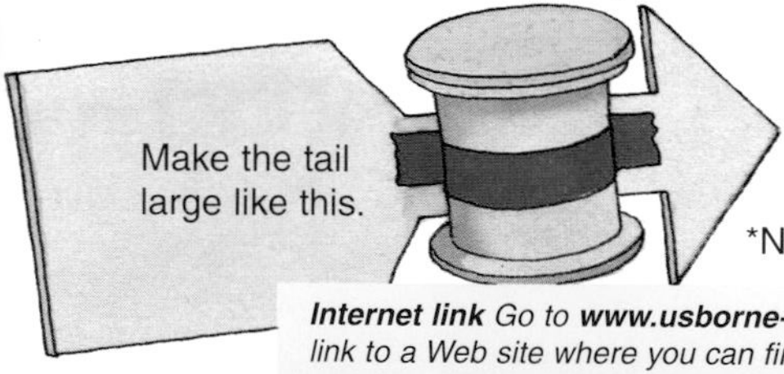

Make the tail large like this.

4. Put a blob of Plasticine in the middle and push in the knitting needle, point upward. Put the reel on top.

This arrow shows that the wind is coming from the north.

Use stones to keep the cardboard flat.

The arrow points in the direction the wind is coming from.

You could make a chart like this to show the direction and strength of the wind on different days.

Winds are named after the direction they blow from. For instance, a north wind blows from the north.

*Never look straight at the Sun as it can burn your eyes.

Internet link *Go to* ***www.usborne-quicklinks.com*** *for a link to a Web site where you can find out facts about the wind.*

Air power

You can use air to make things move. Try these ideas, then see if you can find any more ways to use air power.

Sailing boats

Float an empty plastic tub in some water. Try to blow it along.

Now push a knitting needle through some paper to make a sail. Use Plasticine to stand the needle up in the tub.

See how easily you can blow the boat along now.

More air can push against the sail so the boat moves faster. Try different-sized sails to see which works best.

Rocket balloon

Air makes this balloon rocket along.

You need: a long piece of thread, straw, long balloon, sticky tape, peg

Thread the string through the straw. Then tie it between two chairs.

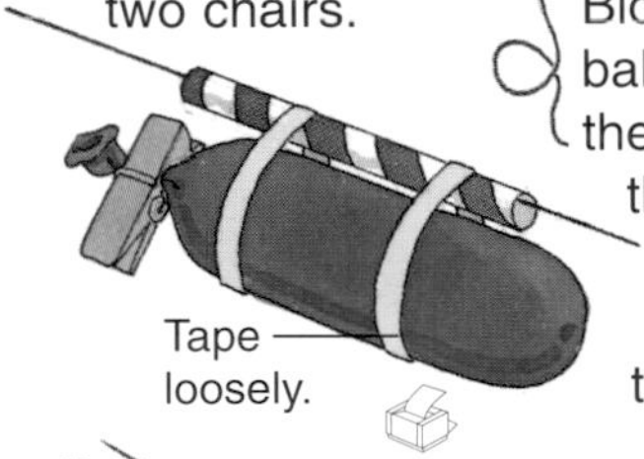

Tape loosely.

Blow up the balloon and peg the end to stop the air coming out. Tape the straw to the balloon.

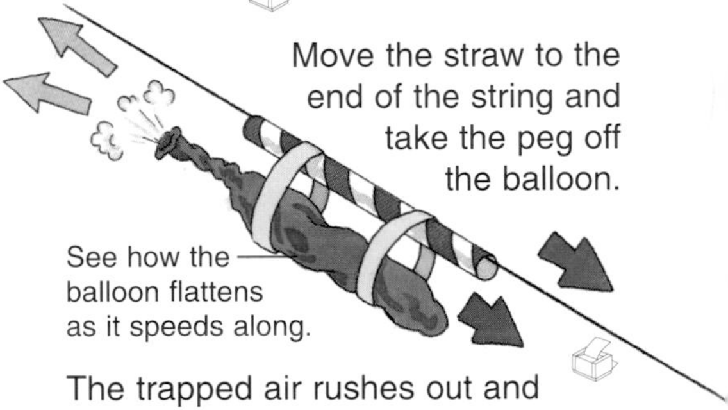

Move the straw to the end of the string and take the peg off the balloon.

See how the balloon flattens as it speeds along.

The trapped air rushes out and makes the balloon move forward.

 Internet link *Go to* ***www.usborne-quicklinks.com*** *for a link to a Web site where you can find out more about the different ways people have used air power.*

Windmills

Windmills were used for grinding corn into flour. The wind turned sails to make machinery work inside.

Wind winch

This model winch can pull things up and down.

You need:
thin cardboard, clay, straw, 2 pegs, thread, 2 cocktail sticks, buttons, pencil, tracing paper, sticky tape

1. Trace the circle shape below on to cardboard. Cut out the middle. Then, cut along the straight lines to make blades.

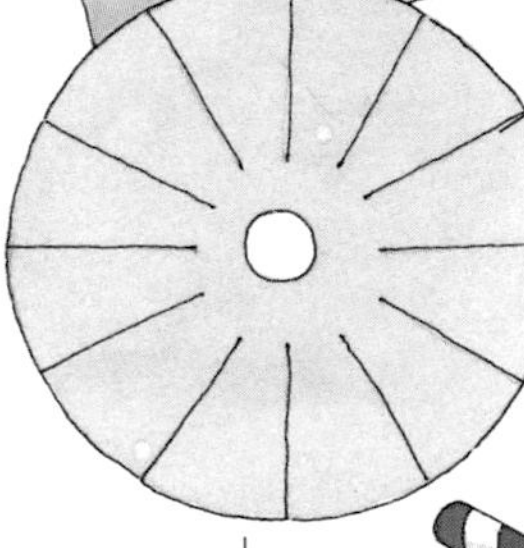

Trace this shape.

2. Bend each blade slightly. Then, push the circle onto a straw. Hold it in place with Plasticine.

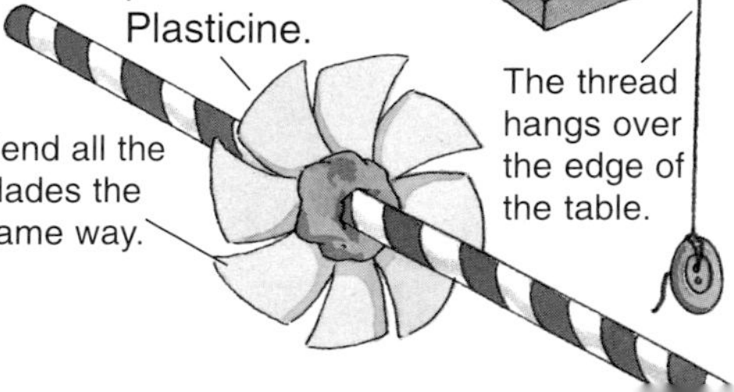

Bend all the blades the same way.

Put the pegs upside down.

3. Use Plasticine to stand the pegs up at the edge of a table, so you can fit the straw between them. Push the cocktail sticks through the pegs, into the straw.

4. Tie or stick a thread to the straw. Tie a button to the thread.

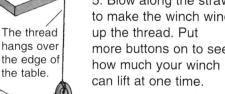

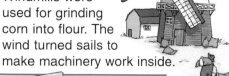

The thread hangs over the edge of the table.

5. Blow along the straw to make the winch wind up the thread. Put more buttons on to see how much your winch can lift at one time.

Moving through air

Some things travel through air better than others. Here you can find out why.

Paper puzzle

Both sheets are the same size.

Tear two sheets of paper from the same pad. Screw one sheet up into a ball.

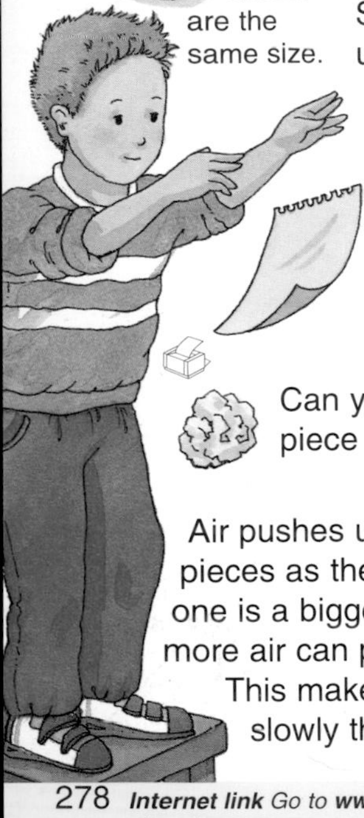

Hold both pieces at the same height and drop them at the same time.

Can you guess which piece will land first?

Air pushes up on the paper pieces as they drop. The flat one is a bigger shape so more air can push against it. This makes it fall more slowly than the ball.

Pyramid pointer

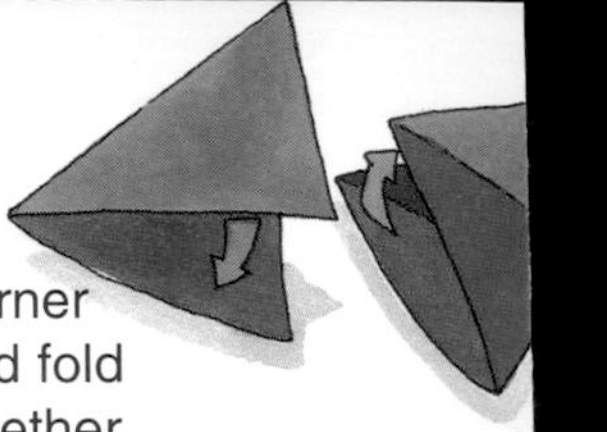

Fold a square of paper in half from corner to corner. Open it and fold the other corners together.

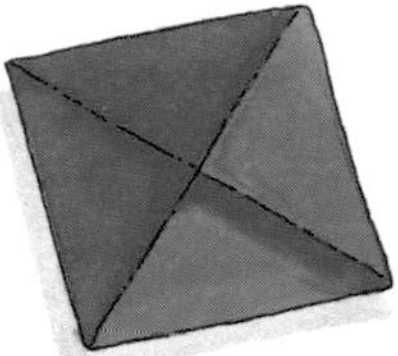

When you open the paper again you see four triangles.

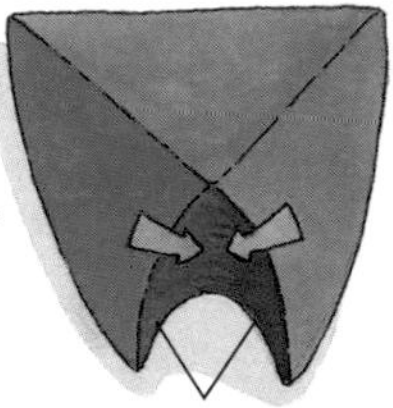

Pinch one triangle in. Push its sides together so you can tape them.

Now drop the finished pyramid several times to see which way up it lands.

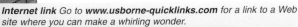

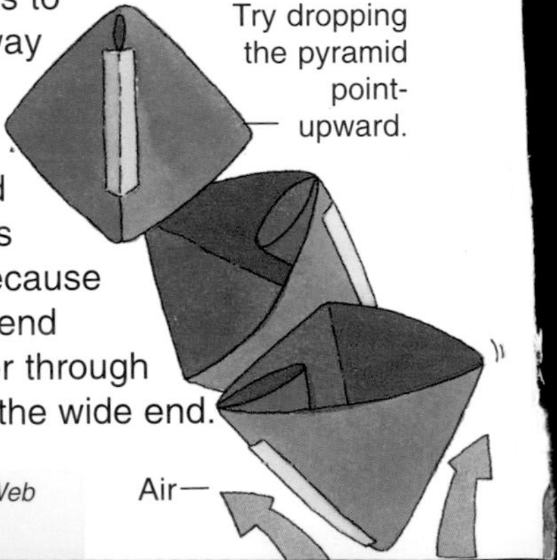

Try dropping the pyramid point-upward.
Air

The pyramid always lands point first because the pointed end moves faster through the air than the wide end.

 Internet link *Go to* ***www.usborne-quicklinks.com*** *for a link to a Web site where you can make a whirling wonder.*

Make a parachute

Parachutes are shaped so that lots of air can push against them.

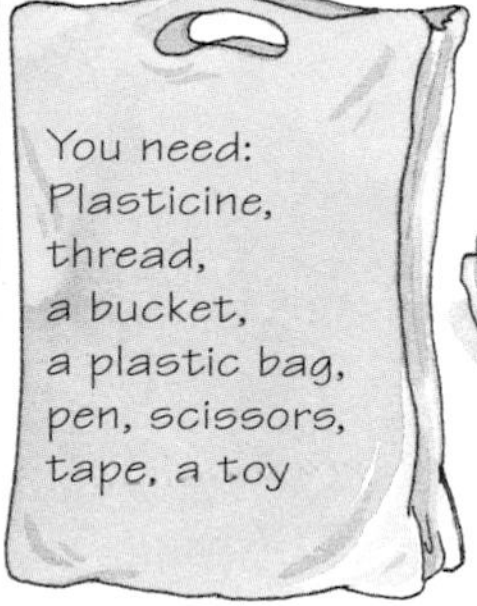

You need:
Plasticine,
thread,
a bucket,
a plastic bag,
pen, scissors,
tape, a toy

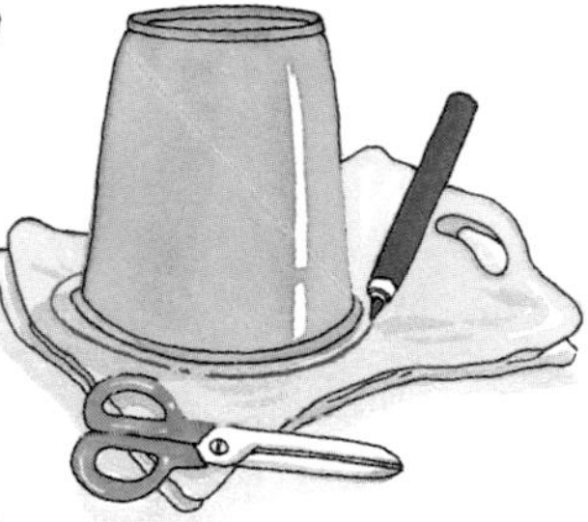

1. Put the bucket on the bag. Draw around it and cut the circle out.

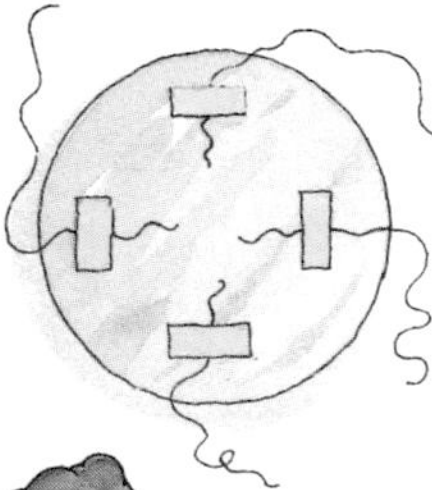

2. Tape four pieces of long thread to the circle like this.

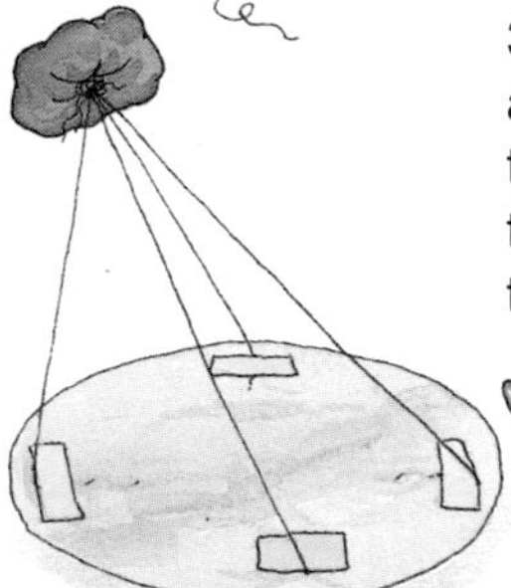

3. Tie the ends together and push the knot into the Plasticine. Press the Plasticine on to the toy.

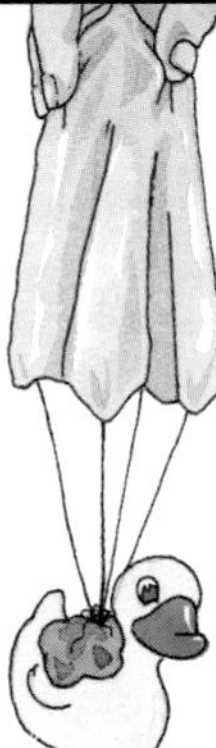

4. Hold the top of the parachute and drop it from a height.

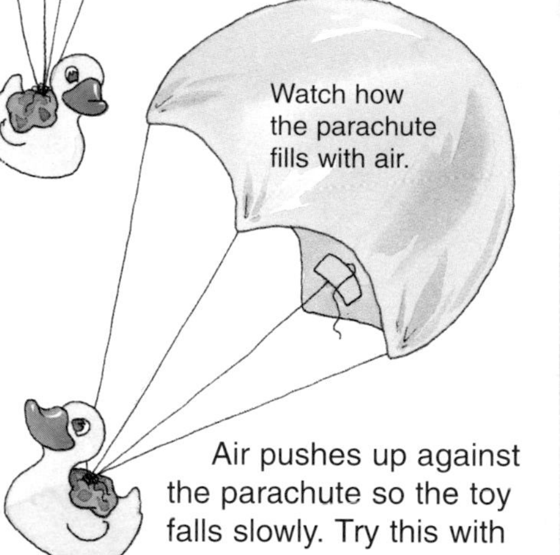
Watch how
the parachute
fills with air.

Air pushes up against the parachute so the toy falls slowly. Try this with slightly heavier toys. Do they fall any faster?

Go-faster shapes

Fast cars have smooth, pointed shapes. The air flows around these shapes instead of against them. Shapes like this are called streamlined.

Flying

Planes can fly because of the way air pushes against them.

Make a glider

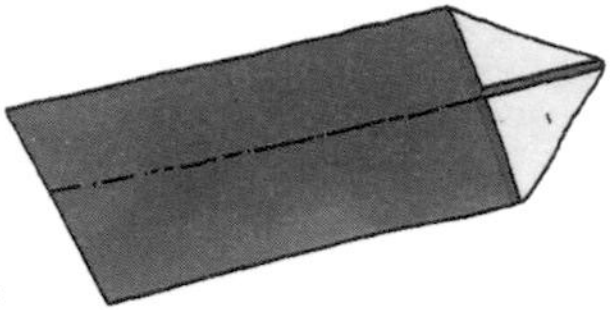

1. Fold a sheet of stiff paper lengthways. Then, open the paper and fold two of the corners inward, as shown above.

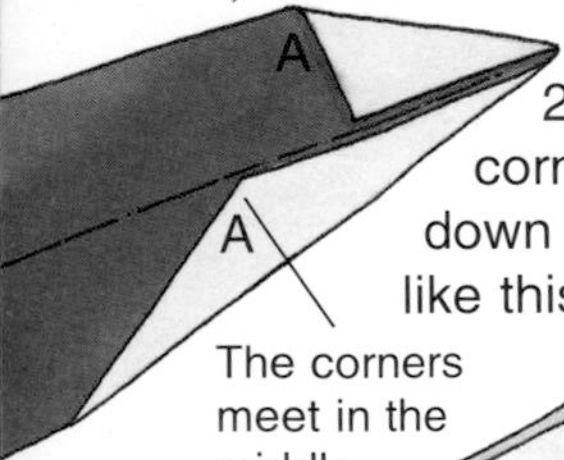

The corners meet in the middle.

2. Fold the new corners marked A down to the middle, like this.

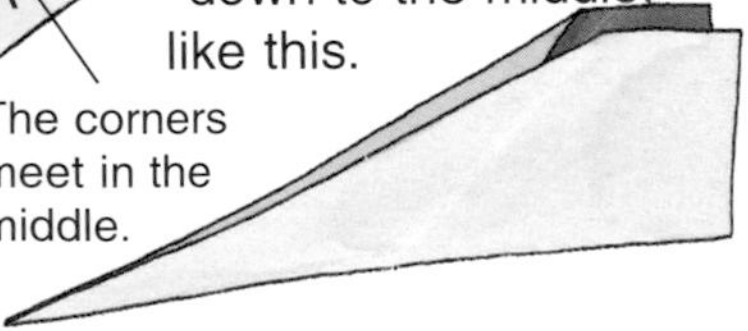

3. Fold both sides of the plane together with the folded corners inside.

4. Then, fold the top edges down to make a wing on each side.

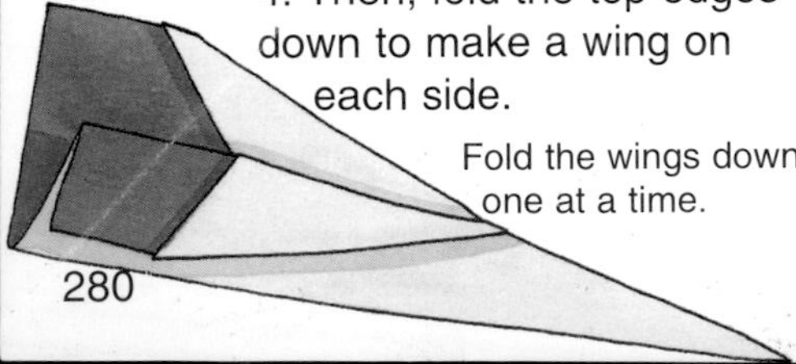

Fold the wings down one at a time.

5. Make a rudder by folding a small square of paper into a triangle.

Fold the corners together.

6. Glue the rudder between the wings at the back of the plane. Cut slits to make one flap in the rudder and one on each wing.

Flying the glider

Try throwing the glider gently forward.

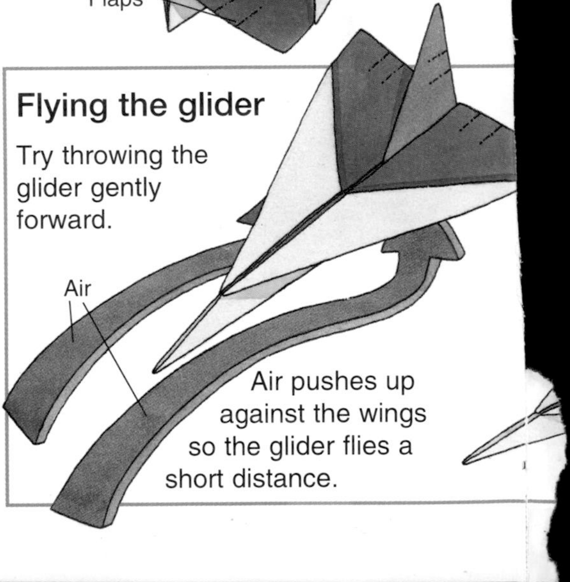

Air pushes up against the wings so the glider flies a short distance.

Rising paper

Hold the edge of a sheet of thin paper just beneath your mouth. Blow hard across the top of the paper.

The paper rises because the air beneath pushes harder than the fast-moving air above.

How planes fly

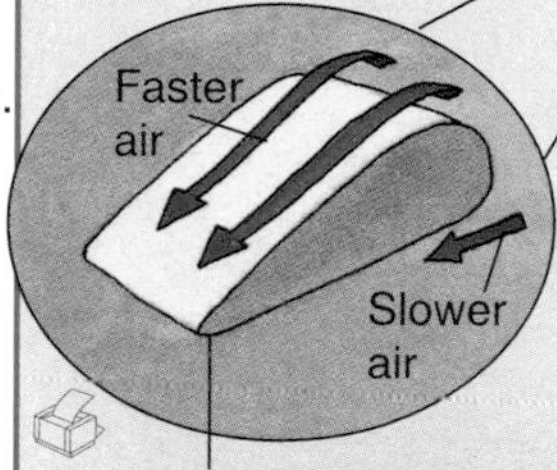

Planes have wings which are curved on top. When the plane moves, the air travels faster across the curved top.

This shows a slice through the wing.

The slower-moving air beneath pushes harder than the air above. This lifts the heavy plane up so it can fly.

Bend the rudder flap to the right. How does the plane fly now? What happens if you bend the flap to the left?

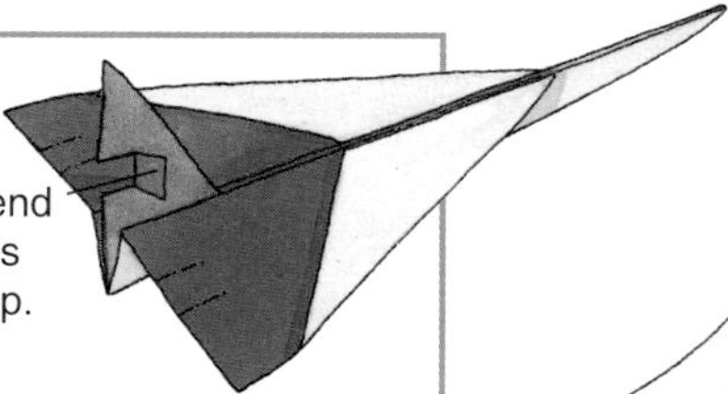

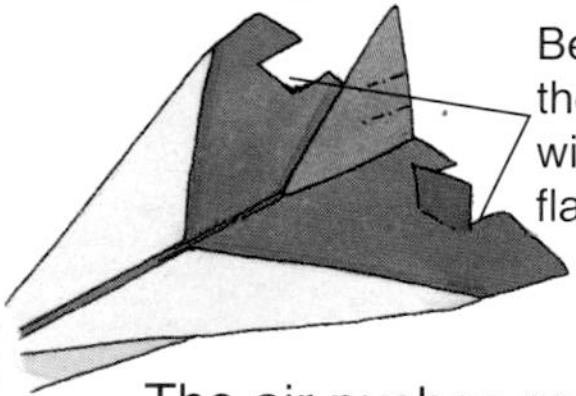

Fly the plane with both wing flaps up and then down. Try again with one flap up and down.

The air pushes against the flaps, making the glider turn, climb or dive.

How pilots steer

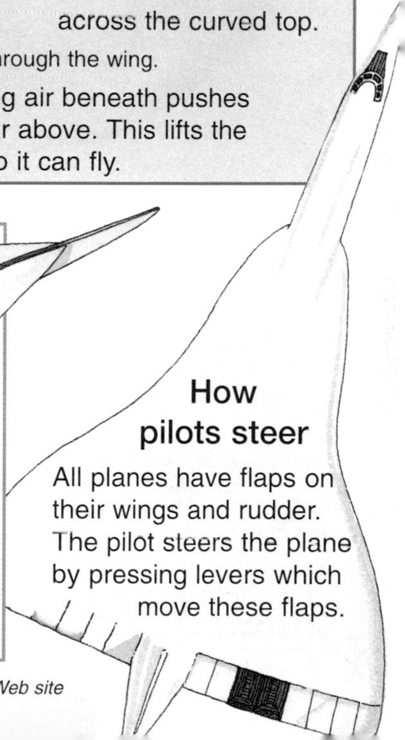

All planes have flaps on their wings and rudder. The pilot steers the plane by pressing levers which move these flaps.

Internet link *Go to* ***www.usborne-quicklinks.com*** *for a link to a Web site where you can find out how things can fly.*

Breathing air

Your body needs air all the time. You get it by breathing in.

Counting breaths

For this experiment, ask a friend to time you with a watch that shows seconds.

Stand still and count the number of breaths you take in 30 seconds. Write this down.

You could make a chart like this.

Then, run on the spot. Count your breaths again for 30 seconds. Is there a difference?

Your body uses part of the air you breathe in to help make energy. You need more energy when you run so you breathe faster.

Breathing bags

The air is made up of a mixture of gases. One of them is called oxygen. This is the part your body uses.

When you breathe in, you suck air into two spongy bags called lungs. They pass oxygen from the air into your body. You breathe out the rest of the air.

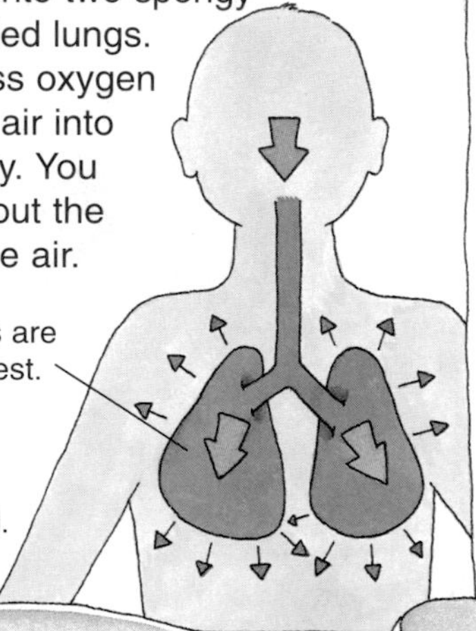

Your lungs are in your chest.

Oxygen travels in your blood.

Cleaning air

Your nose is full of tiny hairs. These trap dust from the air to keep you from breathing it in.

 Internet link *Go to* ***www.usborne-quicklinks.com*** *for a link to a Web site where you can find out what is in the air you breathe.*

How much can you breathe?

Here is a way to measure how much air your lungs can hold. Get a friend to help you try it.

Put your hand over the top until the neck is underwater.

1. Fill a plastic bottle full of water and push it neckdown into a big bowl of water.

2. Turn the bottle upside-down, keeping the neck underwater. Push a bendy straw into the neck.

Be careful not to squash the straw.

3. Take a deep breath and blow gently down the straw.

The air goes to the top of the bottle.
One person holds the straw in place.

The space at the top of the bottle shows how much air you breathe out. Let your friend try this experiment. See who breathes out the most air.

Water in the air

Breathe on a window. Can you see or feel anything on the glass?

Does the glass feel wet?

There is water in the air. When air meets a cold surface, this water appears as tiny drops.

Sound and air

See how the band moves.

Try these experiments to find out how sound is made and how it travels through the air.

Shaking sound

Stretch an elastic band between your fingers and twang it to make a sound.

The band vibrates, which means it moves back and forth quickly. Sound is made when something vibrates.

How you make sound

Put your fingers on the lump in the middle of your throat and see what you can feel when you sing.

When you make a sound, parts in your throat vibrate. You can feel them shaking.

Sound-catcher

Smooth some newspaper over one end of a cardboard tube and tape it in place.

Sing through the tube and feel the paper at the same time.

The paper must be tight and flat.

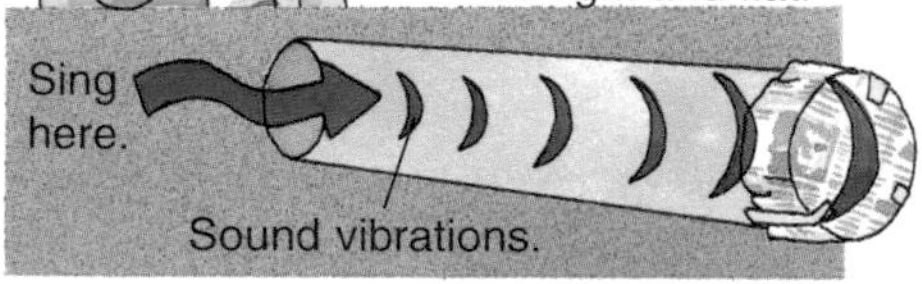

The sound you make sends vibrations through the air in the tube. These make the paper shake.

Silent space

Out in space there is no noise because there is no air. Sound vibrations cannot travel through empty space.

Bottle music

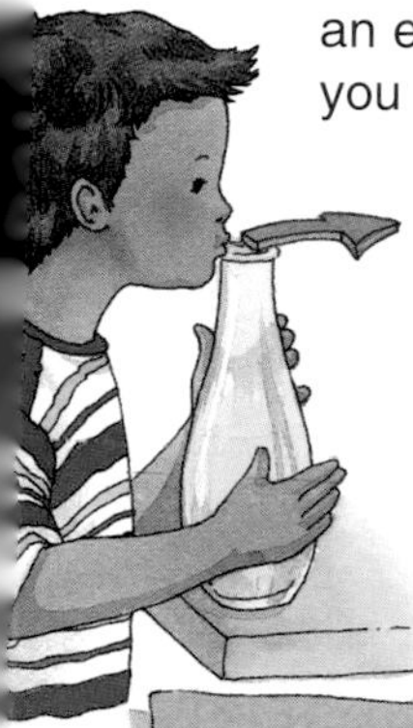

Blow across the top of an empty bottle. See if you can make a sound.

When you blow across the top, you make the air inside vibrate inside the bottle. It makes a noise.

Put different amounts of water in the bottle. See if the sound changes.

The water pushes out some of the air.

The more water you put in, the less air there is left in the bottle. Smaller amounts of air vibrate more quickly and this makes a higher sound.

Musical pipes

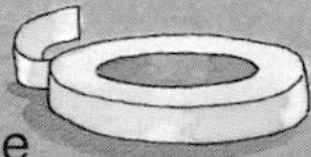

Lots of musical instruments make sounds because air vibrates inside them. Here is one you can make.

Your breath makes air vibrate inside the straws.

1. Cut some straws to different lengths. Starting with the shortest, lay them one by one on a piece of sticky tape.

Leave the longest straws till last.

2. Place another piece of sticky tape on top. Hold the row up and blow across each straw. See which makes the highest sound.

Internet link *Go to* **www.usborne-quicklinks.com** *for a link to a Web site where you can find out how to make another sound from a straw.*

How the experiments work

These pages give more detailed explanations of how the experiments in this section work. To find out even more about the experiments, visit the Web sites recommended. For links to all these Web sites, go to **www.usborne-quicklinks.com**

Air all around (pages 266-267)

Air, like other gases, does not have a fixed shape. It spreads out to fill any available space so nothing is really empty. Air cannot escape from the atmosphere as the force of gravity keeps it from floating away from the Earth.

Air that pushes (pages 268-269)

Gases exert pressure in all directions. The pressure is affected by the amount of gas in a given space. When air is pumped into a tyre, the valve keeps the air from escaping. As more and more air is pumped into the enclosed space, its pressure increases and it pushes strongly on the tyre, keeping it inflated.

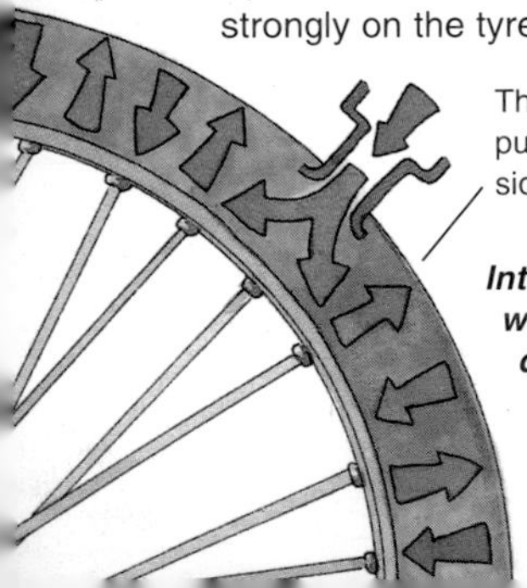

The trapped air pushes against the sides of the tyre.

Internet link *Go to* ***www.usborne-quicklinks.com*** *for a link to a Web site where you can find out more about air pressure.*

Changing size (pages270-271)

Air is made up of tiny particles called molecules. When air is heated, its molecules move more quickly and spread out, so a given amount of air takes up more space. If the air is contained so it cannot expand, its pressure increases. When air is cooled, its molecules slow down and move nearer to each other. Its pressure then decreases.

Rising air (pages 272-273)

Because air molecules spread out when heated, a certain volume of hot air is lighter than the same volume of cold air. This makes the hot air rise, and float above the cold air.

Internet link *Go to* ***www.usborne-quicklinks.com*** *for a link to a Web site where you can take a virtual flight in a hot air balloon.*

Wind (pages 274-275)

The wind frequently changes its direction and speed. The faster a wind moves, the more strongly its effects are felt.

Air power (pages 276-277)

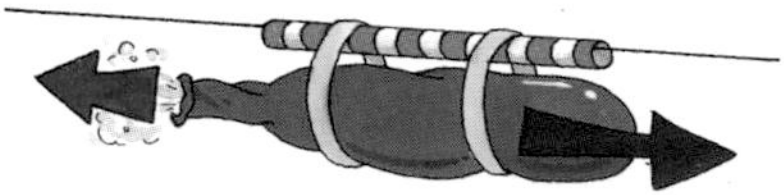

The air inside the rocket balloon is under greater pressure than the air outside.

When the peg is taken off, the pressurized air rushes out of the balloon. Newton's third scientific law states that to every action there is an equal and opposite reaction. The balloon obeys this law by moving in the opposite direction to the escaping air.

Moving through air (pages 278-279)

When things move through air, they have to overcome the air pressure rushing against them. This slowing-down effect of the air is called air resistance. Some shapes encounter more air resistance than others.

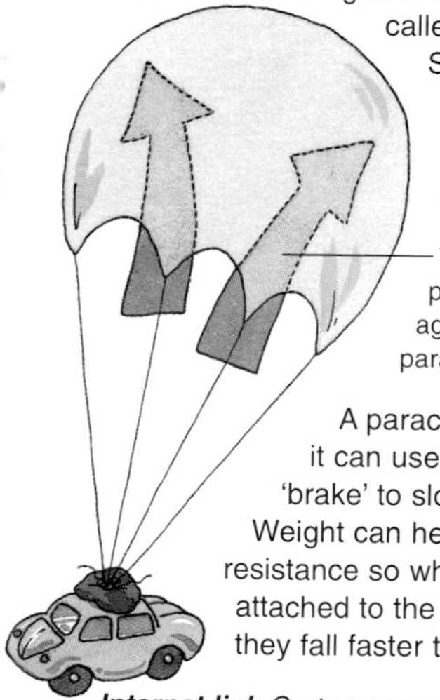

Trapped air pushes hard against a parachute.

A parachute is shaped so it can use air resistance as a 'brake' to slow down a fall. Weight can help to overcome air resistance so when heavier toys are attached to the model parachute they fall faster than light toys.

Internet link *Go to* ***www.usborne-quicklinks.com*** *for a link to a Web site where you can try some simple air experiments.*

Flying (pages 280-281)

The fast-flowing air above a plane's wing is at a lower pressure than the slower-moving air beneath. The difference in pressure results in a "lift" which is strong enough to support the weight of the plane.

Internet link *Go to* ***www.usborne-quicklinks.com*** *for a link to a Web site where you can read a brief history of flight.*

Breathing (pages 282-283)

When air is taken into your lungs, some of the oxygen dissolves into your bloodstream. The blood carries oxygen to every cell in your body and takes carbon dioxide gas (a waste-product of the cells) back to the lungs. The carbon dioxide is exhaled together with the parts of the air, such as nitrogen gas, that the body cannot use.

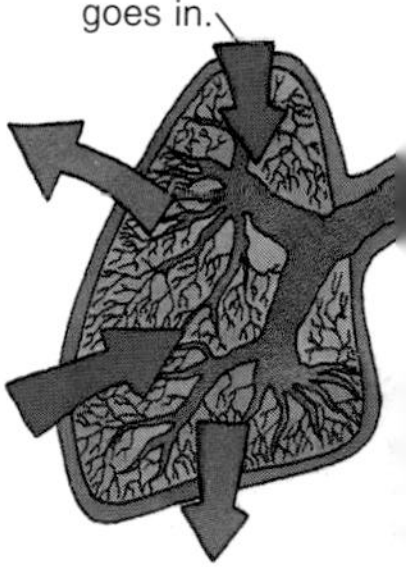

Carbon dioxide goes in.
Oxygen goes out.

Sound (pages 284-285)

Sound is a form of travelling energy produced when an object vibrates. The vibrations travel through the air and make your eardrum begin to vibrate. Your nervous system registers these vibrations as sound.

Internet link *Go to* ***www.usborne-quicklinks.com*** *for a link to a Web site where you can watch a short movie about sound.*

Index

Cover design by Russell Punter and cover illustration by Christyan Fox. With thanks to Susanna Davidson.

First published in 2002 by Usborne Publishing Ltd, Usborne House, 83-85 Saffron Hill, London EC1N 8RT, England. **www.usborne.com**